"Witches, drool-worthy warriors, and hot passion that will have readers reaching for a cool drink. Cheyenne McCray has created a fantastic and magical world where both the hero and heroine are strong and are willing to fight the darkness that threatens their worlds." —*A Romance Review*

FORBIDDEN MAGIC

"McCray will thrill and entrance you!"
—Sabrina Jeffries, *New York Times* bestselling author

"A yummy hot fudge sundae of a book!"
—MaryJanice Davidson,
New York Times bestselling author

"*Charmed* meets Kim Harrison's witch series, but with a heavy dose of erotica on top!"
—Lyndsay Sands, *New York Times* bestselling author

"Wildly erotic and dangerously sensual, this explosive paranormal thriller sizzles. McCray erupts on the scene with one of the sexiest stories of the year. Her darkly dramatic world is one readers won't mind visiting again . . . McCray knows how to make a reader sweat—either from spine-tingling suspense or soul-singeing sex . . . McCray cleverly combines present-day reality with mythological fantasy to create a world where beings of lore exist—and visit the earthly realm." —*Romantic Times BOOKreviews*

"McCray's paranormal masterpiece is not for the fainthearted. The battle between good and evil is brought to the reader in vivid and riveting detail to the point where the reader is drawn into the pages of this bewitching and seductive fantasy that delivers plenty of action-packed sequences and arousing love scenes." —*Rendezvous*

Other Novels by

CHEYENNE McCRAY

PARANORMAL ROMANCE

Wicked Magic

Seduced by Magic

Forbidden Magic

ROMANTIC SUSPENSE

Moving Target

Chosen Prey

ANTHOLOGY

No Rest for the Witches

Available from St. Martin's Paperbacks

SHADOW *Magic*

Cheyenne McCray

St. Martin's Paperbacks

This is a work of fiction. All of the characters, organizations and events portrayed in this novel are either products of the author's imagination or are used fictitiously.

SHADOW MAGIC

Copyright © 2008 by Cheyenne McCray.
Excerpt from *Dark Magic* copyright © 2008 by Cheyenne McCray.

ISBN: 0-312-94958-8
EAN: 978-0-312-94958-7

Printed in the United States of America

St. Martin's Paperbacks edition / May 2008

St. Martin's Paperbacks are published by St. Martin's Press, 175 Fifth Avenue, New York, NY 10010.

10 9 8 7 6 5 4 3 2 1

With all my love to Anna Windsor.
Best friend, confidante, writing partner.
I couldn't do this without you.

ACKNOWLEDGMENTS

Thank you to all of my readers. You're the reason I'm here and I love you all.

Many thanks to Grace Marzioli for her fabulous fashion advice.

Cassie Ryan, Tee O'Fallon, Anna Windsor—you are my rocks. And damn, does it hurt when you drop them on me. Love you!

Judi McCoy, love you for the stickies and for being such a great friend—despite the fact that no one dies in your books and I can't say that's true in mine. Thanks to the sticky gals, Kayce Lassiter, Peggy Parsons, Magon Kinzie, and Sue Palumbo. Alcatraz will never be the same.

A toast to the Butterscotch Martini Girls, Tina Gerow, Isabella Clayton, Dani Petrone, Brit Blaise, Lynne Logan, and Kayce Lassiter, as well as Kayla Janz. You all are amazing, and thank you for everything!

To my agent, Nancy Yost, who knows how to brighten my day even when she confuses the hell out of me.

And to my editor, Monique Patterson, Queen of the Fomorii—I mean Goddess of Editing.

CHAPTER ONE

PAYBACKS ARE A BITCH.

And Hannah Wentworth would see to it that Ceithlenn, a dark goddess from Underworld, paid. Big time.

Banshee, Hannah's falcon familiar, made a soft cry and gripped her shirt tighter in his talons, reminding her of where she was and why she had come to this secluded pond deep in the forest of Otherworld.

Those . . . feelings she'd been having.

Ever since she'd been forced to leave San Francisco, Hannah's instincts had told her things were about to get worse. Impossibly more dangerous.

Whatever was coming, Hannah wasn't about to face it blind or unaware. She would find out what she could, or die trying.

Hannah knelt on the damp grass beside the pond and dropped the pack she held. She dug through the leather bag until she found her scrying mirror then drew it out and settled it on the grass in front of her.

Smells of moss and rich wet earth mingled with the scents of evergreens and wildflowers as she focused on the mirror. A breeze ruffled Banshee's feathers, and stirred her dark hair and the shock of blond that swept down one side of her face. A night bird began its evening song, and Hannah thought she heard Fae voices joining in.

Her grandmother had given her the scrying instrument

after Hannah left her socialite mother to live with her father. The strength of Hannah's innate talent for alomancy, using the mirror and sea salt crystals to scry, had astonished the high priestess of her D'Anu Coven. Hannah's power over this form of divination as well as her connection to the Dragon Elementals grew greater as time passed.

The ornate ebony wood frame was fashioned of two Dragons, each biting the tail of the other so that it was a never-ending circle. Hannah rubbed her thumb over one of the intricate carvings. Ebony was the most powerful magical wood and was associated with all of the Elements—Earth, Air, Fire, and Water—and aided her in her communication with the Dragons.

They were her totem and always had been. Even her falcon familiar was the living embodiment of Dragons in her world.

Hannah tried not to grind her teeth at the thought that she and her Coven sisters had been forced to flee their homes in San Francisco for Otherworld, just days ago.

No time for that now. Deep breath. We are *going to figure out how to toast that goddess-bitch.*

She gripped the soft grass in her fingers as she looked over the mirror. Only Hannah could "see" in the black glass within the ebony frame when she scried.

Hannah pulled a vial of salt crystals from her pack and tugged out the cork, which she then set aside. She leaned forward so that she looked directly over the mirror, her hair swinging forward at the sides of her face. The mirror didn't show her or Banshee's reflections.

She concentrated with everything she had, pushing out all other thoughts to still her mind and prepare herself for the vision to come. Silently, she asked for the aid of the Dragon Elementals and the great Druid Ancestors, and she called on Banshee's powers to strengthen her own.

The falcon's magic joined hers as it flowed through her body.

Come on . . .

Her heart rate picked up as it always did before she scried something monumental. The world closed in on her until all that remained was her, Banshee, and the mirror. The forest's sounds and smells vanished and it was as if she floated outside her body.

Time slowed. She tilted the vial and studied the patterns of the salt crystals in the air as they spilled out of the vial and onto the mirror. The vial slipped from her fingers, dropped onto the grass, and rolled away as she braced her hands to either side of the mirror and analyzed those patterns, too.

The thrumming of her heart grew even more rapid until it felt as if her entire body throbbed.

Images appeared in the mirror and she tumbled, tumbled into the vision, all five senses, body and mind and soul, as if the events she visioned were truly happening. As if she were truly there.

Her heart nearly stopped beating.

Rain pounded down so hard it soaked her to her skin, chilling her, and she had difficulty seeing. But through the downpour she made out humans fleeing from a San Francisco tourist pier. Their terror flooded Hannah so deeply she felt it in her bones. Blood and death and the acrid odor of fear mixed with the rotten-fish stench.

Fomorii demons.

Magic sparked at her fingertips as she caught sight of malformed shapes attacking humans. A scream rose in her throat.

But then something enormous appeared, coming closer. A blast of fire bellowed from it as it spread its wings.

The Fire Dragon. An Elemental.

Terrorizing humans.

No! Not possible.

Inside her vision, Hannah heard herself screaming, begging the Dragon to stop.

And then it turned its fire on her. Heat slammed into her and she screamed again.

Hannah jerked out of the vision and with a gasp she

almost fell backward. It took her a moment to realize she was in the present again. Her clothes were dry. She no longer felt as if she were burning from the blast of flames that had engulfed her in the vision.

The images whirled in her mind.

No sense. They make no sense.

She wrapped her arms around herself and shook her head. Her eyes were moist as if she had felt an emotion deep enough that a tear had wet each eye.

She never cried. Ever. Not since she was a child and had had to live through all of her mother's choices. She had no tears, wanted no tears. Nothing could make her cry.

Hannah lowered her eyelashes as she looked at the mirror again. It was cold, no vision remaining. But the pattern of the salt crystals remained the same. Whatever change was coming, it involved her totems.

Especially the Fire Dragon.

Banshee gripped her shoulder tighter and she winced as his talons went through her shirt and bit into her flesh. Her familiar gave a cry, more than likely sensing her fear and confusion.

"I'm fine, Banshee." Hannah raised her hand to his beak and he nuzzled his head against her fingers.

She eased into full reality and after a few moments realized that it was nearly dark. How long had she been in the vision? It had seemed like only minutes, but the remnants of sunlight had vanished, leaving only a veil of murky twilight.

Blessed Anu, her heart wouldn't stop pounding and her mind wouldn't stop whirling. Hannah bit the inside of her cheek and stuffed her things into her bag after dribbling the salt crystals from the mirror back into their vial.

Hair prickled at the nape of Hannah's neck.

She went still.

Someone or something was watching her.

Hannah dropped her pack to free her hands so that she could use her magic if she needed to.

She twisted to the right, her hands ready. And caught her breath.

Through the gloom Hannah saw a tall, powerful-looking man. The sudden urges rushing through her body made her breath catch. His broad chest was bare save for straps that crisscrossed his flesh. Gems on the straps glittered in the waning light.

Images flashed through her mind of rubbing her palms over the man's carved biceps, down his flat stomach . . .

She blinked and swallowed, but couldn't take her eyes away from him. Long hair dusted his shoulders, and she wondered how it would feel to run her fingers through the strands that caught the last of the sunlight enough to glimmer slightly. What color was his hair? Dark? Light?

Desire made her shiver as she let her gaze travel lower to where his snug black pants molded to his muscular thighs, trim hips, and—

She swallowed again.

Dear goddess, what had come over her? She couldn't stop looking at him. She felt no fear—more of a recognition. Like she knew this man.

As her gaze moved back up from where his pants were tucked into his boots, she took in the sheathed sword resting on one side of his hips. The sword hilt's gems sparkled like those on his chest straps.

Hannah's gaze met the man's as she finally looked from his body to his face. He had an aristocratic tilt to his head as he stood with his arms crossed over his chest. And studied her.

His gaze was unwavering and her body heated as she realized he had been looking her over as much as she'd been checking him out. Her body was responding to a man she'd never met.

The moon and crescent engraved band on her upper right arm tingled and grew warm against her skin.

In warning?

Hannah raised her chin and narrowed her eyes as her thoughts came back into focus and she tightenened her grip on reality. Who did this man think he was, watching her like this? Was he one of the D'Danann?

Somehow she didn't think so.

She opened her mouth to demand that he tell her who he was and inform him that he had no business watching her.

But he turned and melted away into the darkness.

THE FOLLOWING MORNING, HANNAH stood in an open area of the woods, her face tilted up as she studied the unfamiliar crystal-blue sky. She frowned as she lowered her head and looked into the forest. The two D'Danann warriors and Rhiannon were late joining her so they could make the journey to the Drow realm.

Goddess bless it, she hated to be kept waiting.

Hannah whistled and held out her arm. Banshee answered with a screech and sailed in a wide circle over the forest before he landed with delicate precision on her outstretched forearm. The crow-sized falcon knew how to rest his talons on her bare skin without hurting her. Although sometimes he would grip tightly enough to get his point across when he felt Hannah needed an attitude adjustment.

Banshee had something in his hooked beak and dropped it at her feet.

Hannah glanced down. "Ugh." A dead mouse. "You know I'm not crazy about your version of presents."

As he responded, Banshee raised his wings and kept his cry to a decibel that wouldn't hurt her eardrums.

Hannah stroked the black feathers on his head and cheeks that made him look like he was wearing a helmet. "I think you do it just to gross me out."

If birds could have an amused twinkle in their eye, Banshee did.

Like all peregrines, he was striking in appearance. He had slate-blue upper parts with bluish speckled bars across his white chest and on his undersides from wing tip to wing tip.

Banshee worked his way up her bare arm to her shoulder. Hannah brushed back the natural shock of blond that swept over her brows and curved along one side of her face. The thick streak was a stark contrast to the rest of her dark hair. It hung in a straight but sophisticated cut, styled by the best—at Joseph Cappucci's Salon and Spa near Union Square in San Francisco.

San Francisco. Her home. Hannah clenched her jaw as Banshee reached her shoulder. Thanks to that goddess-bitch, it was likely that Hannah and the other D'Anu witches wouldn't be returning to their former lives anytime in the near future.

Returning to their former lives . . . as if that would ever be possible. Nothing could be the same after what Ceithlenn had done.

Still, Hannah closed her eyes and pictured herself on Market Street during rush hour. She missed it all. Every bit of it. Bumping into other people as she walked through the crowds. Stopping by her favorite bakery for an éclair. Having a Frappuccino at Starbucks. What she wouldn't give for a Venti double caramel with an extra shot of espresso right about now.

With a sigh she shook her head, opened her eyes, and looked in the direction of the D'Danann village. *Definitely no Starbucks in Otherworld.*

After Banshee ruffled his feathers and settled himself, Hannah hitched up the small leather pack higher on her opposite shoulder and waited for her companions, one of whom was another gray magic witch, Rhiannon.

Hannah's Coven practiced gray magic, unlike all other D'Anu Covens that believed only in white magic. For some of Hannah's Coven sisters, maintaining the fine balance between gray and black was a fierce struggle. Hannah was certain that none of her sister witches would cross the line.

But sometimes . . . Hannah worried about Rhiannon and Mackenzie. The way the witches fought with their magic was maybe too intense. Too close to the dark.

Hannah shook her head. "Mackenzie and Rhiannon are fine."

Once Hannah had become a gray magic witch, she'd had no problems, no guilt, in using a power that could save lives.

With her strength of will and her utter confidence in herself, she knew she would *never* cross the line to black magic.

Faint voices caught Hannah's attention. It was time to head to the transference stone and make their way to the realm of the Dark Elves, the Drow.

In the distance, Hannah could make out Rhiannon and her husband—a Tuatha D'Danann warrior named Keir—as they walked through the forest toward her.

Eavan, also a D'Danann warrior, accompanied them. The infuriating man wouldn't stop chasing her. Although he was charming, sexy, and exceptionally good-looking, she didn't plan on having anything to do with him, much less *any* male in Otherworld.

This wasn't her home. Unlike four of her Coven sisters, she refused to get entangled in some romantic mess that would pull her between two worlds. She'd seen enough of that thanks to her mother. And thanks to her mother's choices.

Her chest constricted at the thought of her less than loving childhood.

Deep breath. Calm and controlled. She never lost her cool in front of other people and she wasn't about to now.

As her companions neared, Hannah rubbed the moon and crescent engraved band that encircled her upper right arm. The gold band was a symbol of her Pagan ancestry, and through a special ceremony it had been imbued with ancient magic. She'd had it designed as a gift to herself when she'd guided her software corporation past the twenty-five-million-dollar mark.

Her company . . . Hannah's whole body went rigid and she clenched her teeth. What was happening now to the company she'd built from the bottom up?

She let her hand fall away from her armband. The moon and crescent were for intuition and fulfillment, success and optimism.

Right now she was a little low on optimism and could use all the help she could get. Not to mention the reminder of what it felt like to be in control of her life. Of any damned thing.

Banshee gripped her shoulder tighter with his talons, bringing her firmly back to the present. She straightened her spine as Rhiannon, Eavan, and Keir finally reached her.

The tension radiating from Rhiannon when she approached kicked up Hannah's own. She and Rhiannon had never found common ground, and frankly, had never liked each other. But they were sister D'Anu witches, and Hannah respected Rhiannon for her magic, her talents, her dedication, and her love for her sister witches.

"Are you ready?" Rhiannon asked Hannah, managing to keep her tone civil. Morning sunlight gleamed on Rhiannon's chin-length auburn hair and her green eyes held a hint of irritation. She wore a leather outfit like that of the D'Danann warriors.

When Hannah and her sister witches fled from San Francisco a week ago, they hadn't been able to pack much, which had limited their wardrobes considerably. The choice had been peasant dresses like the women in the village, or the leathers of the male and female D'Danann warriors.

Leather won out with all the D'Anu witches.

It'd be a real pain fighting in a long skirt.

"I've been waiting for you for a good half hour." Hannah resisted tugging down her own leather shirt. So much for her Vera Wang tailored slacks and Dior blouses. Her Jimmy Choos and Pradas were back in San Francisco, but at least she had her Arche running shoes and didn't have to wear D'Danann boots.

Rhiannon brushed her palms against her pants, her expression turning from irritated to anxious. The demon scars on one of her cheeks stood out a little more as her face paled. Rhiannon was no doubt nervous because the four of them were about to come face-to-face with Rhiannon's newly discovered father, the king of the Drow.

Hannah wondered how she'd feel if she found out her father was one of the Dark Elves—and a traitor.

A determined look came into Rhiannon's eyes. "Let's do it then."

The four strode through the thick forest. Only the light weight of Banshee on her shoulder, and the slight bump of her pack against her hip as she walked, kept Hannah's thoughts grounded.

"A waste of time." Keir's expression was thunderous, which was not unusual for the six-foot-six warrior. "I find it unlikely the stubborn bastard will agree to join our battle."

Rhiannon frowned as she looked up at her husband and she sounded edgy and unsure as she spoke. "Even though he said no before, maybe this time Garran—my father—will agree."

Hannah held back her own opinions. It wouldn't do any good to rail again about not trusting the Dark Elves. Two of their sister witches insisted they could and should give the traitorous bastards a chance. Hannah considered the fact that the Drow had sided with the warlock Darkwolf at one time. No, thank you. It didn't matter that they'd had a change of heart later on.

But the D'Anu witches, Tuatha D'Danann warriors of Otherworld, and the Paranormal Special Forces of San Francisco desperately needed the help of the Dark Elves against Ceithlenn and the Fomorii.

If only they could convince the Drow king to commit his forces to battle.

This time they would.

This time they *had* to.

The moment the trees parted to reveal a meadow and the transference stone, Hannah's gaze riveted on a woman who stood on the opposite side of the stone. Hannah couldn't help but catch her breath in surprise and something like wonder.

Stunning. The woman was absolutely stunning. No high fashion model could begin to compare.

It was impossible to look away from her. She . . . glowed. Or was it the air around her that did? Such blue, blue eyes. Long, flaxen hair hung in a waterfall of silk to her toes, and she had delicate pointed ears. Her filmy clothing ruffled in the soft wind like the leaves of nearby trees.

The woman stood in her bare feet beside a bridge that

spanned a small stream. Water made a tinkling sound as it trickled over stones. The scent of wildflowers and rain-cleansed air swept through the meadow.

Hannah cocked her head. This must be the Great Guardian her sister witches had spoken of countless times. An Elvin woman of indeterminable age, who was reputed to be wise, intuitive, and prophetic.

Strange warmth flowed through Hannah as she stepped closer to her companions. Vaguely she was aware of Keir and Eavan laying their weapons on the ground before the Guardian.

"Rise," the Great Guardian said in a voice that was like a song to Hannah's ears.

It was then she realized all of her companions had bowed. Rippling warmth spread along Hannah's skin. With her up-bringing, she had been taught to never bow to anyone but a queen or king of a foreign country. This Elvin woman was far more powerful than any royalty Hannah had met, and a part of her wished she had bowed with her companions.

The Great Guardian smiled, her gaze lingering on Hannah.

Some strange force drew Hannah toward the woman and Hannah didn't resist. She walked closer to the Guardian until they were only a few feet apart. Banshee stirred on Hannah's shoulder, but didn't react with alarm.

"Much troubles your soul, reluctant traveler," the Elvin woman said, her words directed to Hannah. "Tell me what burdens you."

Hannah held back the sudden diatribe that rose up in her throat. *What burdens me? Let's see . . . my Top Ten, or the whole freaking list?*

"Speak freely." The Guardian's gaze firmly held Hannah's and a pulling sensation tugged against her mind.

There was simply no choice but to answer. Words spilled out so fast Hannah almost couldn't believe she was saying them.

"To start with, who wouldn't be upset if their world was falling apart, overrun by a goddess-bitch and a slew of demons?" Hannah's voice held a bite that she hadn't intended, but she went on. "We've lost our homes and had to flee to Otherworld. But more importantly, thousands, *thousands* are dead because of Ceithlenn. Not to mention that we can't get any Anu-blessed help from the armies here, except a few D'Danann."

Hannah's control had nearly shattered, which shocked her like a jolt to her chest and caused her to step back. Banshee sent a warm wave of his magic through Hannah and she sensed his attempt to calm her. Still, she felt anything but.

The Guardian's expression remained serene. Despite her respect for the Elvin woman, Hannah fought not to ball her fists at her sides from the frustration, anger, and fear boiling up inside of her. It was all she could do to keep her own expression as collected and controlled as possible.

"You have much to be angry about." The Guardian's blue gaze continued to hold Hannah's. "You seek the Drow once again for aid. Perhaps you will find some solace for your rage in those dark places below our ground."

That's supposed to make me feel better?

Hannah's belly clenched. More words bubbled up inside her, angry words, but the Guardian had already turned to Rhiannon.

"Your father represents his people, and he must have a reason to lead them into battle. It is true the Drow lean toward what benefits them. It is their way, one we must respect."

"Respect?" Rhiannon's cheeks flushed. "How can I respect a race that isn't willing to help others for the sake of the common good, rather than for their own gain?" She propped her hands on her hips. "Even if I am part Drow, I can't accept that."

"You must." The Guardian looked from Rhiannon to Hannah. "Tell King Garran it has been decided that, providing the Drow help in the battle against Ceithlenn, he will get what he most desires for his people. Conditionally. And he must come to me alone to receive my gift."

Following a brief moment of shock that the Light Elves would help the Drow, a twinge of hope sparked in Hannah's belly. "We'll tell him."

"Thank you, Guardian." Rhiannon gave an audible sigh of relief. "Anything that can help us defeat Ceithlenn is a good thing."

"Anything?" The Great Guardian's gaze moved from Rhiannon to Keir to Eavan and finally landed on Hannah. "Think well on choices you may be forced to make."

As she continued to study Hannah, the Guardian added, "You will know what you must do in the far reaches of the ground, Hannah."

Hannah blinked. Confusion tumbled through her like a landslide.

Before any of them could respond, the Guardian turned, stepped onto the bridge, and faded from sight.

For a moment, Hannah and her companions remained quiet. Only the sounds of wind whistling through branches and birds singing interrupted the silence. The breeze ruffled flower petals and dandelion fluff floated in the air.

"*Why* does she do that?" Rhiannon grumbled and marched to the transference stone. "I hate it when she speaks in riddles."

Light laughter tinkled through the surrounding forest but was gone almost as soon as Hannah heard it.

Rhiannon apparently wasn't wasting any time. She stepped onto the stone, Keir following as he held her hand. Rhiannon looked from Hannah to Eavan and said, "Hold tight."

Hannah watched as Rhiannon's and Keir's forms wavered like sunshine on the surface of a pond, and then they were gone.

Eavan looked down at Hannah and seemed confused. "Hold tight?"

Hannah raised her fingers to Banshee's beak and he nuzzled his head against them. "It means to wait for her and she'll be right back."

"Ah." The warrior's eyes were deep brown, an arresting

contrast to his white-blond hair. "Then we have a moment to ourselves," he said in the deep Irish brogue of the D'Danann. "A moment for you to tell me why you avoid me so?"

I don't have time or mental space for this right now.

Hannah met his gaze as she lowered her hand. "I made it a policy not to date anyone who flies."

He raised an eyebrow. D'Danann were powerful Fae warriors who had the ability to unfold their great wings when they wished to, and then to tuck them away so that they vanished as if they didn't exist.

She mentally shook her head at the thought of any of her acquaintances in the city getting a good look at a man with wings. She almost smiled. Wouldn't that set them on their asses?

Eavan opened his mouth as if to say something when Rhiannon's form wavered on the transference stone.

"Time for you to head back to the village," Hannah said to Banshee. "It's not natural for you to go underground."

She had the strangest sense that she wouldn't be seeing him for a while. An empty feeling settled in her belly. Banshee had become a part of her when she was thirteen, when he had appeared out of the night sky just before she'd performed a moon ceremony alone. When he'd landed on her chest of ritual tools, she'd known instantly he was a witch's familiar. He had filled her with the strength of his magic, imbuing her with warmth and power and heightening her senses.

Sometimes she wondered what witch had belonged to Banshee, and he to her. Somewhere in the world that witch had likely passed on to Summerland. What had brought Banshee to Hannah, she didn't know, but she'd thanked the goddess Anu many times that he had come.

The falcon made a low sound and tugged at her hair with his beak, and she knew it was to reassure her. She held out her arm and he sidestepped until he was far enough away from her face to spread his wings. He pushed away from her arm as he took flight and Hannah watched him for a moment as he circled above her before vanishing beyond the forest. She swallowed back a feeling of loneliness that crowded her throat.

Hannah secured her pack on her shoulder, turned back to the transference stone, and headed onto it so that she stood beside Rhiannon. The strength of the tension between the two of them collided and Rhiannon took a step aside and cleared her throat. She always made it clear that she hated for most people to invade her personal space.

Hannah knew she was pushing buttons whenever she got too close to Rhiannon. Right now they didn't have time for her phobia, or whatever it was.

"You're just going to have to let me inside that little box of yours," Hannah said, "if we're going to get there anytime soon."

"Whatever." Rhiannon's eyes sparked before she looked at Eavan. "Come on, I can take both of you." With an expression of distaste directed toward Hannah, Rhiannon held out one of her hands to Hannah, and her other to Eavan.

Currents of discomfort ran through Hannah's arm as she clasped Rhiannon's cool hand. Hannah wondered if the dark Shadows inside of Rhiannon were reacting to her in some way, since Rhiannon didn't really want to be touching her.

After seeing in the last battle what the power of those Shadows could do, Hannah felt more than a stirring of unease, like something crawling, under her skin. What if Rhiannon lost control over the Shadows she had inherited from her Drow father?

Maybe going on the transference stone with Rhiannon was a bad idea.

Maybe it was a terrible idea.

"Here we go." Rhiannon clenched Hannah's hand.

The world went hazy then black. Hannah couldn't hear, couldn't see, and her skin numbed.

For a flash, Hannah couldn't feel Rhiannon's hand, and a burst of fear clawed at her throat. What if she became lost in whatever kind of vortex Rhiannon was taking them through?

Bright light suddenly shone in Hannah's eyes and

Rhiannon's hand grasped hers hard enough to scrunch her bones together. Hannah's feet met grass, and she was certain she would have tipped over if Rhiannon hadn't had a hold on her.

Hannah composed herself and shook her hand free of Rhiannon's. She glanced at her companions and saw that Eavan had made it as well, although he looked a little tipsy himself.

Keir stood beneath an apple tree at the center of the meadow. A rock outcropping took up a great stretch of room on one side. From the top tier of the rocks, a waterfall spilled into a couple of pools before disappearing into the ground, and the place smelled of grass and flowers that were being tended by a group of tiny Faeries.

Hannah hadn't been here before, but one of her sister witches, Copper Ashcroft, had been trapped here for over a year. Hannah glanced up at the apple tree. No wonder Copper wouldn't eat anything made with apples.

Hannah noticed that Rhiannon blinked as if the sunlight bothered her, and her skin was already starting to redden. Rhiannon had always had some sensitivity to the sun, and it wasn't until she learned she was half Drow that she discovered why.

In a voice that lacked enthusiasm, Rhiannon said, "Come on," and gestured for everyone to follow.

Hannah flexed her hands at her sides as if she were about to battle the Drow.

The Dark Elves weren't to be trusted, and Hannah wasn't about to start.

CHAPTER TWO

RHIANNON LED HANNAH, EAVAN, and Keir around the outcropping of boulders. Beside a pine tree was a flat, rectangular rock surface. It was the shape and size of a large door and surrounded by dirt, no grass. The flat stone had strange markings scratched into the surface along all sides.

Without looking at her companions, Rhiannon stomped on the door five times—probably with a little more force than was necessary—then stepped back.

A fraction of a moment passed before the stone door shuddered and started moving across the ground, to the left. It made horrid screeching sounds as it slid to the side, causing chill bumps to rise on Hannah's skin. If she had any say, first thing she'd do was have that door greased.

Keir insisted on leading and stepped onto a set of stone stairs that disappeared into the darkness of the Drow realm. Only one person could walk down the stairs at a time. Rhiannon then Hannah followed Keir, with Eavan taking up the rear. Torches flamed to life along the walls the moment Keir's boot hit the first step. Hannah blinked as her eyes adjusted to the change from sunlight to near darkness.

Cool air touched her cheeks and her hair lifted slightly from her shoulders as a breeze rushed up from below. As she made her way down, Hannah avoided touching the dirt walls. The last thing she wanted to do was get filthy. The passageway smelled of damp earth and moss, not unpleasant scents—but it was still dirt.

The only sounds were Rhiannon's and her own breathing, the slight noise of small stones and dirt shifting under their shoes, and the snap and hiss of the torches. The D'Danann were eerily silent as always.

After what seemed an eternity, when they were deep underground, the four of them stepped off the stairs into a large, circular hall. Only a few torches were lit, giving them just enough light to see. Hannah's gaze swept the room, taking in the forms of warriors carved into the walls in all manner of action.

Her heart jumped a little when four men melted from the partial darkness—two on either side of Hannah and her companions.

She contained her surprise at how stunningly handsome each one of the Dark Elves was despite their soft-toned bluish-gray skin. Amazingly, their skin color suited them. Their tall, muscular physiques were so well defined they could have been sculpted from marble. Shining hair rested on or fell below their broad shoulders, their hair in shades ranging from silvery blue to gray to black around their pointed ears.

Leather straps attached to breastplates crisscrossed the Dark Elves' bare chests. They also wore metal shoulder plates and snug leather pants. Quivers with arrows were secured to their backs. The arrows looked to be created from pewter and probably some other alloy to strengthen them.

Hannah narrowed her gaze. The detailed edges of their shoulder and breastplates were twenty-four-karat pure white gold with touches of yellow gold. If anything, she knew her fine metals and gems. Each of the Dark Elves wore a small fortune.

"Keir of the D'Danann, who may we have the pleasure of meeting today?" asked a warrior with a deep voice and an unusual accent as he and one of his cohorts blocked the way.

Keir turned slightly to allow the Drow to see the rest of

the group behind him. "You should remember the king's daughter, Rhiannon. Our companions are Hannah of the D'Anu and Eavan of the D'Danann."

"Forgive us, Princess," the deep-voiced Drow said. Each man bowed to Rhiannon. "If we had seen you, we would have taken you to the king at once."

Even in the dim lighting Hannah saw Rhiannon's cheeks redden. "Yeah. Well. We would like to see Garran, my, ah, father, right away."

A small burst of adrenaline heightened Hannah's senses at the realization they were about to meet the infamous king of the Drow. Rhiannon's discomfort was obvious and Hannah found herself feeling a little sorry for her even though they didn't get along. To find out the king of the Drow was her father—Rhiannon must have been torn in so many different directions.

The men bowed again, then turned and led the way as Hannah, Rhiannon, Keir, and Eavan followed.

Hannah raised her eyebrows when they were taken to a chamber that resembled half of a geode. The entire room sparkled from the natural crystals, including the ceiling. At the back of the room was a door that looked to be made of obsidian. An oval black granite table, surrounded by high-backed padded granite seats, took up one side of the room. Freeform carvings of Drow warriors graced the chamber.

A large, black padded granite throne commanded the center of the room. A matching smaller throne stood to the side of the larger one.

Hannah's throat grew dry and she felt a quivering sensation under her skin at the sight of the man reclining on the larger throne.

Bless it! Her body's reaction to the sight of him must have been due to the legendary magic of the Dark Elves that supposedly captivated a woman to the point she never wanted to leave the Drow realm.

Absurd.

The more she studied him, the more she realized there

was something . . . familiar about this man. His powerful build and the way he held his head at a regal angle.

Hair rose along her arms.

The man who watched me at the pond.

She knew it with every fiber of her being. A combination of lust and fascination tingled along her nerve endings and she bit the inside of her cheek to try to rein in her bizarre reactions.

The man, whom she could only assume was the king, was even more handsome, more gorgeous, than she had thought him to be when she saw him last night. He looked as if he could be a model for a world-class gym—despite the fact that he had bluish-gray skin, more gray than blue.

Now she knew the color of his hair, a sinful fall of silvery-blue that rested on his shoulderplates. Through the strands she saw his pointed ears, and the craziest image of running her tongue over those curves and points rolled through her mind.

King Garran had the most incredible eyes—beautiful liquid silver. The kind of eyes she imagined would turn to steel-gray when he was angry . . . or aroused.

Every sensibility within her went on vacation as she moved her gaze from those amazing eyes.

His features—so strong, so well-defined they appeared even more aristocratic than last night. Just the way he held himself and the air of absolute confidence and cunning intelligence that surrounded him caused desire to stir in her belly. He was a man who knew what he wanted and knew how to get it. Those qualities had always been a huge turn-on with Hannah.

She had no doubt he was a man even sronger and more virile than could be imagined.

Her gaze moved to the shoulderplates covering the broad expanse of his shoulders. Gem-encrusted leather straps crisscrossed his smooth, sculpted chest, and like last night she wondered how it would feel to brush her palms over the skin that stretched over such taut muscles.

She almost felt dizzy with lust as she looked from his chest to his rippled abs and on down . . . good goddess, the man had to be huge. Her mouth watered as she imagined touching all of him, every bit of him, including his powerful thighs and no doubt a taut ass to die for. He had probably lived for centuries, maybe millennia, but the Drow king looked no older than his mid-to-late thirties.

Drow king.

Hannah snapped her gaze to meet the liquid silver eyes of the king. Eyes that held both the promise of hot, sweaty sex, and also a tinge of amusement.

Drow magic. He's using his magic to make me want him so badly I can hardly stand it.

She swallowed and tried to sort out what was real. It felt so real. Every bit of desire flooding through her.

It can't be. It must be Drow magic.

Hannah straightened her spine as she clenched her jaw and fisted her hands at her sides.

Got. To. Get. A. Grip.

It seemed like she'd been staring at King Garran for hours, but it had probably only been a couple of minutes.

But in those minutes . . .

To Hannah's relief, the king looked lazily from her to Rhiannon.

Rhiannon stepped forward. She held her chin up as the king rose and walked down the dais toward his daughter.

Focus. Concentrate on the reason we're here.

"Rhiannon." He caught his daughter's hands. "You have come to see me."

King Garran's unusual accent and sensual voice caused a thrill to travel down Hannah's spine.

Rhiannon cleared her throat. "Yes. And to ask the same favor of you again."

Garran paused, then gave a nod, his expression thoughtful as he released her hands. "Allow me to meet your companions."

As Rhiannon turned to introduce the three of them, Hannah met Garran's gaze.

Their surroundings seemed to vanish as his liquid silver

eyes drew her in. Rhiannon's voice buzzed in Hannah's ears, but Garran didn't look away from her.

Garran came toward Hannah with the grace of a predator, every muscle in his body flexing with his movements. He rested one of his hands on his sword hilt.

When Garran reached her, Hannah found it hard to breathe. She didn't know what was happening to her, but she didn't care for it. These sensations were touching her with a warmth that felt as if it were wrapping its way around her very soul. It was on a level she knew really wasn't Drow magic at all.

What in Anu's name is going on?

She gathered her usual cool reserve and gave him what she hoped was a "back off" stare.

He took her hand and a jolt of *something* shot through her as he raised her hand to his mouth and brushed his lips across her skin. The warmth inside her both tightened and expanded at the same time, nearly overwhelming her.

When the Drow king raised his head, his expression was so sensual that she felt as though she could dissolve on the spot. Melt into a pool like the liquid silver of his eyes.

She swallowed and bit the inside of her cheek. *Hard.*

He didn't release her hand. "The woman of mystery," he said softly, so that she was certain only she heard. His sensuous Elvin accent sent a thrill through her belly. The accent wasn't Irish like the D'Danann's. More old-world, as those who lived in the days of King Arthur might have spoken. "What is your name?" he asked in a louder tone of voice.

Words almost wouldn't come to her. "Hannah Wentworth." She snatched her hand away then struggled not to clench it at her side. "Of the gray magic D'Anu witches." Why she didn't say anything about last night at the pond, she wasn't sure. And why he didn't seem inclined to talk about it added to her confusion.

"It is most certainly my pleasure." Garran held her gaze for a moment then turned to Keir and they clasped each other in that centuries-old hand-to-elbow handshake. "Keir, D'Danann."

He released Keir and offered his hand to Eavan, who hesitated before accepting it and returned the same hand-to-elbow grip.

"King Garran," Eavan said with a slight nod as they released each other. Hannah detected a note of hostility in his tone and wondered if it had anything to do with the king flirting with her.

Garran met Eavan's gaze. "And you are Eavan of the D'Danann, as my daughter said."

Had Rhiannon introduced Eavan? Hannah's ears had been buzzing so loudly she hadn't heard a word Rhiannon said.

Garran turned to his daughter and smiled. "Please. Join me. We were just about to feast."

Keir put his arm around Rhiannon's shoulders. Before she realized what he was doing, Garran touched Hannah's elbow and directed her out of the chamber and into the hall. Her stomach twisted into a knot just from that small touch as he guided her across the great circular hall and into another chamber that was obviously a banquet room. The table was large, rectangular, and could probably seat fifty people.

After releasing Hannah's arm, Garran drew back a chair that stood beside the largest chair at the head of the table, and Hannah sat on it. Amazingly, the padded leather was as soft and smooth as a velvet night sky, and so comfortable Hannah couldn't help but relax.

Garran then seated Rhiannon directly across from Hannah, on the other side of the table, and Keir pulled out the seat beside her. Eavan eased next to Hannah as Garran took the chair at the head of the table.

For the first time in her life, Hannah was nervous around a man. Beneath the table she dug her fingernails into her pack that she held in her lap, trying to get her feelings under control.

The long table quickly filled with Dark Elves, all male. Where were the women?

While Hannah did her best not to look at Garran, his deep

voice reminded her of summer nights and star-filled skies. It flooded her senses as he spoke to some of those gathered around the table.

Before she knew it, servers had placed trenchers before each person and the table was laden with platters of chicken, beef, and pork. The scents were enough to cause Hannah's mouth to water. Bowls of potatoes, sugar snap peas, and yellow squash were arranged around the meat dishes, along with fresh fruit and large hunks of cheese and bread. The bread smelled warm and freshly baked.

The entire time, Hannah was far too aware of Garran. She felt odd—jittery—in his presence but flushed with heat.

No man had ever made her feel that kind of electricity sizzling under her skin just from being close to him. How could she feel this way when he was one of the Dark Elves, a being who couldn't be trusted? A traitor.

And he has blue skin, for the goddess's sake!

From the other side of her, she sensed Eavan's tension and decided to ignore him, too.

As Garran spoke with Rhiannon, she couldn't help but listen to his rich voice. Hannah tried to stay completely aloof, but it was difficult as she noticed his soft smile and gentle manner as he talked with his daughter. Rhiannon seemed to have set their differences and her anger aside for the moment as her father told her stories of the mother she never knew, and of his love for them both.

A sigh came out of nowhere and Hannah tried to hold it in as her thoughts brushed her own childhood.

The dull roar of conversation rolled over Hannah as she tore tiny pieces off a chunk of bread and let them fall onto her trencher. In some ways she was like Rhiannon. Hannah had never known a true home, and what a real family was like.

Instead, she had spent her childhood being dragged around by her mother who went from husband to husband to husband. Selena Wentworth was born of "old money," and had spent it lavishly. Her husbands each demanded alimony once Selena divorced them and moved on to the next man.

She paid the alimony without batting an eyelash or putting a dent in her checking account.

Hannah tore off bigger pieces of bread until there was nothing left in her hands. She fought back the childish feelings that tightened her stomach as she thought about her mother. A mother who would rather attend parties, luncheons, and social gatherings than spend time with her own daughter.

Hannah sucked in her breath. What in Anu's name was she doing? Thinking? She was no longer that little girl who needed attention and never received it.

"Why did I not see you at my daughter and Keir's joining, Hannah?" Garran asked, drawing her away and giving her a reprieve from the unwanted thoughts. His rich voice flowed over her like honey.

She frowned as she worked to regain her composure and force better forgotten memories away. "I was at the wedding."

"You must have left the room." Garran leaned closer to her. "I would have seen you." He lowered his voice another octave. "*Sensed* you. Like last night."

Something inside her told her she would have felt him, too. The innate power of his presence made her dizzy, and that was enough to make her grind her teeth. *Was* he using Drow magic on her?

"Why were you watching me last night?" she asked, keeping her expression neutral and her voice just as low as his.

"It is not often one comes across such beauty. And magic." Garran gave her a lazy look as his gaze slid from her face to her breasts, and then his eyes met hers again. His slow perusal caused her nipples to tighten and ache against her will. The corner of his mouth curved into a sinful smile. "I wager you have many surprises."

GARRAN'S LIPS TWITCHED AS he studied the beautiful woman who looked at him with such disdain.

Hannah Wentworth might not wish to be attracted to him, but in every fiber of his being he held certainty that she was.

Hannah's dark brown gaze moved from his eyes, down his chest, to his abs. Fortunately she could not see beneath the table, unless that was one of her D'Anu talents. He had to refrain from shifting in his chair as her gaze traveled over his body. Instead, he leaned back, propped his elbows on the chair's arms, and steepled his fingers.

She brought her eyes back to his. "My talents would be wasted here," she said, then turned to speak to the D'Danann warrior on the other side of her.

Garran did smile then. This woman was not easily rattled or embarrassed, something he found more than intriguing. Her mere presence heightened his senses. The soft scent of her skin—woman, and something light, clean, and fresh. Need vibrated through his body, deep and carnal.

The intriguing woman was one of the most beautiful creatures he had ever had the pleasure of meeting. A woman meant to be savored as a man would enjoy a fine Faerie-made honeyed mead.

He would start with brushing his lips over the line of her delicate brow while sifting his fingers through the blond lock that was so distinctive against her dark hair. His teeth would find her earlobe and she would give a soft cry as he nipped it then slipped his tongue inside.

When his mouth finally met her soft lips, he would taste her like a hummingbird might relish nectar from a bloom. His tongue would move with hers and their lips would meet and meet again.

The din at the meal table faded as he focused intently on Hannah until he was certain he could hear Hannah's every breath with every rise and fall of her chest. His gaze settled on her breasts and he lowered his lids as he smiled his sexual promise when she glanced at him. Her cheeks had the slightest tinge of pink as her nipples grew obviously harder, pushing even more against the cloth covering them.

Cloth he wanted to peel away so that he could suckle, lick and bite those nipples.

He noticed the catch in her breath as she looked away. She reached one hand up and slid her fingers over her gold armband in what appeared to be a nervous movement. He shifted in his seat as his erection grew when he imagined her fingers stroking his cock in the same way.

Garran let his gaze drift from her breasts to her small waist and pictured her naked body. He would stroke her flat belly, the curve of her waist to her hips and then he would spread her thighs wide. He could almost feel his hands sliding beneath her ass as he buried his face against her folds.

He imagined how sweet her flavor would be, smooth and rich on his tongue.

Gods, he wanted her. Wanted to taste her sweetness. Wanted to feel her slim body beneath his as she cried his name.

When he came to his senses, the noise in the room gradually returned to his hearing. The bellows of laughter he had pushed out of his consciousness now rang in his ears, hiding the sound of her breathing and the rapid beat of her heart.

His gaze moved from her to her companion and he narrowed his eyes. The man sitting beside Hannah clearly desired her. A moment's anger at the D'Danann warrior traveled through Garran, an unfamiliar feeling of jealousy. But the feeling quickly diminished as he saw that Hannah was dismissing the man, just as she had dismissed Garran.

But unlike her reaction to him, Garran felt no currents of attraction between her and the D'Danann. At least not on Hannah's part.

Instead, the sexual awareness remained between Garran and Hannah. Tangible, strong threads that could easily be woven into a tight rope.

Hannah turned her attention to her trencher and frowned at the pieces of bread she had shredded on it before looking at the rest of the food on the table. More raucous laughter broke out from the opposite end, but the D'Danann and D'Anu did not join in. They appeared far too serious.

Hannah took a few grapes and a bit of cheese, but merely picked at her food as he watched.

Garran's gaze settled on his daughter who sat on the other side of him. She looked so much like her mother that every time he saw her, his chest seized and he felt that lonely ache that sometimes took residence in his heart.

Since the time Rhiannon's mother had passed on to Summerland, no woman had attracted him like his daughter's companion, this Hannah Wentworth.

No one, until this fresh, exciting D'Anu witch.

Oh, he had enjoyed attempting to seduce Copper Ashcroft when she had been trapped in Otherworld. But the fascination had been nothing like what he felt at this moment. With Copper it had been mere flirtation.

It had been nothing like what stirred inside him now— such intense feelings of desire along with the need to possess. He had never experienced such an incredible attraction as he felt at this moment.

Garran, who normally had no difficulty in focusing on whatever task was at hand, had to struggle to take his focus off Hannah to where it belonged.

He could ill afford such a distraction as Hannah, especially with so many weighty matters at hand.

Garran smiled as he studied his daughter. They had spoken of her mother and earlier he had shared some of the joyful memories with Rhiannon. But he had not yet touched on her life now.

He laid his hand over Rhiannon's where it rested on the table. "Are you happy with your mate?"

Rhiannon had been focused on the D'Danann, Keir, and she cut her gaze to Garran. She cleared her throat and nodded. "I am. Very happy."

He offered her a smile and squeezed her fingers. "Then I am pleased for you."

"Thank you." She looked uncomfortable with his hand on

hers and he released it before selecting a hunk of white cheese and setting it in his trencher beside his healthy serving of pork.

"We will eat." He tore off a piece of bread from a loaf that sat before him and brought the piece close to his mouth. "Then we will talk about why you have truly come to see me."

AFTER DINNER, ONLY HANNAH and her companions remained seated at the table with Garran.

The king had introduced them to each member of his "Directorate," something like a high council, and they met the leaders of the order, Sepan and Hark, along with Garran's First and Second in Command, Vidar and Carden. The men had made it clear they expected to stay for the discussion with the witches and the D'Danann, but Garran had dismissed all of them.

Now just two guards were positioned to either side of the door inside the room, and two on each side of the door in the great hall.

The dishes had been swept away and all that was left behind on the smooth, clean table were tankards of mead that had been placed in front of each person.

Garran leaned back in his chair in a casual pose, his elbow resting on one arm of the chair while his free hand stroked his chin. No longer did Hannah see the teasing light that had been in his liquid silver eyes, but the seriousness of a warrior, a king.

"You have come once again to seek the aid of the Drow." Garran looked to Rhiannon and to each of her three companions in turn. "Tell me why my people should assist you?"

Rhiannon frowned. Hannah felt a pinch in her gut that told her this wasn't going to be as easy as she'd begun to hope.

Hannah thought it best to speak first and start with the urgency of their situation. "Ceithlenn has killed thousands in our city," she said. "Somehow the goddess collects their souls and the souls make her stronger—strong enough that she was able to bring her husband from Underworld."

Astonishment showed on Garran's face. "Balor? In your San Francisco Otherworld. At this moment?"

Rhiannon nodded and gripped her tankard in both hands. "The god is searching for his eye. Darkwolf still wears the eye on a chain around his neck, and if Balor gets a hold of it . . ."

"All who stand in his way will perish," Garran said in a flat tone.

"That's why we need your assistance." Hannah relaxed her hands when she realized she was clenching them on the tabletop. "We can't do it alone."

Rhiannon leaned forward in her chair and pushed her mead out of her way. "There are only a handful of us—the D'Anu witches, what D'Danann warriors the Chieftains will give us, and the San Francisco Paranormal Special Forces."

"But this matter does not concern us." Garran's voice remained calm and Hannah's temper rose in a slow burn. "Balor is not in Otherworld," he added before taking a drink of his mead.

Rhiannon's face turned nearly scarlet and her scars stood out against her cheek. "Don't you care about me and those I love? You're supposed to be my father. Won't you help your own daughter?"

As he studied Rhiannon, Garran said softly, "*I* would." Then he raised his voice as he thumped his tankard on the tabletop. "But I am the king of the Dark Elves and I bear the responsibility of making the decisions as to what is best for my people."

"The good of the few outweighs the good of the many?" Hannah's back was rigid as she spoke. "That is such—such—"

"Bullshit," Rhiannon said, her green eyes burning with fire. "Thousands, if not *millions,* need you. That is the many. You are the few."

Keir's expression had turned thunderous and Eavan narrowed his gaze. Likely they were reining themselves in from locking horns with Garran.

It was obvious that no matter how hard they pleaded, Garran wasn't going to budge. Hannah looked at Rhiannon, who nodded.

Hannah leaned forward in her seat, her eyes fixed on Garran's. "What if we were able to offer something to *your* people in return for helping *our* people?"

"Then you would have my interest, as king as well as a father and a man." Garran drummed his fingers on the arm of his chair. "What do you bring to barter?"

Hannah took a deep breath. "The Great Guardian said she will give you something you want for your people in exchange for helping us."

Garran stopped drumming his fingers. Shock registered along the strong lines of his face, making Hannah wonder what could be so important that it would affect the king so strongly. "The Guardian said this?" he asked, a hard edge to his tone.

Rhiannon wrapped her hand around her tankard again, but didn't take a drink. "The Guardian met us at the transference stone right before we came here."

Irritation was evident in Garran's expression. "You failed to mention her offer immediately, for what reason?"

Rhiannon sounded like she was talking through gritted teeth. "Because I wanted to know if you would do it out of the goodness of your heart. Apparently you don't have one."

Garran's look turned thoughtful for a moment as he met his daughter's gaze. He glanced toward Hannah again. "What exactly did the Elvin Guardian say?"

"You'll be given something for aiding us, something your people want." Hannah swept the lock of blond from her face to join her dark hair. "Conditionally."

Rhiannon added, "She said you have to go alone to talk to her."

Garran leaned back in his chair again and stroked his

chin with one hand while his stare seemed to travel somewhere in the distance, as if he didn't see any of them at that moment.

Finally, he shifted in his seat and looked to each member of Hannah's group. "I will visit the Guardian to hear what promise she can make me and my people. Then I will make my decision."

Rhiannon's shoulders relaxed and the tension coiled inside Hannah unwound a little.

"But I have my own condition." He looked to each person. "One of you will stay with my people and serve as liaison to yours."

Hannah frowned. "Why?"

"My reasons are my own. That is my condition." He turned his gaze on Hannah. "One of you will stay here while I talk to the Guardian. And if we go to battle alongside your people, that person will remain with the Drow and at my side during the war. Do you accept?"

It couldn't be Keir or Rhiannon—neither of them should be separated like that. And Eavan . . . Hannah glanced at him. Definitely not the liaison type.

Yes, *she* needed to do what was necessary to help out an entire city, if not an entire world.

"I'll do it," she said before anyone else could respond. "I'm the best woman for the job."

A pleased smile crept over Garran's features even as Eavan growled, "I forbid it. I will stay."

Hannah swung her gaze to Eavan, fury burning her insides. "Do not *ever* think you can tell me what I can or can't do. I will stay and that is absolutely final."

Eavan opened his mouth to say something but she let her expression speak louder than her words. "You do *not* want to argue with me."

She cut her gaze back to Garran. "I have my own condition." The coiled tension in Hannah's belly magnified and she had to force her hands to relax on the tabletop. "*No one* is to attempt to use *any* Drow magic on me."

A slight smile curved the corner of Garran's mouth. "Done."

"No godsdamn way," Eavan said as he stood. His chair almost toppled, but Hannah caught it with a quick tug using a rope of her magic.

"Sit, Eavan." Hannah's glare met Eavan's as he shot his gaze toward hers. "I made the choice. If it's the only way we're going to get the help we need, then I'll do it."

"Then I will stay, too." Eavan made a low growling noise in his throat, his expression thunderous as he scowled.

Garran's voice was firm. "Not more than one of your delegation."

"It will be me." Hannah looked at Garran who was once again casually relaxed in his chair with a hint of humor in his smile.

When Hannah glanced at Rhiannon, she saw that Rhiannon's lips were parted and she was staring at Garran.

"You should all go back now." Hannah pushed her chair from the table. "You have a lot of work to do if we're going to fight Ceithlenn in San Francisco." She caught Garran's eye as he got to his feet. "And we have a lot to do here to make it happen."

If eyes could literally twinkle, Garran's did.

Eavan grumbled a lot more and Rhiannon scowled, while Keir had the same dark expression that he always did.

Except when he gazed at Rhiannon. When Keir looked at Rhiannon, it was like the whole world revolved around her and as if she were something treasured and precious to him.

Sometimes Hannah wondered what it would be like to have a man look at her like that.

Right. She shook her hair back as they reached the stairs. After all the men who had run through her mother's fingers like water, and had taken all they could from her, Hannah didn't believe very strongly in solid, real, loving relationships. She had seen four of her sister D'Anu witches find men who seemed to fit the bill, but she knew it was different for them. She was Selena Wentworth's daughter. *She* was different.

Hannah's muscles tensed as she spoke to Rhiannon. "I need you to watch over Banshee while I'm gone. Take him to San Francisco when you go back. Please."

Rhiannon looked surprised and paused a moment before she said, "No problem. I'll make sure he's taken care of."

A feeling of relief mingled with sadness flowed through Hannah. She hadn't been parted from Banshee since he had first come to her. Not like this—for who knew how long. "Thank you," Hannah said before she took a step back.

"Are you certain?" Eavan's expression softened and his eyes appeared concerned when he turned to Hannah. A part of her felt touched that he was worried about her.

"Of course." She forced a smile. "I'm always confident in my choices."

Sure you are, her mind whispered, and she mentally slapped it down.

Eavan gave a single nod before stepping onto the stairs that eventually led up into the sunlight.

"I will see you soon, daughter," Garran said when Rhiannon glanced at him.

She studied him for a long moment before she went up the stairs behind Eavan.

Keir did that old handshake with Garran before following Rhiannon.

Keep cool.

Hannah resisted fidgeting and tugging down on her leather shirt. "Are you going to see the Great Guardian now?"

His silvery-blue hair shimmered in the low lighting when he shook his head. "When it is dark, sweet one."

"Excuse me?" Hannah folded her arms across her chest. "My name is *Hannah.*"

Sweet one, my—

Garran looked like he wanted to laugh. "Come. Let me show you our realm. If you are to serve as liaison, then you must know and understand my people, at least at a basic level."

CHAPTER THREE

RICH SCENTS OF EARTH and minerals swirled in the cool air brushing Hannah's skin as she walked beside the king. She gripped the strap of her pack tight before releasing some of the tension coiled inside her and letting her hand fall away.

They strode across the great round hall with numerous doors around its circumference. Her shoes made soft sounds against the marble, but Garran was as silent as the D'Danann.

Despite the fact that his skin was a bluish-gray, the man was gorgeous. It would have been impossible not to appreciate the litheness of his movements, his grace—and power. Power in every flex of his muscles, in the way he held his head, in his very presence. He was a king in every sense of the word.

Garran paused and gestured to the excellent carvings on the walls. "Some of our finest craftsmen created these grand works of art."

The carvings were mostly of male warriors in battle. Then heat burned Hannah's skin as she slowly looked around the enormous circular hall. Were women kneeling to the men in some of the artwork? *Oh, my goddess.* Most of the Drow women even wore collars.

Hannah's gaze snapped to Garran's. Heat flared her body and she clenched her hands at her sides. "Don't you dare tell me"—she pointed to the carvings—"that Dark Elves treat women as subservient?"

Garran raised an eyebrow. "It is our lifestyle."

"Oh, no." She shook her head as she ground her teeth. "You *cannot* make me believe female Drow enjoy being treated like that."

His shrug was casual. "They would have it no other way."

Hannah considered decking him. Or better yet, using her magic to make *him* a collar—and a leash. "You probably don't give them a choice."

"Certainly we do." He tried taking her by the elbow and guiding her to a door, but she jerked away from his touch. "However, it is a rare thing for a woman to choose not to serve a Master."

A Master?

The thought of Garran on the floor with the magical collar and rope was looking better and better.

He swept his arm out in front of him, indicating they should go through a large arched doorway that spun off from the great hall. "You will see."

Her lips tight with anger, Hannah walked beside Garran as they entered an underground city. For the moment awe replaced her anger.

Stalactites spotted with glowing lichen projected down from the great cavern. The entire ceiling sparkled and more lichen caused a blue glow to give a soft light to the city.

Homes clung to rock outcroppings and footpaths wended their way around the cavern walls. Most of the city was spread out across the smooth, obviously well-worn floor of the cavern. Narrow streets wound from one building to the next. It reminded her of the D'Danann village, yet not.

Wonderful aromas spilled from shops that sold bread and other bakery goods, including what smelled like coffeecake. Hannah's mouth watered even though she was still full from dinner.

All she saw were males who gave low nods to Garran as she and Garran passed them. In turn he inclined his head and greeted each person by name. The respect in their gazes and voices, and the way they responded to him with their gestures and expressions, told her how well they thought of their king.

Where are the women?

As they strolled—Garran acknowledging every male they walked by—they came across a butcher shop, a place that offered leather goods, as well as a smithy that made the breast and shoulder plates most of the warriors wore. It seemed everything one could think of could be found in this underground city.

Except a Starbucks.

She shook her head. First thing she was going to do when life returned to "normal" in San Francisco would be to buy one of those Frappuccinos she'd been craving.

Her gaze riveted on a glittering blanket of gems ahead in a windowless display. Goddess, a fortune in jewelry was spread out. Diamonds the size of eggs, rubies as big as a fist.

Gem-encrusted leather collars?

Hannah's head snapped up. She brushed her crescent and moon armband with her fingers before dropping her hand to her side as she caught sight of a few women on the path in the direction she and Garran had been heading.

The women were so scantily clad they might as well have been wearing nothing. Practically sheer tops were so short they exposed the roundness of the underside of the women's breasts and the filmy material hardly covered their nipples. They also wore short gauzy skirts that hardly reached the bottoms of their ass cheeks.

Most of the women wore collars.

Collars, for Anu's sake! Like dogs or other animals, they wore collars and *served a Master.*

Heat filled her as she watched the women. Their skin was smooth and supple in the cavern's soft lighting, their curves in all the right places—their bodies virtually perfect.

A couple of the women whispered to each other when they saw their king with Hannah and they bowed to him almost shyly. But otherwise the women smiled, talked, and laughed among themselves. Despite the fact they wore collars, they appeared . . . happy.

"Explain to me," Hannah said through gritted teeth, "why these women allow themselves to be collared and why they are practically naked. Are they sex slaves or something?"

"The collar means a woman belongs to a Master." Garran came up short and they stopped in front of the jewelry store as he glanced down at Hannah. His expression softened. "Sex is important to any consenting adult relationship, but our way of life is not 'all about sex' as you would say."

Hannah braced her hands on her hips as she glared up at him. He was so damned tall she had to tilt her head. "Then what is it about?"

"Come." He touched his hand on her elbow. "We will talk."

One thing Hannah *never* did was cause a scene in public. She clamped her jaws shut as she realized that was what she'd just about done. She blanked her expression and held her carriage high as she usually did.

Garran guided her past a fish market, the scents reminding her of home and the wind off the bay, calling up memories of her old life and a twinge in her belly. They strolled beyond the market to a display of wooden figurines and children's toys. Then the smells of fresh fish and wood drifted away as they continued on to what appeared to be a park.

Children wearing rough-spun tunics and pants laughed and played on the flat, moss-covered rocky area filled with boulders and stone statues. Hannah couldn't help a smile as she and Garran stopped outside the park and watched the children racing, kicking black leather balls, climbing boulders, or sitting cross-legged on the mossy ground playing with toys. They had wooden dolls and figures including something that looked like the ugliest troll she could imagine. Some of the male dolls were dressed like warriors wearing breastplates and leather chest straps, and even leather pants. The female dolls tended to have iridescent clothing that shimmered in the blue lichen lighting.

Barbie and G.I. Joe had nothing on these dolls.

Hannah touched one of the smooth boulders surrounding the park. "I never thought about Elves having children."

When she glanced up at Garran, he wore an amused expression. "Did you think we are created from stone?"

"Actually, I had been wondering if *you* were." She turned her attention back to the park. Several women were dressed in a little more clothing than the ladies Hannah had seen in the village, but they still wore collars. They sat on rock benches at various places around the area, many talking as their children played.

A pinging sensation bounced around in Hannah's heart. The mothers looked so happy, as did the children. Hannah hadn't had the kind of childhood where she was allowed to play with other children. She'd been sheltered, watched by a nanny, then sent to boarding schools where fraternization was discouraged.

One of the children threw a baseball-sized black leather ball that overshot the kid he'd been throwing the ball to. It rushed straight for Hannah. Garran snapped his hand up and caught the ball before it would have slammed into her face.

Relief whooshed through her. That would have hurt like hell.

A young boy dressed in a royal-blue tunic and pants trotted toward them with a chagrined expression. "I—I didn't mean to—"

Garran squatted so he was eye level with the boy and handed him the ball. "You have great strength, Jalen." The boy clutched the ball to his chest and looked at Garran with wide blue eyes. Garran placed his hand on the boy's left arm. "Continue your practice, most especially your control. One day you will make a fine warrior."

Jalen nodded hard enough that his blue hair fell into his eyes. "Yes, my lord."

Garran eased to his feet and gestured to the park. "Enjoy your game of *carta*."

The boy nodded again before whirling and bolting to

where other boys and girls had stopped playing and were staring at Garran. Some waved and gave shy smiles and Garran acknowledged them with a slight incline of his head.

It was odd seeing Garran as more than a king and a warrior. A strange whirling gripped her insides and she had no idea why.

She let her gaze drift from Garran to the boys and girls. "They're beautiful."

"Children among Dark Elves are rare," he said softly, with what sounded like a touch of longing, and she moved her gaze toward him. "They are much treasured."

The distant look in his eyes surprised her for a moment before she realized he was probably thinking of his own daughter, Rhiannon, who had been raised among humans and kept far from him—in San Francisco. A part of Hannah melted and it took a lot of effort to make herself return to the subject that still bothered her.

"You haven't explained this whole Master/slave thing," she said, and his attention cut to her.

"Our women are not slaves." His words had a hard edge to them and he had an even harder look in his eyes. "It is an exchange of power, protection, and pleasure if you will."

Hannah frowned. "I'm not following you."

Garran folded his arms and leaned his hip against one of the larger boulders. "Our men are far stronger physically than our women. They rely on us for protection and to provide for them."

She crossed her own arms beneath her breasts and her frown turned into a scowl. "So the males make them walk around with hardly anything on, wearing collars, and calling them *Master*?"

"In turn," Garran continued as his gaze held hers, "the woman holds the power to give the man pleasure."

Her cheeks heated as her anger rose. "So this *is* all about sex."

He shook his head, his silvery-blue hair shimmering in the soft glow given off by the lichen above. "A Drow female who serves a Master has the power to please him in all aspects of his life. Family, home, and yes, sex."

Hannah huffed out her breath. "I don't get it."

Garran took her by the elbow again. They walked along a path and she tried to calm down about the whole woman-serving-a-man thing. *Barbaric*.

He came to a stop in front of another jeweler's display. He glanced at one of the gem-studded collars then turned his gaze on her. "Wouldn't you enjoy belonging to someone, Hannah Wentworth?"

Belong to someone? Having a Master? More heat flushed over her and her whole body tensed. "I want to talk to you," she said, nearly grinding her teeth as she spoke. "In private."

He winked and smiled, and she thought again about using her magic as a rope and collar.

As the heat in her body ramped up even more, she and Garran walked from the city through a honeycomb of passageways. They entered a dim hallway where arches opened in various directions, and he led her through one of the arches. The whole time they walked, Hannah's temper mounted.

They eventually reached the end of a short hall that led to a door on the right. The sound of rushing water met Hannah's ears as he drew her into a chamber.

A bedroom—likely his. In the far corner, water tumbled from a high rock, spilling into a pool the size of a sauna. Tapestries of Drow warriors in battle draped the walls. Rugs lay scattered on the floor in the same rich colors as the tapestries. On one wall hung swords, a quiver of arrows, and a bow, along with other weapons. All would be incredibly expensive in her world. The metals and gems glittered in the soft blue lighting shining from lichen on the ceiling over their heads.

A huge bed that looked as if it had been carved from an enormous round stone commanded the center of the room. "You sleep in a rock?" she muttered. "I shouldn't be surprised."

"Try it." Garran moved closer to her and she felt the power of his presence grasping hold of her like a tight embrace. "The bed is quite soft." He reached up and trailed the knuckles of one of his hands down her bare arm. "Almost as soft as your skin."

Immediately a jolt, like spellfire, shot through her body from the places he touched. Goose bumps pebbled her skin and she pushed his hand away as she backed up.

She let her anger replace her awareness of him as a man. Her voice lowered to a growl. "No wonder you were all sent to live underground. All of this 'woman serving a Master and who holds the power' stuff is crap. You're barbaric heathens."

Garran's eyes darkened, no amusement, no teasing left in his gaze. She almost took another step away from him as a chill traced her spine.

"It is not for you or any others to judge our lifestyle." His jaw tightened and the temperature in the room dropped as if winter had shrouded the last whispers of fall. "The Elders are judgmental, hypocritical bastards who had no right to do this to my people."

Hannah swallowed hard as she resisted rubbing her arms from the chill. The realization that he was right hit her like a snowball to her belly, icing her insides. She had always held to the strong belief that no one group had the right to judge what another race did, or to dictate what those people could or could not do, or banish the race because they were different.

As long as it was consensual, this Master thing was really none of her business or anyone else's. If it was true slavery, though, that was a whole different ballgame.

Hannah let out a breath and she could see it in the icy air. This time she did rub her arms with both hands. The band on her upper arm chilled from the cold and she started to shake. Somehow Garran had changed the temperature with his anger and his Drow magic.

"You're right." Her teeth chattered as she spoke. "I have no right to judge you or any of the Dark Elves. As long as the women are happy with it, then it's nobody's business but your own."

The air in the room warmed dramatically as Garran's expression softened and his jaw relaxed. "Do you say this from fear? Or do you believe it to be true?"

"I have mixed feelings." The goose bumps on her arms vanished as the temperature warmed. "I don't agree with it, but when you put it that way, you're right. No race should be banished or segregated for their lifestyle."

Then she thought of the Fomorii and she scowled. "Unless the race is like the demons from Underworld, creatures that murder and feed off other beings."

He gave a slow nod. "Then you do understand."

She relaxed her arms at her sides. "I don't agree with your lifestyle, but I understand a little better." Her frown returned as she held his gaze. "But don't you ask me if I want to belong to anyone again. Especially in public—if you want all your manly parts to remain intact."

Garran smiled and reached up to trail his fingers through her hair. "Agreed."

A shiver racked her body, and this time not from any chill in the room. His hand slid from her hair as she stepped back, needing to get away from his touch.

"What I really don't understand," she said, letting her voice harden again, "is why you chose to help open the door to Underworld."

Garran's muscles flexed when he tensed and his jaw tightened. "I was promised that my people would have what they most desire—to again walk in the light." He moved his hand to his chest. "To no longer be marked as we are."

Her heart caught in her throat. Marked for their choice in lifestyle?

He brought his fingers to his head and raked them through his silvery-blue hair. "Agreeing to such a bargain to open the door was a mistake that I realized almost too late." His gaze slipped away and pain was etched across his features. "For some it *was* too late."

Garran shook his head as though shaking off a bad dream. "Balor would never have granted us our former lives as promised by Darkwolf. I sensed it in Ceithlenn's thoughts the moment she escaped through the door."

"You helped set her free." A surge of anger rose in Hannah again, despite the pain on Garran's strong features. "You should have been helping us return her to Underworld all along. Or kill her."

Garran stepped forward and brought his hand up to finger the lock of blond hair curving along one side of her face. The way he kept touching her—it made it so hard to think. "I know this, Hannah Wentworth." His voice was low, soft. "But I serve my people and they come first. Can you not understand that?"

"I'll have to think about it." The flames in her chest didn't want to recede. "A lot."

She wasn't sure she could come to terms with his original choices. First, he had sided with Darkwolf and opened the door to Underworld—which in itself she found nearly unforgivable. So what if he had realized his mistake and helped close it again? The damage had been done. Ceithlenn was free.

Then Garran made the choice to not aid those in the battle in San Francisco, even though he had helped let the dark goddess out.

How could anyone accept or forgive those decisions? It wasn't until he was offered something that he even considered helping her city and people in a mess he helped cause.

But now that she'd met Garran, heard his side of the story . . . goddess, she was confused. And confusion wasn't something she liked. Not at all.

He studied her, his face so close to hers now that she felt his warm breath on her cheeks. A shock of desire hit her straight in her belly and the power of it nearly made her stagger backward.

Dear Anu. He must be using Drow magic and I'm not as immune as I thought I was.

"I have more to show you." He gave her his usual cocky grin, and she straightened and raised her chin, forcing the lust and need away. "You do not yet know our primary means of commerce—a most important aspect of the society you will have to represent to your people, should we form an alliance."

Commerce. Money. Business.

Yes.

Now here was something Hannah could sink her teeth into. And maybe observe without wanting to emasculate her host.

Garran's hand was warm and big around hers and she didn't try to shake off his hold as he led her out of his chamber, down the hallways, and to the great round hall. This time she ignored the carvings on the walls of the collared women bowing to warriors, and concentrated on where they were going next.

After they crossed the hall, they entered a carved-out tunnel that smelled of dark earth and minerals. She'd never been claustrophobic, but the walls seemed to close in on her, and she was relieved when they left the tunnel and entered a cavern.

"Beautiful," she murmured as she took in the massive space. They stood on a platform in the middle of a huge sparkling cavern. "And amazing."

Otherworld was truly a place filled with surprises and this was no exception. Veins of white and yellow gold marked the earthen and rock walls. Rubies, emeralds, and other gems that had to be worth billions were organized in huge mounds, far below where they stood. If she and Garran continued on the path leading from the platform, they would wind down in a slow circle until they reached the bottom where Drow workers toiled.

Overhead hung stalactites that shimmered in the low glow filling the cavern. The lighting was created by more of that lichen she'd seen in the city and in Garran's room. Stalagmites also burst up from the cavern floor, and the Drow worked around them.

Some of the Dark Elves sifted the jewels and ore from the

excavated earth. Against one wall stood multiple pickaxes along with buckets and shovels.

The Drow below weren't dressed the same as the warriors. Instead they wore simple gray shirts and pants and most had their hair drawn back with leather ties. She watched as the dusty workers traveled in and out of various tunnels. The passageways were so dark she couldn't see into them.

She looked up at Garran. "What do they use for light?"

He shrugged. "Drow need no light to see by when we dig or travel through tunnels. Our senses guide us. But we do require some, as you can see, in our city and in our pit."

"Why do you need light there?" She tilted her head to the side. "If you don't in the tunnels."

Garran laughed. "To live a comfortable life where we can see clearly and not have to rely on our senses."

"Ah." In the middle of the cavern was a huge area that looked as if the dirt had been freshly turned. "The center of the cavern," she said as she looked from it back to Garran. "Did you mine there, too? The rest of your tunnels lead off, away from the pit, not down into the floor."

Garran rubbed the bridge of his nose with his thumb and forefinger before meeting her gaze again. "That . . . was a mistake." The pain on his face was so intense she felt it all the way to her belly. The roguish look was gone from his eyes and for a moment all she saw was sorrow and remorse.

Hannah shifted her gaze back to the freshly turned earth. "It's where your people dug and found old passageways and caverns that led to the door to Underworld. Copper told me about that." Suddenly Hannah understood Garran's pain, and sorrow touched her soul. "Your brother died down there just weeks ago—murdered by a Fomorii demon."

"Yes," Garran said quietly when she looked at him.

Hannah didn't know what to do or say. With her upbringing, she'd never been the huggy-touchy type, but right now the urge to comfort Garran was almost overwhelming. And she didn't have the slightest idea what to do about it.

He took her hand and squeezed. "Enough for now."

Garran drew her through the passageway and back to the great hall. Without saying anything more, he led her to another hallway and then to another room with a waterfall tumbling over rocks in one corner. The water splashed into a roughly circular pool, much like that in Garran's chamber. The room was decorated in navy blue velvet and gold brocade with beautiful tapestries gracing the walls.

"Where do you get all of these—these things?" Hannah asked as he released her hand and she stepped onto a navy and gold patterned rug. Her experienced eye told her the rug was so well made it could have been Persian. She walked to a bed that was much like Garran's, and rubbed her hand over the velvet coverlet. "And the food—things that are raised aboveground? Like the vegetables we ate for dinner and the fish in the market?"

She turned to Garran to see him with his shoulder hitched against the chamber's doorway, his arms across his chest. There was no longer pain in his expression. Instead he smiled as if he were entertained by her question. "Did you think we would eat bats and grubs?"

Her normal aplomb returned. She could give as good as she got. "Of course."

This time he laughed out loud. "At night we barter with various beings that live on the surface." His eyes suddenly held a dark, smoldering look. "As you can imagine, we have much to offer."

"You certainly do." Hannah held his gaze. "Gold and gemstones, of course."

Garran studied her for a long moment

Breathing didn't come easy and her heart pounded so hard her chest hurt as her gaze locked with his. Intense desire flooded through her like she'd never felt before. Her nipples hardened and ached and a tingle traveled from her belly to between her thighs.

The roguish glint returned to his eyes as they traveled over her body, making her wish she was naked and it was his hands instead of only his gaze stroking her.

Who was this Hannah who was being totally turned on by the king of the Dark Elves?

"Stop it." She sucked much-needed air into her lungs. "You're using Drow magic on me."

The corner of his mouth quirked. "So you desire me."

Mentally attempting to douse the flare of lust coursing through her, she narrowed her gaze and glared at him. "You promised you wouldn't."

It was as if a rope bound her, tugging at her, trying to draw her to him with his gaze. "I used no magic. Something exists between us, a magic we share."

"Not possible." Hannah licked her moist lips and wiped her damp palms on her leather pants. She straightened and glared at him. "I don't believe you."

Garran's expression turned hard, angry even. "I gave you my word, Hannah Wentworth." He moved forward and she took a step back to find herself pinned against the wall. "I never break my vows."

"Yeah, right." The desire she'd been feeling spiked and she shivered all over as she looked at him. "*Stop* it."

In a fast movement he had his hands braced on the wall, over her head. She was a fairly tall woman at five eight, but he towered over her, his masculine scent surrounding her, his entire presence dominating her.

A tangle of thoughts swirled through her mind.

Duck under one of his arms.

Punch him.

Knee him in the groin.

Kiss him.

It was the last option that pressed against her mind, bending her brain so that she almost couldn't think any longer. Her gaze settled on his lips before she looked up to meet his liquid silver eyes.

"Nothing's going to happen," she finally managed to get out, her voice low and husky. "No way."

His expression was still hard and he moved his face closer to hers. A shiver racked her body when he lightly brushed her lips with his before he drew back. "It will." To her surprise he pushed away from the wall, taking his warmth and the power of his presence with him. "But not now."

Hannah's composure had eroded so completely from the lust and desire that she had to fight to regain a semblance of that composure.

"It is time I visit the Guardian." Garran glanced at the doorway. "You may retire here while I am gone."

She wasn't about to argue. At this moment she needed time alone, time to compose herself.

"Rest well," he said before he turned and strode out of the room.

Hannah stared after him. He was delicious—the way he moved, the flex of muscles in his back and shoulders, his snug leather pants molding to what looked like a very tight ass . . .

All too soon he had vanished from sight.

She shook her head to rattle the thoughts out.

Drow magic.

But he had given his word, and she believed him. She actually believed that this man, someone she'd always thought to be a traitor due to past events, was truthful.

At least in this.

The strength of Garran's character—from her usually right-on intuition—told her he was a good man, even if she didn't agree with what he'd done before she'd met him. He did what was in the best interests of his people.

She rubbed her temple with one hand as she shut the arched wooden door with her other then walked to the bed and perched on the edge of it. She couldn't get the man out of her mind. She could imagine the feel of his lips . . . what he would taste like . . . how it would feel with his mouth on her breasts . . . the silk of his hair in her hands . . . his thick hardness pressed against her belly . . .

Hannah squeezed her eyes tight and took a deep breath.

Tomorrow. Tomorrow things would be different. She

would act the diplomat, maintaining the five Cs. Calm. Cool. Composed. Collected. Controlled.

She opened her eyes again and stared at a tapestry of a Drow couple, and the collar around the woman's neck.

Or not.

CHAPTER FOUR

IN HER HUMAN FORM, Ceithlenn struggled to catch her breath as she stayed in the shadows, away from the lights illuminating the sidewalks and street. Fuck, but she was weak. Her legs trembled, as rubbery as Underworld grubs, and her normally keen sight wavered.

Fury at her drained and vulnerable state boiled in a heated pool in her belly.

The D'Anu witches, the D'Danann warriors, the human cops. This was their fault. She would make them all pay for what they had done.

And Darkwolf. His betrayal will cost him dearly.

But first, she had to regain the full strength of her powers. Then she would deal with them.

Ceithlenn's neck seemed to barely support her head as she turned her attention to the top of the rolling San Francisco street. Soon a pair of guardsmen would patrol the silent area and when Ceithlenn dealt with them, she would replenish her power and her magic for another night.

For now I must rest. Conserve my strength for what is most important.

She sucked in a deep breath as she leaned back against the brick wall next to the window of the small neighborhood grocery store. What her body wanted to do was slide down to the sidewalk, curl up into a ball, and sleep. She clenched her teeth and braced her palms flat on the brick wall, the roughness of it biting her flesh as she forced herself to relax.

"Balor," she whispered to the night. "I will find you soon, my love."

Ceithlenn put her fingertips to her temples and bowed her head. She brought forth an image of her beloved husband. His muscular form, the strong lines of his jaw and his cheekbones, and the empty eye socket in the middle of his forehead.

"Where are you?" Her words drifted away with the ocean-scented breeze.

With her eyes still shut tight, she focused. Sent waves of energy, as much as she could release without sacrificing all of her strength. Her mind skimmed city streets, homes, buildings.

Nowhere! She couldn't sense him at all.

An ache twisted inside her as if a Fomorii demon had wrapped its claws around her heart. *Balor*. He had been forced to transport somewhere in this city moments after he arrived.

I must find him. I must!

A shriek almost ripped from within her and she barely choked it down. She moved her fingertips from her forehead and clenched her hands into fists as she tipped her head back to look up at the fog-obscured sky.

"Where. Are. You?" she said through clenched teeth. "I need you."

Something blocked her mental powers. Or Balor was somewhere her mind could not reach.

If only bringing her beloved husband from Underworld had not depleted most of her strength and left her with little power. Since that day, feeding off human flesh and taking human souls gave her just enough of that strength and power to last from one night to the next.

Instead of being able to gather great quantities of souls to replenish herself, she had only been able to dine on and claim the souls of two humans at a time, no more.

Not enough. *Not enough!*

Even though she gained strength whenever she claimed humans for food and souls, if she attempted to take any more, it only replaced what power she had to use to steal the second pair.

It was driving her out of her mind.

Not for long, though. She knew deep in her gut that she would find a way to come back into her full powers.

She filled her lungs again and cleared her mind as best she could. What energy she did have she held in reserve to change from her pitiful human shell. She would return to her glorious goddess form when she was ready to attack the guardsmen who would be patrolling the street at any time.

The sharp snap of boot steps against concrete echoed up the incline of the steep street and relief flowed over her. Much longer, and she didn't know if she'd have the power to take their lives.

The pair of military guards appeared at the crest of the hill. She managed a smile at the thought that *she* was the reason for the government's implementation of martial law. *She* was responsible for the almost silenced city.

As the guardsmen approached, their images became clearer to her bleary sight. Both wore tan and brown camouflage and smelled of sweat, and one of them stank of cigarettes.

Keeping to the darkness, Ceithlenn let the men pass her. She pushed away from the brick wall and stepped from the shadows behind them. She kicked a stone from the sidewalk and it clattered as it bounced and rolled across the asphalt street.

The click and snapping sounds of the guardsmen's rifles bit the quiet night as the men whirled and trained their weapons on her.

The guards remained stiff-shouldered as one of the men shouted, "Don't move. Hands above your head."

Ceithlenn obeyed. In her Sara form, dressed in human jeans and a T-shirt, with her short, punk-red bobbed hair, she knew she appeared innocent and just as weak as she'd been feeling.

In anticipation of her meal, adrenaline shot through her veins and what strength and power she still commanded came to her in a rush.

"State your name," the same guardsman demanded. He wore a military cap and the bill shadowed his eyes. "And state your reason for being out of your home."

"Sara Jones." Ceithlenn used the name of the warlock whose body she had joined with. She took a step forward but stopped at the sound of another sharp click of their rifles. She didn't think they would shoot, but if they did her human shell would likely not survive. And that meant Ceithlenn's death as well because she wasn't in her goddess form.

She had no problem faking the tremble in her voice as she continued, drawing on the lingering memories of Sara Jones, still stored in the occupied brain. "My sister is pregnant and her water broke. The baby is two months too soon. Our phone—we can't get it to work."

"State your place of residence," the same man demanded with no compassion and Ceithlenn decided she would kill him first.

The heat of her anger almost caused her hair to flame and her incisors to lengthen. She didn't have time for this shit. She controlled her transformation—barely.

"Two houses down." Ceithlenn put all the pleading she could into her voice. "We live in an apartment above a garage. I'm begging you. That's why I came to find some guardsmen. To see if you can get someone to help my sister and her baby."

The man who was about to be eaten alive motioned with his gun. "Face forward. Keep your hands up and I'll follow you." To the other soldier he said, "Radio for a doctor and backup."

Ceithlenn's entire body shook with the force of her rage. This was taking too much of her precious time and strength. She ground her teeth and turned so her back was to the men. The second guardsman spoke into the shoulder radio she'd noticed earlier. Ceithlenn concentrated on throwing enough magic at the men to block the transmission. Crackling noises and static came from the radio as the second man repeatedly tried to make contact.

I will kill the first one twice. And another time for good measure. She moved slowly forward so the guardsmen would get closer. *Just like I will kill all the fucking witches and D'Danann when my full powers return.* Her thoughts turned blacker as she thought of Darkwolf, the warlock who had betrayed her and Balor. *I have something special in store for that traitor.*

She had to find the double-dealing warlock. The bastard who had Balor's eye. The eye, once returned to the empty socket in the middle of Balor's forehead, would easily win this war for them. With one glance of his mighty eye, Balor would lay waste to all within his sight.

And then, with their army of Fomorii demons, she and Balor would slay any who barred their path to the Old World. In Ireland they would rule again as gods as they had two millennia ago.

Ceithlenn focused on the sound of the boot steps coming up behind her.

"Move it," the soon-to-be-dead guardsman growled and nudged her with the barrel of his rifle.

In that moment, Ceithlenn couldn't have controlled the change if she wanted to. She shrieked and her hair flamed with the full force of her fury. In less than the time it took to blink her incisors lengthened, her claws extended, and her leathery wings unfurled.

She whirled and projected her magic at the guardsmen.

Both men froze. Only their eyes moved. The terror reflected in those depths fed her, made her stronger.

Ceithlenn hissed as she grabbed the one closest to her by his neck and raised him up so his boots dangled above the sidewalk.

She easily flung him so that he landed on his side, his head making a cracking sound against the sidewalk as his rifle thunked and rattled on the concrete before it settled. He lay on his side now, frozen but facing her, fear even more pronounced in his gaze.

The second guardsman remained stiff and unable to move—all but his eyes.

With a wicked grin, Ceithlenn looked from the first guardsman to the other. "On second thought," she said in a low purr to the guardsman on the ground, "I will eat this one before you, and you will watch as I dine on his flesh, his blood, his soul. Your fear will feed me as you witness your own fate."

Ceithlenn scratched her nails down the second guardsman's neck and found his strong pulse. She nuzzled his neck and inhaled before sinking her fangs into the sweet flesh. She ripped a chunk away and slowly savored it as the luscious taste of blood gushed down her chin.

When she finished eating the flesh from their bones and drinking their blood, she would take their souls and regain some of her magic. She sighed at the blissful flavor of human meat and the intoxicating smell of fear.

Silent screams from both men added fuel to her hunger and she pressed herself tighter to the second guardsman before she sank her fangs into him again.

CHAPTER FIVE

JAKE MACGREGOR'S MUSCLES BUNCHED beneath his T-shirt and overshirt. It was all Jake could do to restrain himself from slugging a hole in the wall of his sorry excuse for an office. Or knocking one of the many stacks of file folders on his desktop across the room.

As captain of the San Francisco PSF—Paranormal Special Forces—Jake was expected to clean up this whole goddamned mess with Ceithlenn and the demons.

Immediately. Without the D'Anu and the D'Danann.

Jake gripped the Styrofoam coffee cup on his desk and crushed it in his fist, realizing too late it still contained a quarter cup of cold coffee.

"Goddamnit," he growled. The smell of black coffee rolled out along with the liquid that came just about too close to his laptop.

He slapped scrap paper on the mess and pushed as much of the coffee as he could into a waste can he grabbed from beneath the desk. Damnit, no napkins, no tissue. But he could use a towel from his gym bag.

It was almost surprising he didn't take off the desk's laminate top as hard as Jake rubbed the remnants of the coffee off his desk with the hand towel he snatched out of his bag. When he finished, he wiped the coffee off his hands just as hard.

Not too much over a week ago, the day after *it* all went

down, Jake had helped the witches make their escape with the D'Danann to that whatever-the-hell-it-was Otherworld place. He'd been in touch with the D'Anu witch, Silver, and the D'Danann warrior, Hawk, since then, working out the details of getting all of the witches and D'Danann back to San Francisco and setting up shop. But it hadn't happened yet.

Jake glanced at a framed picture on one of his walls. From the time he was old enough to grasp the concept of baseball, he'd been a diehard Giants fan. The photo was of the San Francisco Giants, taken the last time the team had won the World Series. A close friend, Raul Jimenez, who'd been a star right-fielder with the Giants, had given Jake the picture. It was probably worth thousands—the photo was signed by every member of the team.

Most of whom were now dead.

That World Series Championship win came before Ceithlenn, the bitch goddess, had murdered thousands in the Giants' stadium. Including his friend Raul and other members of the team.

That ever-present empty place in Jake's gut grew larger with every person the goddess murdered.

Locals had continued to call the stadium Candlestick Park, despite the stadium having been rebuilt and moved into the city—and renamed depending on what corporation was sponsoring it. Once it had been called Monster Park, named after a sponsor's product.

How fucking appropriate.

Now, with the taint of what the goddess had done, the park held terrifying memories for the citizens of San Francisco. Jake couldn't imagine calling it Candlestick Park again.

A knock on the doorframe caught Jake's attention and he turned to see Lieutenant Landers in the doorway, holding a newspaper. Like most of his officers, she looked like hell with blackish-blue circles under her blue eyes and exhaustion darkening her expression.

"Got word, Captain." Landers's short blond hair was

ruffled as if she'd just rubbed her hand over it. "Our new HQ is ready for occupation."

Thank God. Jake gave a sharp nod as he balled up the coffee-stained towel and tossed it into a corner. "Make sure every last one of our officers packs their crap and gets it to the warehouse on the QT, and in a hurry," he said. "Grab only what's absolutely necessary to the mission."

It hadn't taken a hell of a lot to convince the owner to turn the pier warehouse over to the PSF. Martial law, combined with the police department's authority to commandeer property under extreme circumstances, gave them all the power they required.

"You've got it." Landers didn't move from the doorway. Instead she extended the newspaper she'd been holding and he took it from her. "Another one."

"Shit." He slammed the latest newspaper on top of his desk, where the spilt coffee had been. The newspaper's headline screeched BIOTERRORISM STILL SUSPECT IN STADIUM SLAUGHTER.

"No kidding, Captain," she said with her usual fire back in her voice. "A big steaming pile of it."

Every one of his officers knew that bioterrorism had nothing to do with what had happened in the baseball stadium where thousands of withered husks had been recovered. Husks of humans whose souls had been stolen by Ceithlenn.

Souls that had helped her bring an ancient god named Balor to San Francisco.

Jake pinched the bridge of his nose and rubbed his burning eyes. He couldn't remember the last time he'd had a good night's sleep. Maybe five months ago when all this freakish shit started happening?

He shook his head as he looked up and met her gaze. "Thanks, Landers."

"We'll get the sonsofbitches." Her expression turned hard, her anger unwavering. Like him, she'd seen too many of their officers, countless men and women, die at the hands of the demons and the goddess. "One way or another, they'll all pay."

His own expression was probably hard as granite. "Every last one of them."

When she left, Jake turned his back on the door and braced one hand on the wall next to the lone window of his office. For a long moment he stared out at the prime view of the pollution-coated block wall of the building across the street. He needed to get together his own belongings to hole up in the warehouse on the pier with the rest of his officers. Construction workers had been hard at it 24/7 getting the place prepared for the move. 'Bout time it was ready.

Ceithlenn. He could never quite get the image of that flame-haired, leather-winged bitch out of his mind. Or the hideous malformed demons she commanded. At times it was like they were all in some surreal dream and none of this was real.

Christ, after months of working with the D'Anu witches and those winged warriors from Otherworld, he still had a hard time believing it all. Even after battling the demons himself.

To think it all started with one power-hungry warlock, Darkwolf, who'd summoned the demons from Underworld. Teams of officers, witches, and warriors had tried to find Darkwolf. Last thing they knew, the warlock had kept the eye and vanished from the massacre. Darkwolf had taken Junga, the demon queen, with him.

"What black magic can Darkwolf do with that eye?" Jake muttered aloud. "Is the bastard going to give it to Balor or keep it for himself?"

Jake faced the door of his office as he scrubbed his hand over his stubbled cheeks then pinched the bridge of his nose again with his thumb and forefinger. A goddamned nightmare. All of it.

Fredrickson popped his head in the doorway.

"What?" Jake snapped at the officer.

With a jerk of his thumb, looking totally unfazed by Jake's mood, the redheaded Frederickson gestured behind him. "Marsten needs you in weapons. And it's not good," he said before ducking back out of the doorway.

Jake growled beneath his breath, anger simmering under his skin like fire over kindling. It hadn't been his fucking day since sometime last September. He stormed out of his office, past cubicles of officers packing what they'd need for the move, as he headed to the expanded weapons area.

"Marsten." Jake strode into a room with the sharp tang of metal and chemicals in the air. He approached the burly dark-haired cop. "Status."

Marsten shook his head. "These demon heart-seeking bullets. We need more military supplies to make them, but they're giving us hell."

"What the f—" Jake ground his teeth. "What's the problem?"

Marsten's expression was dark, furious. "Some military higher-up here in the city is putting a stop to what he considers 'unnecessary expenses.' "

Jake let out a stream of curses, his entire body wound tight enough that it was a miracle he didn't *really* split the seams of his shirt. And this time he came closer to putting his fist through a wall.

"Ceithlenn's got something to do with this," Jake said when he reined back what he could of his temper. "This pretty much proves she's got Fomorii placed in strategic positions, like we thought."

Which was exactly why they'd kept the move to the warehouse secret from anyone outside the PSF. *No one* could be trusted. The way the demons could take over a human's body and life—Jake wouldn't even know if one of his own officers had been compromised.

Jake drew his Glock from the holster beneath the overshirt. He removed the cartridge loaded with heart-seeking bullets used to fight Fomorii, and slipped out one of the bullets and held it up to the light.

Using his weaponry knowledge and skills from being Special Ops in the Marines, Jake had designed the bullets and had given the schematics to the weapons lab. The bullets were created using a special microchip that detected a demon's, or even a human's heartbeat. After hitting its target, the microchip sent a powerful electric current straight to the beating heart, zapping it so hard it exploded.

Marsten just watched Jake as he looked at the translucent head and studied the red liquid swirling around the microchip. The liquid served as a conductor to make the current even stronger upon impact. Top secret military advances had given the PSF's weapons labs what they needed to develop the heart-seeking bullets. The only way to kill a Fomorii was to blow out its heart or take off its head. Jake and his officers went for the heart and left the beheading to the D'Danann.

But if they lost their source of materials to make the bullets, Jake and his officers might just have to learn how to take up fighting with swords like those Fae warriors.

Yeah, and maybe we'll all sprout wings, too.

"We have to circumvent law enforcement and military in San Francisco." Jake managed to keep his voice low and controlled as he returned the bullet to the cartridge and loaded his Glock. "One way or another we'll obtain what we need."

"You've got it, Captain." Marsten took his cell phone from the clip on his belt. "I have a few contacts outside of the city who couldn't possibly have been near one of the Fomorii."

"Do it." Jake left the room and headed toward his own office. Familiar smells hit him—old carpeting and coffee that had been sitting on the warmer too long.

His gaze roamed the room. His department's staff had been quadrupled with officers from all over the Bay Area, and still it wasn't nearly enough. The PSF lab techs had been working overtime making more of the heart-seeking bullets and trying to design other weapons that might give the PSF a fighting chance.

For a moment Jake paused as his mind worked over possibilities for newer, better weapons. He'd drawn up a couple of schematics on his laptop, but what he'd come up with so far wouldn't stop Bugs Bunny.

The demon Tasers and the special pepper spray that had been created from his designs and know-how had to be used at close range and only gave the officer enough time to fire off another round of the heart-seeking bullets if the bullets didn't find their target the first time.

No way was he giving an inch on those bullets. They'd get the materials. And the wheels in his mind would just keep on whirring overtime on coming up with something that could stop a god. Or goddess. Or both.

Meanwhile, the D'Anu and D'Danann were supposed to be doing their damnedest to get some kind of help from Otherworld. He hoped to hell it would be soon.

When Jake reached the door to his office, he came to a stop, his gut tightening with concern and instant primal need.

Kat DeLuca perched on the edge of his desk, her long legs crossed at her knees, her slim skirt hiked up just enough to reveal a good portion of her thighs. She'd pushed away his mountain of files and his laptop so that the top of the desk was mostly bare.

Jake's throat was dry as he focused on her dark eyes and not her legs. Or her small, firm breasts that swelled beneath the silk blouse covering them. Or rather he tried not to focus on them. He swallowed. "You shouldn't be out of your condo."

"I'm a reporter." She braced her palms to either side of her on the laminate surface of his desk, her brows narrowing as she frowned. "I have every right to be gathering facts and presenting them to the public."

"Christ." Jake shut his office door and locked it behind him. "We've been through this before. It's not about rights. It's about safety."

Her scowl deepened. It only made her look more beautiful, but she had a reporter's hard edge to her tone as she spoke. "Until I get some answers, we're going to go through it again. And again."

It wasn't more than three steps from the door to his desk. He caught her face in his hands and pressed his mouth hard against her soft lips before raising his head and staring at her intently. "You don't know what the hell is out there, Kat."

"Then tell me." She brought her hands up and placed them over his. "I deserve to know what's happening."

Jake sucked in his breath as he stared at the gorgeous woman whose face graced the screen of the nightly news. Her familiar perfume swept over him—a scent as exotic as she was. Like green tea and ginseng. He rubbed one of his thumbs across her cheek, her olive complexion smooth, unmarred. The thought of one of those demons getting their hands on her seared his insides like a blowtorch.

"That's territory you know I can't cross with you." Jake slid his hands from her face to her shoulders and she gripped his T-shirt in her fists. "When we started dating a year ago, we agreed not to discuss work."

"Damnit, Jake." Kat tugged at his T-shirt. "This is different."

"Just believe me when I tell you it's not safe." He squeezed her shoulders tight, but she didn't even wince. He hardened his voice. "Nowhere is safe, except your home. Jesus, Kat, you shouldn't even be going to the news station."

"What's it been?" Her features softened and she released his T-shirt and slid her palms down his abs toward the waistband of his jeans. "Five, maybe six months since you started acting edgy and disappearing for days, now weeks." She uncrossed her legs and spread her thighs as she grasped the waistband of his jeans and pulled him to her. "I can't remember the last time we had sex."

Jake groaned, his thoughts going blank as she unfastened the button of his jeans and tugged the zipper down over the briefs covering his now swelling cock.

Wild, raging, primal need took over his mind, his body. Animal instincts that he couldn't control if he wanted to. And God, he didn't want to.

He shoved up Kat's blouse and unfastened the front clasp of her lacy bra as she wrapped her fingers around his erection. In seconds he had her flat on her back on his desk, her skirt pushed up to her waist, and the thin strip of material covering her folds pulled aside.

In one, hard thrust, he buried himself deep within her wet core. Kat gasped and arched her back, raising her breasts up, capturing his attention.

It felt so good being inside her. He gripped both of her breasts and began teasing her nipples as she moaned and thrashed beneath him like the wildcat she was. She hooked her ankles behind his ass, drawing him closer.

All the pent-up frustration they both felt fueled the frenzy of their sex. He fucked her hard and fast and it was only moments before she gave a cry that he smothered with his palm.

Her pussy gripped his cock and he clamped his jaws tight to keep from shouting as he climaxed. He shuddered as he poured himself into her.

For a moment their combined breathing was loud in the stillness of his office as he tried to slow his heartbeat. He braced his hands on the desk before pulling away and tucking his cock back into his briefs and fastening his jeans.

Kat's eyes were heavy-lidded as she rested on her elbows and looked up at him. "Come home with me."

Jake sighed and helped Kat off the desk and she arranged her clothing. She looked a little rumpled and he smoothed her short hair with his fingers before he brought her close to him in a tight hug. The smell of sex and her exotic scent had his cock hardening again.

"I'm sorry, baby, but I can't," he said quietly. "I'm not going to be around for awhile."

She went completely quiet and he drew back to look down at her. The softness that had been on her features vanished. "Where will you be?"

"Don't ask." Jake settled his hands on her waist. "And I have no idea how long I'll be gone." He ground his teeth as the war they were waging against Ceithlenn and the demons came more sharply into focus. "But it'll be as long as it takes."

"Our relationship is off the record, Jake." Kat stepped away smoothing her slightly creased skirt as she frowned. "If we really have any kind of relationship."

Jake felt like shouting, but he kept his voice controlled. "Stay at home as much as you can. I'm dead serious."

She studied him for a long moment. "You do what you have to do. I do what I have to."

"Damnit, Kat." He followed as she turned away and unlocked the door. "Can't you listen to me on this? Trust me?"

Kat wrapped her fingers around the doorknob before pulling the door open. She paused and looked up at him. "Trust goes both ways," she said then turned and strode through the doorway.

Jake stared at her as she walked away, her chin tilted up and her backbone rigid. He clenched and unclenched his fists at his sides before reaching behind the door for his gym bag.

Other than tackling a demon barehanded, right now there was only one way to work out the frustration, anger, and concern that was about to send him over the fucking edge.

After slamming his office door behind him, he headed through the cubicle maze to make his way to the department's gym. He'd pump iron until his muscles gave out. Then hopefully one of his jujitsu sparring partners would be around and he could kick some ass.

CHAPTER SIX

GARRAN WALKED OUT OF the Drow realm and into the night, one hand resting on his sword hilt. Starlight and soft breezes greeted him, along with scents of freedom. The outdoors—pine trees, grass, wildflowers, berries, deer, wolves . . . the remnants of sunshine even had a smell to it.

For a moment anger caused his muscles to tighten. The Elvin Elders had banished the Drow for their darker ways. The Elders forced the Drow to live belowground using a great spell to make the Dark Elves' skin and eyes intolerant to sunlight. Their skin tones had even been changed to separate the Dark Elves from those who considered themselves to be of the light.

Self-righteous godsdamn bastards. Garran's muscles bunched with the need to hit something. The pine tree looked like a good target, but no doubt a Dryad—a keeper of the trees—would be furious and he'd have *her* to contend with.

Garran and his people had refused to bend to the will of the Elders. The Drow *would not* give up their ways, their lifestyle, their darker use of magic—although it caused the Elders to force them belowground.

The Great Guardian . . . she was a creature far above the Elders, the greatest being of the light. And yet she had done nothing to stop the Elders.

Garran ground his teeth. The only reason he had agreed

to meet with the Guardian was for the sake of his daughter and his people.

After the stone door screeched to a close, he sucked in a deep breath and pictured the transference stone and the meadow where the flat, circular stone had been placed many millennia ago.

The Guardian would be there. No matter when one arrived, if she wanted to speak with a being, she would somehow know when to appear.

With a mere thought, his body traveled through the doorway in time and space that took him to the transference stone. He felt the stone beneath his feet the moment he arrived and he opened his eyes.

His gaze met the Great Guardian's eyes, which were an incredible blue color. Like the finest, clearest sapphires the Dark Elves mined. Starlight mingled with a slice of moonlight softly spilled over her features. As Drow, he could have seen her in pure darkness. But the touch of moonlight turned her aura from gold to silver and she was beautiful beyond words.

Despite centuries of anger directed at the Elders, Garran could hold no grudge against the Great Guardian. He slowly knelt and laid his sword at her feet.

"Rise, King Garran of the Drow." Her melodic voice flowed over his skin like cool water in an underground pool.

He rose to his full height and sheathed his sword at the same time he faced the beautiful Guardian. Such awe filled him that he had no words for a moment.

Her clear blue eyes met his. "You have come to see me about the war against Ceithlenn in the San Francisco Otherworld."

The Guardian was tall, but Garran stood a few inches taller and he looked down at her. "You spoke to the D'Anu and D'Danann about rewarding my people with what I want most for them. This, provided the Drow aid the D'Anu and D'Danann in their battles."

"Conditionally." Her placid expression did not change.

Heat stirred in Garran's gut. "You know the Dark Elves' greatest wish is to walk again in the light. What condition would you put on this?"

"The Drow will be gifted the freedom to walk in early morning and early evening." The Elvin woman seemed to glow a little brighter. "When aboveground, the Drow will have the same skin and hair tones they possessed before being banished."

"Gifted?" He scowled and the heat flowed from his gut throughout his body. "It is our due. The Elders had no right to lay such a curse as they have upon my people."

"It is the best I have to offer you." Her expression remained placid. "If your people stay out beyond the allotted time, they will first have sensitivity to the sunlight, and if they ignore the condition, they shall turn to ash."

"This is as far as you will bend?" Garran couldn't stop from clenching his fists at his sides. "Why this condition?"

The trees themselves seemed to sigh as a breeze lifted his hair from his shoulder plates. "To do otherwise would destroy the balance in Otherworld," she said. "It would wreak havoc amongst all species."

Garran narrowed his brows. "What you speak of is nonsense."

The Guardian gave a gentle smile. "What was, what is, and what is to come, is as it is meant to be."

"You do naught but speak in riddles." He kept his voice steady despite the anger tightening his skin. "The outcome of this war—you have already seen it?"

"No." She paused a moment before she continued. "The past, what occurs now . . . all has meaning. It is as the gods have determined it should be based on our choices. The choices we make in the present will determine what the future is to be."

Garran's head ached and he resisted the urge to rub his temples. "Should we join this war, how would we have the might to eliminate their foes?"

"The humans are not to kill too great a number of the

Fomorii." The Guardian's words seemed to have a little more steel to them. "It is another act that would upset the balance in Otherworld and Underworld."

"Not destroy all the Fomorii we can?" He narrowed his eyes, his thoughts darkening. "How then will we rid the San Francisco Otherworld of the demons?"

"I will offer you my own gift." The Great Guardian's expression did not waver, but Garran felt a subtle change in the energy surrounding them. The fine hairs on his arms rose as he waited. "When in the presence of the Fomorii, *you* will have the power to transport large groups of the demons to Underworld with a thought."

The Guardian's words seemed almost surreal. "It cannot be so easy," he said.

"It comes at a great cost to you, King Garran." Her words hung like a sword suspended in the air between them.

The world seemed to shift a little. The night stilled, unnaturally quiet, and he barely heard the trickle of the stream. "What is this cost?"

"The first time you choose to use this power, it will weaken you and your own powers." She never moved her gaze from his. "The second time illness shall overcome you and dilute your magic until you are well."

His throat tightened as he waited for her next edict.

"The third occurrence could cost you far more." She paused. "It could mean your life." Her words sank into him like liquid metal seeping into his skin then solidifying, weighting his entire body. "Only one thing can save you should you choose to use this power thrice."

As a warrior, Garran did not fear death. However, he did fear leaving his people without a leader. Naught but weeks ago, the Fomorii had murdered his brother, the next in line for the throne. The beasts had also murdered the second and third in command.

If Garran died without a trained replacement . . .

The Orb of Aithne. As long as the new king had the orb and was trained in its use . . .

"And what might the saving grace be?" He cleared his nearly closed-off throat. "Should I use the gift all three times."

Another sigh of a breeze ruffled tree leaves and the hem of the Guardian's long gown. "This knowledge could prevent you from attaining it if you know in advance."

For a long moment Garran weighed his decision. Always he based his choices on what benefited the Drow. When he had at one time sided with Darkwolf, he had done so because of the very same promise—only through Darkwolf, Balor had promised the full light of day with no conditions.

Garran studied the Great Guardian as he considered his decision. She waited, patient and unmoving.

To sacrifice his own life . . . was that act in the best interest of the Dark Elves?

And for his daughter and her people?

Yes.

Finally he spoke, and when he did his words and tone rang with authority. "I accept."

The Guardian did not acknowledge him with a word or a movement. Instead, her glow expanded into a sudden brilliant flash that encompassed him. He ground his teeth as such incredible power flooded him that pain shot to his very soul. Every muscle in his body tightened and he felt as if his bones might snap, one by one.

He bore the pain without a sound. Confidence in his decision gave him strength and he combined that strength with the magic filling him.

When the bright light finally faded, until only the Great Guardian wore a silver glow, sweat coated Garran's body and his muscles ached. His eyes were so dry they felt gritty when he blinked.

"You alone, King Garran, now have the ability to walk in the sunlight," she said quietly. "At all times of the day."

Shock coursed through him at the unexpected divulgement. To again feel full sunlight on his face? The thought caused a different kind of warmth to flow through him as he imagined such a blessing placed upon him.

But what of his people? What right did he have to such a gift if his people were not awarded the same?

"Once you have used the powerful endowment I have given you, should you survive, you shall again return to live amongst your people as one of the Dark Elves," she added. "You will then only be able to enjoy the light in the early morning and early evening. Your senses will tell you and your people when it is time to return to the Drow realm."

Garran had no words of his own as the Great Guardian's avowal settled on him like a cloak.

The Guardian continued, "You must always keep the D'Anu witch, Hannah, at your side. Do not think to separate yourself from her. The magical bond you create when you and she work as one will award you each with more power."

Strange that Hannah was the one who answered his demand that one of the companions remain in the Drow realm as part of his own condition. Apparently it had been the Guardian's magic already at work.

But to keep her with him at all times . . .

He clenched his sword hilt. "I would not put the witch in danger."

The Guardian's expression remained firm. "As I said, you must keep her by your side if you wish to turn the tide of this war."

A long moment passed before Garran could answer. "Thank you, my lady." He inclined his head in acknowledgment. "We will aid the D'Anu, D'Danann, and humans in their battles against the Underworld evils inhabiting their world."

"Prepare at once." The great Elvin woman spread her hands out, palms up. "Once you have informed the D'Anu and D'Danann of your decision, it shall be time to travel to the San Francisco Otherworld."

Still stunned by all of the Guardian's revelations, Garran bowed from his shoulders.

"One more thing you must heed."

Garran sucked in his breath as his eyes met hers. Not another godsdamn condition.

Her sapphire eyes darkened. "You must tell no one beforehand of your ability to transfer the Fomorii to Underworld."

Garran let the thought roll through his mind. Hers was not an unreasonable request. As a leader himself, he well understood the jealousies and conflicts that could arise if people perceived their ruler to be playing favorites. He inclined his head again. "Yes, my lady."

She smiled and it was as if the stars shone from the sky above to light her features. "I wish you well."

Garran watched as the Great Guardian turned away, crossed the small bridge, and vanished.

The ramifications of what he'd just agreed to hit him like the slam of a troll's club against his chest. He would need to ensure Vidar would be a good and just ruler in Garran's stead.

With no time to do it.

After the deaths of his brother, Naal, and his Second and Third in Command during the opening of the door to Underworld, Garran had made Vidar his First in Command. Weeks ago Garran had begun to groom Vidar to take his place should anything happen to him. He respected the sharp-witted, sharp-tongued warrior, but his gut told him that Vidar was not prepared to take on such a great responsibility for any length of time. Not yet.

Godsdamn, but he should have spent more time with Vidar's training, no matter that it had been just weeks.

Garran stood at the center of the transference stone, his hand still resting on the hilt of his sword. It had been so long since the Elders had changed his skin tone and hair. He almost did not remember what he looked like before he and his people had been banished.

What would it be like to walk in daylight again? To feel the sun's yellow heat on his skin?

A twist in his gut followed vivid images of himself and his people as they once were. Longing flowed through him, and he was not entirely sure why. They had made good lives for themselves belowground and had existed in their realm for centuries.

Had he made the right decision? Was it enough for his people to enjoy what sunlight they could before being sent belowground again?

No time for those thoughts. Garran shook his head. He had work to accomplish before he delivered his decision to his daughter and her companions.

He closed his eyes and visualized the meadow over the Drow realm and his body shimmered and vanished from the transference stone.

After traveling through the dark void, he returned in moments a step away from the door above his home. He opened his eyes and paused to study the dark place he had not seen bathed in sunlight for centuries.

The gifts the Great Guardian had given him . . .

Yes. He had made the right decision. He would be able to not only help *his* people, but his daughter and *her* people as well. The thought warmed his chest and he smiled.

After he made his way down the stone stairs to the great hall, Garran ordered one of his guards to summon Vidar. The warrior was to return from the training cavern where he worked with their army, to meet with Garran in the throne/strategy chamber.

Garran settled himself on his throne, rested one elbow on an armrest and stroked his chin.

Once he discussed his plans with his Directorate and those in his command, he would go to the D'Danann village.

When he traveled to the San Francisco Otherworld, he would meet with the D'Danann and D'Anu to discuss tactics. Without telling the witches or warriors of his ability, he had to find a way to get the Fomorii gathered in one place at the same time. He would transfer them all at once and not use the power thrice. Certainly, he would determine how to accomplish this and not leave his people without an experienced leader.

Vidar strode into the throne room and bowed. Garran

acknowledged his First in Command with a slight nod, then pushed himself off his throne and stepped down from the dais and faced Vidar.

The warrior had black hair and blacker eyes, and his skin was slightly bluer in hue than Garran's. Physically, Vidar's strength nearly matched Garran's. But not his magic. Vidar also did not have the powerful yet diplomatic presence a ruler of the Drow needed. At times Vidar was easy to anger and that anger could disrupt his magic.

"I will be leaving soon." Garran studied Vidar's expression. "While I am gone you will serve as Steward in my place."

Vidar's dark eyes narrowed as he met Garran's. "May I ask, my king, where you are going and how long you will be away?"

"It is an acceptable question." Garran turned from Vidar, his hands behind his back as he eyed the obsidian door. "To the San Francisco Otherworld to aid in the battle against Ceithlenn and the Fomorii."

"Your Highness." Vidar's tone held a hard edge to it. "You cannot put yourself in harm's way. *I* will lead the army and do as you bid." Vidar insisting he should lead the army in Garran's stead was an excellent quality in a First in Command. Garran expected no less.

Still, Garran faced Vidar again and stated, "I go alone. No questions. No answers will be given."

Vidar raised his chin. "My king, we cannot afford the chance that you might lose your life. As your First, I insist—"

Garran held up his hand, halting Vidar's speech. Despite his approval of Vidar's desire to protect his king, Garran did not have time to waste on futile arguments. "As I said, you will serve as Steward."

Vidar set his jaw but he bowed in acknowledgment before meeting Garran's gaze again. "I will gather the Directorate so that we might make arrangements." Vidar's expression was harder than Garran believed it should have been when one was speaking to his king. "They will not approve."

"Your place is to do as I command." Garran tightened his

jaw. "As you well know, I need no approval. I am king and my word is law. But yes, summon the Directorate."

"It will be done, my king." The harsh look on Vidar's features did not lessen, but he bowed from the shoulders once again before rising, turning away, and striding out the door.

Garran narrowed his gaze as he watched Vidar retreat. When he had the opportunity to work with his First alone, Garran would discuss Vidar's impertinence. *That* was unacceptable.

For the sake of the guards standing inside the doorway, Garran did not let his frustration show. He kept his head high, his hands behind his back, as he waited for the Directorate to convene at the strategy table.

As he paced, his thoughts churned over what he must do before he left Otherworld. Vidar's training. Ensuring the preparation of his warriors for battle.

One by one, the wisest and eldest of the Dark Elves entered the chamber. As was true of all Elves, whether dark or light, each man looked to be the same age as Garran despite being centuries or many millennia older. As usual, the members of the Directorate wore simple black tunics, breeches, and boots.

When they were all assembled and seated, including Vidar, Garran remained standing. He moved his gaze from one Directorate member to the next, meeting each man's eyes.

"Shortly, after I have visited the D'Danann village, I will travel to the San Francisco Otherworld." Garran kept his expression firm, hard. "Alone."

The reactions to his announcement were immediate— stunned expressions to a one.

But before anyone could respond, Garran continued, "I cannot give you my reasons—not yet. I will join the D'Anu and D'Danann in their battle against Ceithlenn."

Garran raised his voice over the angry words that began to spill from the Directorate members' lips. "Vidar shall serve as Steward in my absence, and Carden will be his First in Command. Carden will assemble an army prepared to go to war against Ceithlenn and the Fomorii when I give the order."

Sepan, the second in line to be Head of the Order of the Directorates, stood, his chair rumbling over the granite floor as he pushed it back. His gray eyes flashed and his silver hair glinted in the light refracting from the chamber's crystal walls and ceiling.

Sepan banged his fist on the table. "We cannot allow it. It is wrong, as wrong as when you endangered yourself fighting the demons when the door to Underworld was opened. Even then you had an army at your back. To go alone to this San Francisco Otherworld is preposterous!"

"You forget yourself." Garran's temper rose, heating him as he met Sepan's unflinching gaze. "I am king. I have made a choice for the good of my people and I will not waver from that decision."

"What choice is that?" Hark, the Head of the Order, maintained his placid expression where Sepan's was filled with fury.

"I cannot tell you at this time." Garran looked from one member of the Directorate to another. "This is how it will be. Again, as I have said, Vidar shall serve as Steward while I am gone." His gaze rested on Vidar. "And if my life should end, Vidar will no longer be Steward. He shall become king of the Dark Elves."

Shock registered on every man's face, including Vidar's, who said, "I must refuse this—this—"

"Command." Garran folded his arms across his chest. "I will again remind you, Vidar, that as your king my word is law. You will be a just and honorable king should I die."

The silence in the room was so deafening that Garran's ears rang. He faced his Directorates. Most members of the Directorate managed to school their expressions.

Sepan was not one of those. He broke the silence, his gray eyes dark with undisguised fury. He bent where he stood and placed his palms on the table. "You have made this decision without our counsel."

"I find your disrespectfulness intolerable." Garran steeled his own gaze. "I am king. It is best you all remember this." He looked at Vidar, who now had a shrewd gleam in his eyes that made Garran pause.

He didn't have time to second-guess himself, but he intended to have a stern and frank talk with Vidar before he left for the San Francisco Otherworld. "Have Carden prepare the army," Garran continued. "I will give word when it is time for battle."

"Yes, my king," Vidar said, this time without as much heat in his voice.

After looking to the members of the Directorate and holding each member's gaze for a firm moment, Garran said, "I must rest as I have much to attend to before I leave."

His mind already churning over what needed to be accomplished prior to his departure, Garran turned and strode out the door.

CHAPTER SEVEN

HANNAH WOKE TO THE feeling that someone was watching her. For a moment she lay still and kept her eyes shut and her breathing steady. The drum of the waterfall was all she heard, but a presence nearby caused her to shiver.

"You are awake," came a man's smooth, rich voice. "It is time for us to go." A laugh, then he added, "Unless you prefer I join you in bed?"

Garran.

She opened her eyes to see him standing over her, his usual teasing smile on his face.

"In your dreams, blue boy." Hannah pushed herself to a sitting position on the bed. She'd lain down moments after Garran had left her. The bed was so comfortable it had drawn her into sleep as soon as she settled on the mattress and she felt as if she'd slept forever.

"Go where?" she asked, holding back a yawn.

He extended his hand. "To see my daughter and her people. Your people."

Rumpled, irritated, and in need of a bath, Hannah ignored his hand. Even though she'd been tired, she hated that she'd fallen asleep in her clothing. Ugh. It didn't matter to her the warrior gear was Fae made and all she had to do was think the Fae word for "clean" and it would be as good as new again. She preferred to sleep in something soft and silky and bathe first thing in the morning.

She sighed. Soft and silky. Otherworld was sorely lacking a Victoria's Secret.

Goddess, what she would give to be in her own bed and take a shower in her own bathroom. Then perhaps putting on a Chloé blouse and her Jean-Paul Gaultier pinstriped jacket and slacks.

"Well?" Garran's lips were still quirked into a smile. "Must I carry you out of your chamber so that we might make our way to the village?"

She glared at him before she cast a glance to the corner where the waterfall tumbled from a rock shelf into a pool. Two fat pottery containers sat on a flat stone to the side, probably some kind of bathing gel. The slight tang of sulfur hung in the room and she assumed the water was from an underground hot spring.

Thank the Ancestors.

Hannah pushed the covers aside and was just about to climb out of bed when it occurred to her. She met Garran's gaze. "You didn't tell me what your decision is."

"You didn't ask." His expression grew serious. "But yes, my people will join yours in the battle against Ceithlenn and the Fomorii.

Relief swept through Hannah. "Thank the goddess."

"Now we go to your people," he said.

"Before I go *anywhere*"—she swung her legs over the side of the bed—"I'm taking a shower."

His teasing smile returned. "Would you like—"

"No." Hannah got to her feet and ignored his sexy grin. "I don't need your 'help.' I need you to get out of the room, let me take my shower, and then we can go."

"As you wish." Garran winked before leaving the room and closing the door behind him.

Hannah rolled her eyes. *Goddess help me. Why did I agree to be his liaison?*

She had no blessed clue.

Okay, she did.

If she had left it up to Eavan, they might be going to war,

all right. But it would be the Dark Elves against the D'Danann and D'Anu instead of Ceithlenn and the Fomorii.

With a shake of her head, Hannah started stripping out of her clothing, *really* looking forward to that shower.

GARRAN WAITED BESIDE HANNAH'S doorway, his back against the wall, his arms folded across his chest.

Still smiling from enjoyment at teasing Hannah's prickly outer shell, he shook his head. His senses told him there was far more to Hannah Wentworth than she wanted anyone to see.

His skin felt drawn tight over his muscles as he turned his thoughts to traveling to the D'Danann village. Elves going into the thick of the Fae warriors was not done.

Regardless, Garran had gone to the home of the D'Danann to see his daughter take the D'Danann warrior Keir as her mate.

Today he would go to tell the D'Danann and D'Anu his decision.

It was not long before the door opened, the scents of Elvin-made bathing gel preceding her into the hallway. The same gel was always kept by the bathing pools and waterfalls, but it smelled different on each person who used it.

He inhaled the perfume of moonlight and cherry blossoms that now scented Hannah's soft skin.

She had her leather bag over one shoulder. "I feel *so* much better." She pulled her dark hair out of the collar of her shirt so that it flowed freely about her shoulders. The unusual blond lock edging one side of her face against her dark hair added to her loveliness. "Now what?"

Garran had to focus his thoughts, tearing them away from Hannah's beauty to consider what he needed to accomplish before they left for the D'Danann village. "First I must visit my troops."

Hannah fell into step beside him as they walked through the maze of passageways leading to Drow homes and sleeping quarters, and farther on to the village.

"I'll get to see Banshee sooner than I thought." Hannah sounded pleased and he glanced down to catch the first glimpse of happiness he had seen on her face since she arrived. From the way she immediately calmed her expression, he had a feeling she kept her emotions well schooled. And that true joy was not something she had often experienced.

Why?

Then Garran realized what Hannah had said and thoughts of a quite ugly and more difficult race of Fae beings came to mind. Not only were Banshees formidable opponents, but they had a screech loud enough to render a man unconscious. Many a male had woken hanging upside down in a tree, bound from head to foot.

He almost shuddered. Thank the gods he had been spared that fate.

"Why are you so anxious to see a Banshee?" Garran watched Hannah's face and saw pleasure play over her features before it vanished again.

"Banshee is my familiar." She glanced up at him. "He's a peregrine falcon."

"Ah." Garran nodded his understanding and smiled at the irony. In Otherworld, Banshees had familiars, too. "You named him?"

Hannah shook her head. "He told me his name—sort of. I scried it in my mirror when he first came to me."

She appeared somewhat more animated as she answered his questions about how long the falcon had been with her and how she used a mirror to scry, and she mentioned that Dragon Elementals helped her visions and enhanced her magic. She paused though, and her features paled as if something suddenly bothered her that she wasn't sharing with him.

She shook her head and said, "I don't know why in the world I'm telling you all of this."

He raised his brows. "Why not?"

Hannah gave a not-so-casual shrug. "I don't talk to anyone about my relationship with Banshee or my scrying talent."

She cocked her head as her gaze met his. "Are you using some kind of Drow magic to drag this all out of me?"

Garran laughed. "No, sweet one." His words grew serious as he continued, "I believe it is merely a connection you and I share."

This time she looked up at the ceiling of the passageway and said, "Goddess, help me. The man is delusional."

He snorted back another laugh. The witch was definitely amusing at times.

They entered the Drow village.

Garran inclined his head to those whose paths he crossed, acknowledging every individual with a slightly shuttered expression. As king, he was accessible to his people, but he maintained an appropriate amount of emotional and physical distance.

Hannah was as regal as any queen with her bearing and her polite responses to all of his people who greeted them. Like him, she kept a certain distance from most of the world, quite naturally.

Some people could never adjust to the rigors of ruling a kingdom. Others were born to it.

Garran liked what he saw in her.

As they strode through the village, he found himself lingering over thoughts of having the opportunity to spend more time with Hannah. His attraction to the human witch was beyond the physical. It was as though his soul recognized her in ways he could not fathom.

Clean air constantly swirled through the cavern, blown in through natural vents in the rock ceiling. Occasionally, he would catch the scents of pine and wildflowers, and it would send a hollow ache through his belly, reminding him of Rhiannon's mother and his love for her. That love had not waned, and never would.

With Hannah's entrance into his life, he wondered for the first time in many years if it was possible to love another as much as he had loved Rhiannon's mother.

Garran blew his breath out in a rush. He barely knew Hannah. It was certainly a mystery why his thoughts traveled in such directions.

Yet not, his own voice echoed inside his mind.

He shook his head as they continued through the village and into another honeycomb of passageways that led to the training cavern.

Swords clanging, arrows whistling through the air, light banter, and shouted orders bounced off passageway walls as Garran and Hannah neared the cavern. When they reached the location his army used to hone their skills, he paused in the great archway and folded his arms. Hannah came up short beside him.

As usual, before he had the opportunity to watch unobserved, the sentries recognized his presence.

"King Garran," one of the men pronounced, and every warrior in the cavern stopped what he was doing. Each gave a bow as absolute silence fell on Garran's ears.

He held back a sigh. Just once he would like to arrive unnoticed.

Garran raised his hand in acknowledgment. "Resume." The chamber amplified his voice as he gave the order.

The men immediately returned to their activities, but without the previous raillery.

Sometimes being king . . . was not easy.

Garran's brother, Naal, had been his closest friend. After Naal was murdered, Garran found it difficult to interact socially with his men. He had lost his only true friend when Naal died, and the person he most trusted as go-between with his warriors and other subjects.

Garran raised his chin and placed his hands behind his back as he waited for Vidar to approach.

Vidar bowed from his shoulders before rising. "Yes, my king?"

"I leave now for the D'Danann village." Garran met Vidar's dark gaze. "I will return before dawn."

Vidar gestured to the warriors practicing with swords and bows. "One of our men should accompany you."

"No." Garran gave a nod toward Hannah. "Only the D'Anu witch shall go with me."

Something flickered in Vidar's black eyes when he looked at Hannah that caused Garran to narrow his gaze. He did not like the shadows that darkened Vidar's expression.

Godsdamn. Garran ground his teeth. When he returned from the D'Danann village, he had much to discuss with his First.

After taking a moment to speak with Vidar, Garran chose to converse with Carden, his Second in Command, as well as two other legion leaders.

Carden was perhaps five centuries younger than Garran while Vidar was older than Garran by a few decades.

Garran had been watching Carden and Vidar since his brother had passed on to Summerland. When Naal, in addition to Garran's Second and Third Commanders, died in the battle at the door to Underworld, both Carden and Vidar had moved up in rank. Vidar from Fourth to become Garran's First and Carden from Fifth to Garran's Second.

Vidar was a shrewd opponent—Garran's best swordsman. The First in Command led his legion with a firm hand and his men served him with dedication and loyalty.

Carden excelled with both the sword and at archery, was sharp-witted, and commanded his legion with authority and fairness.

With his brother's death so recent, Garran had not had the opportunity to truly work with each man to analyze their strengths and weaknesses.

Garran sucked in his breath as he fought back hot waves of anger at himself. *Arrogance. Fucking arrogance.* He had thought himself to have much time to make decisions.

Now he was left with no time.

No time at all.

When finished with Carden and the other two men, Garran

escorted Hannah from the training cavern into a passageway that led to the great hall. She had remained silently at his side as he had given instructions on battle preparation and discussed strategy with his men.

"That Vidar." Hannah's brow furrowed when Garran glanced down at her. "He sure didn't seem to like me. And the others weren't so friendly, either."

"Drow warriors do not approve of women being in the training cavern," Garran said, although his thoughts consistently turned in another direction. "Women are meant to remain in their homes or in the village."

Hannah came to a complete stop and he had to pull up short. Her expression turned furious and she balled her fists at her sides. "I cannot believe—"

Garran put his fingers to her lips. "We have discussed this, Hannah. Regardless of your personal feelings, this is *our* way of life."

His groin tightened as he let his fingertips slide down the curve of her neck. Her pupils dilated as she stepped back, and he noticed her shiver. His touch, that slight connection between them, had affected her, too.

"You're right." Hannah's throat worked as she swallowed. "It pisses me off, but it's not my place to judge you or your people."

"Thank you." Garran resumed his steady pace toward the great hall, and Hannah jogged up to his side then had to double her steps to keep up with him.

HANNAH TOOK A DEEP breath of fresh air as they climbed the stairs out of the Drow realm and stepped into the darkening evening. She shuddered as the door scraped closed behind them and wondered if WD-40 worked on rock. Maybe some heavier oil.

She frowned. "It's already night?"

"You slept the night and most of the day through." Garran

moved beside her. "By the time you finished your shower and I met with my men, it was evening once again."

"I never sleep more than six hours at a time." She glanced up at him and cocked one eyebrow. "No Drow magic?"

He gave her a wicked look. "If it had been up to me, I would have kept you occupied throughout the day."

"I'll just bet you would have," she grumbled.

She hitched her pack higher on her shoulder as she looked up at the sky and the stars starting to peek through the growing darkness.

Over the horizon the slightest wisps of pink remained in the sky, leftovers from what had probably been a beautiful sunset.

"What do you miss most about not being able to come out during the day?" Hannah asked as they moved away from the door.

Garran was silent for a moment. Likely she'd touched a sore spot. Then he took her hand and she experienced a bizarre quivering at the electric zing the contact sent through her body.

"Seeing a beautiful woman with sunlight in her hair." His low voice caressed her skin, causing goose bumps to rise on her arms.

Absolutely no response would come to her mind as the intensity of his gaze said that he meant her. He wanted to see *her* in the sunshine.

He smiled and clasped her other hand and squeezed them both. From the way he was looking at her she thought he might kiss her. And in the magic of the moment, in the night, she wanted him to.

Instead, he said, "Close your eyes and picture the transference stone."

Oddly, a sense of disappointment flowed through Hannah as she obeyed and tried to prepare herself for the trip. Last time she had been with Rhiannon, afraid the witch's Shadows might want to tear her apart or leave her in that vast blackness.

Now she was with Garran, somehow trusting him so completely that she didn't understand the why or how of it—and he no doubt had even more Shadow magic than the half-blood witch, his daughter.

In the next moment it was as if her head were spinning. The void they entered swallowed her gasp. Seconds later her feet landed on something solid and her disorientation caused her to stumble into Garran's arms and against his warm body.

Hannah opened her eyes and looked up at him. Crazy sensations, like small bursts of fireworks, centered in her abdomen. She parted her lips and Garran's gaze focused on them, his expression hungry and filled with desire. The rising moon shed enough light to bring his features into sharp relief. The strength of his jaw, his high cheekbones, the firmness of his lips. Even his eyes appeared more like liquid silver than ever.

Garran's gem-encrusted leather straps rubbed her chest and his sword hilt bumped her hip. He pressed his very firm erection against her belly and she let out a little gasp that wasn't lost in some kind of void this time. His hair was more silver now and it drifted over his shoulder plates as the grass- and wildflower-scented breeze swirled around them.

Blood rushed in Hannah's ears, so loudly that the songs of night birds and Faerie song faded away. He released her hands and slid his palms over her skin until he reached her upper arms and gripped them tight.

All thoughts left her mind save one—she wanted Garran to kiss her. Wanted to feel his lips on hers and taste him as he slipped his tongue inside her mouth.

"Hannah . . ." he whispered as he lowered his head.

A screech sliced the night.

CHAPTER EIGHT

HANNAH JERKED FROM GARRAN'S arms at the sound of the familiar cry.

Whatever spell had been between her and Garran vanished as Banshee's shriek brought her back to reality.

Garran wore a puzzled expression as she stepped away, but he didn't try to stop her. He loosened his grip on her upper arms and let his hands drop so that they were at his sides.

"My familiar." Her throat was tight and dry as she met his gaze. "Banshee."

Garran didn't say anything as she turned her attention to the sky. The falcon let out another cry of greeting as he circled high overhead, his form small and dark between the moon and where she stood. Banshee was both diurnal and nocturnal and he had a sixth sense when it came to Hannah.

She held out her arm and Banshee arrowed toward her at what would have been an alarming rate if she didn't know him so well. Peregrine falcons could travel at speeds well over two hundred miles an hour when diving for their prey.

He slowed to land gently on her bare forearm. True happiness bubbled up inside her at seeing her friend, her companion. Time passed oddly in Otherworld. It hadn't been long since she'd left for the Drow realm, but it seemed like it had been ages.

Banshee eased up her arm to her shoulder, his eyes focused

on Garran as if determining whether he was friend or foe. She wanted to laugh, but managed to hold it back.

"Garran, this is Banshee." The falcon settled himself on her right shoulder, the one opposite Garran. "Banshee, meet the king of the Drow."

Banshee and Garran locked gazes, then to Hannah's surprise, Garran gave a slight nod and the falcon bobbed his head. Through the magical connection she had with her familiar, she sensed that Banshee hadn't made up his mind whether or not he approved of Garran but did wish to show him respect.

Hannah got the feeling it had more to do with her coming close to kissing the Drow king than anything else. From Garran's expression it looked like he didn't appreciate the interruption.

She held back a smirk. *Males.*

Banshee nuzzled her neck with his head and Garran clasped her hand. It felt natural. Right.

What's wrong with this picture, Hannah Wentworth?

While they walked into the forest, she almost laughed at the fact he kept calling her "sweet one." Instead, she said, "That's the last thing I am—sweet. I'm considered a ball-busting bitch in my 'Otherworld,' and I don't apologize for it. That's how I've gotten where I am today." She frowned. "Where I was."

Her company had never been far from her mind. What in the Ancestors' names was happening to her company and her employees right now?

Garran broke into her thoughts. "I find that most difficult to believe. That anyone would think of you in such terms."

This time she did laugh, but it was humorless. "Believe it." She sidestepped a bush as leaves crunched beneath her shoes. Garran made no sound as he walked, just as he hadn't in his own realm. "I'm not exactly the girl-next-door type."

"I am not sure what you mean by that expression," he said. "I think of your appearance as strong, capable, regal."

Hannah blinked and looked up into his eyes. "Regal?"

His expression remained thoughtful as he nodded. "However, despite such a hard exterior, inside you are a warm, loving woman."

She turned her gaze straight ahead into the dark forest as her face felt as though her skin had tightened over her cheekbones. "I don't know what the hell you're talking about." She adjusted the strap of her pack with her free hand and Banshee had to sidestep her fingers. "I am who I am."

"You are more than you think you are." Garran squeezed her other hand as she tried to pull away from his grasp. "Tell me of your childhood."

Hannah ground her teeth and this time tried to yank her hand away from his, but couldn't. Damn, he was strong. "There's nothing to tell."

His voice was low, soothing. "I want to know."

Hannah's thoughts whirled and she almost stumbled over a tree root, but Garran kept her steady. Some compelling force took hold of her, drew the words from her, just as when she met the Great Guardian.

"I had a rough childhood." Hannah's laugh was cynical as her body tensed. "No, that's not exactly right. Most people would believe I lived a dream life. I had everything I ever wanted. Every toy, every dress, every perfect thing a child could have. I traveled the world as many times as I wanted and visited any theme park I demanded to be taken to. I had it all."

"Belongings. All that you fancied." He appeared very serious when she glanced up again. "Those things are not what give a person happiness."

"No, they don't." Hannah couldn't hold back the sigh that rushed from her as she faced straight ahead into the dark forest.

"It was much the same for me and my brother," Garran said, and she snapped her attention to him. He gave a casual shrug. "We were the sons of royalty. Anything we commanded was ours."

Surprise filtered through her. She hadn't given his childhood much thought, that he was the son of a king. She kept her gaze on him as he continued.

"Our father was busy with war as Naal and I grew from babes to men." He didn't sound bitter or remorseful, just factual. "In those years, the Elves were always at war when we lived in your Earth Otherworld. Demons. Men. Fae. Gods. If it was not one war it was another."

Amazement at the thought of what Garran had lived through flowed through her. "What happened to your mother and father? When did you become king?"

"They died in a battle against several of the old gods who attacked dishonorably—with no warning. Many of our men, women, and children died." Anger was apparent on Garran's features and in the way he squeezed her hand. "Somewhere around three millennia ago. Give or take a few centuries."

"I'm sorry" seemed like a trite thing to say at that moment, so Hannah said nothing.

He relaxed his grip on her hand but continued to hold it. "Continue with your story." A kingly demand.

She hated talking about her childhood—she never did. But after what he'd shared, her own childhood woes seemed insignificant.

Yet thinking about it and saying the words still caused her chest to tighten. "I grew up with a mother I rarely saw. From the time I was born, one nanny after another raised me. When I began to get used to the new nanny, my mother would get rid of her and hire another.

"I think she resented getting pregnant with me." Hannah's lips quirked, but again she felt no humor. "Probably the stretch marks."

Garran raised a brow when she glanced at him.

"Selena Wentworth is definitely a socialite in every sense of the word. That's all she cares about. Parties, status, the best clothes, the nicest cars, the most luxurious homes— having more money than anyone else." Banshee gripped Hannah's shoulder and she sensed waves of comfort coming from him.

Fireflies danced to her right in interesting patterns and she realized they were Faeries, not fireflies. Maybe having their version of a Fae celebration.

"Continue," Garran said in that same commanding voice that propelled her forward.

Hell, she'd gone this far. Why not all the way?

"When I was old enough, my mother sent me to boarding schools, which meant she didn't have to deal with me for most of the year."

Hannah inhaled the clean forest air. Sometime during their short journey, holding Garran's hand had begun to feel natural, as if he belonged right there, and she had to shake the strange thoughts off. "When I hit thirteen I started to do the rebellion thing," she added.

Garran smiled, the kind of smile people shared when they understood one another. "My mother and father were forced to deal with my insurgence before I reached adulthood. Many years passed before I realized that during that short time in my life I rebelled because I wanted my father's attention."

Hannah nodded. "I really went at it in school. Talking back to my teachers, sneaking out of the dorms at night, and refusing to do what they told me. I never let my grades drop, but I gave everyone so much hell they were constantly calling my mother.

"That got her attention." Ahead Hannah could see the lights of the D'Danann village. "She decided she'd had enough, so she sent me packing to live with my father."

Garran guided her forward, along a maze of a path. "Was living with your father difficult as well?"

"It was certainly different." Hannah cocked her head. "My father was a male version of my mother. *Mr.* Socialite. But what he did that turned my life around was to introduce me to my heritage by letting me spend time with a grandmother I'd never known. She taught me about my D'Anu ancestry and I became an apprentice."

The trials of her upbringing truly seemed minor in the

scheme of things. "I know so many people have it worse in one way or another." Hannah lowered her voice the closer they got to the village. She didn't want to be overheard by her sister witches—she'd never shared any of the facts of her childhood with them. "But it sucked at the time, and, yeah, it influenced my life. Like I said, I am who I am."

He brought her to a stop at the edge of the forest as raucous laughter spilled into the night from one of the taverns.

Garran lowered his head and lightly brushed his lips over hers. When he drew away she could barely catch her breath. She could only stare up at him.

"As I told you before, Hannah Wentworth"—he skimmed his knuckles over her cheek—"you are far more than you think you are."

Two leather-clad D'Danann warriors with grim expressions emerged from the shadows, their swords unsheathed. The women warriors' sudden appearance startled Hannah into almost dropping her pack. Garran maintained his grip on her hand and Banshee ruffled his feathers.

"You are not welcome, King Garran," the redheaded warrior said, her sword raised.

"You were allowed to witness your daughter's joining with Keir, but we will not let you trespass again," the second D'Danann, a blond, said while narrowing her eyes.

Banshee made a low sound that indicated his disapproval. Hannah scowled and started to tell the warriors where they could put those swords.

With a calm expression, Garran looked from warrior to warrior. "I am here to see the D'Anu and D'Danann who fight the Otherworld battle. Send word to them that I am here."

Neither woman so much as twitched. "The witch may pass, but you will not," the blond said.

"Oh, for Anu's sake." Hannah pushed herself between the women, in front of Garran. "We have business to take care of to help in the war in San Francisco. Garran stays with me."

"Very well." The redhead tipped her chin. "One of us will accompany you and the Drow to the training yards where the commanders are." Her gaze met Garran's. "And we will ensure the Drow king is well guarded."

Hannah wanted to growl. This rivalry was absurd.

Instead, she ignored the woman and shoved her way past the warriors, Garran at her side. With the silence of the Fae and Elves, one of the warriors followed close behind— Hannah only knew because she cast a glance over her shoulder and saw the redhead, who still bore her sword.

Garran said nothing and his expression was well schooled as they headed toward the training yards. Banshee continued to make low sounds of disapproval. Hannah was surprised that her familiar was siding with Garran, yet not. The falcon was so in tune with her decisions and feelings that he normally didn't question her choices. Even if he was a little jealous and possessive.

When they arrived, they stood at the entrance to the main yard as warriors left to summon Keir and Tiernan at their homes, and yet another warrior went to assemble the D'Anu witches in one of the taverns.

Hannah wanted to snap at all the warriors for acting as if Garran were a plague, but she gritted her teeth and waited beside the calm-looking Drow king.

Finally, she and Garran were escorted to one of the village's many taverns. It was less crowded and therefore had a more subdued atmosphere.

Banshee gave a cry and took to the air before she and Garran headed in. She watched Banshee for a moment, her heart twisting as he joined with the night, then she followed Garran.

At once they were greeted by Hannah's D'Anu Coven sisters, those who were not presently in San Francisco. As Hannah and Garran entered the tavern, two of the three leaders of the D'Danann contingent to San Francisco walked through the door behind them—Tiernan and Keir. They were so silent she hadn't realized they were there until they gathered in the entrance beside the witches. By his nod to each man and his expression, she was certain Garran had sensed them even if she hadn't.

Hannah tried to keep from standing so rigidly as Cassia and Copper greeted her with a hug. She'd never been crazy about how touchy-feely most of the group was. Rhiannon kept her normal distance which was fine by Hannah.

They moved to a long, polished wooden table lined with chairs. Garran sat beside her and Rhiannon was directly across from them with Keir at her side. Hannah set her pack down by her feet.

This tavern was so unlike the pub the D'Danann normally frequented, which had rough wooden tables with benches. Instead of smelling of ale and roasted meats, the air was mostly perfumed with the scents of baked desserts, such as apple pies and cinnamon pastries.

Copper always grimaced when she came into this tavern, thanks to her aversion to apples. A tavern maid they had become quite familiar with over the past week or so delivered tankards of ale. By now the servers knew better than to give Copper the apple ale, so they always brought her something that smelled of grapes.

"Are Silver, Alyssa, Mackenzie, and Sydney still scouting out San Francisco with the D'Danann they took with them?" Hannah asked Cassia after Hannah took a drink of the crisp apple-flavored ale.

The beautiful, ethereal-looking half-Elvin witch folded her hands on the table in front of her tankard. "We'll join them tomorrow."

Rhiannon cut through the chitchat and looked across the table at Garran. "What's your decision?"

He studied her for a long moment. "We will fight beside your people. You have all the resources the Drow can lend."

Silence and a collective sigh of relief seemed to travel around the table.

Rhiannon closed her green eyes for a moment before opening them and looking at her father. "Thank you," she said quietly.

Garran's response was a single nod.

"Now we've got to plan how this is all going to go down." Copper fiddled with the end of her long braid and thunked her ankle cast on the floor as she shifted in her chair. She frowned. "The Drow can only fight after dark."

"That is correct." Garran looked to each person at the table. His silvery-blue hair and bluish-gray skin was a contrast to the hair and skin of those around him, yet Hannah now didn't see him as any different from every other man and woman in the tavern.

Garran continued speaking. "I will go alone to your San Francisco Otherworld and make my assessments. My men will be prepared to fight when the time is appropriate."

"Jake said the new headquarters is ready." Copper studied Garran. "Including the room you're going to stay in during the day when the sun is out so that you won't fry to a crisp."

"My appreciation," Garran said, yet there was a light to his eyes that intrigued Hannah. As if he were looking forward to this, sunshine or no.

"We're leaving to head back to the city first thing in the morning." Copper leaned against her husband, Tiernan, and the blond warrior draped his arm around her shoulders. "Thank goodness the D'Danann found their blessed Cauldron of Dagda," Copper added as she looked from one warrior to the next. "Now we won't have to spend so much time figuring out how to feed these bottomless pits."

Hannah looked at Garran. "Are Drow as insatiable as D'Danann?"

He gave her a sensual look that made her nipples tighten. "Always."

Her cheeks heated and she elbowed him. "I meant food."

Garran chuckled and Copper snickered. "Yeah, it was getting hard to find enough, ah, *food,* to feed all the D'Danann," Copper said with a grin.

"When all of the witches get together, we'll grab our personal items—clothes and stuff—and take them to HQ," Copper said. "If you don't mind, we'll use our magic to get into your house and gather what jeans and T-shirts you have."

"Jeans and T-shirts." Hannah sighed. "Guess Stella Mc-Cartney and Derek Lam attire won't cut it when it comes to battling Ceithlenn and the Fomorii." She glanced down at her leathers and couldn't help a quirk of a smile when she looked back at Copper. "But how about something silky from Victoria's to go under them?"

"You've got it." Copper laughed and then sobered, her easy smile melting into a frown. "We'll use our glamours to make sure no one sees and recognizes us when we get back to the city. According to Jake, martial law is in full effect. Especially since two soldiers were attacked and eaten alive on a street in the city the other night."

Rhiannon visibly shuddered and her skin paled. "After having visions of Ceithlenn doing exactly that, I have no doubt it was her."

The thought of what Ceithlenn had done to those soldiers made Hannah's stomach churn and fire heat her body.

"What about the white magic D'Anu witches?" Hannah asked as it occurred to her that she hadn't heard what had happened to the High Priestess and her Coven after the last battle. "Janis Arrowsmith and the others? Even though they were only healing the injured and not fighting, they were seen on national television, too."

"According to Jake," Copper said, "all thirteen white witches have been taken into protective custody and put in safe houses until the authorities are assured they're not in any danger."

"I still can't believe that Sara was Janis's apprentice." Rhiannon tapped her fingers on the smooth tabletop. "She just doesn't *get* that Sara isn't Sara anymore. Ceithlenn is only using Sara's human shell."

"I should have severed Ceithlenn's head from her shoulders when I had the opportunity," Keir growled.

Rhiannon rubbed her husband's arm. "How could you know Janis would throw herself across Ceithlenn-Sara's body? None of us did." Rhiannon looked at Garran. "If I'd learned how to control my Shadows better, maybe the goddess would already be back in Underworld."

"It *was not* your fault." Copper frowned as she looked from Rhiannon to Keir. "Either of you. So stop blaming yourselves."

The group was quiet for a moment. Around them floated conversation that Hannah hadn't even noticed until now, coming from other tavern patrons who were talking in a low hum.

Garran broke their group's silence. "Hannah and I will travel back to my realm before we leave for San Francisco."

Apparently Garran intended to follow through with keeping her as his liaison. For some reason, the idea didn't bother her at all. What was stranger, far more bizarre, was how she was almost looking forward to their journey back to the Dark Elves' realm.

Somewhere along the way aliens had stolen her brain and she had no idea where they'd hidden it.

To Rhiannon, Garran said, "May we speak alone, my daughter?"

She hesitated only a moment then pushed her chair back to stand before Garran escorted her to a small table in the corner.

Hannah turned her gaze to the big rough, scarred warrior, Keir, who was Rhiannon's husband. Hannah had referred to him as a Neanderthal on prior occasions—he was completely barbaric as far as she was concerned.

So it was to her surprise that a thoughtful-looking Keir picked up his tankard and said, "It is time for Rhiannon and her father to heal," before taking a swallow of his ale.

CHAPTER NINE

GARRAN STUDIED RHIANNON AS they sat alone, across from one another in the tavern. Warmth and pride filled his chest as he smiled at his daughter.

Rhiannon looked so relieved, as if the mightiest of weights had been raised from her shoulders. "Thank you again."

Garran reached across the small table and clasped her hand in his. They both looked down at their joined hands, the tone of his bluish-gray skin so different from her pale flesh. She didn't draw away and their eyes met again.

"Understand this, daughter." Garran squeezed her fingers lightly. "I would go to the farthest reaches of Otherworld for you." Despite his words, Rhiannon's expression turned sad, as if disbelieving. He squeezed her fingers tighter. "You must understand, too, that while I would do this for you, I could not involve my people if it did not benefit them. I am their king, and I am also your father. For them I must make decisions that take precedence over my own feelings, desires, needs."

Rhiannon remained silent, but her gaze still held his. She sounded as if her throat were dry when she spoke. "I get it now, and I'm sorry I judged your actions so harshly."

Her throat worked as she swallowed and continued, "But being Drow . . . I'm having a hard time separating what's good and bad." Her voice grew hoarser as she spoke. "The

Shadows inside me that I inherited from you—they helped me a couple of times, but they've done harm, too. Before I started to control them, they almost killed Keir. How can I believe there isn't some evil inside of them?"

She frowned and tugged her hand. He let it slide from his, feeling a sense of loss, that his flesh and blood did not accept him as he was.

"I am who I am. That will never change." A deep sigh rose within him and he let it out in a slow exhale. "It is my wish that one day you will embrace your heritage."

Rhiannon appeared nervous now, as if she might jump and bolt away. "I have to think about it some more. I've only known about you, have only known you, and have only known I'm half Drow for a really short time." She glanced toward the table of warriors and witches who were talking among themselves before looking back at him. "It's not so easy for me, can *you* understand that? You deal in dark magic and that mark has been left on me."

"But not black magic, remember that," Garran said. "The difference is great."

"Is it?" Rhiannon's chin-length hair swung as she shook her head back and forth. "I just don't know what to believe right now."

Garran leaned forward, his forearms braced on the table. "You must make your choices. I will love you no matter what those choices might be. Come to me if and when you are ready. I will be waiting, as I waited for your mother all those years ago."

Rhiannon's eyes grew watery, as if she were fighting back tears. Despite her torn expression, she didn't say anything and simply nodded before slipping out of her chair and going back to her husband and the other witches and warriors.

Garran looked across the tavern, barely noticing what was around him. Rhiannon's rejection dug at his gut like a cold blade.

Perhaps one day she would understand him . . . Perhaps not.

His only choice now was to be at Rhiannon's side when he was able to, as a father should. Beyond that, it was up to her whether or not she would accept her Drow heritage. And accept him.

HANNAH SAID HER GOODBYES to her Coven sisters and Banshee again before she and Garran made their way back to the Drow realm. She would be seeing them the following day, but somehow it felt like it would be longer, as if they would be worlds away. Truly they would be, once the witches were in San Francisco and Hannah was still with Garran in Otherworld. But it wouldn't be for long.

Hannah adjusted the shoulder strap of her pack. "How did your talk go with Rhiannon?" she asked Garran as they neared the transference stone, the Great Guardian nowhere in sight.

Garran let out a long sigh and took Hannah's hand. She squeezed his fingers, hoping that gave him some comfort. "Rhiannon is my daughter. I wish only for her happiness."

Hannah looked into the night as they continued walking. Moonlight dripped like silver tears over leaves and grass. "I don't understand why I've come around to understanding and accepting you faster than your own daughter," she said quietly.

Garran brought her to a stop and took both of her hands, forcing her to look up at him. "You and I share a different bond." His tone and his gaze were serious, none of the teasing light in his eyes. "Ours is a meeting of souls."

Hannah shivered and looked away from his intense expression at the same time she tried to step back. Right now she wanted to finish what they'd started before Banshee had interrupted—a kiss that she desired with everything she had. But if she admitted it to herself, she needed more than a kiss. Much, much more.

This craving her body had for him was insane.

When Garran drew her into his embrace and forced her to

look at him again, she didn't stop him. His body was warm and solid against hers as he buried his hand in her hair and cupped the back of her head. His eyes still held hers as he used his other hand to grip one of her ass cheeks and draw her snug against him, pressing his cock hard to her belly.

Hannah's breathing grew heavier, her heart pounding a little faster as he focused on her lips.

Fierce, hard, fast, like the warrior he was, he took possession of her mouth. He clenched his hand in her hair and held her so tightly that the straps crisscrossing his chest hurt as they smashed her breasts.

His taste—so earthy and masculine—drove her senses wild. She braced her palms on his cool metal shoulder plates, and kissed him back with the same passion.

Her senses spun, need spiking so badly she wanted to crawl up his powerful body and wrap her thighs around his hips. And they weren't in the Drow realm. Every bit of the desire she'd had for him on this short journey to and from the D'Danann village proved he had never used magic to make her want him.

Not that she doubted his word. If nothing else, she sensed he was a good man, an honest man.

With a low groan, Garran abruptly stopped the kiss. Her lips felt swollen and she wasn't sure she could breathe properly. His eyes were the same color as the moonlight as he looked down at her with so much passion that she reached up to kiss him again.

But he surprised her by stepping away and holding her at arm's length. There was no doubt he wanted her. It was in his eyes, the way he looked at her, the roughness of his breathing.

Instead of taking the kiss any further, he reached out and grasped her hand. "Let us go back to my realm," he said just before everything whirled and they entered the dark void of the transference.

The void swallowed her scream before they abruptly appeared in the meadow. She stumbled into Garran again, almost dropping her pack.

He held her for a brief moment then disappointment slid through her veins as he drew back, took her hand again, and brought her the few steps to the door to the Drow realm.

She shuddered at the sound of the rock door opening. "We definitely need to find some kind of lube to get rid of that horrid sound," she said as they started down the stairs. She almost came to a stop after the words left her mouth. What was she thinking? Once they left for San Francisco, she was never coming back.

Silence draped them like a soft, comfortable cloak as they made their way down the stairs, deep into the depths of the Drow realm. They were immediately greeted by Garran's guards. He merely responded with a nod before placing his hand at the base of her spine and guiding her to one of the doors leading from the great hall.

Her heart beat faster as he led her along passageways they'd been through before. Was he taking her to his own chamber?

Warmth traveled through her body all the way to her nipples. Erotic thoughts of her and Garran—naked and in bed together—wended their way through her mind. She met his liquid silver gaze as they walked and she knew he sensed every lustful urge rising up within her.

The line of his jaw tensed and he looked away from her as they continued down a passageway. Cool, crisp air flowed over her, but she felt hot. So, so hot for Garran.

They reached the room she had slept in last night. Instead of leading her into the room, he brought her to a stop in the doorway.

Garran grasped her by her shoulders. In a harsh clash, his mouth met hers and she shivered at the firmness of his body and the leather straps against her breasts.

She gasped into his mouth when his callused hands moved beneath her shirt and roamed her body, up and down her back from her shoulder blades to her waist, stirring more lust within her. She moaned into his mouth with an urgency of her own as his fingers moved up to brush the sides of her breasts. Thrills shot straight to her belly as his thumbs found her nipples.

The intensity of the passion swirling inside her at that moment nearly took her breath away. Why Garran? She hadn't felt this way around any man, not one, and she'd dated and had sex with a lot of wealthy, gorgeous, successful men.

By the goddess, she wanted more than just a kiss from Garran. Who cared that she barely knew him? She always got what she wanted, and right now she wanted *him.*

Garran drew away from her and wild, primal need stirred in his liquid silver eyes.

Her voice was husky as she started to tell him she wanted him to take her to bed. "Garran—"

"Shhh." He put his fingertips to her mouth, silencing her. "Rest now. We shall leave on the morrow."

Hannah blinked, too stunned to move as he replaced his fingers with a brush of his lips.

As he released her and backed away, he gave her a devastatingly sexy smile then a roguish wink before turning and striding away from the room.

For a moment, Hannah stared at the place he'd been standing before her temper flared and heat raced over her.

"Bastard." She ground her teeth and slammed the door, the hard thunk resounding through the chamber. She dropped her pack as she glared at the door.

Yeah, they'd leave tomorrow. After she killed him.

THE PAIN IN GARRAN'S groin as he strode from Hannah's chamber made it difficult to walk. He had come so close to taking her. Holding himself back had required more effort and restraint than he had thought he possessed.

He would bed Hannah, but not until her trust in him was complete, and there was no doubt in her mind he did not use Drow magic to make her desire him so.

And when he was certain she felt the same soul-bond that he did.

He forced his thoughts to the task at hand. Before he rested, a discussion with Vidar was called for.

When he reached the Great Hall, Garran had one of his guards summon Vidar. Garran waited in his throne room, unable to hold back his frown as he glanced to the throne where the Orb was kept safe and hidden in the secret recesses of the armrest.

Was Vidar ready to receive the training from the Orb of Aithne?

Garran fully faced the throne and closed his eyes for a moment before opening them. No, he would wait. Once he had assessed the situation in the San Francisco Otherworld, he would return and determine if Vidar had served well in his absence. It was truly the best option Garran had at the time to weigh his decisions.

Garran took the steps up the dais to his throne and reclined with one elbow on the chair's armrest as he stroked his chin.

When Vidar entered the chamber, he bowed then stood with a wide stance, his hands behind his back. His expression remained clear and respectful. No insolence, arrogance, or disrespect was in his eyes.

Still, Garran felt something out of place. Off. Yes, when he returned shortly, he would further evaluate Vidar's performance.

"I leave on the morrow with the D'Anu witch." Garran removed his hand from his chin and placed both forearms on the armrests. "I will take residence with the D'Danann, witches, and human forces who prepare now to again battle Ceithlenn."

"Yes, my king." Vidar's tone was calm, even. "Are you certain we cannot send one of our best warriors to accompany you?"

Garran nearly sighed. If it was not for the Great Guardian's declaration that he was not to inform anyone of his gifted power, he would take one of the men with him. As it was, he could ill afford to have a warrior shadowing him as he attempted to carry out his task.

"Perhaps upon my return, after I have determined our best course of action," Garran finally said.

Vidar maintained a look of calm. "It would be for the best, my lord."

Garran steeled his own expression. "However, at this moment I must have a word with you about your disrespectfulness for the D'Anu witch, Hannah."

Annoyance flashed across Vidar's features and a muscle along his jaw twitched. "A woman has no place in the warriors' training chamber. Nor should she be allowed to feast with the Directorate and warriors when council is convened."

A slow burn crawled up Garran's spine and he barely restrained his anger. "It is not your decision to make. If I deem it so, that women may attend whatever I choose, then it shall be. You *will* offer only the utmost respect to both of the witches—Hannah and my daughter Rhiannon—when either are in your presence."

Vidar paused longer than Garran thought appropriate, but the First in Command said, "Yes, my lord. It shall be so."

Garran kept his eyes on the warrior. "See to it that Carden's training as your First is well attended to."

If Vidar was annoyed in any fashion, he did not show it. "At once, my lord."

With a nod, Garran gestured to the doorway. "You may leave to attend to your duties."

Vidar bowed, then turned and walked out the doorway of the throne room, his spine and posture rigid, almost wooden.

Garran narrowed his eyes. Yes, he must return from the San Francisco Otherworld soon to monitor Vidar and his training.

CHAPTER TEN

DARKWOLF ALMOST DROPPED TO his knees, barely keeping to his feet in the small apartment. His mind swam and he struggled to focus on Elizabeth-Junga, the former queen of the Fomorii.

The weight of Balor's eye was becoming increasingly difficult to carry and the pain in his head more intense. The stone eye, hanging from a chain at his throat, grew heavier, as if the ancient god himself yanked it toward the ground.

Somewhere, the god slogged through the sewers. That much Darkwolf's scrying had told him.

Balor would never stop searching for Darkwolf and the eye. Not until the eye was destroyed, sent to Underworld, or the god found him.

Perhaps if his Clan still existed, Darkwolf could have gathered the warlocks, and together they might have used their black magic . . . but to do what?

It didn't matter, anyway. Ceithlenn had murdered most of his Clan and the rest had fled the city when she arrived.

Elizabeth pursed her lips and studied him. He preferred to think of her as the beautiful Elizabeth Black rather than the Fomorii demon that had taken over her body. As Elizabeth her scent was intoxicating—of woman and soft musky perfume.

Thank the gods she didn't smell like the Fomorii did when they were in their demon form. All Fomorii smelled only of their host when in a human shell.

"Can you do something—anything?" Elizabeth crossed her arms over her chest. "You're a warlock. You brought me and my kind to this world, can you not send the eye back?"

A flash of anger at her question made his headache worse. Darkwolf ground his teeth and went to the window of the small apartment they had taken over, his back to her.

What Elizabeth—Junga—had done to rid the place of its former renters, he didn't want to know or think about. For now, it was theirs to use until Balor closed in on them again.

Darkwolf braced his hands on the wooden window frame, near the lock. He stared at the empty street and the cracked sidewalks spotted with black crap, no doubt most of it discarded chewing gum trod on by countless people over countless years.

Every day the anger burning within Darkwolf grew hotter and the pain in his head greater. One day he might lose control of that anger and use the power of the eye for himself.

Why not use it? Why suffer this torment day by day? He'd shrouded the eye as best he could with his own magic to keep Balor from finding him quickly. But what if Darkwolf discovered a way to use it against the god?

When Darkwolf found the eye on the shores of Ireland, he'd been a white witch known as Kevin Richards. Darkwolf had been so overcome with the power of the eye, with the greed that had gripped his soul, that he'd been oblivious to everything but bringing the Fomorii and Balor to this world.

But now that Ceithlenn had arrived, everything had changed. Something inside him had snapped when she used him, dominated him, forced him into sexual acts that left him feeling more unclean than even the horrid things he had done while under the powerful influence of Balor's eye.

Power that Darkwolf had used willingly.

He gripped the sill so tightly his fingernails dug into the aging wood and his jaws ached from clenching them.

Darkwolf released the sill to turn and face Elizabeth, meeting her blue eyes. "If I could rid myself of the eye, I would," he said through gritted teeth. "You know that."

She pushed one of her hands through her thick, glossy black hair. "There must be some way that you can dispense with the gods-be-damned thing."

His mind returned again to his darkest thoughts. "Or just maybe I can use it for myself. Screw Balor and hiding it from him."

Elizabeth dropped her hand to her side, her eyes widening. "Do you think that's possible?"

"Hell if I know." The pain in his head grew greater. He had to relieve it before he went mad. "But I do know what I want now."

The only thing that lessened his pain daily was unleashing his power on Elizabeth, sexually dominating her, fulfilling them both. She always took him willingly, her desire as insatiable as his.

Lust darkened her eyes and her nipples beaded beneath the T-shirt she was dressed in now. Instead of the tailored, fitted suits she'd worn before, as Elizabeth Black, she had finally settled for more practical clothing—jeans, T-shirts, and running shoes.

He'd preferred it when he could shove up her skirt and sink his cock into her tight core whenever he wanted to. But he could still fuck her hard and fast no matter how she was dressed.

And right now he needed just that.

Elizabeth wet her lips with her tongue as he strode from the window, across the cramped living room. As soon as he reached her, he grabbed her shining black hair in one fist, yanked her to him, and grasped her ass with his free hand. He ground his cock against her belly as he claimed her mouth. At the same time a growl rose in his throat.

Whenever he took her a feral, primal need overcame him that made every other thing around them vanish. The eye no longer weighed him down, and he no longer felt Balor's presence. If he could be inside Elizabeth constantly to keep it all at bay, he would.

He jerked her T-shirt from where it was tucked into her

jeans and shoved it over her breasts. He palmed them, her hard nipples pressing against his hands. Following his orders, she never wore underwear, so there was no bra to get in his way.

The anger that had been simmering in him made him growl again and he bit her lower lip hard enough to make her cry out. The taste of blood heightened his lust and he bit her again.

Elizabeth's hands went to work, stroking his cock through his jeans and then unfastening the top button. The zipper slid apart as she forced it down and freed his erection.

Darkwolf released his hold on her lower lip, licking the blood away before jerking her long hair hard, forcing her to her knees. She whimpered, but he knew she loved it when he mastered her.

"I want you to go down on me before I let you have my cock in your pussy." He pushed his erection against her lips.

Without hesitation she parted her lips and slipped him inside until she reached the back of her throat. With his hands clenched in her hair, he started thrusting in and out of her mouth.

She worked his erection with one hand while fondling his balls with her other. At the same time she sucked his cock like no one else ever had. She made soft whimpering and moaning sounds as she bobbed her head and looked up at him with her startling blue eyes.

He watched his moist erection slide in and out of her mouth and that turned him on even more. Her shirt was still up, over her bouncing breasts, her nipples large and taut, making him want to suck and bite them.

The heat in his balls intensified and his sac drew up. Elizabeth applied deep suction and he lost it. Semen spurted down her throat and his mind spun with the power of his orgasm. The pulsing of his cock inside her mouth sent spasm after spasm through him.

She continued sucking as he pressed his groin to her face, and she wrung every last drop from him.

Darkwolf resisted the urge to fall to his knees. He let go of her hair only long enough to grab her shoulders and jerk her to her feet.

"What do you want, Elizabeth?" he said as his cock rubbed against her jeans and began to grow erect again. "Tell me exactly what you want me to do to you."

"Fuck me and spank me so hard it hurts." Her cheeks were flushed, her pupils dilated, and her breasts rose and fell at a rapid pace.

Another growl rose up in Darkwolf. He knew what she wanted, but he liked to hear it from her. He jerked her T-shirt over her head, unbuttoned her jeans and unzipped them, before pushing the jeans to her thighs.

"On your hands and knees." It made his cock harder to give her orders that she immediately obeyed.

Elizabeth dropped to her knees as he shoved her down by her shoulders and then she planted her palms on the worn carpeting. She spread her thighs as far as the jeans would allow and he knelt behind her. Should he take her in the ass or her pussy? She liked it both ways and the pain of his entry in her tight ass was something she craved.

But today he wanted the slickness and warmth of her pussy. He positioned his erection at the opening of her core, grabbed her hips, and slammed into her.

Elizabeth cried out from the power of his thrust then shouted again when he slapped one of her ass cheeks with his palm.

Damn, her snug channel gripped his cock so tightly it took effort not to come too fast. He spanked her other ass cheek, enjoying the sting against his palm as she whimpered from the pain of his slap. Again and again he spanked her. Her cries and whimpers and the sight of his handprints on her ass made the need to come more intense.

The stone eye swung against his chest as he rocked back and forth. It was cushioned by the magic he shrouded it with, but still he was aware of it.

He drove into her over and over and spanked her harder

and harder. She screamed when she climaxed, her skin flushing pink from her orgasm. Her whole body shuddered and her pussy clamped down on his cock with every tremor that racked her frame. He forced himself to hold back his orgasm, wanting her to enjoy her own as he drew out her climax until she couldn't stand it anymore.

When she finally sobbed and begged him to stop, he thrust several times more then shouted and dug his fingers into her firm ass cheeks. His cock throbbed inside her pussy, which continued to squeeze down on him with her ongoing contractions.

For that moment in time all he did was let the pleasure wash over him. He closed his eyes hoping that it would last. That he could put off the inevitable just a little longer.

When the orgasm started to fade away, the pain in his head and the weight of the eye slammed into him. He collapsed on Elizabeth's back, forcing her down to her belly.

The pain was so great that all he could do was lie there until he had the strength to take control again.

CHAPTER ELEVEN

THE FOLLOWING DAY BEFORE it grew too close to dawn, Garran escorted Hannah to his throne room. He had found the spark of anger in her eyes amusing as she practically slammed the door to her chamber in his face before taking her shower. Again he had waited until she had refreshed herself and came out of the room, her pack over her shoulder.

When they reached the smooth, obsidian granite door in his throne room, he raised his hand. His palm warmed as his magic flowed from his hand in a glittering dark cloud and opened the heavy door. No one but one of the Drow could open this doorway to those from Otherworlds.

He took Hannah into the small room that contained a circular transference stone, similar to the one the Great Guardian allowed the Fae and other beings to use as long as they had Elvin escorts.

"You need some light in here. And a heater," Hannah grumbled as she rubbed her bare arms. He could see her skin had pebbled like gooseflesh from the chill in the chamber.

Using his magic again, he closed the granite door. Total darkness shrouded them, but his Drow sight allowed him to see clearly and he took her hand in his.

"Light, Garran. You might be able to see, but I can't." She tried to jerk her hand away from his, obviously still irritated with him from leaving her filled with desire last night. But he gripped her fingers and refused to release her.

"Close your eyes." He watched her in the darkness as she looked up at him. "Now. Then hold on to me as I take us to your Otherworld."

She scowled at him but closed her eyes. The sound of the catch in her breath was lost as he guided them through the void to the Drow door to San Francisco. All it required of him was a thought of where they should be, and in moments they arrived.

Hannah grabbed onto his arm when their feet hit the rocky beach in the darkness beneath a pier. He looked down to see her blink and her lips part as she stared out at the bay.

She flashed what he was certain was a rare smile. "I'm home." Her smile faded as she stared out into the distance to the lights of Alcatraz Island. "As much of a home as it can be right now."

Garran tugged her hand and drew her from beneath the pier, past the giant round pilings, and into the foggy night. He sucked in the scent of brine mixed with the city's pollution that assaulted his sensitive sense of smell. He didn't smell the strong rotten-fish odor of the Fomorii, so the beasts were not close. At this moment.

But he did catch faint feminine perfume on the air, the scent of Fae, and the lingering smell of man.

Rocks and pebbles crunched beneath Hannah's shoes, her breathing elevated, and he sensed her pleasure at returning to her city.

"You're late," came his daughter's voice, and he smiled. Rhiannon might have her mother's looks, but she had *his* occasional temper and impatience.

Hannah yanked her hand from his as soon as they heard Rhiannon's voice, and even in the near darkness he could see a slight flush creep up her neck.

Amused at her obvious embarrassment at being caught holding his hand, he followed Hannah up the only slope that led from the beach to the wooden pier and to the asphalt. A single light pole stood off to the side. Rhiannon and Keir waited just outside of the glow. Rhiannon was no longer in her D'Danann leathers, but in human clothing, as was Keir.

"It's getting close to sunrise." Rhiannon looked to the east. "We've got to get you to the warehouse."

"Do not fear." Garran stared in the direction the sun would grace the sky. Anticipation skittered along his skin at the graying atmosphere and the faint pink glow just over the horizon.

"What do you mean, 'Do not fear?' " Hannah's voice rose and he detected concern. Concern that made him smile again. She might not wish it, but already she had begun to care for him.

"No kidding. Hurry." Even Rhiannon had urgency to her voice that warmed his chest.

The Great Guardian had only commanded him to not share with anyone that he had the power to send the demons back to Underworld. She had not told him to hide the fact that he could now walk in the sun. Which would be obvious once he began working with the D'Anu, D'Danann, and their human law enforcement officers.

As he stood on the pier and stared into the east, his skin did not tingle. In Otherworld, that would be a signal it was time to go belowground. If one of the Dark Elves ignored the sign, as soon as the sun rose all that remained of him would be ash.

"Now that you're here to help, you are *so* not going to fry," Rhiannon said as she came up beside him.

He looked down and admired the spark in his daughter's eyes and in her spirit.

"The Great Guardian has granted me a gift." His words echoed on the pier as he looked from Rhiannon to Hannah. "As long as I am here, assisting you and your people, I am able to walk in the sun."

Hannah's eyes widened and Rhiannon's jaw dropped. "Really?" she asked.

He answered by looking to the east again.

It seemed an eternity passed, but it truly was not long before rays of morning light peeked through the fog.

As if only for him, the mist melted away and the sunrise burst clearly over the horizon. Oranges, yellows. So beautiful.

His eyes did not burn or water. His skin did not heat. Rather, other feelings altogether suffused his body. The rush of magic flowed through him as the sun fully appeared.

Behind him, Hannah and Rhiannon both voiced their surprise with a "What in the goddess's name?" from Rhiannon and a "I don't believe it" from Hannah. He knew he now looked as he had before being banished with his people. His skin and hair were returning to their former tones.

But for the moment only the rising sun captured his attention. Its warmth touched his face and he closed his eyes to absorb the feeling, to remember it always.

When he opened his eyes again, the sun was brighter. He held his palms up and looked at his skin. Pale as he remembered. His hair was long enough he could see the white-blond shade of it resting against his shoulder plates. He dropped his hands to his sides and turned to face his daughter, Hannah, and Keir. They all appeared to be too stunned to speak.

"I think it is time you showed me your headquarters."

ANTICIPATION TIGHTENED HANNAH'S BELLY as Rhiannon and Keir escorted her and Garran to a warehouse positioned along the wharf. From the outside the tin siding was rusted and neglected, and the building had a abandoned look to it.

This was apparently their new "home" thanks to the battle with Ceithlenn.

That had taken place in the middle of a baseball stadium. On national TV.

A battle that had left thousands dead and fingers pointed at the witches—the very reason the witches had been forced to flee to Otherworld.

But now they were back and ready to fight again.

Keir opened a side door and she stepped inside, along with Rhiannon and the suddenly very different-looking Garran.

No . . . he truly wasn't so different than before—his body was still sculpted perfection, his features proud and kingly, and his stride was that of a warrior. But his hair was white-blond instead of silvery-gray, and his skin was almost as fair as the Great Guardian's. His eyes were the same liquid silver that enraptured her when she looked at him.

She wanted him, and she still couldn't believe he had left her last night.

Uncontrollable thoughts of being in bed with Garran made her mind swim. They were no longer in the Drow realm, so her lust for him definitely had nothing to do with the legendary magic of the Dark Elves. She wasn't sure what to make of those feelings except that she wanted to have wild, incredible sex with him.

When they entered the warehouse, Hannah's lips parted in amazement. She paused just inside the doorway of the warehouse before they were noticed, taking in everything. Organized chaos dominated the large place, which was divided in half by newly erected walls to her left. The windows were a little cloudy, but allowed sunshine to stream through. They were high enough that those inside couldn't be seen from the outside—unless they could fly like the D'Danann.

The walls, concrete floor, and surrounding equipment looked as if they had been cleaned efficiently. A combination of smells, including new wood and sawdust, patchouli incense, and lemon oil hung in the air.

D'Danann, D'Anu, and the Paranormal Special Forces were in various groups, obviously engaged in strategy sessions.

"Garran?" Copper's voice came from the side and Hannah turned to look at her sister D'Anu witch. She was staring at Garran in openmouthed astonishment. "It's you—but the sunlight—your skin—your hair . . ."

Hannah glanced up at Garran who winked at Copper. "I have come to do your bidding. How would you have me assist you?"

Copper blinked, snapped her jaws shut, and approached, limping a little in her ankle cast. Then with a grin, she said, "How cool. You can walk in the daylight."

Behind Copper stood her husband, Tiernan. The blond warrior stepped forward and took the Drow King's arm in the hand-to-elbow grip. "We are pleased you have chosen to join us."

"As am I," Garran said with a genuine smile as he and Tiernan released each other.

Then came a round of greetings and handshakes among the D'Danann and D'Anu who had not been in Otherworld last night. They were also welcomed by Jake Macgregor, captain of the San Francisco Paranormal Special Forces.

"We've started calling ourselves the Alliance," Copper said after the introductions were made. "Short for Unified Otherworlds Alliance." She grinned. "We couldn't keep calling ourselves the D'Anu, D'Danann, and PSF team—too much of a mouthful. And now with the Drow helping out, referring to our team as the Alliance will make things a lot simpler."

"Great idea," Hannah said, and Garran nodded.

Even though his expression remained kingly, Hannah sensed that he was pleased his people were counted as members of the Alliance.

Hannah glanced around the warehouse, taking in more details. Numerous humans dressed in PSF gear were working on various things like weaponry and training.

The PSF had a lot of disadvantages since they were human and had no magical abilities that enabled them to battle powerful magical beings. But the PSF officers had developed weapons that gave them a fighting chance, and Hannah knew they were working on finding other ways to help win the war.

Hannah was drawn in with Rhiannon, Keir, and Garran.

The D'Danann were dressed in jeans and T-shirts rather than their warrior leathers so that they could more easily go out among humans. But Hannah could tell them from the PSF by subtle things, like the way they walked, the power in their presences. The long and shoulder-length hair helped, but there was something *more* about them.

The only human here who rivaled the D'Danann in physical appearance and presence was Jake Macgregor. Other good-looking officers were in the room, many as powerfully built as Jake, but there was something special about him, too. Not to mention his sexy dark looks, his blue eyes, and the fact that he was built like a linebacker.

As always, Hannah stiffened when her sister D'Anu witches came over to hug her. Damn her childhood. Damn her mother, her family and friends, for never hugging. Why did she have to feel so abnormal? Just the thought of being close to these people made her feel crushed and breathless and trapped.

But Garran . . .

She closed her eyes.

She'd figure out Garran later.

Banshee's welcoming cry echoed in the warehouse. Hannah smiled and extended her arm as she tilted her head back to see her familiar circling above her. He glided to an easy landing on her arm and she stroked the feathers at the back of his neck.

"I missed you," she said even though she'd seen him just yesterday.

"I'll show you around, and then we need to scry," Silver said, interrupting Hannah's focus on Banshee.

Hannah nodded and the falcon pushed away from her arm and took flight. She watched him as he flapped his beautiful wings and sailed up to rest on one of the rafters.

The witches left Garran and the D'Danann behind, including Silver's husband, a warrior named Hawk.

Silver's gaze was warm as she smiled at Hannah. Silver was so beautiful with her gray, almond-shaped eyes and her long silvery-blond hair that spilled softly past her shoulders. She was pregnant but her belly had only grown into a small pooch.

Silver and Copper, who were blood sisters, escorted Hannah around the huge warehouse. PSF officers used one section to design their special equipment while another area was used for planning and strategy sessions. To Hannah's surprise, a darkened room had been built with special jail cells. It smelled odd, of metal and something undefinable.

"They're created to neutralize magic." Silver gestured to the bars. "A few of the Fae who live in Golden Gate Park came to us and suggested it." Her eyes were wide with what appeared to be amazement. "They helped us build it in a matter of hours, and then they vanished."

Surprise made Hannah shake her head with wonder. She'd never heard of the Earth-bound magical creatures helping beyond answering summons during certain moon ceremonies. They often lent their magic to aid the witches in various causes, but to leave the park itself?

Silver and Copper led Hannah through the rest of the warehouse. One half was still under construction with workers building walls and making rooms with no ceilings. The warehouse was huge enough to make *lots* of rooms. Everyone was using sleeping bags instead of mattresses to sleep on the concrete floors. Roughing it, most definitely.

The sisters also showed Hannah the special room that had been built for Garran to stay in during daylight hours, but now that he was able to be in the sunlight, it wouldn't be necessary.

Hannah was immensely grateful there were a couple of bathrooms and showers already constructed in the warehouse.

When they were done with the tour, Copper and Silver drew Hannah into one of the many rooms that looked as newly built as the rooms in the rest of the warehouse, but more "finished."

"Since you're here now, it's a good opportunity to scry,"

Silver said as they closed the door behind them. "It's been a while since all of us have been together."

Hannah hitched up the pack that held her scrying tools. A little normalcy would be welcome right about now.

Smells of incense and scented candles met her senses as soon as they'd walked through the door of the kitchen. Patchouli, sandalwood, pine, and cedar incense. Rose, cinnamon, and chamomile candles. Safflower, almond, and hazelnut oils. And then there was the blessedly wonderful smells of freshly baked cinnamon rolls and bread. All familiar scents that filled her with a sense of being home, even though they were far from a real home.

The room was amazingly beautiful considering they were in a warehouse.

Two large, industrial ovens crouched directly across the room from the door, and to the right stood two big refrigerators. White cabinets took up the remainder of three sides of the room, in a U-shape.

A giant cauldron with golden steam rising from it sat on one counter. Even from across the room, Hannah could smell fresh breads, roasted meats, and cooked vegetables emanating from it.

"The Cauldron of Dagda." Silver caught Hannah's attention when she spoke. Silver rested one hand on her belly while she gestured to the cauldron with her other hand. "Thank the goddess it was finally located in Otherworld. It was getting harder and harder to find enough food to feed these bottomless pits called the D'Danann."

"Now that *is* a blessing," Hannah said with a smile.

Dried herbs hung from a rope slung across one corner of the room. On the counter sat candles, clear vials of oils, fat pottery jars no doubt containing magical creams, and a Dragon vase holding sticks of incense from its gaping jaws. Tools of their craft were arranged neatly on every countertop. Except for the left side of the ovens, where an array of cinnamon rolls, baked breads, potpies, and other delicious things stood cooling. Surely Cassia's handiwork.

Speaking of the mysterious witch—Hannah's eyes met Cassia's blue ones, and once again the wisdom in the blond half-Elvin witch's eyes amazed Hannah. For a time Cassia had served as an apprentice to the D'Anu, not revealing what a truly powerful being she was. Still, no one knew the extent of her magic, and when asked, Cassia gave noncommittal answers.

Where once Cassia had acted bumbling, unsure, and "common," she now had an ethereal, elegant look to her and she was beyond graceful. She had a calmness and strength that all the witches leaned on. Cassia cooked and healed, but Hannah was certain there was so much more to her.

Hannah tore her gaze from Cassia's. A long oval table took up one side of the room, and the other witches were already assembling around it. At the center of the table a cone of incense burned in a Dragon holder. Mulberry scented for protection, strength, and divination.

Rhiannon sat at one end of the table, her arms folded across her chest as she leaned back in her chair with her eyes closed and her chin-length auburn hair tucked behind her ears. Her gift was visioning the future.

Alyssa worried her lower lip and studied the candle in front of her. Soft brown curls bobbed around her pale cheeks.

Raven-haired and lavender-eyed Sydney adjusted her elegant glasses before settling into her seat close to a silver consecrated bowl of water and three fat candles.

Silver stood in front of her pewter cauldron, rather than taking a seat. The snake bracelet winding its way up her wrist glinted in the light.

Hannah met Mackenzie's usually mischievous blue eyes. The witch pushed her blond hair behind her shoulders before she began shuffling her deck of tarot cards so fast she appeared nervous.

Cassia was the last of the eight witches to settle in a chair and she rested her bag of rune stones on the table.

Slim, athletic Copper sat with her forearms on the black laminate table and her hands clasped as she looked at

Hannah. Soon, no doubt, Copper would be able to remove the ankle cast that she'd had since she crushed her ankle due to the battle to close and keep the door closed to Underworld. Copper's ability was dream-visions, so she had no visible tools.

Besides Copper and Rhiannon, Hannah was the only one at that moment who didn't have scrying materials out. She raised her pack and withdrew her black Dragon mirror and the vial of salt crystals and arranged them on the table.

"What about Darkwolf?" Hannah asked after she set her pack on the concrete floor beside her chair. "Is he still on the run from Ceithlenn?"

"According to our scrying, and"—Silver glanced at Sydney—"Conlan and Sydney saw him firsthand battling and then escaping from Balor." Silver returned her gaze to Hannah's. "We think he's not on their side anymore. But we don't know *what* he's up to, if he plans to do anything with the eye, or if he's even a threat."

"So basically Darkwolf's a loose cannon," Copper said.

Hannah looked at each of her sister witches. "Who's going to start scrying?"

"I might as well." Copper clenched her hands on the table in front of her as she leaned forward. "I've been having dream-visions that haven't made a whole lot of sense. Last night's was the clearest so far, although I don't know what it means." She frowned and looked at Hannah. "I saw a strange black sphere, something dark and shadowy, but I could tell you and someone else were inside the bubble."

Hannah resisted rubbing her arms as a chill slid over her skin. Copper shrugged, but Hannah could tell it wasn't done casually. "I know it's not much." Copper tugged her long copper-colored braid over her shoulder. "But that's all that has come to me."

Rhiannon opened her eyes and tipped her head forward as she looked at Hannah. No hostility was in Rhiannon's expression, only thoughtfulness and puzzlement. "I see you with King Garran—my father. You're on rocks, near water—

an island, I think—and you're in danger." Rhiannon looked concerned as she studied Hannah. "Very serious danger. I just can't see what."

Hannah did her best to remain calm and to not acknowledge the sharp edge of fear knifing through her. Before, their visions tended to be more general, encompassing them all. This was the first time Hannah had been the focus of Rhiannon's and Copper's visions.

Everyone looked at Hannah for a moment before Alyssa picked up a match lying in front of her and struck it on a porous stone. The sharp tang of sulfur mixed with the blueberry scent of the blue candle Alyssa lit. "I chose blue for hope, spirituality, and protection . . ."

Her words trailed off as she stared into the candle flame. Alyssa had always been the most sensitive, almost fragile, of all the gray magic D'Anu. Hannah had never said anything to any of her sister witches, but she'd always worried more about Alyssa than anyone else. The worry came from flashes Hannah had seen in her scrying mirror, feelings she'd had when she was close to Alyssa.

Alyssa straightened in her seat and took a deep breath before blowing out the candle. She closed her eyes for a moment, a pained expression on her face.

Not a good sign.

The silence in the kitchen was so great that Hannah could hear the rumble of conversation, banging sounds, and other activity outside the room that she hadn't been paying attention to before.

Finally, Alyssa opened her eyes and met Hannah's gaze. Alyssa's soft brown eyes looked a little glassy and Hannah's belly sank. From years of practice at keeping her expression unreadable, Hannah kept the growing fear off her own face.

Alyssa took another audible breath. "Something's going to happen, Hannah, and you're going to be in the middle of it. Unless we can change the future, something's going to happen between you, Garran, and Ceithlenn."

Hannah merely nodded before she turned her steady gaze

to Sydney. The lavender-eyed witch calmly looked away from Hannah and struck a match before lighting one of the candles between her and the bowl of consecrated water. The citrus scent of the orange candle energized Hannah, sending a burst of strength through her. Orange candles were for success, strength, and fire.

Candlelight reflected on Sydney's glasses as she looked at Hannah and said, "I think I chose the appropriate candles for this divination."

Hannah simply gave a single nod before Sydney lit a gold candle, which signified not only wealth and abundance, but connection with the divine, the goddess Anu. The third candle Sydney lit was black, a color she always used. It had strong magic for banishment and protection from unseen forces.

Sydney raised the orange candle and tipped it so that its wax dribbled into the bowl of water. After frowning at the patterns for a moment, she raised the gold candle and poured the wax from it into the bowl. She only waited a few seconds before adding wax from the black candle. She set that candle down, studied the wax in the water a little longer, then blew out all three candles that sat in front of her. Remnants of smoke drifted away.

Sydney's throat worked as she folded her arms on the table and looked at Hannah. She tried a gentle smile. "Looks like you're the star today." Her smile faltered. "This war is going to hurt you in many ways. Perhaps physically, mentally— stressful situations that will challenge you and put you in much danger." She glanced at the bowl again before returning her gaze to Hannah's. "I see all of us in trouble, but you're at the center. You and someone very, very close to you."

Hannah raised her eyebrows. She'd never been truly close to anyone—she kept people at a distance. As much as she loved her Coven sisters, she didn't even let them get too near emotionally.

"Well, this is all very interesting." Hannah kept her tone dry. "What do you have to say, Mackenzie?"

Hannah's sister witch didn't answer. She simply dealt her tarot cards in her favorite spread, a Celtic cross. She quietly flipped each card over and looked down at it before turning over the next and the next until she'd revealed all ten cards.

She pursed her lips. "I see a lot of conflict within you, Hannah. In the way you look at what's around you now, and how you will view things in the future." Mackenzie studied the cards again.

Hannah's throat felt so dry it hurt. What could *that* possibly mean?

Mackenzie's blue eyes met Hannah's. "You will go on a quest. I can't tell whether this is something you do willingly, or something you're forced to do. I can't see if you're successful."

Hannah couldn't think of anything to say, so she turned to Cassia who was already tumbling her rune stones onto the black tabletop.

It only took a moment before Cassia looked up, but she moved her gaze to each witch in the group instead of just focusing on Hannah like everyone else had. "The Alliance is facing an enormous battle ahead, and we *will* need the aid of the Drow, just as we had thought."

Cassia cocked her head as she studied the stones. "Something strange and unusual is on the horizon, but all we can do is wait and see what that is and be prepared to deal with it the best we can."

"How do we prepare to deal with something when we don't even know what that something is?" Hannah asked, tucking her single shock of blond hair behind her ear.

Cassia's turquoise eyes remained steady, calm, like . . . Like what? "We have to face this as it comes. I can't see any other way."

Hannah resisted a frustrated huff and snatched up her vial of salt crystals. While taking a deep breath, she uncorked the vial and set the cork aside. She squeezed her eyes shut and said a soft chant in her mind to the Dragon Elementals, asking their assistance.

Her heart seized at the memory of the last time she scried, in Otherworld. And the Fire Dragon . . .

The vision had to have been wrong. She swallowed and called to the Dragons.

Warmth and certainty spread through her when she knew the Dragons were with her in spirit.

But were all four there? By the goddess Anu, she couldn't tell.

What was important now was what her scrying would tell her at this moment.

Hannah opened her eyes before tilting the vial and letting the salt crystals tumble onto the mirror.

As always, time slowed, sounds and the world around her vanished until she was shrouded in darkness. All that remained was her and the patterns the salt made in the air as they fell and then the patterns created when they tinkled against the black glass.

In the mirror she stood on something—a platform?—that rose high enough she could see the glittering city stretching out below her.

Hannah's heart rate kicked up so fast her chest hurt. She couldn't move, couldn't use her magic, couldn't even speak—or scream. Which she wanted to do when her gaze landed on a dark shape in front of her.

Ceithlenn, the goddess from Underworld. The evil soul—stealing, murdering bitch. Anger rose up in Hannah swift and strong, so strong her body vibrated with it. But she couldn't move. She was frozen in place.

The dark goddess smiled, her red eyes boring into Hannah's. Ceithlenn took a step toward her.

Hannah's whole body burned as if she were on fire and she writhed from pain searing her entire being. It wouldn't stop. She couldn't escape.

Everything went black.

Hannah gasped as she was jerked out of the vision. It felt like she had pulled her face out of a vat of water. She mentally found herself back in the kitchen, surrounded by her sister witches.

She'd never felt so out of control, never felt like falling completely apart after having a vision.

It was as if the black glass of her scrying mirror had shattered, and she along with it.

CHAPTER TWELVE

WHILE THE WITCHES DISAPPEARED into the kitchen for one of their scrying sessions, Jake got his first good look at the king of the Dark Elves.

Garran stood in the center of the planning area of the warehouse with his arms folded across his massive chest and over his jewel-studded leather chest straps. Some of the D'Danann warriors, as well as Jake and a few PSF officers had gathered around the Drow king.

The man had the bearing of someone who knew what he wanted and without question expected to get it. Likely an obnoxious sonofabitch.

With his cop's instincts, Jake automatically catalogued Garran's appearance. At the same time he tried to keep his face expressionless as he analyzed the king.

Garran was as tall as Jake and most of the D'Danann, putting him at about six-six. The king had fair unblemished skin with no lines at the corners of his silvery eyes. His pointed ears were exposed through his long blond hair, his hair hanging to the metal plates that rested on his broad shoulders.

Along with the leather straps crisscrossing his chest, Garran wore black leather pants and boots that were similar to what the D'Danann usually wore. A sword with a jewel-encrusted hilt was strapped to one side of his hips and a long dagger sheathed to his other side.

Garran had the solid build of an athlete, not as overbuilt

as a guy who spent his time at the gym bench-pressing. The king definitely looked like someone who'd be a challenge to take down in a fair fight.

From what Jake had been told about the Drow, they were anything but fair. They used dark magic and a guy could never be certain about which side the Dark Elves were fighting on—good or evil.

And something in Garran's shrewd, intelligent, and assessing gaze told Jake that the king was hiding something. Keeping some kind of truth from all of them.

After Tiernan and Keir greeted Garran with a strange hand-to-elbow grip, the rest of the D'Danann returned to their duties and Jake indicated to his officers to do the same.

When just Hawk, Garran, and Jake remained, they headed to the huge backlit computerized map table currently showing the San Francisco Bay shoreline and Alcatraz Island. Immediately Hawk pored over the map, but Garran and Jake continued to size each other up.

"You speak for humans?" Garran said as he rested his hand on his sword hilt. He had an unusual accent. Different from the Irish brogue of the D'Danann.

Automatically, Jake had the urge to put his hand at his gun holster, but forced himself to relax. "You could say I represent at least a portion of the human population, yeah. I'm basically a police commander."

"Commander." Garran studied Jake with his strange silver eyes. "Your followers do as you will them to, then. You are a great leader amongst your people."

"I'm the Paranormal Special Forces captain." Wondering where this conversation was headed, Jake leaned his hip against the map table. "I'm in charge of one branch of law enforcement."

The king's gaze never wavered. "Yet you are the sole representative of humans in this battle?"

Jake kept his gaze focused and unwavering on Garran even as he frowned to himself. "I guess you could say that."

Garran gave a slow nod and extended his hand. Jake

pushed away from the table and reached to shake the king's hand, but he grasped Jake's arm in that same odd way the D'Danann and Garran had greeted each other.

Garran had a firm grip and he gave a low nod before raising his head and looking at Jake again. "It is my pleasure to meet the leader of the humans."

Jake opened his mouth to correct the king, then shut it. Let the guy think whatever the hell he wanted to. Maybe it was better this way.

He turned to look at the map table at the same time Garran did.

For the first time it occurred to Jake that as far as all the Otherworlders were concerned, he was the "representative" from the non-magical human race. When he thought about it, all along they'd been treating him with the deference they might treat the king of another race of beings.

Weight settled on Jake's shoulders and he frowned. He wasn't sure exactly how he felt about that realization.

CHAPTER THIRTEEN

GARRAN PUZZLED OVER THE best move to utilize the Great Guardian's gift as he looked from Jake Macgregor of the human law enforcement to Hawk of the D'Danann.

"It would be most advantageous," Hawk said with a scowl, "to attack the Fomorii and Ceithlenn while they hide below this island."

"Yeah, getting rid of them in one fell swoop would solve our problems—if it's possible." Jake glanced again at the what the human had called a "computerized" map they had been studying. He cut his gaze from Hawk to Garran. "Unless the Drow are good long-distance swimmers, and the D'Danann can fight in the water once they fly to the island, a battle with the demons over there is nearly impossible."

Jake clenched his fist on the map table as he continued, "Alcatraz was chosen to house a prison because it is virtually impossible to penetrate. No escape. No entrance." He gestured to the area where the island was situated. "We have no way of getting a large enough number of us there to attack them in that underground cavern Ceithlenn created."

Hawk nodded. "If what the witches scried in the past is true, then the host of demons is most definitely at this location."

"We've seen the witches in action over the past months." Jake rose and folded his arms across his chest. "I'm betting on them."

"Aye." Hawk glanced over his shoulder in the direction of the room the witches were scrying in this very moment, then looked back at Jake and Garran.

Thoughts churned through Garran's mind. If he could reach that island and use the power the Great Guardian had given him, he could end the war. As simple as that.

Jake's frustrated huff brought Garran's attention back to him. The human continued, "The only way I can think of is to get the U.S. Air Force to bomb the whole damned island. A couple of missiles and the island and everything below it would be decimated."

Garran opened his mouth to tell them of the Great Guardian's words of warning, that not all the Fomorii could be killed without destroying the balance in Otherworld.

He clamped his mouth shut. Absolutely no way existed to rid themselves of the Fomorii without Garran sending them back with the power the Guardian had given him. If he spoke of her warning, it would perhaps leave those fighting Ceithlenn with a feeling of hopelessness—how could they send the Fomorii back to Underworld themselves?

Damn the Underworlds at the Guardian's insistence he tell no one about his power. Now he was forced to accomplish his task before a way was found to completely destroy the demons.

"Of course to blow up one of the most famous national monuments in the freaking world," Jake said, "I'd have to go through a hundred channels to convince everyone up to the President that there really are *demons* beneath Alcatraz." Jake continued with a look of pure frustration on his face. "I can't even get them to believe that what they saw on television during the baseball game was real.

"Not that I can blame them for refusing to believe that some flame-haired goddess-bitch sucked the souls of every living being in those stands while the Alliance fought off the Fomorii on the field." Jake clenched his fists on the map table. "No matter how many times they analyze the televised events, they just don't *get* it. The official consensus is that every station televising the game had some kind of high-tech interference that was fed a hoax, a cover-up, for what really happened. Damn near everyone believes it was bioterrorism."

"Fools." Hawk braced his hands on the table. "If your military will not do as we need them to, then we must find a way to draw the demons out." He looked at Garran. "At night when the Drow can battle with us."

Garran gave a slow nod. "We will fight by your side until we draw our final breaths."

"Let's hope it doesn't come to that." Jake glanced around the warehouse at those toiling in one manner or another, and Garran followed his gaze.

"Tonight we've all got to get some sleep." Jake scrubbed his hand over his stubbled jaw. The man's eyes were red and he looked exhausted. "Tomorrow we'll figure out some way to draw the demons out."

"Aye." Hawk blew out an audible breath. "All members of the Alliance have had little rest since Ceithlenn's last attack."

Garran only nodded once again. Now that he knew where the Fomorii were hiding, he could deal with them himself.

IT WAS LATE WHEN Garran set out on his mission. Without a sound, he slipped through the warehouse.

When he was halfway from the room he'd been given and the warehouse door, Garran caught Hannah's sweet womanly scent behind him before she spoke. "Where are you going?"

He stopped without looking at her. He had hoped to avoid this situation.

"I said, where are you going?" Her voice grew sharper and held a hint of irritation.

He looked over his shoulder. Gods, she was beautiful with her brown eyes, the lock of blond hair outlining one side of her face against her dark brown hair. He wanted her over and over again, and hoped he would survive his mission to come back and take her to bed to do just that.

"I wish to explore the area." He looked toward the door again. "I will need to be familiar with it before I bring the Drow to fight."

He felt Hannah's presence grow nearer. "I'll go with you," she said, close enough that he imagined her warm breath on his neck. "The D'Danann warriors guarding the door inside and out wouldn't let you past them without me."

Garran faced her. "I will shroud myself with Drow magic. It will not be necessary for you to join me."

She frowned. "I'm still coming with you."

"No." He put force behind the word as he met her eyes. "I go alone."

"Why?" She braced her hands on her hips and arched a brow.

Garran rubbed his eyes with his thumb and forefinger. The words of the Great Guardian came to him, about keeping Hannah at his side. But he had no intention of taking her with him this night no matter what the Guardian said.

"I wish to be alone." He dropped his hand away from his eyes and firmed his expression as he said the words in a tone meant to eliminate further conversation.

"I *am* coming with you." With her chin tilted up, both fire and ice in her gaze, she sounded and looked like a ruler, imperious and regal, a queen.

She would make a fine queen, indeed.

He shook the thoughts from his head at the same time he made the motion to tell her no. But by the look in her eyes and on her expression, he knew it was a battle lost.

He sighed. "Come, then, quietly. I will shroud us both in my magic."

The cloud he enveloped them with was hazy as they walked to the door guarded by a pair of D'Danann warriors. From the corner of his eye, he saw Hannah's surprised expression when he faced each warrior and moved his hand in a circular motion, his palm facing each man. As intended, they were oblivious to his and Hannah's presence and didn't even move when Garran opened the door.

At the same time Garran turned the cool knob, he let a swell of his dark magic touch each of the warriors standing guard on the outside of the door.

Hannah looked at him in amazement as they exited the warehouse and the warriors did not so much as look at them. The door made no sound as it closed.

A nearby light from a lamppost cast shadows on Hannah's face as he looked down at her as they walked away from the warehouse.

"Pretty neat trick," she said, although she didn't look pleased. "The Dark Elves could attack us so easily just by doing what you just did."

Garran shook his head. "Only the king holds such power. It is passed on from king to king as a protective measure, given from the Orb of Aithne."

She cocked her head as they made their way silently to the pier. "The Orb of what?"

"Aithne." He gestured in the direction they had come from this morning. "We must go."

Her frown was darker now, and she came to a stop directly beneath the lamppost. They were still shrouded by his magic.

"We're not just out for a stroll, are we," she stated.

"I will explain." He touched her elbow and guided her in the direction of the pier. "Come."

Hannah seemed to accept that. For now.

She looked him over as they walked. "You looked good before in your Drow garb, but you're pretty hot in human clothing, too."

Garran cocked one eyebrow as he glanced down at her. Before most had settled in for the night, the witches had hunted for human clothing for Garran so that he "wouldn't stick out" in the human world. He wore what they called a T-shirt and jeans, but his feet were still clad in his supple leather boots. It felt odd not wearing his shoulder plates or leather chest straps, and the T-shirt felt confining hiding so much of his skin. Yet, at the same time the clothing was comfortable. He had left his sword behind but had a lengthy dagger strapped to his side.

"You cannot get enough of me." He let his tone drop low and seductive, with a hint of amusement. "I believe that is why you desire to join me this night."

"You wish, blue boy." Hannah appeared unaffected when he glanced at her. "I'm just keeping an eye on you."

He smiled as he looked down at the beautiful woman beside him. Despite the fact he'd had no intentions of bringing her with him, it felt pleasant to have her at his side. "Then you do not trust me."

"Not for a moment."

At that he laughed, the sound echoing through the night, joining the subdued sounds of the city behind them, a city that was still under martial law.

Fog absorbed most of the moon's light and he reached for her hand to make sure she didn't trip in the near darkness.

At first she stiffened but gradually relaxed as they walked. He gripped her cool hand tighter in his then sent magic from his hand to suffuse her body with warmth.

She glanced up at him. "So where are we *really* going?"

Garran did not answer and she did not press him as they walked hand in hand from the warehouse toward the pier. Smells of the city's pollution mixed with the scent of brine on the air. Otherworld was so clean in contrast that the smells of this human city nearly clogged his senses.

Hannah's sigh joined the gentle slap of waves against the pier as they neared it. He led her onto the pier and her shoes made soft sounds on the wood. As he was Elvin, his movements were always silent, much like the Fae.

When they reached the end of the pier facing Alcatraz Island, he turned to her. He took both of her hands in his, raised them, and pressed his lips to her knuckles.

Hannah closed her eyes and made a soft little groan. "If you're trying to seduce me, it's working."

Garran raised his head and laughed, and she opened her eyes. He released her hands and drew her into his embrace. Again she stiffened but gradually relaxed as he held her tightly, making it clear he was not going to release her for that moment in time. He rubbed his hands over her back and she wrapped her arms around his waist, settling her face against his chest.

He buried his nose in her hair, the clean, womanly scent chasing away some of the smells of brine and fish.

The thought of fish gave him pause—the Fomorii smelled of rotten fish, but a strong stench. If he left Hannah, what if she was attacked by one or more of the demons that might be in the city?

At the realization his chest ached and he felt as if a knot had formed in his throat. He could not leave her . . . but he should not take her . . .

Or could he, and still keep her safe? Was that what the Great Guardian had intended when she told him to keep Hannah close?

Garran cleared his throat, stepped away from Hannah, and clasped her upper arms with his hands. She felt small and fragile in his larger grip, not the strong woman he knew her to be.

"I have a mission to complete," he said, his voice low in the night. "I would rather return you to the headquarters, where I know you will be safe, than to take you with me."

Hannah shook her head, a stubborn glint in her eyes. "I don't know what in the Ancestors' names you're talking about, but you're not leaving me behind."

Garran closed his eyes for a moment, searching inside himself for the magic the Great Guardian had given him. It survived deep in his chest, a ball of liquid power that gave him inexplicable energy and strength he had never felt before.

To get to the island, though, he would have to use his own dark magic. The Drow never used black magic, but their powers edged close to that ever-deep precipice.

He opened his eyes to see Hannah's brows narrowed and a firm but questioning look on her features.

"What's going on?" She shook out of his embrace and his hands fell to his sides. He missed her warmth at once, missed touching her softness and having her head resting against his chest.

He pushed his hand through his hair. His skin tones had returned to the bluish-gray of the Drow and his hair was silvery-blue again. Apparently his skin and hair only changed to its former tones during daylight hours.

A foghorn sounded in the night as a great ship passed in front of them, temporarily obscuring the island from his gaze. Great swells of water rolled from the ship toward the shore, the waves slapping sand and pebbles beneath the pier.

"I cannot explain why, but I must go to the Fomorii lair now." He brushed his knuckles across her cheek. "I do not want to put you in danger."

"You're insane." She brought her hand up to the moon and crescent armband she always wore. It was the only nervous movement he had noticed she made on occasion. "I can't let you do that."

"You cannot stop me." He almost smiled when her fingertips crackled with her sparkling green magic. He had seen two of the witches use their powers when the door to Underworld was opened then closed, and he knew the witches could be quite formidable.

"Do you want to bet I can't stop—" she started when he released his magic.

Hannah gasped as he surrounded them in a dark sphere, a *geodess,* weaving a spell into the fabric of power. He laced within it a command to take them to Alcatraz, and then a spell to return them to the shores of San Francisco. The Great Guardian had said he would be weak after he used the magical gift, and he wanted to make sure he had a way to bring Hannah and himself back safely. If he could leave her in a bubble of protection on the pier while he was gone, he would, but his power would not extend so far, and still retain enough magic for the return trip.

With a mental command the *geodess* rose and Hannah dropped onto her backside with the movement. She let out a sound of surprise. He used his powers to guide the sphere onto the water where it bobbed in the wake created by the ship that had passed by.

Concern and perhaps fear crossed her features as she got to her haunches on the curved floor of the sphere that was firm beneath his feet. He knelt beside her. She looked away from him and pressed her palm against the side of the *geodess*. His magic rippled beneath her hand and she shivered before cutting her gaze back to him.

"We are in what my people refer to as a *geodess*," he said as he met her eyes. "It will take us safely to our destination and return us to our origin when the mission is complete."

The dark sphere began to float toward the island as he pushed it with his magic. He took Hannah's hand in his and this time her muscles didn't tighten. Instead she sat by him in silence for a few moments before squeezing his hand in return.

"Mission . . ." she said in a concerned tone. "What could the two of us possibly do"—she gestured toward the island—"against all of those demons?"

"Trust me." It was all he could say as he studied her features in the darkness.

"Guess I don't have a choice." She shivered and he drew her into his embrace, surrounding both of them with heat.

The *geodess* continued to skim the water as it made its way to the island.

When he sensed the island was near, he murmured, "We have arrived," and her body tensed.

"You're really going to go through with this—whatever it is you're planning to do." She scooted away from him and he let her, even though he didn't want to.

Garran looked through the dark sphere as they approached a sheer rock side of the island.

He looked from the island back to her. "This is something I must do. Something that will benefit all."

Hannah grasped her belly with her arm for a moment as if it hurt. Then she dropped her hands to her sides, straightened her spine, and pushed back her shoulders, like a warrior ready to do battle. "You're the boss. Let's do it."

Garran focused on the rocks, using his senses with the might of his dark magic to reach out and find the opening to the cavern that would lead to the Fomorii lair. When his slow exploration did not reveal anything, he strengthened his search. At his mental command a dark layer of power burst from him, through the sphere, and wrapped itself around the island.

Immediately he located the opening to the cavern—and the Fomorii guards posted around it.

He would have to eliminate the demon guards without alerting the rest of the Fomorii. He had expected that, but had also hoped the demons would be too cocksure of themselves to believe they needed a guard.

Hannah sat on her haunches at his side, her palms braced on her thighs. "I don't see anything. It's so blessed dark."

With his Drow vision, Garran could see every rock, every pebble as they drew closer—as well as the Fomorii guards. Not to mention their rotten-fish stench was so powerful one could not miss them. He guided the sphere close to the rock face so that he would not be seen once he left its safety. He intended to leave Hannah in the *geodess*.

He studied the opening to the cavern. It was low to the water, a lip jutting from it that would allow him to climb in and out. The overhang hid the opening effectively. He would have to lower himself from the overhang to the shelf.

Black power surrounded the opening. No doubt Ceithlenn had created the cavern with her magic.

"Four of the demons are guarding the entrance." He rubbed his jaw. "I need to do away with them before I enter the cavern." He looked down at her. "I will leave you here, where you will be safe."

"Like hell." Green magic sparked at her fingertips. "Where you go, I go."

If he had the extra power he would need to do it, he would bind her inside the *geodess* until he finished his task. As it was, he was using most of his dark magic to maintain the sphere itself. No matter the outcome—if he died—the *geodess* was spelled to return to the pier they had left from. Hannah would be able to move in and out of it at will.

He took her by the shoulders and looked into her dark eyes. "If anything should happen to me, return to this *geodess* and it will take you to your city." He gave her a slight shake. "You *will* do as I command."

Fire snapped in her gaze and she narrowed her brows. She shrugged out of his hold and pushed him away by placing her hands on his chest and shoving. "I'll do whatever *I* think is best. Not what you tell me to do."

He stared at her a long moment before glancing to the steep rock near the entrance, then back to her. What would he do with this stubborn woman?

The only thing he could. Keep her at his side. For now. "Remember that all you need to do is climb onto the *geodess* and it will embrace you and take you home."

Hannah didn't answer. Instead she raised her hand and a soft green glow emanated from her palm, giving her enough light to analyze the rock face.

"Your sister witches used magic ropes in the battle at the door to Underworld." Garran remembered how the witches had utilized the ropes as well as a net and shields. "Is this one of your talents as well?"

"Not a problem." She stood, the sphere steady beneath her feet. "I have plenty of talents."

"Good. You will need your ropes to climb down the rock face and return to the *geodess*." The memory of the brightness of the witch magic he'd seen came to him. "Is it possible for you to dim your magic so that it cannot easily be seen?"

Hannah nodded, still not looking at him. "How do I get out of here?"

"Hold on to me." Garran shot out a dark stream of magic at the same time he grasped Hannah by her waist. The stream wrapped itself around a large boulder far overhead and he gave the mental order for his magic to pull them up the sheer side of the island.

She gripped him tight with one arm while she held her other palm out, magic sparking at her fingertips, obviously ready to use her powers.

They pushed through the wall of the *geodess,* which felt like passing grasping hands trying to hold them in. He ordered the magic to still and remain in place as he left a piece of his powers behind.

Rough winds batted them against the side of the rocky wall as they rose and small stones trickled down to the water, the tiny sounds loud in the still night. He didn't pause and they continued to rise. The icy winds whipped their hair about their faces and he again used his magic to chase away the chill.

Just as they came close to reaching the surface they would climb onto, the demon stench grew stronger.

A Fomorii appeared.

It looked directly at them.

The demon opened its mouth as if to give warning to its fellow Fomorii.

Hannah shot a sparkling green magic rope out so fast Garran barely saw it skim through the air.

The rope spun around the demon's head and mouth, choking off any cry it would have made.

The rope continued to wrap itself around the Fomorii's entire body, and the demon dropped. It would have made a thud, but another burst of power emanated from Hannah that cushioned the demon's fall so that there was only silence.

"You are truly a talented witch," Garran said in a low voice as he pulled them close enough that they could crawl onto the rocky ground.

She grunted as he helped push her up far enough that she was able to roll onto the ground. "I told you not to underestimate me," she whispered.

"Indeed." His muscles strained as he grasped the rock to pull himself all the way up. The words of the Great Guardian came to him again—that he and Hannah would be stronger together. It seemed the Guardian had been correct.

Still, he did not like putting Hannah in such danger.

When they were both on their feet, they looked down at the demon bound by her magic. "Goddess, that thing stinks." She gestured toward it with an expression of distaste. "Be my guest."

Garran unsheathed the long dagger at his side. The demon's eyes bulged, but it was so tightly bound that it could not move a fraction.

As he did not have his sword to slice the demon's head from its body, Garran chose the only other way to kill a Fomorii. The dagger slipped between the magic ropes and it took only a swift movement to remove the Fomorii's black heart.

Garran flipped the heart aside with his dagger. The heart made a squishing sound as it hit the rocks before it turned to silt. The demon's body also collapsed into the fine, dark substance that blew away on the harsh winds. Hannah drew her magic back inside her. Garran kept his dagger unsheathed.

"I can subdue two at once now that both of my hands are free," she said, and he acknowledged her with a nod.

Hannah followed as he moved through the near darkness toward the three remaining Fomorii guards. Lights from around the former prison gave enough light so that Hannah could no doubt see well enough. He hoped she would be able to keep from making any noise and not stir any rocks as they crept forward.

The Fomorii rotten-fish malodor grew so great it was near to overpowering. It came not only from the demons guarding the entrance, but from the cavern hidden below the island.

He glanced at Hannah, whose nose wrinkled as if she was trying to avoid sucking in too much of the foul air. She had both hands raised, prepared to release her magic ropes.

When the three demons came into view, Garran's eyes met Hannah's and he gave a clipped nod.

They looked forward, and as one released their magic.

Two of the demons dropped silently to the ground as one of Hannah's ropes completely subdued one Fomorii, and Garran's power wrapped itself around the other.

But Hannah's rope missed the third demon's mouth.

Its roar shattered the night air and Garran's scalp prickled as he cursed.

"Bless it," Hannah said in a hoarse whisper as she dropped the third demon and gagged it with her magic. Garran quickly cut out the hearts of the three demon guards.

But it was too late.

Other Fomorii had heard the lone guard's fierce growl.

Answering roars came from the cavern below.

CHAPTER FOURTEEN

GARRAN'S MUSCLES TENSED AND his gut churned. Godsdamn. Now he must face the beasts head-on, rather than making the stealthy entrance he had intended.

"Stay," he commanded Hannah, and flung up a black barrier of magic that she would not be able to pass through.

"Bastard!" Her voice was muted as she thumped her fists on the shadow shield, an expression of fury on her features.

It was close enough that he would be able to maintain the shield with his magic and still have enough to do what he had to.

Without pause, he rushed toward the roars, hooked a stream of dark magic around a pair of boulders. He held on to it with one hand, his dagger in his other, and flung himself down from the barrier into the cavern.

As he swung into the entrance, he slammed his booted feet into the first demon, sending the beast flying. A second Fomorii roared and reached for Garran, but he dug the demon's heart out with a quick twist of his blade. Another came at Garran from behind, and he whirled, slicing the demon across the throat, but his dagger was not long enough to behead it. The demon healed almost at once and lunged for Garran.

At the same time he battled, he analyzed the cavern. To his right were rocks he could climb, a series of rocks that led to a shelf.

Garran cut the heart from another Fomorii, turning the beast into silt. He stepped back toward the rocks, still facing the oncoming demons. The damned beasts had tipped their claws in iron, as he'd been told, and iron was deadly to Fae and Elves. One slice of their claws could render him helpless—or kill him.

Determination roared through his veins as he threw up a shadow shield between himself and the oncoming demons. The two shields he had created, and the large amount of magic he'd left behind to maintain the sphere, had stretched his powers thin.

He scrambled up the rocks, dagger in one hand as his other grabbed for purchase. His breathing was heavy and his heart raced. It was all he could do to hold the wall up between Hannah and the entrance to the cavern, and the one between himself and the Fomorii.

Below, demons growled and screeched so loudly the cavern echoed with it. The Fomorii were hideous—some orange, others green, purple, red, or blue. They had multiple limbs and eyes, and their claws all glinted from the iron they had been tipped in.

Some of the demons tried to climb the rock wall to reach Garran, but he pushed forward, his target the shelf above the floor of the cavern. The closer he got to it, the deeper the sense of evil he felt. No doubt Ceithlenn. He hoped to the gods she was here so that he could send her back with the Fomorii—if she didn't kill him first.

Rocks bit into his palms as he pulled himself upward and then forward, driving himself toward his destination. Shrieks from the demons nearly deafened him and his nose clogged and eyes watered from the rotten-fish stench. Just as he tumbled onto the ledge, his power holding the shields in place snapped.

Garran fell, his face hitting the stone shelf. *So much for Elvin grace,* was the fleeting thought that slipped through his mind.

While the Fomorii rushed him from the left and other

demons attempted to climb from below, Garran pushed himself to his feet. He stretched his body to his full height. The dagger clattered to the rock shelf when he dropped it.

At the same time he was all too aware of everything going on around him, and of the demons nearing him.

He closed his eyes and blocked everything out. He dug deep inside his soul for the magic the Guardian had given him.

It was there, swirling, waiting to break free.

Garran thrust his chest out, expanded his arms, saw every Fomorii in the cavern with his mind's eye.

Power burst from him. So intense, so hot, he thought he might burn away.

He opened his eyes as his body shook with magic to see the cavern bathed in silver light. It glittered, bounced off every surface in the cavern, almost blindingly so.

With all his might he focused on sending the Fomorii back to Underworld.

Pain shot through his head. His body.

He put more force into the power of his gift.

The demons vanished.

The cavern was empty.

Complete silence.

Exhaustion and pain slammed into Garran and he crumpled to the rock shelf.

THE SHIELD HOLDING HANNAH dissolved as she banged on it. Off balance, she stumbled forward and dropped on one knee on the hard rock. Pain shot through her knee.

She scrambled to her feet and headed toward the roars.

Oh, goddess. What am I doing? What is Garran doing?

Was it a good sign that the beasts still roared in the cavern below? That Garran still survived?

The strength of her fear for Garran burned in her chest. Anger, too, that he had done this—but she would deal with that later. Providing he survived whatever crazy plan he'd had in his mind when he brought them here. She'd kill him herself if they made it out of here alive.

Hannah ran toward the boulder where Garran had used his magic to climb down. She tripped over a rock but kept herself from falling by bracing her hands on the boulder.

A plan formed in her mind.

Her heart pounded so loud her ears throbbed, but the roars and shrieks of the demons still cut through. The Fomorii stench was overwhelming and she wanted to clap her hand over her nose.

Instead, she whipped a thick rope of magic from her palm and wrapped it around the boulders. When she slid down the rope she would be prepared to throw up a spellshield to protect herself and Garran. If she had to, she'd use spellfire to knock the demons out of her way so that she could reach Garran.

How they would get out alive, she wasn't sure, but she could protect them, and fight if necessary.

Heart still pounding like crazy, she readied herself on the overhang. She gripped the magic rope in both fists.

Sudden silence filled her ears as she swung down.

Shock coursed through her as she landed on the lip of the cavern entrance. She clung to the rope, unable to pry her fingers from it as she stared into the enormous space.

No demons. Nothing.

At her feet were a few piles of silt from demons that had been killed, but in the cavern—*nothing*.

No more roars or screeches, or the horrid odor of the Fomorii—only a little bit of it lingered. All she heard were waves rolling up to the far end of the lip that extended out toward the water.

Garran. Where's Garran?

Her throat grew dry and knots twisted her stomach as she searched the cavern with her gaze. The Fomorii had vanished. Had Garran, too?

Hannah's own breath nearly strangled her when she saw

Garran's body on a rock shelf. He'd collapsed on his side and wasn't moving.

She looked at the rocks between her and Garran. There was a good climb between the two of them, but she pushed herself forward and scrambled up the rocks. Their sharpness bit into her palms, and shards of pain splintered through her every time one of her knees hit the jagged stone.

Her breathing grew harsher as she made her way toward Garran. His bluish-gray complexion looked pale and his eyes were closed. He was lying on his side, his features slack.

She climbed over the last rock and hurried to Garran's side. She dropped to her haunches next to him. Her hands trembled as she raised them over his body and sent her healing magic from her palms to Garran's body.

At once she felt his lifeforce. It was strong, his heart beating a steady rhythm. Relief flowed through her like a warm wave.

Through her magic she felt that his powers had been drained. Something more was there, too, but she couldn't tell what it was. She sent strong healing energy from her body, through her hands, and into his prone form. Her green magic sparkled between them and he stirred.

Even as more relief poured through her like wine warming her belly, she continued to heal him as best she could. Cassia would know what to do once Hannah managed to get Garran to her.

She glanced at the rocky path she'd taken to get to him and wondered how in Anu's name she was going to get Garran to the sphere.

His hand suddenly clasped around her wrist, startling her and bringing her attention to him. His eyes were open and for a moment she stared into their liquid silver depths.

Hannah's first instinct was to kiss him, her second to slap him for putting himself in so much danger.

But where had the danger gone?

The healing magic she'd been using faded back into her

body. She glared at him and braced her hands on her hips as she rested on her haunches. "Idiot."

He smiled, the same sexy, cocky smile that told her he was going to be okay.

"You could have been killed by all those . . ." She slowly swept her gaze over the cavern. "Demons," she finished, not really knowing what else to say.

Had the cavern already been empty? Were just a few here that Garran had fought with hand to hand?

But why was he lying on this rock shelf, passed out?

What had happened?

Garran pushed himself to a sitting position and braced himself on the rock shelf with one hand. "They are gone."

"How many? And how?" She wrinkled her brow and looked around the cavern again, feeling as if a Fomorii might just pop up out of nowhere. "I don't understand."

Garran said nothing as he got to his knees and then to his feet. He wavered, as if he were tipsy, and she hurried to her feet, afraid he might fall off the edge of the rock shelf.

She wrapped her arm around his waist. "Lean on me."

"I am fine." He took a step forward and staggered a little, almost making her fall with him. "I *will* be fine," he amended with a smile at her.

"With you injured, how are we supposed to get out of here?" She moved with him as he took a step forward. "I don't suppose you can create one of those floaty balls, or order the one you left behind to come and get us."

"My powers have lessened." He took another step toward the rock they would need to climb on. "From this distance I don't have the strength to bring the *geodess* to us."

She released him as he reached the rock and he started to climb. His biceps bulged as his arms trembled with the effort, the muscles in his back flexing beneath his T-shirt.

What had this great Elvin warrior done to be so weak?

"Was Ceithlenn here?" Hannah followed as he made slow progress along the rocks that led back to the entrance. "Did she make all the Fomorii disappear?"

"She was not here." Garran's boot slipped on a rock as he crept forward. "I fear she is still in your city."

Hannah's gut twisted at the mention of Ceithlenn still in San Francisco. "If she didn't do this . . . what happened?"

"I do not have the strength for speech." His voice did sound weak as he moved on.

Hannah clamped her lips shut. This entire thing had been crazy, from the moment they left the pier until now. In some unbelievable way, Garran had something to do with the disappearance of the demons. She just didn't know how.

Unless they hadn't been there to begin with? Her skin went cold. Did that mean more demons were in the city than they'd thought?

Their progress was agonizingly slow and Hannah's stomach constantly churned, as if Ceithlenn might appear. Hannah wasn't sure she could shield herself and Garran against an onslaught of the dark goddess's magical powers or her ability to suck up souls. Hannah flinched at the thought of what the goddess had done to all those people at the stadium and acid rose up in her throat.

To keep their souls—the D'Danann, D'Anu, and PSF officers—from being taken by the goddess, the Great Guardian had created an elixir from an Amarant, an exceedingly powerful, magical precursor of the everlasting, never-fading amaranth they knew here. The Guardian had provided a flagon that contained a magical potion made from the rare Amarant that bloomed only in Otherworld. Unfortunately there wasn't enough to put in the city's water supply to save everyone in San Francisco.

As far as Hannah knew, she was still protected from losing her soul. She studied Garran as he moved ahead of her. He wasn't safe from that fate since he hadn't been around when they'd taken the elixir. When they got back—and they *would* get back—she'd have to see if Cassia had more in that flagon.

Blessed Anu, it seemed to take forever and a week to reach the lip of the cave's entrance but they finally did. Garran sat for a moment on the last rock he had stepped on. Hannah settled beside him and noticed his skin was slick with a sheen of sweat and his chest rose and fell with each harsh breath. He still looked pale—more so than he did when he was in the daylight and his skin and hair color changed.

Water pushed back and forth from the rock just below the lip of the cavern's entrance. As they sat on the rocks for a moment, Hannah thought about the change in his skin tones and hair when he was in the daylight. He had been magnificent. Beautiful yet dangerous. His hair had gleamed white-gold in the sunrise and his skin had been almost the same color as the Great Guardian's. Fair, but a little darker than hers.

She studied him as he sat beside her, still the proud, strong, dangerous warrior king despite the fact that somehow he'd been weakened. And he was gorgeous—even with his skin color again the Drow shade of bluish gray and with his silvery-blue hair. It was beautiful as it rested on his shoulders. His liquid silver eyes, powerful build, and regal bearing were enough to take a woman's breath away. She wanted to reach up and trace his ear to its point and down . . .

Garran looked at her with his slow, lazy perusal that made her body tighten and the place between her thighs ache.

With a slight smile to his lips, he looked to the mouth of the cave. Immediately she sensed him using his powers—the darkness and strength of it made her shiver.

The magic faded and he took her hand as they both rose to their feet. He looked beyond tired as they walked to the short drop-off to the water. When she peeked over, the black sphere was waiting for them.

"So you did have some magic left," she said.

"When I came close enough to it, I was able to draw the *geodess*." He looked down as if he weren't sure how he was going to climb the distance. He frowned and took Hannah's hand. "We will have to jump."

Hannah gripped Garran's hand tighter. "We won't bounce off?"

He shook his head. Before she had time to realize what he was doing, he pulled her to the edge of the entrance—and jumped, bringing her with him.

A cry ripped from her as they fell. When they hit the bubble, it cushioned their fall then immediately sucked them inside. Garran and Hannah landed on their asses and her head knocked against his.

"Ow." She rolled away and rubbed the temple that had struck him. "You're thickheaded in more ways than one."

His lips curved into a slight smile as he closed his eyes and his body went slack.

Hannah's heart jumped and she immediately used her magic to examine him. He was fine. He just needed to recover from—from whatever had happened back there.

She kept her hand on his chest, feeling the hardness through his T-shirt. Thank Anu the Fomorii hadn't gotten their claws into him.

The sphere rocked, spun a little, causing her to feel a bit dizzy, then slowly began moving toward San Francisco. The spell that had woven the *geodess* together didn't seem as strong as it had before. She could see through the walls and it wasn't as dark. It also moved more slowly.

She glanced at Garran, who remained passed out on the floor of the sphere. A grasping sensation made her belly squeeze tight as the bubble slowed even more and seemed to sink a little. She looked around at the walls that grew lighter with every second.

Her belly clenched again—and then she knew exactly what to do. She raised her hands and released her green magic, creating a spellshield all around them and intertwining it with Garran's magic. She shivered at the darkness of the power he'd used to create the sphere. It wasn't black, but it was so, so dark.

Confidence remained in Hannah that even combining her gray magic with Garran's dark, she'd never fall so far out of line that she would cross into black magic. It simply wasn't an option.

With her magic joining his, she could see outside the bubble. The lights of San Francisco sparkled against the skyline, growing larger as the sphere started skimming the water, heading closer to the city.

On the journey back, she kept one of her palms on Garran's chest, feeling his heartbeat. She resisted cupping his smooth jaw then running her fingers through his hair.

Hannah rolled her eyes up to the domed ceiling of the sphere. Since when had she started getting mushy like that? For the Ancestors' sake, he was one of the Dark Elves.

She looked down at Garran and her heart softened.

The *geodess* bumped into something, jarring Hannah so that she fell across Garran. He opened his eyes as she started to push herself up.

Those mesmerizing, liquid silver eyes . . .

Garran caught her face in his hands and brought her to him so that their lips met, and Hannah sighed. He kissed her softly then gently rose so that the two of them sat face-to-face before he looked at the sphere.

He frowned as he reached out and touched the wall that now swirled with both his dark magic and her green power. "My spell failed?"

"It just needed a little reinforcement." Hannah's gaze found the dock that was now above their heads. There was no rocky shore, just wooden pilings and a sheer wall. "I don't suppose you can get this thing to go up again, can you?"

When she returned her gaze to Garran's he was shaking his head, a frustrated, angry expression on his features. "My powers have never been weak in all my years." He clenched his fist on his thigh.

She put her hand on his fist. "It happens to the best of us."

His voice came out in a low growl. "Not *me*."

"Well, guess you're not so perfect after all." She pushed herself to her feet and glared at him. "Maybe you're a little like everyone else."

Garran glared back, but she looked upward at one of the dock's reinforcements. She raised her hand and let loose a magic rope that glittered in the night. The rope wrapped around a wooden pole protruding from the edge of the dock.

Without waiting for he-man, she grasped the rope and started to pull herself up. She wrapped her legs around it and her arms strained from holding her own weight as she inched her way higher. It would sure be handy to have Garran's power and have the rope draw her up the way his magic had at the island.

When she reached the walkway she paused. How was she going to swing herself onto the dock?

She let out a little yelp as she felt pressure on her rear. Like a hand was pushing on her ass, she began to rise until she could climb fully on to the walkway. She looked down to see, as she'd expected, Garran sending some of his magic up to help her. So he wasn't *totally* depleted. That was good.

He grabbed her magic rope and began making his way up. His muscles bulged in all the right places. It would have made her mouth water if she wasn't so concerned for him. His jaw was tense in the soft light coming from the pier. Whatever had happened in the Fomorii lair had really zapped his strength.

When he reached the top of the rope, she started to grab his hand to help him the rest of the way up, but with one powerful move he swung himself up and onto the pier. He flipped and landed on his back and let out a low groan as he stared up at the foggy night sky.

Hannah leaned over the side of the pier to watch the *geodess* fade and diminish as Garran pulled his magic back into himself, and she drew hers back inside her.

She remained on her ass for a moment before pushing herself to her feet and looking down at Garran. "I think we need to get back and get to bed."

This time his look was entirely too seductive. "It will be my pleasure."

Hannah shook her head and smiled. "Let's see if you can get your butt back to the warehouse."

He got to his feet and she pretended not to notice that he was still wobbly. His warrior pride was probably killing him.

Exhaustion made her lean into Garran, who wrapped his arm around her shoulders as if knowing she needed his support. More likely they needed each other's support. It was probably close to midnight.

When they finally reached the warehouse, they bypassed the D'Danann warrior guards with Garran's shroud and entered the building.

When they were a good distance away from the entryway, Garran dropped the shroud.

They came to a complete stop as Hawk, Rhiannon, and Jake stepped through the kitchen door. Without hesitation, the three strode toward Hannah and Garran. Each of them wore an expression ranging from concern to questioning to angry.

Goddess, I so *do not need this right now.*

"Why aren't you all in bed?" Hannah asked, feeling grumpy and irritable, as the three reached her and Garran. "It's late."

"Where've you been?" Jake looked from Garran to Hannah, his voice filled with mistrust.

"I had a strong vision." Rhiannon looked slightly rumpled with her chin-length hair ruffled. She was barefoot, wearing a pair of faded blue jeans and a bright pink T-shirt. "You both went to Alcatraz tonight."

"Yes." All weariness vanished from Garran's voice as he straightened to his full height, looking every bit the powerful warrior.

Jake glanced at Hannah, who sighed. "There and back again."

"But what my vision showed me . . ." Rhiannon shook her head as in disbelief. "The cavern was filled with Fomorii. You were there, Garran, with all the demons—and then they just vanished. Every last demon that was in the cavern."

"Is this the case?" Jake narrowed his gaze at Garran.

Hannah wondered exactly what he would say. *She* had no idea what had occurred in that cavern.

Garran appeared calm, as if nothing had happened. "Rhiannon's vision is correct." He met his daughter's gaze. "I was in the cavern and the demons did vanish."

Rhiannon, Hawk, and Jake looked at one another with astonished expressions before returning their gazes to Hannah and Garran.

"It's true." Exhaustion was catching up with Hannah. She felt it to her bones, like each one was made of lead. "I heard a massive amount of roars and shrieks, but I didn't get into the cavern until after the Fomorii were gone. I found Garran unconscious and no signs of the demons."

"Care to explain?" Jake's sharp tone had Hannah wondering what had him on edge. "Did *you* do something to the Fomorii?"

"All I am able to tell you is that the demons have returned to Underworld," Garran said clearly, and Hannah looked up at him in surprise.

He knows they were sent to Underworld? How?

Jake folded his arms across his chest and shook his head. "I'll believe it when I see it."

"As you will." Garran kept his gaze focused on the three. Small lines had formed at the outside corners of his eyes, and Hannah realized it was a sign he was tired. "But now Hannah and I must retire. We have had no sleep for many hours."

Hawk's jaw tensed. "How did this happen? How do you have this knowledge the Fomorii returned to Underworld?"

Garran's gaze didn't waver from Hawk's. "I cannot say."

"You can't or won't?" Jake asked.

"For the blessed goddess's sake." Hannah's head ached and her temper soared as she glared at both Hawk and Jake. "Isn't it good enough for you that the demons are gone?"

"For all we know, he had something to do with hiding the demons"—Jake's eyes flashed his skepticism—"not sending them back to Underworld."

"Believe what you will." Garran's voice remained so even

that Hannah didn't understand how he accomplished it. She was totally about to lose her composure, and she prided herself on keeping it together. "But for now, as I said, Hannah and I require sleep."

Rhiannon pushed aside Hawk and Jake and glared up at each of them. "Give it a rest for now. If it'll make you feel better, we can go to Alcatraz ourselves and check it out."

Before she tugged Jake and Hawk away, Rhiannon told two D'Danann that Hannah and Garran needed someplace to lie down for a good, long sleep, a place where they wouldn't be disturbed.

One of the warriors led them to an empty "room" that was simply a place with plywood walls, a door, and no ceiling.

Oops. One room.

Good enough.

When the D'Danann warrior left, Hannah and Garran sank onto the concrete floor, and she realized she didn't give a damn where they lay down, so long as they got some rest. But the warrior came back with a couple of sleeping bags and Hannah thanked him before he closed the door.

As soon as she and Garran rolled out the sleeping bags, side by side, and settled on them, he pulled her close, so that her head rested on his chest.

Odd, but she didn't want to separate herself from him. Instead she had the intense desire to be as near him as possible.

Hannah let all thoughts of missing demons and arguing men float away from her mind.

She closed her eyes and immediately slipped into darkness.

CHAPTER FIFTEEN

CEITHLENN APPRAISED HER NEW living arrangement. She had saved her strength by having the Fomorii do the work in securing the opulent location—the way a ruler should.

The wooden blinds of the new luxury apartment were slightly open, allowing strips of moonlight to line the burgundy carpeting at an angle. The Fomorii she had brought with her had just finished overtaking the bodies of the man and woman who had lived in this apartment before Ceithlenn made it her home.

Smells of food still simmering in the kitchen made her stomach churn. The demons would be happy to eat whatever the humans had been cooking, but Ceithlenn had no stomach for it.

She wanted flesh. Human flesh.

And their souls, she needed their souls.

Her muscles actually ached from the weakness that continued to master her body as she waited for a group of Fomorii to return with food for herself and for the demons. They could all stand to fill up on what they preferred to eat.

Ceithlenn shook her short punk-red hair back. She was in her human form, the warlock formerly known as Sara, which she found much easier to maintain while she struggled with her powers. In the cavern, where over half of her Fomorii legion remained, she always appeared as her true goddess self.

To see her as such struck fear in the hearts of the demons and other beasts and helped her control them.

The smells coming from the kitchen—Polish sausage along with boiled potatoes and cabbage, her Sara-self told her—now gave her the urge to vomit. If she wasn't waiting for the five Fomorii to return to her with her true dinner, she would leave this foul-smelling place until it was cleaned up and aired out.

A smile of satisfaction curved her lips. Almost half her legion of Fomorii had infiltrated San Francisco. The demons had taken over the bodies of highly placed military and law enforcement officials, as well as those of senators, congressmen, wealthy businessmen and women. Anyone in anyplace where she could get a foothold to be prepared for her next attack.

Soon, because of her newfound control, martial law would be lifted so that humans would again roam the streets at all times. Events would be held such as rallies and parades. Those with great wealth would ensure the events carried on, and the military and law enforcement branches would not stop them.

She sensed the return of the Fomorii and that alone gave her strength—to know she would dine and regain at least some power.

The time when she and Balor would again rule over the Old World, including Ireland, would soon come. With no interferences from any of the gods and goddesses who had left for Otherworld when she and Balor were banished to Underworld.

Ceithlenn scowled as she summoned some of the last vestiges of her strength to jerk open the door with her magic, allowing the Fomorii to stumble in with their prey. As usual, she had chosen nighttime for their feeding. But instead of having her demons travel a distance away, so as not to raise suspicion, this time she didn't care. The food they pushed in through the door were humans obtained from other apartments in the building.

The Fomorii remained in their demon forms as they pulled, shoved, or carried the humans into the apartment. The five Fomorii each carried two of the pathetic creatures so that there were ten in all. The demons dumped the humans in the middle of the burgundy carpeting. The Fomorii had used human methods to restrain the creatures to bring Ceithlenn fresh food, binding their bodies and muzzling their mouths with duct tape.

Ceithlenn salivated at the sight of the bound and gagged people and she sucked in a deep breath of the sweet smell of their succulent flesh combined with the even sweeter scent of their fear.

"Ah . . . this one." Ceithlenn knelt before the largest of the humans. His fat spilled over the waistband of his gray sweatpants.

She summoned some of the strength she had left to transform into her goddess form and watched as the humans' eyes widened in even more terror. Within mere seconds, her hair turned to flame, large leathery wings sprouted from her back, her hands extended into claws, and her teeth lengthened into sharp fangs.

"This one, and"—she smiled as she pointed to a businessman in a two-piece suit—"that one are mine. You may share the rest."

Before Ceithlenn even had the opportunity to feed, the demons had already started. Smells of blood and flesh served as an aphrodisiac that caused her belly to rumble.

And then she was rocked to her very core.

Souls rushed at her. Souls of the humans the Fomorii were killing. Strands and puffs of white and gray entered her body—*souls*.

Always before, she'd had to *take* souls by murdering the humans herself. This time, her demons making the kills released the souls and Ceithlenn could draw them in faster and easier than ever before.

As the sound of muffled screams, growling, smacking, and of flesh being torn from bone met her ears, Ceithlenn closed her eyes and sucked in the humans' essences. Power flooded her, filled her, so great that all weakness and exhaustion vanished.

Pure euphoria lifted her and her formerly clouded mind cleared.

She scraped her claws along the fat man's throat.

A vision slammed into her and she almost collapsed.

Her cavern. The one she had created below Alcatraz Island.

Empty.

No Fomorii. No Basilisks. No Handai. None of the three-headed dogs of Underworld.

Only vast emptiness.

A shudder of fury shook her body.

She shrieked and barely recognized that the room had gone silent at the sound of her scream.

Ceithlenn wrapped her wings around her body and transferred to the cavern.

She arrived on the shelf she always used to preside over her legions.

The cavern was empty.

Just as she had envisioned.

Another shriek tore from her throat and she shoved herself from her perch, taking flight. The fury roiling up inside her caused her to feel as if her entire body burned with flame like her hair. Her vision grew even redder than usual when in her goddess form and her claws had extended until they hurt.

She soared around the empty cavern, somehow knowing her legions had been sent back to Underworld. But how could such a great feat have been accomplished?

The stench of the Fomorii had faded and she smelled only the bay outside the cavern—

And something more.

Something that gave her pause.

Human.

Elvin.

Both had been in her cavern. How many?

Ceithlenn gave another cry and made a round of the cavern again.

Something caught her eye. Metal.

She flew to the rock shelf where a long dagger had been discarded. When she landed, she picked up the weapon by the hilt and almost dropped it. Elvin made. But not of the Light Elves. She would not have been able to hold it if it had been one of theirs.

No, this blade could only have been fashioned by the Dark Elves.

Traitors!

The Drow had turned on Balor, the Fomorii, and Ceithlenn when the door to Underworld had been opened.

She raised the blade to her nose and caught a strong scent. Definitely Drow.

With her eyes closed, she gripped the hilt of the blade and searched for the memory of the weapon.

The darkness behind her eyelids exploded into images.

Garran. King Garran of the Dark Elves had wielded this very blade.

Her fury grew hotter with every image her vision revealed, of what had taken place in this cavern. Garran fighting the Fomorii. Fending them off alone. Garran scrambling over the rocks. Reaching this very spot. Standing. Delving inside himself for magic.

A great burst of power encompassing the entire cavern. So powerful that even the image almost knocked Ceithlenn against the wall.

Silver brightness faded.

The cavern empty.

Garran collapsing.

Darkness.

Ceithlenn's hand shook so hard with fury that she almost dropped the blade, but she maintained her grip and felt Garran stir. He heard a female voice.

Opened his eyes.

And saw one of the D'Anu witches.

It was one of the witches Ceithlenn had battled in the stadium.

The witch's name came from Garran's mind.

Hannah. A D'Anu witch who communed with the Dragon Elementals, their power strong within her.

Dragons . . .

And this witch meant something to King Garran.

Deep inside, his soul recognized her as his mate.

Ceithlenn's eyes snapped open and she narrowed them.

She knew exactly what she was going to do to the fucking King of the Dark Elves.

CHAPTER SIXTEEN

ICE-COLD WIND TUGGED AT Jake's hair and felt bracing against his skin as the PSF's streamlined watercraft headed toward Alcatraz Island in the fog-shrouded night. Thousands of lights glittered from Marin County ahead, and from the shores of San Francisco, which they had left behind them.

Rhiannon stood beside Jake, her hands tucked into the pockets of her bomber jacket. As soon as a couple of the D'Danann got Hannah and Garran settled in the back rooms of the warehouse, Jake and his team had left to check out Garran's story.

Jake furrowed his brow as he gripped the boat's cold handrail while they neared the island. What would they find? The night smelled of brine—but none of that strong rotten fish stench of the Fomorii was present.

Or the stench of evil magic that he caught whenever Ceithlenn was near—not at all the same as the Fomorii stench. The goddess's power was as evil-smelling as the magic that had slaughtered his men in a small Middle Eastern village when Jake had been Special Ops in the Marines. The foul odor always made him want to puke.

Yeah, magic definitely had a smell all to its own, depending on what kind of magic. The D'Danann and D'Anu had a different magical scent, a kind of signature. It was fresh—almost like the wind after a good rain.

The magic of the Dark Elves was more puzzling. Since

they weren't necessarily evil, they didn't smell like Ceith-lenn. But they didn't smell like the "good magic" beings, ei-ther. More mossy and earthy with a hint of an unidentifiable spice.

Jake glanced over his shoulder at those who accompanied him on the mission tonight. His elite team included five of his officers as well as Rhiannon of the D'Anu; along with Hawk, Tiernan, Eavan, and Keir of the D'Danann.

"I don't understand why you feel the need to do this." Rhi-annon's words were almost whipped away by the wind as he turned his head to meet her eyes that were dark in the night.

"I have to see for myself that Garran's story isn't a lie." Jake glanced to Alcatraz Island then back to Rhiannon. "At least we can verify that the Fomorii that were in the cavern are gone—if that part of his story is true."

However, if the demons *were* there, Jake and his team would get the hell out in a hurry.

Irritation darkened Rhiannon's eyes. "Hannah backed up what Garran said, and my vision told me the same thing."

"For all we know, Garran could have put some kind of dark spell on Hannah and maybe influenced your vision," Jake said. "I wouldn't put it past him." At Rhiannon's frown, Jake added, "No offense, Rhi. I know he's your father . . ."

"But I haven't known him long and he is the king of the Dark Elves." Rhiannon looked thoughtful, as if puzzling out something in her mind. "It sure doesn't make sense how hun-dreds or thousands of man-eating demons could vanish—or how Garran was involved."

"Since you inherited some kind of dark power from him, maybe you can use that connection to sense what really went down at Alcatraz." Jake moved his hands from the cold rail-ing to his pockets. "If the demons *are* gone did Garran use his own dark magic to send the Fomorii somewhere? And if he did, exactly where did he send them?"

Rhiannon stared at the island as it grew larger the closer they got to it. The expression on her face said that she was miles away in her mind.

Without looking at him, she said, "You're right. It doesn't matter that Garran is my father. Do we really know if he's on the up and up?" He barely heard her low voice. "Or could he still be an enemy on Ceithlenn's side? Could he be planning to have his Drow warriors attack us the first chance they get?"

"I don't know," was all Jake could say in response. "All I do know is that we need to cover our asses every step of the way."

Rhiannon gave a slow nod before her eyes met his again. "It's hard for any of us to trust him. But I've had a chance to talk with him some, get to know him a little better since I found out he's my father. Maybe we should give him the benefit of the doubt."

Jake's muscles flexed as he tensed. "I don't want to take any chances and let our guard down."

She stared ahead at the island as they closed in on it. "I understand."

He looked over his shoulder at his officers. The team wore sleek scuba gear designed to keep them warm once they entered the icy water. The boat sliced its way through the swells to the area Rhiannon told them to go. She had visioned they couldn't be seen in that location and it would lead them directly to the mouth of the cavern. Every one of Jake's officers carried a flashlight, a dagger, and a water-resistant handgun at his or her side, the guns loaded with the special heart-seeking bullets. If they needed the weapons, he hoped to God it would be enough.

For a moment Jake's thoughts turned to Kat. He hadn't spoken with her since she'd come to his office. His body heated at the memory of being inside her, yet at the same time concern clenched his heart hard enough it hurt.

What he felt for Kat . . . hell, he had no idea. The sex was great and he admired her wit and intellect. They'd enjoyed each other's company for the first six months or so of their relationship—until all hell had broken loose with the warlocks and the Fomorii. Months ago.

What he did know, was that he cared about Kat and her safety. He prayed like hell the demons wouldn't get a hold of her. She was a high-profile news personality, and there was no telling what Ceithlenn had in mind. The goddess had already infiltrated the government. What about the news?

Yeah, he cared about Kat. But she had never filled the soul-deep emptiness he had carried with him as long as he could remember. With drug addicts for parents and an uncle who kept his mother and father supplied with cocaine, heroin, and alcohol, Jake had never felt like he belonged anywhere or with anyone.

Except for his job. Being a Marine and now working with the Paranormal Special Forces was what kept him going.

The air around Jake seemed to grow colder and he rolled his tense shoulders within his snug jacket. Right now it wasn't doing a damn bit of good to think about Kat or his shitty childhood. He needed to focus on the job.

When he looked toward the railing, Rhiannon faced away from him again, huddled at the bow in her bomber jacket. Her chin-length hair whipped around her face and he saw her shivering from the cold. She had been certain she'd visioned the exact location of the mouth of the cavern. Even though no one had wanted to put Rhiannon in danger, they needed her. The kickass witch refused to be left behind, anyway.

"There." Rhiannon pointed to a sharp ripple of the sheer rock to the left side of the island. "Make your way to the other side, and you'll find it."

When they were close enough to drift near the location Jake ordered the lieutenant to cut the engines. In just a matter of moments, he and five team members dove silently into the bay. The three D'Danann flew overhead, landing where Rhiannon instructed them to.

Jake was first to reach the almost hidden lip of the cavern. He rose out of the water, pushed up his face mask, and listened for the slightest sound of the Fomorii.

Nothing. Only a very faint, lingering demon-stench and a

steady *plop*, *plop* of dripping water from somewhere in the cavern.

Without making a splash or a sound, Jake eased his way onto the cavern's lip and drew his water-safe gun. Once he was on his feet, he peered around an outcropping of rocks, into the cavern.

Even though Rhiannon had visioned that Garran was telling the truth, Jake hadn't been able find it in himself to believe the Drow king without hard proof. He had to check matters out for himself. Call it cop-think, or covering his ass, or looking out for "his people," police and otherwise.

It looked like Garran had been clean.

At least about the Fomorii no longer being in the cavern.

Jake motioned for the others to follow him and signaled to the hovering D'Danann with a wave. Because he was human, he couldn't see the flying warriors when they were in winged form, but he knew they were there. It still jolted Jake every time one of the warriors suddenly appeared next to him.

He led the way into the silent cavern. He pointed to a few piles of silt—dead Fomorii remnants—around the entrance of the cave. But that was it, only a few areas had the silt as if the demons had dropped while battling Garran, as he'd said.

As Jake's team slipped deeper into the cavern, sweeping it with their flashlights, Jake saw there was nothing left. Other than dried feces in one corner, carcasses of what had to be whales and sharks, not another sign of the Fomorii or any other beasts remained.

Hawk came up beside him, followed by Rhiannon. Jake wiped water from his face. "Looks like the sonofabitch was telling the truth."

The D'Danann warrior scanned the cavern. "It appears so."

"Do you really trust Garran?" Jake asked as he studied Hawk.

The warrior paused before he gave a slow nod. "Garran made a great sacrifice to save Silver's sister from the Fomorii and Darkwolf."

Jake shook his head. "I'm not sure I feel the same way."

"Things in Otherworld are never as straightforward as in this place, your Otherworld." Hawk propped one booted foot on a rock as he spoke. "I think you would do well to expand your thinking, to sharpen your instincts about all manner of potential allies.

"Even those with darkness in them," Hawk continued as he gave Rhiannon a pointed glance, "can win through to the light, in the right circumstances."

With a frown, Jake nodded. "Maybe you're right. But for now, let's get the hell out of here." He motioned to his team. "If Ceithlenn shows up or any of the demons, I don't want to be caught with my pants down."

Hawk gave him a curious look then glanced down at Jake's scuba bottoms, but Hawk didn't answer before he started walking toward the entrance.

Jake swept the cavern one more time with his flashlight then followed Hawk and his team out into the bay and the breaking dawn.

CHAPTER SEVENTEEN

HANNAH SCRUNCHED HER BROWS against sunlight meeting her eyelids as she gradually woke, curled up on her side. She raised one eyelid, then quickly shut it as the bright light made her wince. Gradually she got used to the sunshine streaming in from the high windows of the warehouse.

Voices, hammering, a drill, and other sounds echoed in the warehouse and in her head.

Hannah normally woke easily and was surprised by the lethargy that made her feel as if her bones would melt into the cement below the sleeping bag. Maybe not so surprising considering what she and Garran went through last night.

Memories and questions fired through her mind like arrows and her head ached even more from them.

Garran was behind her, she was certain, even though he wasn't touching her.

She rolled over from one side to the other to see Garran watching her, a sensuous smile touching his lips. He had propped one elbow on his sleeping bag, his head in his palm, and was simply watching her with his liquid silver eyes.

Such Elvin beauty stole her breath away. White-blond hair hung straight over his shoulders, his skin was fair yet not pale. His physique, his powerful build, made her want to explore his body with her hands, her tongue, her mouth. Her gaze drifted to the crotch of his jeans and she was rewarded with the outline of a very firm erection.

When she raised her eyes and looked at him again, his gaze had darkened.

"Good morning," she said, her voice soft in the emptiness of the room they had slept in. "Or maybe I should be saying good afternoon."

"It matters not." He raised his hand and slipped his fingers into her hair. "The day is good."

The feel of his fingertips along her skin and then his palm cupping the back of her head made her belly twist. She eased her hand up to trace the curve of one of his pointed ears and he shivered as if the act itself were erotic. She fisted her hand in his T-shirt and pulled him toward her.

When they'd kissed before, it had been wild and passionate on both their sides. This was so tender, gentle, that she could almost forget everything that had happened and all that was around them. She moaned as his mouth moved over hers and he took her lower lip between her teeth and nipped at it, sending a thrill straight to the place between her thighs. She slipped her tongue in to meet with his and tasted the wonderful flavor that was uniquely Garran.

Hannah unclenched his T-shirt and moved her hand lower, down the flatness of his ripped abs to the tough cotton of his jeans. He broke their kiss and groaned as she rubbed his erection, and when she looked up at him he appeared to be almost in pain.

"This human clothing is far too uncomfortable." He shifted his hips and opened his eyes.

Hannah rubbed him harder as she gazed up at him under her lashes. "I think it's because you're too big to fit in your jeans."

Garran grasped her wrist, pulling her hand from his cock, and rolled her onto her back in a fast movement that shook the remaining sleepiness right out of her. He straddled her, holding both of her wrists in his hands. Such big, strong hands.

She squirmed beneath him, wet and aching for him to be inside of her. Would he leave her wanting again? He intertwined

his fingers with hers and held their hands to either side of
her head and brought his mouth to hers again.

"I have never known such beauty." He gently brushed his
lips up and across hers. "You move my very soul when I look
upon you."

"I know you're trying to seduce me," she murmured as he
moved his lips over her jaw to the soft line of her neck. "But
you don't have to go overboard."

Garran nipped at the skin between her shoulder and neck.
"I never say anything I do not mean, Hannah Wentworth."

Another flip inside her stomach made her wonder if she
was losing her mind. The instinct she'd had before, about
him telling the truth, rose up in her, and she couldn't argue
with him.

Frankly, she didn't want to argue. She just wanted him.
And bless it, this time she would have him.

In the social circles she'd frequented, her sexual relationships had been . . . civilized. Garran was anything but. She'd
never felt so hot, so needy, so crazy for a man as she did with
Garran. Her body cried out to have his hands on her, his
mouth on her, his cock to be inside her. She wanted to feel
his hard thrusts as he pounded in and out.

His lips neared her T-shirt-covered nipple and she
squirmed beneath him. "Take my shirt off."

He looked up at her with a predatory smile and released
her hands. "Are you certain this is what you want? Once we
begin, I will not stop until we both have reached completion
with me deep inside you."

Oh, goddess. She squirmed beneath him, the images of
him taking her making her hotter and wetter.

"You'd better make good on your promise." She reached
for the hem of her T-shirt that her sister witches had retrieved
from her home. "Because this time you're not leaving."

Garran's eyes melted into dark pewter as he helped her
strip off the shirt. Thanks be, the witches had brought at least
one of her front-clasp bras and she shrugged it off so that all
she was wearing was her moon and crescent armband.

Garran stroked the armband with his fingertips before taking both of her breasts in his hands and rubbing his thumbs over her nipples hard enough to make her gasp. He scooted down a little more and took one of her nipples in his mouth.

Hannah moaned at the feel of his hot mouth on her nipple and the way he sucked and licked it. He continued to palm her other breast and she arched, wanting him to take more of her. She found she was gripping the sleeping bag in her fists and relaxed them to slip her hands into his silky blond hair.

He moved his mouth to her other nipple, still squeezing her breasts at the same time. Some of his long hair fell over his shoulder and the soft strands tickled and caressed her bare flesh.

The moment his mouth left one of her breasts, and he abandoned it to run his lips down the center of her belly, she shivered. Cool air circulating from giant fans at the ceiling of the warehouse brushed her moist, taut nipples. The sounds she'd heard when she woke up faded into white noise as she focused completely on Garran and what he was doing to her.

His tongue traced a path along the edge of her jeans and she reached for the button to unfasten them.

"No." The word was a soft command and he pushed her hands aside. "I will."

Hannah held her breath as he rose up on his knees and smiled at her. He fumbled a bit with the button of her jeans—no doubt from his unfamiliarity with human clothing—but he was a fast learner. As soon as the button was taken care of, he unzipped her jeans, grasped her panties and the sides of her jeans, and pulled down.

He didn't rush, but he didn't take too long, either. He brought her jeans and panties all the way to her ankles where he stopped long enough to flip off her running shoes, tug her socks from her feet, and then yank the rest of her clothing off.

Leaving her deliciously naked. Hunger grew in Garran's eyes as he forced her knees apart and looked at her folds.

He spoke words in a language she didn't understand as

she warmed under his gaze. Words that seemed almost magical as they came from his lips.

"What did you just say?" she whispered. "What language?"

"Elvin." The way he looked at her when he raised his gaze to meet hers made her thighs quiver and her folds grow wetter. "I said you are a goddess. Beauty beyond any that I have seen before."

Warmth turned to heat and flowed up Hannah from her feet to her scalp. She'd never blushed. It was just a fact of life—she was too distanced from those kinds of emotions. But she was pretty sure that this time she had. Her cheeks felt flushed with heat and her skin burned.

A primal growl rumbled up from Garran's throat and he pushed her legs up so that her knees bent, then spread her thighs farther apart.

Strange quivers that she'd never felt before flipped through her belly—like those butterflies she'd heard about but had never experienced. She bit her lower lip as he scooted down and moved his mouth closer to her folds. His warm breath stroked her and she wanted to scream.

She wasn't about to beg. She never begged. Instead, her whole body remained tense and she waited for his tongue to find her clit.

"What do you want, Hannah?" he murmured as his mouth neared her folds.

"You." She resisted squirming. "Your mouth. On me."

With a satisfied expression he lowered his head and swiped her folds with his tongue.

Hannah shivered and moaned as his mouth took control of her body. She lowered her head and gazed at him, causing more crazy eruptions in her belly as she looked at him licking and sucking her.

His gaze met hers and she could tell he liked her watching him. Her climax built in her belly as he traced her folds with his tongue, circled her clit, then sucked it.

Moan after moan rose up in Hannah as she broke eye

contact with Garran and tipped her head back. She lost herself in the feel of his mouth on her. It felt so good with his head between her thighs, the silk of his hair against her skin and brushing her mound.

He started stroking the skin between her anus and her core with his fingers, a delicious indulgence that caused her to move her hips tighter against his face.

Goddess! She almost lost it when he thrust two, then three fingers up her core and began to slowly move them in and out. His knuckles smacked against her flesh as everything went wild inside her. That floaty, tickling feeling grew in her belly, like butterflies swirling in a small cyclone.

Hannah ground her teeth as she turned her head from one side to the other. She dug her nails into her palms and felt the ache building and building between her thighs. Her breasts— were so sensitive to the slightest stirring of air as Garran licked and sucked her clit until she was half mad.

Her entire body started to tremble and she dug her nails harder into her palms.

Garran began pounding his fingers in and out of her body. Harder, harder yet, as if he were driving his cock in her, thrusting hard. Just the image of him taking her made the butterfly storm inside her swirl and swirl and swirl until she knew she was about to lose it.

She ground her teeth and felt as if her head were going to take flight

Garran growled against her folds and her clit and she was gone.

A sharp cry rose up inside her and she felt the butterflies swirl free from her body. They brushed her skin with their feather-soft wings from her belly to her nipples to her cheeks.

Garran drove her on and on until her always dry eyes almost released a tear or two from the most intense pleasure she'd ever felt in her life.

Gradually, he slowed and her core convulsed around his fingers and her body trembled beneath his mouth. The butterfly flutters faded and she unclenched her hands, and her palms stung from how tightly she'd been digging her nails into them.

A few more swipes and Garran stopped. She tilted her head down to see a very smug grin on his handsome face.

Hannah's heart beat fast and she had to inhale and exhale slowly to catch her breath. He rose up over her and started to fumble with the button of his jeans, getting ready to drive into her.

She shook her head and pressed palms on his chest. "My turn."

He raised an eyebrow, but rolled onto his back when she pushed harder against him. She straddled him and brought her mouth down, gently brushing her lips over his and dipped her tongue into his mouth. She gave a soft moan as he gripped her bare ass while she kissed him. In addition to his taste was her own flavor and the scent of her musk was on his mouth. It did crazy things in her belly again to taste what he had tasted when he'd pleasured her so thoroughly.

His jaw was smooth, no stubble on his face, just pure Elvin beauty. And she wanted to see more of him.

She rose up and grasped his T-shirt, watching his face the entire time she did. He looked so damn sexy and sensual. The warmth of his skin heated her hands as she slowly pushed his shirt up while she let her palms run over his muscles. She took her gaze away from his to look down and watch the flex of his abs, his chest, his shoulders and biceps as he helped her take his shirt completely off.

When he was bare from the waist up, she spared a moment to sit back and study him. His white-blond hair was splayed out behind him and his skin was almost golden in the afternoon light. He was simply perfection.

Just as perfect as he looked with his silvery-blue hair and bluish-gray skin. Either way, he was the most gorgeous man she'd ever known.

Garran reached up and palmed her breasts at the same time he pinched her nipples. Hannah moaned and tilted her head back, enjoying the feel of the insides of her bare thighs snug against his jeans as she straddled him, and the feel of his hands and the cool air caressing her body.

She tilted her head down and kissed him again before scooting down his body, bypassing the button of his jeans, but making sure she ran her hand along the length of his cock, causing him to groan.

"I shall remind you who is king if you continue to torture me so," he said when she met his eyes. Goddess, she loved his accent.

She gave him what she hoped was a regal gaze. "You'll do this my way, Your Majesty."

"You have little time before I take control and fuck you, Hannah." He caught her cheeks in his hand. "And when I fuck you, you will beg me for more."

"I don't beg." She eased away from his hands, down his body to his boots, before meeting his eyes again. "But I do tease."

He raised an eyebrow again, but groaned when she drew her hand down his jeans-covered cock before focusing her attention on one of his boots. They were soft and supple, lace-up boots. She loosened them before sliding each one off and tossing them aside. His bare feet looked so enticing that she ran her index fingers under the arches of both of his feet.

Garran jerked and rose up so fast to capture her wrists in his hands that it caught her by surprise. His expression was far too serious.

"No tickling the king, I take it?" she asked with a smile.

He drew her up his length, her bare body scraping his jeans. "Fucking the king, yes. Tickling, no."

"Then let go." She continued to smile as she shook off his hold. So he was ticklish, was he? She brought her fingers to the button of his jeans. "None of that until I've had my fill."

She glanced up to see him watching her with his intense eyes, and those damned butterfly feelings batted at her insides again. The zipper easily moved downward and she was pleased when she released his thick erection and saw the come already beading at the top.

Goddess, now *that* was a cock.

Instead of stopping to taste him, she tugged on his jeans and he raised his hips up, allowing her to take them all the way off. Her gaze met his. They were both naked, and she wanted to feel him on top of her, inside of her. But first she needed to taste him.

She eased up his smooth body and grasped his cock in one hand. Probably because he was Elvin he had no facial or body hair, which she found incredibly sexy. He was so smooth and powerful looking.

He was also so big it was a wonder that her fingers reached all the way around his erection or that he'd fit inside her. Her thighs grew wetter and she lowered her head and slipped his cock into her mouth.

Pleasure rippled through her like warm water as she watched Garran close his eyes and his jaw tighten. The realization of how much she affected this Elvin king, this man, made her feel heady, like she was caught up in a rolling wave. She fell into the spiraling lust that filled her just by being with him.

The taste of his semen was different. Sweet and salty, yes, but something more—delicious. She sucked him at the same time she worked his cock with one of her hands in tandem with her mouth, and used her other hand to fondle and squeeze his balls. Gently, then harder, then gentle again.

Garran groaned and their eyes met while she moved her mouth up and down his cock. Gone was the teasing, playful look in his gaze. In its place was fire and intensity, burning lust that made her feel on fire just by looking into the liquid silver depths.

She let a little of her sparkling green magic flow from her hands to his cock and balls, adding fuel to the flame.

His eyes widened and his whole body shuddered. "Gods-damnit, Hannah," he said, and grabbed her hair in his fists.

She would have laughed at his look of need that magnified with her magic, but her mouth was filled with his cock. He pumped his hips harder and tensed his jaws, his features harsh and feral.

He was so big, but she took as much of his erection as she could. At the same time she infused her magic into him through his groin, pushing him closer to the edge. Yet she gripped onto the thread of it, holding him back, not letting him reach climax.

Garran seemed to know exactly what she was doing and he growled. "Let me come, now, if you want to be fucked so hard I will take you to Otherworld and back."

Promises . . .

Hannah released a larger burst of magic and let go her hold on his orgasm. He cut back a cry as his body jerked, his hips bucked, and his cock began throbbing. His semen filled her mouth and she closed her eyes as she savored his incredible flavor. She'd never tasted anything like him.

Lost in the feel of pleasuring him, she barely noticed that he'd taken her harder by the hair until he forced her to stop and let his still semierect cock slip from her mouth.

"Mmmmm . . ." She opened her eyes and smiled at him as she licked her lips. "You taste so good." She gave him a sultry look from beneath her lashes. "If all Elves do—"

Garran growled, low and deep. He grabbed her by her upper arms, dragging her naked body over his much larger frame. "I am the only Elvin man you will ever be with." He brought her so that her mouth was close to his. She couldn't look away from the ferocity in his gaze. "The *only man* you will be with again."

Hannah wanted to say, "Yeah, right," but instead she let him kiss her and send her spiraling through another storm.

Once again his kiss was incredible as his hands roamed up her bare back, then down again to cup her ass. Her nipples rubbed his smooth chest and his erection grew to its full length and girth where it rested between her folds. Her core was so wet and ready for him to be inside her that she tried to move so that she could slide his cock in.

He stopped her by gripping her ass tight in his hands. She

raised her head and planted her palms to either side of his neck, and stared down at him.

"You are so beautiful," she murmured before she even realized the words were out.

"Because I am fair when in the light?" he said with a frank look in his gaze.

She shook her head, already having made up her mind what was the truth. "No matter what you look like, you are absolutely beautiful."

Garran kept one hand on her ass, but used his other to brush her hair from her face. "Nothing could be more beautiful than you, Hannah Wentworth."

She smiled and moved one of her hands to where his cock rested between her folds. She grasped his erection and rose up far enough to put it at the entrance to her core, and then sank down on him so that he stretched and filled her and touched her so deeply.

Groans from each of them met and mingled as she began to ride him. He raised his hips to meet her as she slid up and down his shaft. She tilted her head back and grasped her breasts in her hands, pinching and pulling at her nipples as she took him.

The moon and crescent band warmed her upper arm, the magic infused within it responding to the sensations in her body. She released her nipples, lowered herself, and braced her hands on his biceps. The added thrill of them flexing beneath her palms as he thrust in and out of her made her stomach muscles clench.

Hannah rode Garran so hard that perspiration broke out on her skin and her hair grew damp against her forehead. An orgasm rushed toward her as if she were riding the crest of a wave rolling in from the ocean.

Closer and closer the wave came toward the shore. Her whole body felt the movement, the pull of the tide. There was no waiting, no holding back.

The wave rose until it crested and slammed against the shore, breaking her into countless pieces.

Hannah cried out and fell forward against Garran's hard chest, wrapping her arms around his neck and holding on as her body seemed to fly in all directions. Their sweat-slick skin slid against each other as he continued to pump his cock in and out of her.

She was still trying to pull herself together as Garran rolled her onto her back. Her mind swam and her body convulsed as he took control of her, suddenly the king again intent on making her his.

His what?

When she looked up into his eyes his features were blurry but so beautiful he almost glowed.

Even as he continued to take her, the powerful orgasm drifted off and a new one began to build. She didn't know if she could take something of that magnitude again.

But she was sweaty, aching, and *needed* to come again. Garran's expression was so fierce he almost looked angry, and she wondered what he would be like if he was angry. What he would do or say, how he would react.

Fleeting thoughts, all of them. Because her body, mind, and spirit were once again lost in just feeling Garran. Being with him.

The next orgasm built slowly, as if he were somehow holding her back, not letting her come again so quickly.

Dark power snaked from him and wrapped itself around her. Hannah cried out at the feel of it embracing her, pouring into every fiber of her being. The magic caused her entire body to tingle, to come even more alive. So much more alive that she didn't think she could survive the kind of orgasm that it would give her.

She looked into his face as he drove into her, his hips bruising the insides of her thighs with every thrust.

The dark magic—a part of her wasn't sure she should be accepting it so easily. It filled her with a power that almost scared her.

But then she didn't care anymore. She was alive. Truly felt alive for the first time in her life. She accepted everything about her dark king in that moment and wanted all he could give her.

His thrust became harder. His magic more powerful. She felt as though she were being carried away, taken someplace secluded where only the two of them existed.

The power flowed up her like a fountain rising to where it would shoot like a geyser into the sky and fall back to earth in a harsh rush.

"Come with me, Hannah," Garran said, sounding as though he were talking through clenched teeth. "Come with me now."

His dark magic shot with her, and she screamed as it took her so high she didn't think she'd ever come down. Didn't want to come down. But when she did, it was another kind of rush that sent more spasms to her core.

His climax hit and he growled as his cock pulsed and she felt every throb, every bit of his semen shooting inside of her.

After the last twinges of his pulsing cock, Garran groaned. He pulled her onto her side, their legs intertwined, her head resting on one of his biceps, his cock still inside her. She was so exhausted after that incredible bout of sex that her eyelids started to droop—

Until the door opened and Hannah met Rhiannon's horrified gaze—her eyes wide, her lips parted. She and Silver stood in the open doorway.

Heated embarrassment rushed over Hannah.

Rhiannon closed her mouth. Opened it. Her face turned red as she looked at Garran. "I can't—I can't believe— You. *Her?*"

"Come on, Rhiannon." Silver put her arm around Rhiannon's shoulders. "Let's give them some privacy."

Face still bright red, Rhiannon backed out of the room and slammed the door shut.

CHAPTER EIGHTEEN

"WE'VE GOT TO GO." Daggers of pain split Darkwolf's head, causing him to bury his face in his shaking hands.

From the beginning, after he'd been led to the stone eye off the shores of Ireland, he'd experienced severe headaches, as if there were something inside his head trying to stab its way out. Only when the dark god, Balor, influenced Darkwolf through the eye. But those times he'd been able to shield himself from most of the pain, blocking it so that it didn't hurt as badly.

Not anymore.

And it had never been this agonizing.

Even the black magic Darkwolf used to shroud the eye, to slow Balor down, was weakening.

"Shit." Elizabeth's chair screeched across the linoleum, away from the table, the sound causing Darkwolf's head to ache even more. "Can you make it?" Genuine concern was in her voice. Darkwolf could almost believe she was human.

"No choice." Summoning what strength he had, Darkwolf rose and forced himself to concentrate on moving each limb one at a time.

The eye weighed him down, as if he had the Golden Gate Bridge dangling from the chain instead of the stone eye, but he managed to get to his feet. His chair tumbled to the floor with a series of loud thumps as he staggered back.

Balor was so close that Darkwolf was going to lose his

mind if they didn't move on. They had to travel farther away, but he knew they couldn't flee from the city. Deep in his soul, he had no doubt the power of the eye would kill him if he traveled too far from Balor.

Would death be better than this?

Sometimes he thought it would.

He had to figure out a way to get the chain holding the eye off his neck and send it to Otherworld where he hoped they'd destroy it.

How the hell was he going to do that?

Darkwolf raised his head despite the weight of the eye and staggered to the door with Elizabeth. He managed to move his feet, even though it was growing harder to do so every time the god closed in on their location. Stale smells of cigarette smoke and musty furniture battered his senses as he moved through the room.

He would use the power of transference if it wouldn't lead the god to them faster. It seemed to slow Balor down whenever Darkwolf and Junga fled on foot or by other, contemporary means of transportation.

At this moment, Balor was in the sewers directly below the apartments. Darkwolf sensed it with every nerve ending in his body. If the god had the power of his eye, he would already have been in the apartment with Darkwolf.

If Balor had his eye, they'd all be dead.

Elizabeth grabbed Darkwolf's hand and jerked him behind her down the decrepit hallway with its water- and graffiti-stained walls, faded paint, and smells of rat piss.

He found that tiny part of himself that still remained untouched by the god and focused on it. He forced his feet to move and they ran from the third-floor apartment. Darkwolf almost tripped down the stairs, having to hold on to the railing to keep from falling. But he managed it and they made it out of the building and into the pouring rain.

Instantly drenched, they hurried down one sidewalk to another. The rain chilled Darkwolf to the point his teeth chattered. At one time the eye had protected him, keeping him warm, but now he fought against the artifact's power constantly.

The magic now worked against him.

Unless he could learn to control it and make it his own?

At this time of the day there would normally have been packed sidewalks from employees heading home during rush hour. Jostling, talking, or blindly following their normal route. But due to martial law, now few people were out, and even those Darkwolf considered fools. They would be nothing but food for Ceithlenn should she get her claws on them.

National Guard units prowled everywhere. Soldiers stopped people on the street, then motioned with their rifles, ordering the people to go home.

Darkwolf and Elizabeth managed to dodge a few soldiers, but were stopped by more than one. Each time Darkwolf had to use his black magic to twist the officer's mind to forget they existed and to let Elizabeth and him pass.

Even the use of his own magic, magic that had nothing to do with the eye, drained Darkwolf enough that his vision wavered.

Could Balor track him through his own powers now?

Fuck.

They traveled so long and far Darkwolf's feet ached and felt like bricks. The burden of the eye grew lesser the farther from Balor they managed to get, and the pain in Darkwolf's head faded to a harsh throb. They walked and walked through the rain, Darkwolf using his black magic to twist minds whenever he was forced to.

When they had gone as far as the eye would allow them to, South San Francisco, Darkwolf and Elizabeth were beyond exhausted. He felt it to his marrow, as if every one of his bones were being compressed by a vise. It had stopped raining, but he was soaked through and goose bumps rose on his skin.

Elizabeth walked through the gate of a home with a manicured lawn, the metal springs of the gate squeaking as it opened and closed. The sound of her running shoes echoed on the wooden steps in the silence of the night. She knocked on the door. It creaked as it was opened. Voices from Elizabeth and someone stupid enough to open their door to a stranger. The door shut behind Elizabeth. She was in.

Darkwolf waited, squeezed his eyes tight, trying to shut out the images of what Elizabeth—now Junga the demon—was doing to the people inside of that home. He heard a shout, a scream, throaty growling sounds—

Then quiet.

His stomach churned, acid rising up in his throat, the urge to hurl almost overwhelming.

Darkwolf opened his eyes and sucked in a deep breath. He took in the quiet neighborhood, trying to get his mind to move to anything else. Everything had an abandoned look to it, but he knew it was all because of the rampant fear in the city.

Bioterrorism . . . He shook his head. Balor and Ceithlenn were far worse than any threat these people could imagine.

CHAPTER NINETEEN

TOWARD EVENING, AFTER BEING caught in bed with Garran, Hannah was gripped by the urge to scry. She slipped away from all of the clamor and grabbed her pack from the room she and Garran had slept in.

Rain pounded on the warehouse's metal rooftop like percussionists playing snare drums as she headed through the maze of hallways. She searched the recently built rooms for an empty one, void of any personal articles. She'd already taken a shower and had slipped into a fresh set of clothing.

The irony of Rhiannon finding Hannah and Garran in bed together was enough to make Hannah shake her head. It was Rhiannon's father with whom Hannah had started having an affair—and she and Rhiannon barely tolerated each other.

Hannah held her pack tighter as she made her way farther toward the back of the warehouse. She sighed. It was probably time to make nice and not be such a bitch to Rhiannon. Then maybe Rhiannon would stop being a major bitch to Hannah. Maybe.

Garran—he'd been at a loss as to what to say to his newfound daughter about his relations with Hannah, and she'd told him he was on his own. She had no idea, either.

Hannah's shoes made soft sounds on the concrete floor as she walked. Her thoughts turned to Ceithlenn and the Fomorii. Had all those demons truly vanished? Had they been sent to Underworld like Garran said?

If so, how?

Hannah whistled to Banshee. With a low cry, the falcon circled overhead then came to rest gently on her shoulder.

While her familiar stayed with her, Hannah found a small, empty room, and closed the door. It had plain ply-wood walls and a bare floor, not another thing in it. Smells of sawdust and wood made her sneeze before she set down her pack and sat cross-legged beside it. The concrete floor was cool beneath her ass.

Rain drummed on the building even harder, the tin roof and siding causing loud echoes in the room. The sound blended with all of the sawing, drilling, pounding in the background as builders made additional rooms so that this would be an even more secure stronghold for their defenses against Ceithlenn.

As far as magical protections, the witches had used every warding they knew of, and were reasonably confident the magic would keep the Fomorii and Ceithlenn out.

The headquarters was being thrown up in temporary fashion but it would give privacy to those who needed it. Her lips twisted into a wry smile. Locks on the doors would cer-tainly help.

She pulled out her scrying mirror.

It wriggled in her hand.

Banshee let out a sound of surprise and she gasped as she stared at the Dragons—the frame was made of two of the creatures, each biting the tail of the other, and they were moving in a circle.

By the goddess Anu, the Dragons were *moving*.

The mirror almost slipped from her fingers because her hand shook so badly and the handle continued wriggling. Her heart thumped against her breastbone as she managed to set the mirror on the floor without dropping it. As soon as it lay flat, the Dragons stilled in different positions than the one they had always been in before.

For a long moment Hannah just looked at the Dragons, her skin prickling. What did it mean? A chill rolled through her as she realized it had to be a sign. A bad sign.

Banshee ruffled his feathers and with a low cry expressed his concern.

She waited until her hands steadied before she took her vial of sea salt from her pack. The cork made a popping sound when she pulled it out.

Hannah's countless years of controlling her emotions and reactions eroded in those few moments. The hand that held the vial shook, and she grasped her wrist with her other hand and tilted the vial.

The world narrowed to that point where all she saw were the mirror and the salt crystals as each individual grain tumbled down to bounce and settle on the black glass. The cold found her heart as she analyzed the way the grains moved through the air, until the vial was empty, and she set it aside.

The salt crystals stilled the moment they hit the mirror's surface. As she stared at the patterns her heart turned to ice.

Fomorii. Countless. Spread throughout the city in human shells. Former military, law enforcement, and government officials and other individuals with power.

The images shifted. Ceithlenn calling to them, ordering them all to battle, after they had transformed back into their demon forms.

The largest battle the Alliance had ever fought against the evil from Underworld.

Hannah's heart thudded harder.

Where were the Dark Elves?

Innocent people murdered—slashed to ribbons. Gutted. Throats torn out.

A scream rose in Hannah's throat.

Then the image faded and she saw *herself*.

Bound by powerful magic. Trapped with Fomorii.
Facing Ceithlenn.

Hannah snapped out of the vision and collapsed on her side. Banshee took flight before she hit the floor and pain flashed through her upper arm and shoulder. The falcon shrieked so loudly that his cry rang throughout the warehouse.

Sweat rolled down the sides of Hannah's face as she pushed herself back to a sitting position. Heat then chills then heat rolled through her and her arms shook as she braced them to either side of her.

The door opened and a jolt traveled through Hannah. When she cut her gaze to the doorway, Cassia walked in, with her great white wolf familiar, Kael, at her side. Cassia wore jeans and a T-shirt like everyone else since they were at war. In the past Cassia wore only skirts and blouses.

She shut the door behind her and walked to Hannah and settled on the floor across from her and the mirror. Kael remained alert next to Cassia, but sat on his haunches.

Banshee swooped down from overhead and landed on Hannah's sore shoulder just hard enough to make her wince. She sensed his immediate apology.

Hannah avoided looking down at the pattern of crystals on the mirror or the changed Dragons. Instead she focused on Cassia's eyes. "Banshee summoned you?"

The half-Elvin witch nodded. "What happened?"

More sweat rolled down the side of Hannah's face and she wiped it away with the heel of her palm. "The short version is that the other half of Ceithlenn's army is in the city." She swallowed and tried to regain her composure. "And it looks like I'm going to be up front and personal with the goddess."

Cassia studied her then her gaze lowered to land on the mirror. "The Dragons have shifted."

"I don't understand why." Hannah couldn't get herself to look at the mirror or the salt crystals. She also couldn't get herself to tell Cassia about her visions of the Fire Dragon turning against her. "It didn't feel right. Something's wrong."

"A portent." Cassia kept looking at Hannah's mirror, so she finally lowered her eyes to look at it, too.

Nothing had changed, and Hannah's stomach twisted harder. Same message. Needing to get it out of her sight, Hannah scooped up her vial, grabbed the mirror around the handle, and tilted it so that the crystals tinkled back into their container. Every last one of them as always.

When she'd corked and put the vial into her backpack, she reached for the mirror, but Cassia clasped her fingers around Hannah's hand.

"Wait." Cassia released her and Hannah left the mirror on the floor. "We need to speak to the Dragons."

Hannah sat back, her hands resting on her knees, still sitting cross-legged on the floor. She took a deep breath and concentrated on gaining her composure. "What do we need to do?"

"A spell." Cassia cast a circle around them, using her sparking magic and chanting a simple circle-casting spell.

When she finished, she sat beside Kael, cross-legged like Hannah. Cassia braced her palms on her knees just as Hannah had done before speaking.

> *Dragons of darkness and destruction,*
> *we seek your wise counsel and your instruction.*
> *Cassia and Hannah of the D'Anu*
> *ask for your assistance true.*
> *We greet you, Dragons immortal and wise,*
> *Dragons of fire, earth, water, and skies.*
>
> *To block all that is evil is our will.*
> *Your powers are our desires that you fill.*
> *Our loyalty to you, the ancient and wise,*
> *Dragons of fire, earth, water, and skies.*
> *For guiding and protecting we*
> *who love and respect you. So mote it be.*

As soon as Cassia said the last words, the Dragons on the mirror's frame began to move in a circle.

Hannah's heart pounded harder. The black glass of the mirror turned smoky gray, something that had never happened before.

The Dragons swirled faster.

Smoke rose from the mirror, smells of burning wood and ashes rising in the air.

Faster they spun.

Faster.

The mirror splintered, glass exploding in the full radius of the circle Cassia had cast.

Banshee shrieked.

Kael howled.

Hannah threw up her arm to protect her eyes.

She felt nothing, no glass slicing into her body.

She lowered her arm when silence followed the sound of shattering glass and she looked down.

The mirror's black glass was gone. All that remained was the blank, plain frame. The Dragons had vanished, too.

Hannah's whole body trembled and the backs of her eyes burned with tears that could never come. How could the Dragons have abandoned her? What had she done? Why had they left?

Cassia's quiet voice caused Hannah to look up and meet the half-Elvin witch's gaze. "This can be interpreted two ways."

Through the buzzing in Hannah's ears, she barely heard Cassia continue. "Either the Dragons have left to fight for you. Or they have gone to fight for Ceithlenn."

Hannah pushed herself to her feet and walked away, breaking the circle, and feeling shattered to her core.

GARRAN RUBBED HIS TEMPLES. He had no idea how in the name of all the gods he was going to explain what had happened at Alcatraz. The simple fact was, he couldn't.

"They're gone." Rhiannon looked incredulous as she stared at him. She snapped her fingers in the air. "Just like that?"

All of the gray magic D'Anu witches and leaders of the D'Danann warriors had gathered in a newly built common room in the warehouse, as well as Jake Macgregor. Every one of them stared at Garran and Hannah, waiting for a full explanation of what had occurred at the cavern on Alcatraz.

Garran raised his head and let his hand fall from his temple to his side. "As I said when we returned, I can tell you no more than the fact that the demons are gone. They have been sent back to Underworld."

Jake nodded. "We saw for ourselves that the Alcatraz cavern is empty. The Fomorii are gone."

"Not all of them," Hannah said, and Garran cut his attention to her, his body heating at her words. "I just scried and learned that, like we thought, demons are in the city, occupying the bodies of people in high positions. Military. Government. Business." She looked at Jake Macgregor. "Law enforcement." Then she sucked in her breath. "But not as few as we figured. Almost half the original number of Fomorii are here. In the city."

"Fuck." Jake's hands curled into fists. "That's what's been going on. Why things coming down from the top officials don't make sense."

Numbness spread its way through Garran as he stared at Hannah. "Are you certain?"

"Not one single doubt in my mind." If anything, Hannah was impossibly paler, as if all the blood had left her face. "All we can do is prepare for another war. This one's going to be a lot harder to fight."

Hannah explained her divinations, but Garran had a feeling she was leaving something out. Perhaps many things.

When she finished, the witches, warriors, and Jake fired questions at her. She answered all of them with her usual composure and grace. The witches discussed how Hannah's divination connected with theirs from the day prior and asked Hannah if she had additional signs of anything that might happen to her or Garran.

Garran's gaze shot to Hannah. "What are they speaking about?"

"The other night." She briefly met his eyes before looking away from him. "We scried about you and I going to Alcatraz, only we didn't understand it at the time."

"Anything else?" Cassia said quietly as she stroked her wolf.

Hannah avoided Cassia's eyes and shook her head. "Nothing."

Garran narrowed his brows as he looked from Cassia to Hannah. Something was not right. Hannah was lying and Cassia knew it.

As soon as those in the common room had broken into groups to work on various strategies, Garran grabbed Hannah's hand and dragged her down a corridor between a few of the newly built rooms.

Fire simmered under his skin as he sensed her lies. She stumbled when he pulled her down the corridor. When they reached the end of the hallway, she yanked her hand away from his grip and glared up at him.

"What in the name of the Ancestors is your problem?" A little color had returned to stain her cheeks, the red looking bright compared to how pale the rest of her face was.

He narrowed his gaze. "You lied when you were asked if you had scried anything about your future."

Hannah folded her arms across her chest and looked away. "I don't have anything else to say about it."

Garran took her by the shoulders and gripped them tight enough that she returned her gaze to his. "Tell me what else you saw."

Her lips firmed as she tried to jerk out of his hold. "I've told everyone what's relevant to our battle against Ceithlenn. I've hidden nothing important."

She looked away again and he released her shoulders to clasp her face in his hands and forced her to look at him. "Do not lie to me."

Fire sparked in her gaze. She wrapped her fingers around his wrists and tried to pull his hands from her face. "I don't owe you anything, Garran. Don't even think you can tell me what to do."

Garran did the only thing he could think of to let her

know just how much he cared about her and wanted to be there for her. He held her face in his hands and brought his lips hard to her mouth.

At first she fought him, trying to pull his hands from her face, and kicked one of his shins.

Then to his surprise, she began kissing him back with such need and ferocity he could sense every emotion roiling inside her. Anger, fear, hurt.

Why did she feel hurt? The other emotions concerned him, but he did not understand that one.

Hannah released his wrists and wrapped her arms around his neck like she needed something to hold on to. Something to anchor her. He pressed his body against hers as he backed her up against a wall. He moved his hands from her cheeks into her soft hair.

So much fire. So much beauty.

The need to keep her safe so that she would never feel hurt again was so strong his skin burned with it.

Soft moaning sounds rose up from her and she delved her tongue into his mouth then bit his lower lip hard enough that he felt a quick moment of sharp pain. It vanished as she thrust her tongue into his mouth again.

Garran forced himself back to reality, back to what he needed to find out from her. He tore his mouth from hers and slipped his fingers from her hair until his hands rested on her hips. Her lips were moist as she looked up at him with her lovely brown eyes, and she still had her hands linked behind his neck.

"What happened, sweet one?" he asked as he studied her.

Hannah's throat worked and he thought for a moment she was going to refuse him. "They're gone." This time the hurt he had sensed was in her voice, in her eyes. "The Dragons left me. I think—I think I've lost my power to scry."

CHAPTER TWENTY

THE PAIN INSIDE HANNAH'S chest felt as if one of the Dragons had eaten her heart before it abandoned her. Saying the words aloud made her feel naked, stripped bare to her soul.

She pressed her forehead against Garran's shirt and held on to him, not wanting to let go. She wanted him to hold her forever so that she didn't have to face the stark pain of the truth.

The Dragons had left her. Scrying with her mirror had been her only method of divination since she was an apprentice witch, when her grandmother gave her the tools.

Now she had nothing.

Garran was quiet as he embraced her, holding her close, but he couldn't hug her tight enough to chase away the pain.

She clenched her dry eyes shut, but the images of her mirror shattering and the empty frame battered the inside of her mind. What had she done for them to leave her like they had?

Garran stroked her hair, whispering soft words that could only be Elvin. Words of power that flowed through her and lessened her pain until she felt like a boat rocking with soft swells of water beneath her.

Then a new burst of pain slammed down on her that his words couldn't protect her from. For a moment she felt like she was drowning in that water that had been rocking her so gently.

"Hannah." Garran said her name loud enough to drag her from the feeling of being underwater. His sensual Elvin accent drew her. "Look at me."

She didn't want to, but she forced herself to tilt her head and look up at him. His expression, his eyes, seemed to carry part of her pain. She didn't want that. Didn't need anyone to bear this burden for her.

"I'll be all right." She slid her hands down his chest and felt his warmth, his strength, beneath her palms. He smelled so good. Of earth and moss. So grounding and real. She tried a smile, but it didn't work. "I'll figure something out."

"Together." He stroked her face, his expression intent. "But you must tell me what happened."

The day had passed so quickly. The sun was setting, the last rays of sunlight fading away so that the dark windows of the building grew darker and the only illumination came from the warehouse lights above. As she watched Garran, his hair gradually changed until it was silvery-blue, and his skin returned to the bluish gray of the Drow.

She reached up and slid her fingers through some of his long hair lying over one of his shoulders. "I don't want to talk about it now. I just want—need—to rest before we go out on patrol."

His liquid silver eyes remained focused on hers. "For now. Then you will tell me everything."

The weights holding Hannah down were lifted away as he wrapped his arm around her shoulders and started leading her through the maze of rooms to the one they had slept in before.

With no ceiling, the room was still fairly bright. The lights would not be dimmed or turned off until well into the night when everyone needed to rest. In the almost bare room was a pair of rolled-up sleeping bags, Garran's leather clothing, sword, and chest straps. And her pack.

An ache the size of a softball welled up in her throat at the sight of her pack lying next to a pile of her clothing.

Hannah wanted to turn and run the moment she saw it.

She'd left the pack in the room when she walked away

from the broken mirror and the circle. Cassia must have gathered everything together. Hannah glanced away, not wanting to look at it.

"I am sorry to leave you, sweet one." Garran brought her around to face him again and he looked genuinely concerned. "You rest. I must go back to my realm to attend to matters there. It will most likely be morning before I return."

The thought of Garran leaving created a strange sort of hollowness in her belly. But with him gone, it would give her time to do what she needed to. He'd never let her do it alone, and as far as she was concerned, now she had no choice. She had no other way to be of use to her Coven. To humanity.

Hannah took a deep breath, centering herself, drawing on her ability to maintain an air of calm despite the fact she felt anything but. She forced herself to relax her muscles as much as she could.

Together, once she showed him how, they flattened each of the sleeping bags to make a full-sized "bed" with one bag on top of the other. Even though they'd only spent one night together, the arrangement—the two of them sharing a bed—seemed right, for now.

When her thoughts went back to him leaving for the night, her belly clenched. She'd scried him being in some kind of danger, but had believed it was in the future. What if he was heading into that danger now?

Should she go with him? Or try and convene with the goddess Anu, as she planned?

Her heart pounded and her thoughts whirled. It was all so confusing, her mind felt like it was going to fly apart.

Hannah sucked in another deep breath of air as Garran started to strip out of his human clothing to put on his warrior's gear. She knew what she needed, wanted to do, right then and there. She could give him a part of herself to help protect him. After she kicked her running shoes aside and tugged off her socks, she unbuttoned her jeans.

Garran had pulled his boots off, yanked his T-shirt over his head, then stilled when he caught sight of her. She kept her gaze on him as she unzipped her jeans, dropped them to her ankles, and pushed them aside.

His throat worked and his muscles flexed as she pulled her T-shirt over her head, tossed it aside, leaving her in only her bra and panties. She unhooked her bra and flung it on the floor before easing her panties down and stepping out of them.

It was obvious by the darkness in his eyes and the intent expression on his face that he wanted her. The tightness in her nipples and the slickness between her thighs grew until the need for Garran was so great she could almost forget everything else.

"I should be leaving." His voice was a husky growl as he unfastened the top button of his jeans. His erection was already a huge outline against the tough cotton material.

"Stay." She took a step toward him. "Just a little while."

It didn't take him more than two seconds to shove down his jeans, kick them aside, and face her in all his naked glory. His silvery-blue hair brushing his shoulders, his bluish-gray skin tightening over rippling muscles, his long thick cock rigid and ready for her.

He was magnificent.

Before she could catch her breath, he reached her and gathered her in his embrace.

Hannah wrapped her arms around his neck and her thighs around his waist as he carried her to the sleeping bags. His thick erection was snug against her belly, making her insides twirl like crazy.

And the expression in his eyes—she'd never had anyone look at her like that before. Like she was the world to him. It didn't matter that it was just sex. For now she could slip into this feeling of being wanted and desired and needed.

Garran settled Hannah on her back, his hips firmly between her thighs as he pressed his weight on her, just enough that she felt protected from the outside world.

Garran brought his mouth to hers and rubbed the length of his erection against her slick folds.

Hannah almost said, "I need you," before she bit it back.

If she didn't need him, though, then what were these feelings rolling through her? Lust? Or something more?

She refused to let any other thoughts cross her mind save for the way Garran was making her body feel right at that moment.

He moved his mouth over hers, kissing her so thoroughly her head spun.

More. She wanted more. And he seemed to sense exactly what it was that she had to have at that moment.

He adjusted himself so that his cock was at the opening of her core, then slid slowly inside her.

A cross between a sigh and a moan escaped Hannah as he gently began to rock inside her. She looked up into his intense eyes as his long, silvery-blue hair slid over her skin, brushing her cheeks and her shoulders.

So slowly he moved, his body feeling almost as if it were a part of hers. She kept her thighs hooked around his hips and gripped his shoulders as she closed her eyes. Focused on the sensations.

And released her magic.

Garran made a sound of surprise as she released her essence, letting a part of herself go to help strengthen him, to help protect him.

He stilled and she opened her eyes. "Don't stop," she whispered. Her green magic glittered around them like a sparkling cloud.

"What are you doing, Hannah?" He remained motionless, deep inside her, his brow furrowed.

"Sharing myself with you." She moved her hands from his powerful shoulders until she was gripping his ass and pressed her hips tighter to his. "Let me."

Garran kept still as he looked down at her. "Only if I can do the same for you."

Before Hannah could respond, Garran let warmth flood from his body to hers and he began sliding in and out with firm, solid strokes. She gasped and cried out at the intensity of the feelings he unleashed inside her. What had been sparkling green around them blended into a fabric of both darkness and light, like the sphere that had carried them back from Alcatraz. Dark and beautiful all at once.

The darkness didn't scare her. It intrigued her and she embraced it, letting it join with her own magic.

The power they created together was beyond anything Hannah had ever imagined. It filled her soul, her heart—her entire being was energized and alive just from the combination of their magic.

She gave him as much as she could of her own essence but every time she did, he would give her just as much of himself. It wasn't draining, it was exciting, thrilling, exhilarating. Enough so that she could only think of him and nothing else. Nothing seemed to exist outside of Garran and her, their bodies and their magic.

His thrusts became harder and more powerful and Hannah gave a small cry every time he drove deep inside her, almost touching her magical core itself.

Warmth and protection flowed around them, a cocoon of pleasure that raised Hannah higher and higher until she thought they might be floating in the air.

Garran's expression tightened at the same time her climax began to spiral and spiral inside her, coming closer to the edge of what felt as if it would be nothing short of an explosion.

Their combined magic had an erotic scent to it. Not just the smells of sex but something deeper and more fulfilling. Frankincense. Honeysuckle. Mint.

Hannah started to writhe beneath Garran, unable to control the magic wanting to burst from every nerve ending in her body. He kissed her, putting power into his kiss, and it was like setting off fireworks inside of her.

She cried out and he stole the cry with an even harder kiss that made the climax tearing through her more extreme. The combination of their magic made the experience so heady, as if at that moment they were more powerful together than they could ever be alone.

Garran shouted as her core continued to contract around his erection. His cock throbbed inside her and she clamped down with her inner muscles, making him give another groan as he pressed his hips tightly to hers and remained motionless.

He braced his arms to either side of her head and held himself up as her mind spun and she tried to focus on his eyes.

Hannah sighed and wrapped her arms around his neck, drawing him to her so that their lips met and he kissed her sweet and slow. Every movement of his lips and tongue caused her core to spasm. She felt so much pleasure that it filled her as if she would never feel pain again.

When Garran drew away, separating their bodies, the real world came crashing back down on her. The connection they'd just made barely cushioned the blow of the memories of what she'd lost today, and what was horrible and wrong in the future.

Garran settled on his side and brushed his knuckles over her face. "When I return, you will talk with me about what troubles you."

She pushed herself to a sitting position as he stood and he took her hand to help her to her feet. Ignoring his statement, she said, "You need to get back to your people."

He grabbed his leather pants. "And you need rest."

Garran would be safe there while she did what she had to do.

She almost reached for her discarded clothing, but she didn't want him to suspect anything, so she picked up one of her red robes instead and slipped it on. "When will you be back?"

He was jerking on his boots. "Before the sun rises."

Hannah nodded.

So would she.

CHAPTER TWENTY-ONE

GARRAN ENTERED HIS THRONE room through the obsidian door to find his First and Second, Vidar and Carden, seated with the two head members of the Directorate, Sepan and Hark. They occupied one end of the large oval strategy table.

The only others in the room were the guards stationed to either side of the door leading into the great hall. Familiar scents of his world met Garran. Earth and minerals carried on a cool breeze coming from the hall.

The sharp words "He should have returned by now," from Sepan, and "What is this madness we are to lend our efforts to?" from Vidar, met his ears as he stepped into the room, and a slow burn began in his chest.

Four chairs scraped the floor as the men stood and each bowed. Varying expressions of respect, concern, and anger were reflected on the faces before him.

"Be seated." Garran took the chair at the head of the table that Vidar had vacated at once, and settled into it as he braced his arms on the granite tabletop. He maintained his calm as he looked from man to man. "How go preparations to aid in the war against Ceithlenn?"

Vidar's disapproving expression was too easy to read. He would not be a good ruler.

Garran resisted grinding his teeth as the burn in his chest became greater.

"Carden has our forces prepared." Vidar leaned back in his chair and folded his arms, an angry, judging posture, causing Garran to narrow his eyes. "Our warriors are ready to do your bidding as soon as you command them to," Vidar added.

Keeping his expression neutral, Garran leveled a long stare at the dark-haired, dark-eyed, fierce warrior who did not back down from his obvious disapproval of Garran's decision to aid in the war against the goddess and demons.

Yes, he would deal with Vidar once they were alone.

Garran's gaze settled on Carden, who had a much more balanced view on most subjects and who was far more respectful. Not to mention he was strong in belief and honorable to the core. Was it too late to replace Vidar with Carden as Steward?

"What brings the Directorate to speak with my First and Second?" Garran said as he looked from Hark's blue eyes to Sepan's gray ones.

Sepan's gray eyes narrowed. "We believed it necessary to convene to discuss the possibility of your failure to return."

Garran studied him for a long moment, then slowly nodded. "This is good. The Directorate and my highest in command should always be prepared for the worst."

His words shocked the four men at the table into silence, which Garran easily filled. "I have been working with the D'Danann, D'Anu witches, and the human law enforcement, the Alliance, to strategize and find a way to eliminate Ceithlenn and the demons."

He looked from one man to the other as he continued, his gut churning at the realization that at least once more he would be forced to use the power the Great Guardian had gifted him with. "Half of the Fomorii have been returned to Underworld." He barely held back a frustrated sigh. "The other half remain in the San Francisco Otherworld."

Hark's gaze widened. "How was it that such a large portion of the Fomorii were returned to Underworld?"

"It does not matter, it is done." Garran maintained his regal position. "What is important now is that the Drow are prepared to fight the Fomorii who remain. It has been divined by the D'Anu witches that a great battle will take place. We will honor our promise and fight by the sides of those we are pledged to."

"A pledge you made without consulting the Directorate." Sepan's voice had a sharper bite to it than was appropriate.

To make his point even clearer, Garran firmed his expression and hardened his tone as he spoke to Sepan. "Lest you have forgotten, I am king." The burn in Garran's chest had spread along his skin. "Make no mistake, Sepan, the Directorate is here to advise should I require it. But the final decisions lie with me."

The older Drow did not back down. "You never gave us the opportunity to advise."

"That is correct." Garran inclined his head in acknowledgment. "I sought counsel with the Great Guardian."

Another silence filled the room and Garran could imagine the crystal walls ringing with that silence. Shock registered on every face in the room.

"You would seek counsel with one of the Light Elves before your Directorate?" Sepan finally sputtered as he leaned back in his chair. "She, above all, could have changed the Elders' minds before they placed the curse over us."

"I still have much respect for the Guardian." Garran kept his temper in check, holding back the fire in his gut. "She requested my audience. I accepted and I chose to follow her wisdom." His eyes remained on Sepan. "All of the Directorate is well aware that when the Great Guardian speaks, it is best to listen."

"That is so," Hark said in his calm tone, as Sepan snapped his gaze to the other member of the Directorate. "She above all is revered."

If it were not for her insistence that he tell no one of the "gift," he would have explained it to his men, but she had made it clear that was not an option.

Garran looked to the two leaders of his Directorate.

"Now I must speak to my First and Second, if you will excuse us."

Sepan still had an entirely unacceptable angry glint to his eyes as he stalked out the door. Garran would deal with him later. Hark merely bowed and left the room.

While the two members of the Directorate exited, Garran allowed himself to mentally touch the link established between himself and Hannah. Now that they had traded essences, Garran could feel Hannah, sense her deep in his gut. But at that moment the link seemed weaker than it had before he had entered the Drow realm. He brushed aside the weakening as a result of his trip back to Otherworld.

When only Carden and Vidar remained, Garran eased back, rested his elbows on his chair's arms and folded his hands on his belly. "What has occurred in my absence?"

As Vidar was First in Command, Carden did not speak—the warrior looked to Vidar to give the report.

"The legions wonder why you left the Drow realm and why we are going to war," Vidar said, his black eyes narrowed.

Garran's chest tightened and he could barely leash the fire in his body. He leaned forward and braced his arms on the table again, this time making no pretense of his displeasure with Vidar.

"And who would have informed the legions of my activities?" Garran nearly bared his teeth. "As my Steward it is your responsibility to keep the legions battle-ready and confident in their leader and his choices."

Vidar raised his chin. "My lord—"

"It is unacceptable that the legions should feel any other way." He narrowed his brows. "You and I have much to discuss after Carden reports to me."

The angry spark in Vidar's eyes wavered. "Yes, my lord."

Garran turned to Carden. "Tell me of the legions' preparations."

Carden was a confident yet respectful warrior, who was several centuries younger than Garran. Carden's blue eyes met Garran's. "All have been practicing for battle daily and are fit and ready to do as you bid." He described the activities of the Dark Elves in detail.

"Good." Garran gave him a nod of approval. "You and I will converse later. For now leave us. Wait in the great hall and I will call for you."

Carden stood and bowed before striding out of the room. Garran excused the guards as well, instructing them to remain out of the throne room but to stay beside the doors.

Garran pushed his chair away from the table, the scratch of the legs against the granite floor loud in the silence. He got to his feet and began pacing the room, his gaze landing on Vidar's arrogant one from time to time.

"My king—" Vidar started when Garran said nothing.

"Silence." Garran's voice was a low roar as he stopped his pacing and riveted his attention on the other warrior. "I have failed. Not only in training, but in choice. You are not fit to serve as Steward in my absence or serve as king should I die and pass to Summerland."

Shock crossed Vidar's features and his skin tinged to a paler shade of blue. He pushed himself up to stand and opened his mouth.

Garran held up his hand, silencing the warrior at the same time he gave him a fierce look. "Sit."

Vidar dropped back into his seat, the thump of the chair loud enough to echo in the chamber.

"These past days, you have proven to me you are not capable of leading our people." Garran walked up to Vidar, resisting the urge to grab the man by the throat with one hand and bring him to his feet. "Carden shall serve as my First and as Steward. I will reassign you to a position more befitting your temper and your failure to respect the needs of your people and the wishes of your king."

Vidar shoved back his chair and stood, his eyes flaring. "You cannot do this."

Garran let another low growl rumble out of his throat. "The gods bear witness to my word and you will not question it any further. You will return to your quarters until my decision has been made as to where you will now serve."

For a moment Vidar stared at him, his hand twitching at his side. Garran rested his palm on the hilt of his sword. He could best Vidar and ten other warriors at one time if it ever proved necessary.

Jaw tensed, Vidar gave a stiff bow, whirled, and strode from the room.

As soon as the warrior left, Garran felt a lessening in the tightness of his chest. He did not doubt his decision to make Carden his First. But what he deplored was his own arrogance in not training a suitable replacement *immediately* after Naal's death, and in not recognizing earlier, or perhaps admitting, that Vidar would have been a poor ruler.

Garran summoned Carden. When the younger warrior walked into the room, his stance was proud, and his presence powerful, but respectful.

Carden lowered his eyes before returning his gaze to Garran's. "My king."

"You will now serve as my First." Garran faced away from the warrior as he climbed the small dais and sat in his throne. Carden's stunned expression greeted Garran when he turned around to recline in his throne.

"My lord?" Carden said.

"I will convene the Directorate immediately and notify them of my decision." Garran reclined in his throne and rested one elbow on the chair's arm, stroking his chin with his fingers. "I will have them see to furthering your training so that you might serve in my stead if something should befall me."

Carden looked too shocked to speak.

"What do you have to say to this duty that I bestow on you?" Garran asked, waiting to gauge Carden's reaction.

The warrior gave a bow before straightening and facing Garran. A noticeable change came over the younger Drow—one that reassured Garran he had made the right decision. Not that he had questioned it once he had realized what had to be done.

Carden's voice was deep, confident. "I will serve our people well during your absence and as your First when you return."

Garran gave a low nod. "Instruct one of the guards to summon the Directorate to convene at once."

His new First in Command obeyed immediately and it was not long before the Directorate gathered around the strategy table. For the most part the expression of each member of the Directorate was serene, noncommittal, non-judgmental, despite what each man may have truly been feeling. Only Sepan's face was openly disapproving.

Carden was the sole warrior in the room and he remained standing at Garran's side when he seated himself at the head of the table.

Garran announced his decision to make Carden First in Command and Steward in his absence. "I shall have you each swear fealty to him should something befall me and I pass on to Summerland."

The silence only lasted a moment before Hark looked directly at Garran. "A wise choice, my king."

While everyone in the Directorate looked on, Hark stood. He withdrew his sword, went to Carden, knelt and laid his sword at the warrior's feet. "You have my loyal service and guidance as Steward in King Garran's absence. If he should pass on to Summerland, I will serve you when you are King of the Dark Elves." He retrieved his sword, sheathed it, and returned to his seat.

Garran looked on in approval as every member of the Directorate repeated the action. The rightness of his decision flowed through Garran like a smooth river that cooled the heat that had burned under his skin since arriving back in his realm.

Carden looked every bit the leader. Tall, proud, yet accepting each man's sworn fealty with a graceful nod.

Sepan was the last to approach Carden. Sepan's expression was unreadable, which pleased Garran. It would not do for any member of the Directorate to show disapproval.

Sepan finished, and all of the Directorate seated themselves. Garran opened his mouth to speak when a sudden feeling like a knife slicing into his gut caused him to grip the armrests of the chair so tightly his knuckles make cracking sounds.

He steeled his expression as sweat broke out on his face and the room faded. His connection to Hannah felt as if it were being stretched so thin that it would be ripped from him. He sensed and felt her anger, fear, pain, anguish, and he was nearly blinded by it.

"My king?" Carden's voice jerked Garran back to the present even though Hannah's emotions roiled through him as if they were his own.

"I must go." Garran pushed his chair back, and everyone stood with him.

"My lord—" Sepan started.

Garran cut him short. "See to Carden's training at once. And find a suitable position for Vidar, one that will not humiliate him, if at all possible."

Before anyone could respond, Garran turned his back on them, strode across the room and through the black granite door.

He slammed it behind him, stood on the transference stone, and focused on his tie to Hannah and her emotions to take him to her.

CHAPTER TWENTY-TWO

AFTER PAYING THE TAXI driver and watching him until the red of his taillights vanished, Hannah walked alongside the road in the darkness.

Small rocks shifted and crunched beneath her running shoes and she hefted her pack higher on her shoulder. She continued until she reached the hidden road that would take her to the sacred stretch of beach known only to the D'Anu witches.

City lights glittered behind her, and to the north stretched the beautiful Golden Gate Bridge as it carried its much lighter than normal traffic to and from Marin County. To the east of the bridge was Alcatraz, but right now she didn't want to think about the horrors that had manifested below it. Or the fact that the demons weren't all gone from the city yet. Somehow the rest of the demons had to be eliminated. If only she knew how the first bunch had been sent back to Underworld.

Right here, right now, breathing in the salt of the ocean, smelling the nearby cypress, feeling the clean air blowing in off the water across her face and lifting her hair, and hearing the slam of waves against the shore, all seemed so ordinary, solid, real. How could bizarre and horrible things be happening while such normalcy surrounded her?

But the pack over Hannah's shoulder felt alien now that her scrying tools had been destroyed. The pack weighed her down enough that she felt as if she would tip over. And she knew that feeling wasn't from the extra contents now filling it.

She hadn't wanted to touch the pack, but she needed it to carry the other tools for the ceremony she had to perform. The vial and the broken, empty frame remained buried at the bottom of the bag—apparently put there by Cassia. Hannah hadn't been able to get herself to pull them out and throw them away—to even touch them.

Dragons had always been with her, especially Fire Dragons. Why then had her mirror Dragons left her? Why had the mirror shattered?

Hannah spun a ball of green magic in her palm to help light the way as she took one step after another down the short twisting road. She missed Banshee, and would have sneaked him out with her if it wasn't for the fact that a taxi driver wasn't likely to be too happy with a falcon in his cab. It had been all she could do to take the necessary supplies from the kitchen and slip out of the warehouse without waking up any of the other witches.

The D'Danann who'd guarded the doors leading outside— she'd been shocked her glamour worked against them because a witch's glamour normally only worked with humans. But apparently Garran's magic infused with her own allowed her to pass by the warrior Fae undetected.

Hannah tried to force down the hard lump that had taken permanent residence in her throat as she came to the footpath veering away from the hidden road. Even with only the gentle light of her magic, she was sure-footed, walking without conscious thought. Instead, images of her scrying mirror shattering and the Dragons leaving battered her mind.

The time she had spent with Garran was the only thing that had soothed her. She had wanted to give to him, to protect him, but he wouldn't take without giving back. Had he lost any of his personal magical strength? She hoped to the goddess not.

Hannah had shared enough of her magic that she'd

weakened herself, which was one reason why she had come to this place of power. Not only did she need to convene with the goddess and the Elementals, she needed to rejuvenate.

Sand shifted beneath Hannah's running shoes and made soft sounds as she walked across the smooth beach that looked completely untouched. No other D'Anu had been here recently. Gentle waves rolled in from the ocean, licking the shore before curling back in on themselves and striking again. Kelp and seashells lay scattered on the shore just above the waterline.

Garran's dark magic stirred inside her as she approached the place where she would perform her ceremony. She didn't fully know how to use it, wasn't sure she should, but his magic was there, waiting.

For a moment she could almost sympathize with Rhiannon, who had fought so long, so hard, against the Drow magic she'd been born with. The dark Elvin power inside Hannah was frightening yet exciting all at once as it stirred like a living thing, churning in her soul and infusing her with its warmth.

When she reached the middle of the beach, Hannah sucked in her breath and dropped her pack. It felt good to be here, to stand beneath the night sky with the new moon hiding behind the fog. The power of the place hummed through her heart and soul.

Hannah set her ball of light on a boulder so that it illuminated the mostly dark beach and she kept a little of her magical focus on it to keep it glowing. She crouched and dug inside her pack for the tools of her craft, making sure not to reach too low and brush her hand over her former scrying mirror. She'd thrown an extra robe on top of both it and the vial of salt crystals, just so she wouldn't have to touch them.

First thing that came to her hand was her small ceremonial sword. She set it on the sand and drew out six candles. Four to set at the cardinal points of the circle and two to perform the ceremony.

She followed that by filling a chalice with water from the ocean, offering a prayer for the Water Dragon's permission.

She then filled a vial with sand, asking the Earth Dragon's permission.

She asked the Fire Dragon to light her myrrh incense and for a moment nothing happened, causing an instant of panic to rise within Hannah. Then the cone of incense began to burn in its Dragon holder, the scent of myrrh rising up to meet her, and she blew out her breath in relief.

Lastly, Hannah coated her body with the frankincense oil and asked the Air Dragon to bless it. A wind whipped up like a small zephyr, flowing over her body in response.

When she was finished, Hannah felt a little relief as she drew out one of the two robes she had brought with her. Her heart clenched again and she held the robe crunched in her fists as she stared out at the ocean. Her heart pounded so hard she felt it throughout her body. Even her eyes ached.

What if the Dragons didn't come? Even though they had graced her by fulfilling her requests in preparing for the ritual, that didn't mean they would actually come.

What if they were to forsake her, too?

Fear had never been a feeling Hannah had allowed. She'd worked too hard to become who she was. Strong. Confident. Controlled.

Right now she felt anything but. At this moment it was like she was that same scared young girl with fear pounding in her veins as she waited for her mother to turn her over to her birth father.

But that had ended up being the best thing that had happened to that point in her life. She had been introduced to her D'Anu heritage and had been embraced like family.

Hannah took off her socks and shoes, careful to avoid getting too much sand in them. She did the same as she stripped out of her clothing, folding everything neatly, until she was naked. She shivered in the cold wind off the ocean, but being a D'Anu witch took away some of the chill, and Garran's magic reduced it even further.

She reached for her red robe and wrapped it around herself, the material soft and smooth against her skin. The moon and crescent armband felt cool against her upper arm, the band the only other thing she was wearing.

When she had all of her tools set up, including her altar, candles at the cardinal points, and had the other items prepared, she stood and stared out at the ocean. She glanced down and slipped her robe off her shoulders and dropped it so that it was a red streak against the gray sand beneath her feet.

Sand slid between her toes and her nipples tightened in the burst of icy air that sluiced over her bare skin. She shivered and picked up her ceremonial sword, unsheathed it, and set the sheath aside. It was small enough that she could carry it in her pack when needed, and not too heavy to use while performing her Dragon ceremonies.

Even so, her arm shook as she raised it and pointed the sword to the east and began to cast her circle with a simple circle-casting chant, starting with asking the Air Elementals for aid. The blue candle for air flamed to life at the east point of the circle. The power of her magic was strong enough that the flame didn't flicker in the wind but burned straight and true.

She moved her sword so that she faced south and her stomach twisted as she called upon the Fire Elementals to light the candle. Relief lessened the knot in her belly when the flame sprouted and didn't waver in the wind.

Hannah continued, pointing her sword to the west. The Water Elementals answered her call, followed by the Earth Elementals when she directed her sword north.

When she finished casting the circle, her heart beat faster. Time to call the Dragons. She paused to thank the goddess Anu and tipped her head back to draw in what power the goddess would lend her.

To her relief, Anu sent some of her strength to Hannah, infusing her body with magic that sent tingles skittering over her skin. When the goddess's power touched what magic Garran had given her, Hannah sensed hesitation, as if the goddess disapproved. But then Hannah's body was encased with strength, strength she would need to call the Dragons.

She thanked Anu and began her chant to bring forth the Dragons.

Standing in the center of the circle, she closed her eyes and crossed her arms over her chest, still holding the sword in one hand, so that she looked like the statue of Isis. She chanted:

Dragons of Earth, Fire, Wind, and Sea,
As your servant I beg you to answer my plea
All-knowing and everlasting, around, within, and
  above,
lend me your strength as I offer you my loyalty and
  love.

Hannah shook not from the cold but from the burning fear in her gut that the Dragons would not answer. She opened her eyes and pointed her sword east. "To me, the purifying power of air, from the Dragon of the East so fair."

She held her breath until golden light glittered before her eyes, then let it ease from her as the wavering form of a glorious golden Dragon appeared. Wind buffeted her body as it swirled from the powerful Elemental and Hannah lowered her sword.

"What seek you, Hannah of the D'Anu?" Instead of a roar, the Dragon's voice was a song on the wind.

She bowed from her shoulders and straightened. "Your guidance. The Dragons that have always been present to assist me when I scry have vanished. My scrying mirror shattered." She hated the tremble in her voice and the loss of confidence. "I don't know what to do."

The Dragon's golden eyes studied her for a long moment. "You must seek the answers inside you, Hannah of the D'Anu. To your own heart you must be true."

She opened her mouth to ask what the great being meant when he vanished into but a few golden sparkles, and then was gone. "Thank you for your words of wisdom." Hannah bowed in the direction the Air Dragon had appeared even though she wasn't so sure about the words or the wisdom. What did the Elemental mean?

Fire Dragons had always been her strength, and her hand shook as she pointed the sword south. "To me, the splendid magical fire power, from the Dragon of the South at this critical hour."

Almost at once flames sprouted from the sand, swirling up until a great red Dragon rose and let out a roar that made Hannah tremble inside and out.

The Dragon spewed flame at Hannah, and a scream rose up in her throat. Only the circle protected her from the fire. Terror scored her like a knife.

Her hand holding the sword lowered to her side as she stared at the Dragon. "Why are you upset with me? How have I displeased you?"

She almost dropped her sword when the Dragon blew flame at her again, this time far more powerfully. And then without a word, the Dragon vanished.

Hannah held in a cry and stumbled back. Sweat rolled down her chilled skin and her entire body shook. She didn't know what to say. Normally she would thank the Dragon for his presence, but she'd never had anything like this happen before when she called on the Dragons for guidance.

Still shaken, she prepared herself for the worst as she turned to the west—afraid that the Water Dragon would ignore her or treat her as the Fire Dragon had. If she had the ability to cry, her face would have been coated with tears.

Wanting to scream, but holding it all inside in a tight ball in her belly, Hannah raised her sword. "To me, the joyous power of water, from the Dragon of the West asks your D'Anu daughter."

From the ocean a great Dragon rolled in with the next wave, raising its head and growing with power as it towered over her. "You have much to fear, Hannah of the D'Anu," came the Dragon's great gurgling voice. "Those of us who would choose to cannot protect you."

"Would you lend me your protection?" Hannah's arm shook as she pointed the sword to the sand.

"Alas, I cannot." The Dragon swiveled its head to where the Fire Dragon had been. "We have been summoned by another far more powerful being who rules both fire and water."

"But—"

The great Dragon shook its head. "Fare thee well, Hannah of the D'Anu."

Her legs wanted to give out as the Water Dragon was swept back out on the waves.

Water and fire. Powerful beings.

The Fomorii were once sea gods, rulers of the water. Ceithlenn was a being with hair of flame—a goddess who must have power over fire.

Hannah almost sank down on the sand. Was there any hope in calling forth the Earth Dragon?

She turned to the north and her hand and voice shook as she held up the sword and spoke. "To me, the magnificent power of Earth, from the Dragon of the north so near my heart."

The ground rumbled. Sand shifted beneath Hannah's feet and she stumbled back a step.

A great green Dragon rose from the earth and sand. When it crouched before her, the Earth Dragon stretched out its tremendous wings and gave a roar like thunder, shaking the ground with its power.

The Dragon lowered its head, weaving back and forth almost like a serpent would and its glowing green eyes nearly mesmerized Hannah.

"Child of Air, Fire, Water, and Earth," the great Dragon rumbled. "It is with great sadness that I see my brethren have forsaken thee."

She simply stared at the Dragon, her lower lip wanting to tremble with the pain of their desertion. The Air Dragon had not deserted her, but had not offered its power, either.

"I will lend you what protection I can," the Earth Dragon said in a low, soothing voice that untied a knot or two from her belly. "But what I have to offer will not see you through your trials. You must find strength in yourself and in those who matter most to you."

The knots retied themselves in her belly and a chill broke out on her skin. Some of the pain faded as the Earth Dragon flapped its massive wings again and a flow of power washed over Hannah. Power that grounded her like the earth itself.

The Earth Dragon's magic combined with her own strained powers, Garran's offerings, and what the Goddess had lent her.

Maybe it would be enough?

It didn't feel like enough.

She clenched the hilt of her ceremonial sword. "With much respect, may I ask who is commanding the Fire and Water Dragons?"

The earth rumbled beneath Hannah's feet and she staggered. "You already know the answer to your question, D'Anu witch."

"Ceithlenn," Hannah whispered.

"I wish you much luck in these coming days, Hannah of the D'Anu." The Earth Dragon settled its wings at its sides and sounded sad as it finished. "Much will be required of you."

The sword fell from Hannah's hand and she watched the Earth Dragon melt back into the sand and vanish.

She dropped to her knees and buried her face in her hands. Oh, goddess, what was she to do?

For what seemed an eternity, she sat there, her dry eyes aching and her heart throbbing, a painful feeling in her chest.

When she had collected herself, gathered her emotions as much as she could, Hannah tugged on her red robe. She took down her circle of protection, started grabbing the tools of her craft, and shoved them into her backpack. Anger tightened the knots in her belly, the anger warring against the hurt, the fear. With the Water and Fire Dragons on Ceithlenn's side, the goddess would be even more powerful than she already was.

She shrugged out of her robe, leaving her naked again. She started to put her T-shirt and jeans on when chilling laughter came from behind her that sent ice down her spine.

She whirled and came face-to-face with Ceithlenn.

The goddess had her claws extended, her hands on her leather-clad hips, her eyes glowing red in the night. Her hair flamed the same color as the Dragon's had earlier, and Ceithlenn spread her batlike wings wide.

Heart pounding so hard she thought her head would explode, Hannah dropped her T-shirt. She raised her hands to throw up a spellshield to protect herself.

Too late!

Ceithlenn spun a red ball of energy around Hannah's naked form that felt like fire burning her skin. She screamed as pain seared her body and she fell to her knees.

Fire licked her as if frying her, yet not. Ceithlenn gave a wicked smile as she watched Hannah.

"D'Anu bitch." The goddess showed her fangs. "If I didn't have special plans for you, I would burn you alive rather than simply inflicting the agony of fire upon you."

Concentrate. Focus. Calm, Hannah attempted to tell herself as she writhed and cried out, trying to get her mind to cooperate as she willed the pain away.

She drew on her own magic, on the Drow powers Garran had given her, on the strength from the goddess Anu, and the magic from the Earth Dragon.

Even as it felt as if her bare flesh were in flames, Hannah managed to wrap herself in the cooling balm of the combined magics, a bubble like the *geodess* forming around her that protected her within the fiery one Ceithlenn had caged her in.

The relief was so great that Hannah collapsed at the bottom of her own bubble of soothing magic. The fire on her skin faded and cool magic rolled over her body.

The dark goddess shrieked, her features contorting and turning even more evil than they already were. The fireball surrounding Hannah's cocoon enlarged.

Sweat from the increasing heat dripped down the side of Hannah's face. So much of her energy had been sapped by Ceithlenn's first attack that it was a struggle to maintain the protection surrounding her.

Ceithlenn planted her hands on her hips and glared at Hannah. "What will be most pleasurable, even more than causing you great pain, is luring your lover to you. And killing him."

Despite the continued heat trying to break through her cocoon, Hannah felt a chill surround her heart. She got to her knees and wrapped her arms across her breasts. "I have no lover."

"I'm not surprised by your desire to protect him." The goddess snorted. "I scried what the Drow king did to my legions and he will pay." She narrowed her evil red eyes and her hair seemed to flame higher. "I will claw out his heart in front of you so that you can watch as he dies."

Horrible images filled Hannah's mind as Ceithlenn continued. "Your so-called 'Alliance' will be busy quite soon with the surprise I have prepared for them while I kill you and the Drow king." The goddess smirked. "It is unfortunate you will not witness the D'Anu deaths at the claws of my demons. Instead you will watch me tear apart your lover."

One thought after another tore through Hannah's soul as terror for Garran and her sister witches screeched through her. What did the goddess have planned for the D'Anu? How could Hannah save them and herself?

Ceithlenn walked closer to the bubble, her hair bright against the foggy sky. She placed her hand against the shield of fire. The goddess bared her fangs.

The evil emanating from her, and the memory of how Ceithlenn ate humans alive, was enough to cause bile to rise in Hannah's throat. The urge to throw up was almost overwhelming.

Hannah swallowed the acid as she tightened her arms across her bare breasts. Still, she kept herself prepared in case she had the opportunity to battle the flame-haired bitch.

Ceithlenn placed both hands on the bubble.

Everything spun.

Hannah couldn't help a scream as the sudden movement slammed her against the side of her protective cocoon. Dark sky, ocean, sand whirled. Fire and blackness all swirled into one dizzying nightmare.

She fell forward when the bubble came to a complete stop. Her mind wouldn't stop spinning and for a moment it was all she could do to maintain her magic shield.

When her mind settled a little, she saw that she was someplace . . . familiar. It took a moment for her scattered senses to realize she was in the observation loggia, the very top of Coit Tower on Telegraph Hill. Instead of the white uncanny glow that always lit the night from the tower, eerie red flooded everything.

The fire sphere was now tall enough for Hannah to stand and she extended her own cocoon, drawing on the power inside her. From the top of the cylindrical tower there was an astounding view of the city and the bay. It had been so long since she'd been here she'd forgotten how incredible the view from the Coit Tower was.

She shook her head, understanding hitting her like a blow to her chest. Ceithlenn had brought her here, an easy trap, a difficult place for her to be rescued—or to escape from.

Red from the flickering flames of the sphere lit the inside of the tower and she gradually realized that Ceithlenn wasn't the only other being there. Hannah's heart knocked against her breastbone when she saw she was surrounded by Fomorii demons salivating and drooling, looking as if they couldn't wait to tear her apart and eat her in tiny pieces. Or large chunks.

When Hannah met Ceithlenn's evil stare, more shock and pain shot through her. The Fire Dragon stood at the goddess's side. The Dragon was normally so enormous that it had to shrink in size to fit inside the tower. The Dragon's red eyes matched Ceithlenn's.

With a roar that reverberated through the night, the

Dragon let loose a stream of fire directly at the sphere surrounding Hannah. The flames joined Ceithlenn's and Hannah screamed as the heat intensified and her cocoon threatened to fail her.

The goddess looked at the Fire Dragon and smiled.

"So it will be," the Dragon said, just before fire shot from its mouth again, engulfing the fire sphere and shattering Hannah's magic.

A louder scream tore from her throat as the fire began burning her alive.

CHAPTER TWENTY-THREE

IT HAD BEEN A hell of a day. Make that a *fucking rotten day*.

Jake clenched the steering wheel of his sports car tighter as he navigated San Francisco streets toward the Alliance's warehouse HQ. He was going to head straight for the weight room and work out until he dropped.

He was sure now that the Fomorii had infiltrated the military and government. "Official" reaction to the current situation only backed that up. Martial law had been lifted as of this evening.

And to top that off, the city government had begun encouraging tourism once again in San Francisco.

"Those responsible have been captured," the officials were saying. *"The threat is gone now that the bioterrorists are locked away."*

Even bogus feed of handcuffed men and women being hauled away in law enforcement vehicles was being shown on news stations around the world.

Jake came to a stop at a streetlight and waited for the red to turn green.

Seeing Kat on the television screen repeating the government's official statements had made everything seem impossibly worse. She'd maintained a reporter's indifferent demeanor as she'd reported the news, and he couldn't help but wonder if a Fomorii had already gotten to her.

Fuck. Jake ground his teeth as the light turned green and he forced the thought from his mind. Kat was okay. She had to be okay.

He wasn't so sure about the safety of the D'Anu "white" witches. They'd been turned out of their safe houses, allowed to return to their homes. The men and women of the Coven were in no way out of danger.

Jake guided his car through the night, closing the distance to the Alliance's warehouse as lights bled by.

Could things get worse, life get more bizarre?

Don't tease God, came the voice of a psychologist in response to Jake's words of a couple of years ago.

Could things get any worse? Jake had said just before he'd left the Corps after that black magic had killed his team.

Apparently they could.

God has some fucking sense of humor.

The fact that he hung out and planned battles with huge men with wings, as well as witches who used spellfire and magic ropes, and now worked with one of the Dark Elves, made him wonder sometimes if he'd lost his sanity. Not to mention dealing with a bitch goddess named Ceithlenn and a shitload of carnivorous demons . . .

Was this what it was like to be locked away in a straitjacket in a white-walled sanitarium while hallucinating?

Don't tease God.

Thoughts of losing his mind aside, he had a pretty good idea of what was going on. No doubt Ceithlenn wanted things to go back to "normal" so that she could have complete access to humans again.

Jake thumped his palm against the steering wheel and ground his teeth harder. Things were getting worse by the moment.

He just about laughed at that understatement of the last couple of centuries.

Jake almost reached headquarters when something flashed red in his rearview and side view mirrors.

Shit.

What now?

He pulled his car over, climbed out in a hurry, and stared up at an eerie red light coming from Coit Tower.

What the hell?

Flashes and sparks erupted from the top and through the upper arched windows. Was the tower on fire?

That's not fire.

Magic. From everything he'd witnessed since working with the D'Anu, he knew magic when he saw it.

Heart rate ratcheting a notch, Jake climbed back into his car. His tires squealed on the asphalt as he spun the vehicle to race through town's maze and up Telegraph Hill. He grabbed the handset for the special radio that he used to contact the warehouse headquarters and called in.

He recognized Cassia's voice as soon as she answered and his heart gave a strange jerk-pull that had nothing to do with the circumstances.

"I need a few warriors at Coit Tower *ASAP*," he practically shouted as he navigated the steep hills on his way.

"Whoever we can spare, we'll send." As usual the half-Elvin witch's voice seemed calm. Too damned calm to suit him. "Some of the Fomorii have attacked the warehouse. Everyone here from the Alliance is fighting off the demons."

"Shit," Jake said before he spoke into the handset again. "Preferably send the D'Danann since they can fly to the top of the tower where the action is."

Cassia said, "I'm heading out now."

As he raced through the city, Jake contacted other PSF officers who weren't staying at the warehouse headquarters 24/7. By the time Jake reached the circular parking lot in front of Coit Tower more red flames and sparks were erupting.

His heart jack hammered even more. The eruptions he saw on top of the Coit Tower were most likely caused by Ceithlenn. He was positive the bitch had set up the Fomorii attack on the Alliance HQ to distract the D'Danann—why, he had no idea.

But I'll sure as hell find out.

The radio crackled and the dispatcher called for units in the vicinity to head to Coit Tower for a possible fire and/or break-in.

Jake radioed in that the PSF was on it and for everyone else to back off.

The dispatcher responded in the negative and said the San Francisco Fire Department was on its way, too.

Jake cursed again and parked as close to the tower as he could.

Didn't these idiots get it yet?

The guys on the SFFD would be just more fodder for Ceithlenn. *Damn!*

He hurried out of his car. More odd flames and sparks flashed at the top of the tower.

His gut churned and he drew his Glock with its special bullets and waited for his officers to arrive. He'd take a few of his men and women with him into the tower and leave the rest to intercept and hopefully turn back—or at least slow down—the regular cops and fire department guys who might just get themselves killed.

Like us.

Like every one of us.

CHAPTER TWENTY-FOUR

BEFORE HE STARTED THE transference, Garran's knees almost buckled at the pain he felt through his link with Hannah.

Fury roared through him. He drew his sword. Caused his dark magic to infuse him, surround him. And followed Hannah's pain from the transference stone.

Red light blinded him. Smells of smoke, fire, and the stench of rotten fish assaulted his senses.

Before he even had the opportunity to assess the situation a ball of fire slammed into the dark shield he had protected himself with.

Hannah. In a ball of flame. Naked. Bare of any protection from the fire.

With a quick sweep of his gaze, he saw that he was in some kind of tower. Fomorii demons surrounded him and Hannah.

Anger arrowed through him as he saw Hannah writhe in the great ball of flame, and he felt the depth of her pain. On the other side of the flames were a Fire Dragon and Ceithlenn. The goddess scowled and flung another fireball at him but it ricocheted off his magic, out of the tower, and exploded, lighting up the dark sky.

Demons dove for Garran, but bounced off the power shielding him. If he did not have the shield up, he could have fought off the demons with his sword, but he would not be protected from Ceithlenn or the Dragon.

Hannah continued to scream and roll in agony in the fire and Garran shook with fury.

Instinct drove him forward. Sword in one fist, he dropped his shield and dove for the ball of flame.

Fire seared his skin as he entered the sphere and the pain he had felt through his connection with Hannah multiplied. His sight blurred as he landed across her legs, bracing his arms and barely keeping his weight from crushing her.

Blocking out as much of the fiery agony as he could, he scooped Hannah in his arms and flung out a dark spell of protection that surrounded them at once, a soothing fabric of magic.

Instantly his body cooled and Hannah stopped screaming. She wrapped her arms around his neck before releasing him at once, as if realizing she did not have time to waste on comfort.

When Hannah was on her feet, he felt her trembling beside him from the power of her pain. From the corner of his eye he saw her hair and naked body were damp from sweat.

Ceithlenn stood outside the bubble and folded her arms in front of her chest. "Now I have both you and the witch," she said, her eyes focused on Garran. "Your powers cannot withstand mine and the Fire Dragon's for long. You will pay for what you have done with my demons."

"No. *You* will pay for all that you have done to the people of this world." Garran prepared himself to use his power gifted to him by the Great Guardian. He might only send a few of the Fomorii to Underworld, but he would rid them of Ceithlenn at the same time he saved Hannah, too.

"Such a cocky Drow bastard." Ceithlenn smirked and walked closer to the fiery sphere. "It seems that I have you at—what would you call it? A disadvantage."

The Guardian's power built within him. He closed his eyelids for just a moment, and as in the cavern, every Fomorii's image and presence firmly imprinted themselves in his mind.

His eyes snapped open and he drew on the power, bringing it from his core and letting the silver magic encase his body so that he glowed with it.

The fiery sphere blew apart into red sparks.

Garran dropped the shield and Fomorii dove for them.

Ceithlenn stumbled backward. "No!" she shouted.

A fraction of a moment before Garran set the Guardian's power free, Ceithlenn wrapped her wings around herself and vanished. Along with the Fire Dragon.

The magic blasted into the Fomorii and, with a thought, Garran sent them all to Underworld.

He felt a moment's triumph at saving Hannah.

A moment's regret at not capturing Ceithlenn.

And a moment's fear at using the power twice—and that he would have to do so a third and final time.

Leaving his people without a trained leader.

All the thoughts raced in his mind right before agony speared his body like a thousand swords. He dropped to the floor of the tower and darkness stole him.

EVERYTHING BOMBARDED HANNAH AT once. The appearance of Garran, the safety and protection of his magic, the fire sphere exploding, Ceithlenn and the Fire Dragon vanishing, blinding silver light—and then the Fomorii demons gone.

Dizziness threatened to overcome her until Garran collapsed.

Hannah cried out and went to her knees beside Garran. She put her hand on his heart and felt instant relief at the strength of its beat. But he was out cold. His skin was clammy and his breathing shallow. The bluish-gray tint of his skin paled so that it was more of a stark bluish white.

The seemingly permanent lump in her throat growing, she held her palms over Garran and let her magic flow to his chest. She put almost everything she had into giving him part of her essence so that she weakened even more.

Nothing. The pallor of his skin didn't change. He didn't move. His chest still rose in shallow puffs.

"Dear Anu." Hannah looked up at the opening at the top

of the tower, up at the night sky. "Please lend me more of your strength to help Garran."

She closed her eyes, but felt nothing.

What was wrong? Why was she failing in so many ways?

Sirens shrieked, and she knew law enforcement would be here soon. She couldn't let them see Garran. A bluish-gray man with silvery-blue hair and pointed ears? Not to mention they were at the top of the tower illegally, and *no one* would believe her story.

"Wake up." She shook Garran's shoulder, hard, but he didn't even stir. "Come on." More urgency infused her voice. "We've got to get out of here."

Not even the flicker of an eyelid.

She whipped her gaze around the tower. They were alone, and she had no idea how she was going to get herself and Garran down from the tower and back to headquarters.

For a brief second, she had the absurd desire to laugh as she thought of herself as Rapunzel, trapped in a tower with no way down. No long hair, either. She did have her magic ropes, but she didn't think she'd ever be able to use them to get Garran down a two hundred foot tall tower, *and* get him back to the warehouse.

The sirens cutting through the night were so close she knew the police had arrived. Hannah peeked out to see police cars approaching and coming to a stop. Strobes flashed red and blue against the white of the tower. The sound of police radios crackling and more sirens met her ears.

Hannah racked her brain. To keep the police from seeing her and Garran, she could hide the two of them with a glamour. With the power Garran had lent her, she was certain the glamour would be strong.

That wouldn't keep police officers from possibly tripping over Garran, though, when they searched the tower. And once the police left, how would she get Garran down? He was too big for her to carry. She looked him over from head to toe. Goddess, was he big.

One thought after another traveled through her head and she discarded each one.

The D'Danann! The great winged Fae warriors could carry Garran with ease.

Could she get their attention? They constantly surveyed the city by flying over it for signs of the Fomorii. As compact as San Francisco was, Coit Tower wasn't that far from the warehouse.

So where were they? The D'Danann should have been investigating the strange activity in the tower by now—all the red magical flames.

What if Ceithlenn came back before she could get Garran out of there?

Knots in her stomach that had never gone away tightened until she thought they might snap. Her flesh still felt as if it were burning and shriveling from the power of the heat that had encased her. She might be imagining it but she thought she smelled smoke mixed with the remnants of the demon's rotten-fish stench.

A sense of urgency rose in her like a hot fountain, bubbling and gurgling and ready to spout out of her. She had to get Garran to Cassia so that she could heal him.

When she got to her feet, Hannah's legs shook enough that for a moment she had to stand still to compose herself. When she was steady enough, she hurried to the side of the tower that looked out in the direction where she'd be able to see the warehouse. The floor was cool beneath her feet and the chill air welcome after what her body had just been through. It was only then that she remembered she was naked. Ceithlenn had caught her at her most vulnerable.

The police car and fire truck flashers were even brighter and she saw a group of firemen breaking into the tower. The fiery sphere was gone, the top of the tower dark, but she was certain they weren't planning on taking any chances.

Another wave of dizziness caused her to hold her hand to

her forehead as she looked down from the two hundred plus height. Not a good idea.

Fear nearly choked her. Goddess! What could she do?

The sensation of someone behind her made her head buzz. With a rush of icy fear Hannah whirled.

Hawk, Keir, and Tiernan.

Relief flooded through Hannah, the ice melting away. The D'Danann had come.

They folded their great feathered wings away so that the wings vanished beneath their shirts.

"What happened?" Hawk said as he knelt beside Garran.

"I'll explain when we get back to headquarters." She glanced toward the stairs that the firemen and cops would use to climb the tower. They wouldn't use the elevator in case of a fire.

Hawk nodded. He and Tiernan picked up Garran's dead weight, Hawk holding Garran under his arms and Tiernan grabbing Garran by his boots. They hoisted Garran, unfurled their wings, and they vanished from sight.

Keir drew off his long black coat and settled it over Hannah's naked shoulders. She stared at him as she pushed her arms through the enormous coat and wrapped it around herself. He kept proving to her he wasn't the barbarian she'd always accused him of being.

She'd been carried by a D'Danann in flight before, but it still sent a burst of nerves through her belly. Keir secured his arm around her waist, spread his great wings, and rose from the top of the tower into the night. Not looking down at the police units and fire trucks, she clung to him as they flew at dizzying heights. Once the D'Danann were in winged form, they could not be seen by the human eye. Anyone they were carrying was also invisible.

Still her heart raced as they flew. The coat flapped in the wind and her hair got in her face.

When she and Keir finally reached the warehouse, Garran had already been taken inside. Hannah hurried in as soon as her feet touched the ground, pushing her hair out of her face at the same time.

Hannah counted her sister witches. Relief flowed through her—they were all there.

Thank the goddess Anu.

The witches looked wound up and had obviously just been in a fight or battle, but they were fine. They were alive.

Hannah thanked the Ancestors, the Elementals, and Anu again.

Ceithlenn had apparently been telling the truth when she said she had a "surprise" in store for the D'Anu—not that Hannah had doubted the evil goddess. It hadn't been a threat. It had been a statement.

Now that she knew her sister witches had survived whatever had happened in Hannah's absence, she had to focus on Garran.

Her heart gave a hard jerk-twist-pull.

At the same time Silver carried some vials of creams and oils, she ushered Hannah down the hallway to the room Hannah had shared with Garran.

When they reached the room, the door was already open and she hurried inside to see Garran stretched out on the sleeping bags, still looking pale and out cold. Silver came into the room with Hannah, and the only other person there was Cassia.

Cassia held her hands over Garran's chest as her healing magic flowed from her to Garran. Her brow was crumpled with concern. "He's very ill, but I'm not sure why."

Hannah cleared her throat. "I think he made more demons disappear."

When Silver and Cassia looked up at Hannah, she continued, feeling as if her words were tumbling over each other like rocks in a landslide. "Ceithlenn and the Fire Dragon had me in a burning ball of fire at the top of Coit Tower and I was surrounded by Fomorii."

Silver's jaw tensed. "The Fomorii that attacked the warehouse were probably just a diversion so the D'Danann couldn't rescue you."

Hannah looked from Silver to Cassia. "Ceithlenn told me—she sent them after all of the D'Anu here."

Silver said, "Explain to us what happened."

"I'm not sure." Hannah looked down at Garran. "He arrived out of the blue and managed to protect me with a shield of his own."

Hannah frowned. "Then a silverish power enveloped him and Ceithlenn seemed frightened. A moment after she vanished, all the Fomorii did, too." She studied Garran. "Then he collapsed."

When Hannah looked up, Silver looked puzzled while Cassia just nodded and continued using her magic on Garran. Silver handed Hannah a vial and when she opened it she smelled cedar wood. It was used for healing, protection, and to drive away evil.

Hannah took the cedar wood oil and touched Garran at his temples and throat. He was wearing his Drow warrior gear, so his chest was bare except for his leather and gem-encrusted straps. Silver helped her to remove the straps and weapons belt, and then Hannah rubbed the cedar oil over his powerful chest, down to the waistband of his leather pants. The air smelled of cedar and Garran's masculine scent.

"I think we've done all we can do for now," Cassia said as she got up. She was wearing a pale blue robe that swirled around her feet when she stood. "I'm certain he'll be all right. It might take a few days of healing, but he'll be as fit as he always was."

The knots in Hannah's stomach got impossibly tighter. "How could you know that?"

Cassia smiled, one of her peaceful smiles that usually had a calming effect. "From what you described I believe I know why this is happening, and why he is ill. If it's so, then he will recover." Cassia's smile faded and she sighed. "This time."

Hannah got to her feet in a rush. "What? What do you mean, 'this time?'."

Cassia shook her head. "It is not for me to tell. You will have to wait until the time is right to learn his secret."

Hannah glared. *Riddling bitch! She's as bad as the Great Guardian and just as immovable. Like a damned piece of witchstone.*

Hannah didn't know what to say as she tried to decipher what Cassia had said. Silver and Cassia left the room, closing the door behind them. Exhausted, every bone in her body weighing her down, with great effort Hannah dropped Keir's coat to the floor and jerked on one of her robes. She stumbled to the sleeping bags, eased down, and curled up beside Garran.

RAIN AND ICE BATTERED Hannah's body and she could barely see through the gray downpour as she ran. Her clothing stuck to her skin, the rain plastered her hair to her face, and pea-sized hail struck her as if someone were throwing small rocks at her.

Her heart raced as she darted through the fog and rain and hail. Her arms and legs hurt from running and her chest ached from her harsh breathing.

She came up short when she reached the pier and she blinked away the rain, unable to believe what she was seeing.

Hundreds and hundreds of demons rose from the bay, scrabbling to gain purchase before flooding the docks crowded with humans.

Terror ripped through Hannah as the Fomorii grabbed people, killing them by snapping their necks, taking out their hearts, or slicing their throats. People screamed and tried to run from the docks, but the demons were too fast. They took down one human after another after another. Blood poured out of the people but the rain washed it from the asphalt streets, concrete sidewalks, and the wooden piers.

Bile rose up in Hannah's throat and the urge to throw up was so strong she didn't think she could hold it back. But she needed to. She needed to figure out what to do to stop these demons.

Hannah's gaze snapped to the sky.

Ceithlenn flapped her huge wings and rose above the beasts.

Like in the baseball stadium, souls shot through the air straight for the goddess. Only these were from humans the

Fomorii were murdering, not souls she was stealing from those still living.

Ceithlenn absorbed the souls, looking more powerful, more terrible with every soul she gathered—her eyes becoming a deeper red, her hair flaming higher, her wings stretching wider, her fangs and claws growing longer.

Hannah tried to scream for help, but no words would come to her mouth. She turned in a full circle, looking around her. Panic rose in her like something trying to rip her from the inside out. Where was everyone? Garran and the Drow weren't there. The entire Alliance was missing.

Hannah's whole body tightened as she came around to face the carnage again.

Garran lay sprawled on the ground, his eyes wide and sightless.

And Ceithlenn was coming straight toward Hannah.

HANNAH CRIED OUT AS she sat up on the sleeping bags. She put her hand to her forehead as if to block out the horrible nightmare. The pounding in her heart was answered by a throbbing in her head, blurring her vision for a moment.

An answering shriek came from Banshee and Hannah looked up to see the falcon familiar circling above her. He glided down and landed on her shoulder, his nails biting through her robe just enough to let her know she was really awake.

She turned her gaze on Garran to see that things hadn't changed—he was out cold and was still flat on his back. Morning sunlight streamed through the high warehouse windows and touched his face. His hair was once again white-blond, his skin fair—but very, very pale.

Banshee took off again, and she sensed he was reassured that she was all right. His concern for her had been palpable when he'd flown down and rested on her shoulder. The falcon flew back up to the rafters as if to watch over all that was going on in the background.

Hannah needed to reassure herself, too, to touch Garran and see that he was okay. The memory of him in her dreams, his sightless eyes, shredded her insides.

She placed her palm on his chest, over his heart, and felt its steady beat. His skin was cool, though, not filled with the warmth it normally had.

A breath of relief escaped her at how true his heartbeat was. She looked down at every perfect feature on his face while keeping her palm on his chest. He was so beautiful, yet rugged and masculine looking at the same time. She moved her hand from his chest and caressed his smooth jaw. Apparently Elves had no facial or bodily hair because she'd noticed none on Garran. Nothing but the beautiful long hair that swept his broad shoulders.

As if he were the male version of Sleeping Beauty and she was a princess come to wake him, she pressed her mouth to his and lightly brushed his lips with hers. His lips were cool, not warm like she was used to, and a combination of disappointment and concern slid through her.

She softly kissed him again and caressed his cheek once more.

Needing to be closer to him, maybe even to help warm and heal him, she lay back down and curled up close to his side, resting her head on his chest so that she could hear his heartbeat.

The memory of the nightmare chilled her, but being close to Garran helped her push the images away.

In the background she heard the usual daytime sounds of talking and construction, but it faded away so that all she heard was Garran's heart beating and the shallow sounds of his breathing. The scent of cedar wood, moss, and earth enveloped her along with his masculine smell. She let it seep into her, comfort her, make her feel as if everything were going to be all right.

Hannah wrapped her arm across Garran's waist, closed her eyes, and slipped into a dreamless sleep.

CHAPTER TWENTY-FIVE

THAT DROW BASTARD HAD tried to send her back to Underworld. Ceithlenn's snarl blasted through the cavern. Fear washed through her like a massive, ice-cold wave. She couldn't go back. Wouldn't go back to Underworld.

Not after everything she and Balor had done to return to the world they had once ruled. Not after the centuries they had spent in the godsforsaken Underworld. Nothing but dank caverns with great stalagmites and stalactites jutting from above and below, black pools that tasted of filth, and the smells—rotten meat, feces, and other horrid odors.

All they'd had to eat were whatever sick creatures inhabited such dark places. All they'd had to rule were Fomorii, Basilisks, Handai, and whatever other fucking beasts had been banished to the same depths as Balor and Ceithlenn.

After she transferred from the tower, she arrived in the empty cavern below Alcatraz. Alone. Even the Fire Dragon had returned to its home.

The fear inside her flickered, burned away by a sizzling, seething fury.

It had taken the souls of countless humans to give her the strength just to bring Balor to this world. Perhaps her powers combined with her husband's would be enough to bring the Fomorii back.

Ceithlenn snarled, knowing she couldn't retrieve them on

her own. For that, she would need warlocks and those useless creatures were either dead or turned traitor.

Crouched on the same rock shelf she had once watched her legions from, her body trembled with the force of her anger. She scratched her nails on the rock at her feet, the sound echoing through the cavern that had once been filled with the grunts and snorts, growls and shrieks, of Underworld creatures. Not only was the place silent, but the smells of the beasts had almost vanished.

She dug the nails of both hands into the solid rock to either side of her, welcome pain shooting through her fingers to her hands.

An attack on San Francisco—that was her next plan. Memories of what she'd done to the humans would have faded in their little minds at least enough to make them less cautious. She'd had Fomorii take over virtually every high-ranking official.

She allowed a wicked grin to creep across her face. Martial law had now been lifted, the city declared "safe."

The demons she had placed at every news station were already reporting the threat was over and law enforcement on all levels would be diligent in protecting San Francisco from further attacks. The film of worthless humans being cuffed and taken into custody had been perfect.

She smiled. Stupid humans. They would resume their lives. Perhaps with some fear, yes, but they would return to their jobs, their daily routines.

Ceithlenn would use the remaining half of her legions to attack the people in the city. With no effort on her part, she would take the souls of the dead and use her powers to find Balor and Darkwolf.

She withdrew her fingernails from the rock and tapped them in a steady drumming sound on the hard surface. Soon she would have to call them all together, every one of her remaining Fomorii, so that they could sweep through the city, giving her power while they murdered human after human.

Once she was again with Balor and he had his eye, she would no longer need the Fomorii, but she preferred to keep her pets to do her will.

A scowl crossed her face as she studied the empty cavern. How had the Drow king been able to send so many of her forces back to Underworld?

She raked her nails across the rock again. Somehow she would learn what weakness went along with such a great power.

CHAPTER TWENTY-SIX

NO OTHER OPTIONS EXISTED. Darkwolf had to use the power of the eye for himself.

Staring at the ceiling, he lay next to Elizabeth on a comfortable bed, in the house they had overtaken. How many people had lived here, he didn't know and didn't want to know. Elizabeth—Junga—had done her job thoroughly and well as usual, leaving no remnants of the former residents behind.

Another stab of pain, like a sword through his head, caused him to squeeze his eyes shut until it receded as much as it was likely to.

Branches screeched across the window in the bedroom. The glow of a streetlight leaked in and caused shadows of the bony tree branches to make patterns on the ceilings and walls. They moved like skeletal fingers reaching for him through the near darkness.

He thought about fucking Elizabeth again to push away the pain and give himself, for the time he was inside her, the feeling of control he no longer had. Her steady breathing told her she was asleep, but she would take him whenever and whatever way he desired.

Instead, his mind turned back to the eye resting on his chest. The purple shroud of his magic glimmered in the dim room, and thank the gods no pulsing red light crept through to tell him Balor was near.

Darkwolf returned to his original thought. He truly had no options left. He had to use the eye himself.

If he dropped the shroud and pulled the essence of the eye into himself, instead of simply augmenting his own magic with it, he knew his power would be great. Great enough to fight Balor himself? Maybe.

Would he become a monster, more terrible than he had been as the High Priest of the Balorite warlocks?

That, too, was possible.

What would he do with that power?

Thoughts of killing, maiming, sacrificing, slid through his mind. Would he commit atrocious acts of violence against humans?

Again?

Or would he use that power to fight Balor and rid this city of the horrible, sickening threat that the god was?

Ceithlenn in her hideous goddess form, and as a human, entered his mind and his gut twisted. Could he use the power against her?

After what she'd done to him . . .

His entire body tensed.

With every fiber of his being he wanted to kill the bitch. Not send her back to Underworld, but *kill* her.

Yes, this was the answer. Every bit of magic and knowledge the eye possessed told him what to do.

Darkwolf smiled and let the shroud fall away—

And let his body absorb all of the magic and the power the eye commanded.

Instant pain seared through him like countless bolts of lightning. He shouted and gave a long cry as agony exploded inside him. Vaguely he was aware of Elizabeth sitting up in bed and her frantic expression.

Darkwolf yelled again as his body contorted and twisted. He held his palms to the sides of his head while pain forced tears from his eyes.

His body began changing, morphing.

Bone popped and shifted and he could feel himself

growing, his body expanding, lengthening. His head smacked into the bed's headboard and his feet hung off the edge of the mattress as he rolled back and forth. He arched as more bolts of pain tore through him and sweat broke out over his skin, drenching him.

The chain holding the eye snapped and the links rattled as it fell to the bed.

The eye—it melded into his flesh, around his heart.

He didn't have to look to know that it had become a part of him.

He shouted again as more muscle and bone shifted, expanded. His jeans and T-shirt cut into his skin. Sounds of ripping and tearing accompanied the feel of clothing shredding and falling away from his body.

The agony went on and on and on.

Finally, the last of the pain faded and Darkwolf slumped on the bed. His mind spun and his body burned hot enough that the sweat began to dry on his skin.

Strength replaced the weakness that had possessed him during the transformation. He rose to a sitting position on the bed, his mind suddenly clear and pain-free for the first time since he'd found the eye on the shores of Ireland.

Years. Years ago.

He looked down at himself and saw purple smoke mixed with a golden glow over his now massive, naked body.

Power flowed through him. Terrible and great power that carried with it heat and anger and the desire to harm. Something. Someone.

Darkwolf breathed at a normal pace but his heart beat stronger than it had before. The sparkles faded as he looked down at his chest, where the eye had been.

It was gone. No, not gone. It permanently encased his heart now.

He closed his eyes and knowledge expanded in his brain. Memories that weren't his own flashed in succession through his mind. Images of wars and power and murder.

The knowledge drew him and he put aside the memories

that weren't his own. Instead he focused on what the eye—the former eye—was telling him.

Where in Balor the power and magic had been contained in the eye, in Darkwolf it had transformed and overtaken his heart. The powers had morphed, too, changing so that Darkwolf's powers were different than Balor's had been.

Darkwolf looked at his arms and hands. What was he capable of now? Did he have the power of a god?

Elizabeth made a sound and Darkwolf turned his head in her direction. Her eyes were wide and her lips parted. He had grown to a height tall enough that he had to look down at her—her small, fragile human shell.

Darkwolf's lips curled into a vicious smile as Elizabeth said in a horrified tone, "What have you done?"

CHAPTER TWENTY-SEVEN

BY THE SLANT OF sunlight streaming through the warehouse windows, Hannah judged it to be afternoon now. Her muscles felt stiff from sleeping so long, and she uncurled her body from where she had been snuggling against Garran.

Hannah raised herself to a sitting position and looked down at him. She frowned. He hadn't moved, not at all, and a strange feeling twisted deep in her belly. What if he didn't wake up?

The overwhelming concern she felt for him turned that twist in her belly into a deep ache. She pushed the thoughts away. He'd be all right. He was just down for the count from doing—from doing whatever it was he'd done.

She held her hand to her arm and touched her moon and crescent armband as she got to her feet. Her red robe was rumpled and she probably looked as bad as she felt—tired and dirty. When she glanced at the place where her clothing was stacked she saw her pack next to her things. She furrowed her brow. The pack was a little sandy and looked bulky, as if everything she'd taken to the shore had been stuffed inside it.

Cassia had probably scried the whole thing and had known where to find Hannah's stuff. She blew out a breath and shook her head. Goddess only knew if they'd ever figure Cassia out. The half-Elvin witch no doubt had far too many secrets inside her as far as Hannah was concerned.

She grabbed some clothing and toiletry items and headed for one of the bathrooms set up in the warehouse, complete with showers. She wasn't in the mood to spend much time showering, so she got in, cleaned up, and was back in the room she shared with Garran in no time.

He was so lifeless looking.

Hannah's damp hair swung forward as she knelt and touched her fingers to the pulse on his neck. Strong as it had been each time. Whatever it was that had knocked him out at least hadn't come close to killing him. The ache that had been in her belly moved up to her throat.

She located the bottles of magical healing oils and grabbed the one that smelled of cedar. She put some on her palms and began rubbing it over his chest. His skin felt warmer under her hands than it had before, which gave her some measure of relief.

While she massaged the healing oil into his skin, Hannah imbued it with her magic, the green sparkles floating between his body and hers. It weakened her a bit, but more importantly, she hoped it would help Garran recover.

When there was nothing left for her to do, she gave him one last look and headed out of the room to locate her Coven sisters.

She reached the kitchen, catching the strong scent of patchouli incense when she opened the door. The other witches were just getting to their feet, their divination tools still on the table.

Pain slammed into her chest as she looked at each one of them. They had divined without her. Then the realization that she had no way to scry now made that mental blow even harder.

Doing her best to keep her expression and her voice calm and controlled, Hannah said, "What did you learn?"

Mackenzie had a hard expression on her face, and her hair was in disarray, as if she'd just run her fingers through her long blond curls. "I saw the Drow—betraying us."

Shock coursed through Hannah, making her scalp prickle.

"I saw the same." Silver rubbed her hand on her abdomen that was just starting to show that she was pregnant. "The Drow attacking us, not the Fomorii."

Rhiannon put her hands on her hips and her green eyes looked like flashing emeralds. Her chin-length hair swung around her face as her gaze met that of each of the Coven sisters. "In my vision, there was something more to it. I can't tell what that is. None of us had unconditionally clear visions that my father will turn on us."

Copper balanced on the foot that didn't have a cast. "Rhiannon's right. My dreams have shown me nothing about Garran being a traitor. He saved my life when the door to Underworld was opened—at the cost of his brother's life— and I don't believe for a minute he'll betray us."

Mackenzie's face flushed. "How do you know he won't use his dark magic to send all of *us* away, just like he did the Fomorii?"

The normally silent Alyssa spoke up in her quiet voice. "How do we know he sent the demons to Underworld, and not someplace to battle us?"

Everyone but Cassia started talking, arguing, and Hannah put her fingertips to her forehead. Helplessness was not something she remembered ever feeling. Before there had always been something backing her up that helped her remain strong and confident. But without her scrying ability . . .

She squeezed her eyes shut. There had to be a way for her to learn what was happening.

The Drow. She had to go to the Dark Elves to see if they could help her find out what was wrong with Garran—and what he'd done. What kind of power he had.

"Stop." Cassia's voice cut across the arguing going on in the kitchen, and everyone fell silent as her turquoise eyes pinned each of them one by one. "Since when do we act in this manner? It has never been so."

Cassia's words and tone had a formal, almost Otherworldly quality to them that Hannah had never heard before. The effect was definitely sobering. Every witch seemed to straighten. Hannah imagined she could actually see minds and emotions clearing.

"You're right." Silver had always been the leader of the group, even though they all turned to Cassia more and more for guidance. Silver pushed her long silvery-blond hair out of her face. "We've got to figure this out together."

While the other witches started discussing their divinations, Hannah gave in to the realization that right now she needed Rhiannon. Of all the D'Anu, Rhiannon was probably the only one who could help Hannah now.

She walked up to Rhiannon, who narrowed her gaze at Hannah. This time Hannah didn't push it and step into what she called Rhiannon's little box—her personal space.

"I need to talk to you." She glanced at the other D'Anu, who were animatedly discussing the divinations. "Alone."

Rhiannon tilted her head to the side. "Why?"

Hannah held back a sound of frustration. "Please. It's about your father."

Rhiannon glanced at the other witches then back to Hannah. "All right."

They slipped out of the kitchen and Hannah led Rhiannon to the quietest place she could find, a small alcove near the strategy/planning area. She gave a nod to Jake Macgregor who watched her and Rhiannon walk across the room. No one else seemed to notice them.

When they were alone, Hannah pushed the blond shock of hair behind her ear and barely kept herself from giving in to a nervous bout of pacing.

Hannah took a deep breath. "I need your help."

Rhiannon immediately had a wary expression. "With what?"

"Your father." Hannah kept her eyes focused on Rhiannon's. "I need to go to the Drow to find out what's happening to Garran. What he's doing and why it hurts him each time."

"That's risky." Rhiannon frowned. "I'm actually beginning to feel like I can trust Garran, but I'm not so sure about the others."

"I know." Hannah felt that ever-present tightening in her gut. "But we need to find out what's going on and this is the only way I can think of doing it."

"Why do you care about my father?" Rhiannon folded her arms across her chest, looked even a little angry. "Back when I first found out who he was, you called him a traitor."

"I did," Hannah said quietly. "But I've changed my mind."

Rhiannon had something between irritation and amusement on her face. As if she had such conflicting emotions she didn't know whether to lash out or laugh. "You care about him."

Hannah paused as she thought about Rhiannon's words and a strange feeling wavered beneath her skin. How had she gone from mistrusting Garran to being so concerned, in such a short amount of time? "Yes, I do," she finally said. "And even though *you* didn't trust him at first, you do now."

Rhiannon paused then nodded. "Yeah. Gut instinct, or something, but somewhere deep inside I'm sure he's not bad."

"I know where the Drow come in to San Francisco," Hannah said. "I need you to help me go through the passage."

Since Rhiannon was half Drow, she was half-Elvin and could pass through this world to Otherworld at transference points. Hannah couldn't because she didn't have any Elvin blood in her.

"We'll have to more or less sneak out of here." Rhiannon looked around them as if to make sure no one was eavesdropping. "If we tell anyone about this, you know they'd never let us go. But I don't know how to get past the D'Danann guards."

"You're part Drow." Hannah glanced in the same direction Rhiannon had before looking back at her. "Your father gave me some of his Drow magic before Ceithlenn captured me. I was able to use his magic with mine to make a glamour strong enough that the D'Danann didn't see me leave."

"I wondered how you got away with that." Rhiannon

wiped her hands on her jeans. "Anything we need to take with us?"

Hannah's lips curved in a wry smile. "Our magic is about all we have to protect us. I don't think either of us are good with a dagger."

"No kidding." Rhiannon smiled back. "We might as well get this done and see if we can get back before anyone gets really worried. Keir will kill me."

Hannah nodded, and as one they each pulled a glamour. Hannah blinked. "*I* can't even see you, Rhiannon."

"Same here." It was strange hearing the disembodied voice. Usually when they pulled a glamour only using their D'Anu magic they could see each other. "I'll go first."

Hannah whispered to Rhiannon which pier they would pass through the door to the Drow realm.

"I know exactly where that is," Rhiannon whispered back.

Because she couldn't see Rhiannon, Hannah waited a second to make sure Rhiannon had passed. Hannah reached out with her new Drow powers and sensed Rhiannon walking in front of her as they made their way through the work areas in the warehouse.

She still ran right into the invisible Rhiannon when she came to a stop as two of the D'Danann passed by. Hannah held back a little more as she made her way to the warehouse door. She ran into Rhiannon again when she got to the door. Rhiannon hissed and Hannah backed up.

"Wait until someone opens the door," Rhiannon whispered.

Hannah rubbed her arms as they waited, her skin shivery with the need to *go*. Finally, one of the D'Danann stepped out and Hannah slipped behind him. She hoped Rhiannon had made it out, too, as she headed toward the dock.

"With me?" Hannah whispered as she walked away from the warehouse.

"You're going to have to drop your glamour once we get near that pier so I can see you and the door."

Not seeing Rhiannon and hearing her speak still made Hannah feel a little unsettled.

When they reached the pier, Hannah said "I think it's safe now," and dropped her glamour.

It was actually a relief to see Rhiannon when she dropped her glamour, too.

Rubble trickled beneath Hannah's running shoes as they climbed down below the wooden planks and around one of the huge pilings. Hannah showed Rhiannon the dirt and rock wall she and Garran had passed through to make it to San Francisco.

Rhiannon grabbed Hannah's hand and said, "Here go the two craziest witches on the planet."

Being in this whole mess together made Hannah feel surprisingly closer to Rhiannon. And when they took that first step straight at the wall, Hannah had full confidence that Rhiannon would get them to the Drow realm.

Hannah closed her eyes. She never felt the earth or rock as they walked forward, hand in hand. But as always, everything went hazy then black. Again, Hannah couldn't hear, couldn't see, and her skin numbed. This time panic didn't rise up in her—fear that Rhiannon would let go. Quiet confidence pushed away some of the numbness.

When their feet met stone, they both stumbled a bit. Smells of damp earth and moss met Hannah's senses and cool air skimmed her bare arms. She opened her eyes and Rhiannon released her hand.

It was so dark that even after blinking a few moments, Hannah still couldn't see. "Should have brought a flashlight."

"I think it's the Drow in me—I see a black door over here."

"That's got to be it."

A thumping sound and then light streamed into the space she and Rhiannon were in. It wasn't too bright, so as they walked through, Hannah easily saw the throne room with its crystal walls, freeform artwork—and a bunch of Dark Elves seated around a great oval table.

Men who stared in their direction with obvious surprise. A couple of the Drow had even risen from their chairs and had unsheathed their swords.

"Princess." One of the Drow bowed after his gaze landed on Rhiannon. The rest of the men stood and bowed, following his lead, and those Drow who had swords out sheathed them.

Hannah glanced at Rhiannon to see her cheeks redden as they always did when she was called "princess." Hannah hid a smile but quickly sobered.

All the Elves had the bluish-gray skin of the Drow, some more blue than others. As usual, their hair color ranged from silver to blue to gray to black. Some work black shirts and pants while one Drow wore the same basic warrior gear as Garran.

The men remained standing as Rhiannon and Hannah approached. One of the Drow stepped forward. He appeared very calm, almost serene, something that didn't gel with her notions of what all Drow were like.

"We are the Drow Directorate," the man said as he swept out his arm, gesturing to the men around the table. "And please meet Carden, King Garran's Steward."

Hannah followed her instinct to bow from the shoulders as Rhiannon did.

When they raised their heads, the Steward, Carden, gave a pleasant smile and offered each of them one of the four empty chairs at the table. Hannah and Rhiannon accepted, and took their seats.

As soon as Rhiannon and Hannah sat, all of the Dark Elves followed suit and the scrape of Hannah's and Rhiannon's chair legs echoed in the room again. The Drow returned to their chairs in silence. Hannah found the silence unnerving and she shivered.

Carden studied Rhiannon and Hannah. "How is the king? Did he send you?"

Hannah looked at Rhiannon whose expression seemed to say, "It's your show."

"The king didn't send me." Hannah was not about to look anything but calm and controlled around these men. There were too many of them for her to announce that Garran was ill. "I need to speak with the Steward and the leader of the Directorate only."

Dark looks from almost all of the men made Hannah feel like shrinking back in her chair, but she kept her spine straight and her chin tilted up.

One of the Drow had a shrewd, not so pleasant expression on his face. He had silver hair and darker silver, almost pewter-colored eyes. "What you have to say can be said to all of us."

"No." Hannah put emphasis on the word. She hoped to the Ancestors that this man with the bad attitude wasn't the leader of the Directorate.

"Sepan," the almost serene man said as he looked at the silver-haired Drow. "Their request is not unreasonable."

"I will remain, Hark." Sepan folded his arms over his chest.

Hannah gave the Drow called Hark her coolest look despite the pounding of her heart. "Are you the leader of the Directorate?"

"I am," Hark said quietly. "You may speak with me and the Steward."

"Thank you." Hannah didn't let her gaze waver when she looked at the man named Sepan, who openly scowled at her. "We appreciate your willingness to accommodate our requests."

She swore she heard a series of growls from the men although they made no other noise as they pushed their chairs away from the table and stood. How did they *do* that? Including Sepan, the men left silently, but their irritation and anger were palpable. She sure hadn't made any friends in that round.

When just the four of them remained, Rhiannon and Hannah both took chairs closer to the head of the table where Hark and Carden sat.

Hannah kept her voice low so that the door guards couldn't hear her. "Garran is ill and we've come to find out if any of you can help us learn what's wrong with him."

Both men appeared stunned. "King Garran is ill?" Carden asked, his voice disbelieving.

"We're pretty sure he'll recover." Hannah held her hands in her lap to keep from fidgeting. "But we don't understand why he's getting ill or what he's doing to cause it."

"I wondered . . ." Carden frowned. "Explain. Please."

Hannah told both men about the disappearance of the Fomorii and how weak Garran had been afterward, and that she hadn't seen what had happened. She went on to describe her capture by Ceithlenn and how Garran had used some kind of silvery power that caused the Fomorii to vanish, then knocked him out cold.

"Is this some kind of magic Dark Elves can use?" Hannah said as she finished and looked at the two men, who looked puzzled. "What's happening to him?"

Hark and Carden glanced at each other. Their gazes returned to Hannah's, and Hark said, "What you have described is no Drow power."

"Could it be a power Garran—my father—had that no one knew about?" Rhiannon asked.

"It is not possible." Hark shook his head. "It is far beyond any ability of the Dark Elves. Even the Light Elves would not have such a great power."

"And the king should never become ill after using Drow magic," Carden said. "The Dark Elves do not experience such weaknesses. Ever."

"Whoa." Rhiannon pushed her chin-length hair out of her face. "None of this is making any sense."

Hannah swallowed, feeling like a fist was in her throat. "Then we need to figure out what's happening. The D'Anu witches have attempted to use their divination powers to learn more, but nothing's matching up."

"Some of the witches have scried things that make the Drow out to be traitors," Rhiannon added.

Carden's face steeled. "Once the king has given his word, he will not go back on it."

"Hannah and I both agree with that." Rhiannon sat straighter in her chair. "So we don't understand these divinations."

"Do you have some way to help us?" Hannah asked.

Hark studied her for a long moment. "Garran gave of his Drow power to you. I see it in your aura."

Unwelcome and unfamiliar heat burned in Hannah's cheeks, as if they could see exactly how Garran had given her power. "Yes," she said.

Hark nodded. "Then we may be able to share visions of the future."

"How?" Rhiannon asked.

Hark pushed his chair away from the table, stood, and extended his hand to Rhiannon. "We need a more private location for this."

Carden stood and took Hannah's hand in his for a moment to help her to her feet. His palm was like Garran's, warm and callused. He smelled different, too. Earthy, but with a hint of an exotic spice.

After releasing Hannah's and Rhiannon's hands, Hark and Carden escorted them across the great hall to one of the corridors Hannah had not explored with Garran. More of the blue lichen glowed overhead on the high ceiling of the passageway so that Hannah could see comfortably.

In the middle of the hallway, Hark stopped at a door, opened it, and let them in. Hannah felt a flutter in her chest at being alone with two Drow. She worried that they might not be exactly what they appeared to be—concerned, considerate, and as anxious as she was to find out what was happening with Garran.

The dim room smelled of unusual spices that Hannah wasn't familiar with. A little like cinnamon perhaps and cardamom. The room was crowded with pieces of furniture jammed up against each other, and bottles, boxes, and other containers covered every surface. A bed took up one end of the room, but it was nowhere near the size of Garran's or even the one in the room she'd slept in the one night she was here.

Hark led the way to a large pillar in the middle of the room. The pillar was about the size of a dinner plate in circumference but reached all the way from the rocky ceiling to the floor. In the dimness of the room, she thought it was made of polished granite.

"Surround the sight-pillar," Hark said.

Hannah frowned, but walked up to it. Hark took her hand on one side, Carden on her other, and they held Rhiannon's hands on the other side of the pillar.

"Stare into the stone with the questions we seek to answer. What is the king doing and why is it making him ill?"

The fluttering in Hannah's chest escalated as she stared at the pillar. She pushed the questions to the forefront of her mind, willing something—anything—to give them answers.

Tingles traveled through the hands of the men on either side of her. She tried not to let it break her concentration as she focused.

She almost stumbled back when the stone turned nearly transparent and dark fog swirled inside it. Hannah felt the fog rolling out from the pillar as it touched her and sank into her. At once her senses seemed keener. The cardamom and cinnamon scents in the room grew stronger, joined with something like bay leaf. She thought she heard the throb of each person's heart, their soft breathing, the rustle of their clothing.

The fog flowing out of the clear column settled over her like a shroud and she shuddered at the icy feeling floating into her bones.

When fog no longer swirled in the column, a scene started to take place. Garran stood in the meadow, speaking with the Great Guardian. Their words played in her mind as they spoke and the scene unfolded. They spoke in another language, probably Elvin, but somehow Hannah understood.

The Great Guardian told Garran how he could conditionally give his people what they wanted most—to walk in the sunlight.

She offered him a special power if he helped in the war against Ceithlenn and the Fomorii. A tremendous power that would allow him to send great numbers of the demons back to Underworld.

Hannah's heart pounded and she could no longer hear anything except the blood rushing in her ears.

It was a "three strikes and you're out" deal.

The first time he used the power he would become weak—just like he had at the Fomorii cavern.

The second time he used the power he would become ill—just like he had in the battle on top of the Coit Tower.

Hannah's heart pounded so hard it hurt as she heard the Great Guardian's next words.

"The third time could cost you much more. It could mean your life. Only one thing can save you should you choose to use this power thrice."

He could die? Garran could die? But something could save him?

"And what might that saving grace be?" Garran was asking in the vision.

"This knowledge could prevent you from attaining it if you know in advance," the Guardian responded.

A scream echoed in Hannah's mind as she silently shouted for Garran to say *"No!"* even though she knew his answer already.

"I accept," Garran said with clear authority in his voice.

You bastard, you bastard! Hannah yelled in her mind.

"He had no right to make such a choice," Carden growled out loud. "His people need him more than we need sunlight."

"We cannot let him use the power a third time," Hark said. Both men were squeezing her hands so tightly Hannah thought her bones would break.

The image faded away and she started to release the hands of the Drow holding hers when another scene unfolded and they all stilled.

In the darkness, with the Golden Gate Bridge in the background, the Drow were waging a battle—

Against the D'Danann and the witches.

A man with black hair, blue skin, and black eyes led the battle.

Drow arrows flew, striking D'Danann. Some of the Drow warriors were decapitated by D'Danann flying over their heads and attacking with their swords.

The D'Anu witches were in the middle of everything, using their magic.

"No!" Hannah shouted as she stumbled back and let go of the hands of the Drow to either side of her. She cut her furious gaze from one man to the other. "You *are* traitors! You *are* going to attack us!"

"Vidar." Carden's jaw was set and he looked furious as his eyes met Hark's. "If he has not already done so, it appears he intends to take a legion of our warriors to battle those Garran vowed to help in the San Francisco Otherworld."

"We must deal with this at once." Hark's anger radiated from him as he strode to the door, Carden at his side. "I hope it is not too late."

Rhiannon and Hannah hurried to catch up to them. "You mean one of your own is taking this other war into his own hands?" Hannah asked, her chest aching even more. "It's not all of the Drow?"

"No." Carden reached the great hall and shouted orders in another language to Drow guards who immediately ran down one of the corridors. He turned to Hannah and Rhiannon. "You had best stay here where you will remain safe," he said before he turned and hurried away with Hark at his side.

Rhiannon and Hannah looked at each other and at the same time said, "Like hell," before they turned and bolted to the black door in the throne room.

CHAPTER TWENTY-EIGHT

"SURE YOU'RE NOT PUSHING it, Macgregor?" Fredrickson stood at the head of the weight bench as he leaned over and spotted Jake from behind. "Can't have our captain killing himself pumping iron." He added with wry amusement, "I think killing you is a Fomorii job."

Jake's muscles quavered a little from the amount of weight he had on the barbell. He merely grunted, both in response to Fredrickson and from the power it took to raise the barbell from its rest. He clenched his jaws as he slowly lowered the barbell just above his chest.

Sweat poured down his face and soaked his T-shirt as he shoved the weight up and brought it back down and up again for a few more reps. He'd been working out a good forty-five minutes and he couldn't get the added problems out of his head.

Now that the government and military leaders—in other words the Fomorii in power—had lifted martial law, people were already out in greater numbers, meaning Ceithlenn had easy access to all the chow she wanted.

The barbell clattered as he racked it before resting and looking up at the high warehouse rafters. Somewhere Alyssa's owl familiar, Echo, gave a long hoot.

A haunting cry that sent a crawling sensation down Jake's spine.

"Finished yet, Captain?" Fredrickson asked, sounding

farther away than he had been. Before Jake could answer a towel hit him square in the face and he heard the lieutenant's muffled laugh. "I say you are."

Jake grabbed the towel and started wiping sweat from his face, neck and arms as he rubbed himself down. Veins stood out on his biceps. In his sleeveless black workout shirt, his eagle, globe, and anchor Marine insignia tattoo flexed with his movements.

It was late, but Jake had needed to work out the frustration of the day. Now the odor of sweat and testosterone added to the familiar smells of wood, the witches' herbs and spices, and the rain-washed scent of "good" magic.

He climbed off the weight bench, pumped up from his workout. The redheaded Fredrickson was wiping off his own sweat but was staring out the door of the weight room. Jake thought he saw one of the witches, but the woman was gone in one blink.

The warehouse was fairly quiet. A lot of the D'Danann were still up—they didn't seem to need as much sleep as humans, or even the witches.

Jake went still as he heard shouting from the entrance.

"The Drow are attacking at the pier!" came the voice of one of the D'Danann warriors.

The Drow?

"What the fuck?" Fredrickson said.

"Goddamn." Jake whirled and ran to his nearby unlocked locker where he stashed his handgun and duty belt while working out.

Fredrickson got to his locker the same time Jake reached his own. It took two minutes tops, for each of them to jerk off their sweatpants and climb into jeans, then buckle their duty belts around their waists. Controlled pandemonium rang through the warehouse. Jake and Fredrickson fastened their Kevlar vests over their soaked T-shirts then shoved their feet into work boots.

Jake had a firm grip on his Glock. His heart had already started a rapid pounding and more adrenaline rushed through him than had been in his body while he was working out.

At the same time Fredrickson and Jake left the workout room, the D'Anu witches flowed from the part of the warehouse where all the bedrooms were. They were fully dressed for the most part—Alyssa was buttoning her jeans and Mackenzie hopping into her shoes. The witches and his officers strapped on their Kevlar vests in a hurry while the D'Danann had already left the building. Most of the witches' familiars were following them.

Jake rushed ahead of his team and the D'Anu witches, taking care when he opened up the door and entered the near darkness. Only a handful of D'Danann remained behind to guard the warehouse.

Shouting, the clang of swords, and other signs of fighting came from around the corner of the warehouse.

"I know I don't have to tell you not to run out in the open," Jake called to the witches as he braced himself and swept the lot with his handgun. No Drow here. "Be careful just the same."

"The Drow use arrows as much as swords." Copper's voice was low, but loud enough for all of the witches and officers to hear. "I've seen them in action and they're deadly."

The sounds of battle grew louder. Jake and the team of officers and witches stayed close to the side of the building until he could see what was going down.

When he reached the corner of the warehouse, he peered around, careful to stay out of sight. In the near darkness the D'Danann fought men with grayish-blue skin—the Drow. Even though he couldn't see them, he could tell some of the D'Danann fought from the air because of the sudden wounds that would appear on the Drow warriors, or the way a couple were beheaded.

The sound of metal striking metal rang out in the night along with shouts, yells, and cries of warriors on both sides. Because they were magical, too, the Drow could see the flying D'Danann who were invisible to Jake.

Several Drow warriors stood back and systematically released arrows, taking down a few of the D'Danann. With absolute precision, some of the D'Danann flipped daggers through the air right into the hearts of the Drow shooting the arrows.

Jake's blood boiled despite the cold air rushing at him and chilling the sweat on his T-shirt. He crouched and motioned for a few of his officers to move and take cover behind a couple of SWAT vehicles and an abandoned wooden building. Silently, like the professionals they were, his officers slipped through the night to hide and to shoot from the best vantage point.

Holding his Glock with both hands, Jake swung around the building and fired.

Apparently the heart-seeking bullets worked as well with the Drow as they did with the Fomorii. He brought down two of the Dark Elves in rapid succession. His officers took out a few more. He didn't have time to be too amazed at how the Drow bodies disappeared into obsidian sparkles, but he took a moment's pleasure in the fact.

Good. That meant the bastards were history.

The shots of the PSF immediately brought the attention of a few of the Drow to Jake and his officers. In nearly lightning-fast motions, the Drow fired arrows that drove into two of Jake's officers. Both men collapsed to the asphalt. One groaned and tried to move while the other remained lifeless where he'd fallen.

Fury burned Jake's gut and he fired around the building again.

It wasn't until then that he saw the D'Anu witches—five of them—headed toward the Dark Elves, each witch surrounded by one of their sparkling magical shields that glowed in the night. Some of them had their familiars at their sides.

Thank God the Drow arrows bounced off the shields.

With his knowledge of how the witches fought, Jake was pretty sure he knew what they planned to do. If they dropped their shields to fight now, they'd be dead. The Dark Elves were too accurate, too fast. Yet he knew the witches weren't stupid and they were damned good fighters. The D'Anu would choose the right moments to use their powers.

The D'Danann continued to battle from above, beheading Drow warriors. Gore splattered in the air and on the ground. The smell of blood and that same earth and moss scent Garran had was strong—only the spice scent Jake associated with the Dark Elves was different with these Drow. Darker somehow.

The Drow shot more D'Danann in the sky. A few D'Danann were killed instantly, bursting into silver sparks. Others slammed to the ground and jerked the arrows out of their bodies. They stumbled to their feet and fought the Drow from the ground.

The magical beings healed pretty fast as long as they weren't beheaded or their hearts ripped or blasted out. So they didn't have to worry about loss of blood—unless their injuries were incredibly severe.

They were fortunate Drow didn't use iron like the Fomorii. No doubt because iron was just as deadly to Elves as to Fae.

But now all the Drow were too close for arrows and used their swords instead.

The witches waited until then to drop their shields and start flinging fireballs and knocking some of the Drow out, while tying others up with their magic ropes. The D'Anu witches didn't kill, but they knew how to incapacitate their opponents pretty damn well. It would have been a plus if the light from their magic affected the Drow like daylight did, but it appeared that wasn't the case.

The familiars did their jobs, too—the Doberman going for one man's jugular; the cat climbing a warrior like a fencepost and going for his eyes; the wolf pouncing on another warrior and driving him onto his back to the ground.

Jake and his officers continued to shoot at the Drow from their positions. Shots rang out through the night along with the continual clanging of swords, the shouts and cries. There wasn't much good they could do at close range while the Drow used swords, except to continue using their handguns.

One particular Drow warrior stood out from the rest and Jake had his sights set on the bastard. By the way he shouted orders, the large blue-skinned, black-haired man was obviously the leader of this group.

The warrior turned his attention to Jake as if hearing his thoughts. With a motion so fast Jake barely saw it, the man drew his bow and released the arrow. It flew through the air, and even though Jake dove for cover, the head of the arrow buried itself in Jake's right biceps. His gun arm.

Jake gritted his teeth, biting back a shout. He did his best to ignore the screaming pain as he snapped the shaft of the arrow and tossed it aside, leaving the arrowhead in his biceps. Sweat broke out on his forehead.

He kept his back against the warehouse, mentally blocking the pain. He took a deep breath, swung around the side of the building, and fired at the leader before the man had a chance to completely dodge the bullet.

It exploded in the Drow's thigh, dropping him to the ground.

Immediately, Copper bound the big man in one of her magic ropes, pinning his arms and hands to his sides.

In one sweep of his gaze, Jake saw that most of the Dark Elves lay wounded on the asphalt, were bound by the witches' magic ropes, or were likely dead and had vanished into black sparkles.

Jake let out a deep breath. The D'Danann, witches, familiars, and PSF officers obviously had everything under control now.

It still pissed him off how the PSF had to rely so much on the D'Danann and witches, but human methods of warfare didn't usually do a whole lot of good against magical beings.

Goddamn, but he had to find the time to work on designs for better weapons for the PSF.

Keir walked up to the blue-skinned leader of the Drow and raised his sword. "We finish this now," he growled.

"Hold on." Copper pushed at Keir's arm. "We should question them to see what in Anu's name is going on. They're supposed to be our allies."

"They are naught but traitors." Keir lowered his sword a little, the scar on his cheek whitening, making him look even more savage.

Keir's head snapped up and the expression on his face changed. His gaze cut across everyone in the lot. "Where is Rhiannon?" he said in a harsh voice, his look showing fierce concern for his wife.

The witches and D'Danann glanced around the bloody area. "Hannah's not here, either," Silver said with a note of panic.

"They didn't leave the warehouse with us." Jake held his hand where the arrow was buried in his biceps, blood coating his palm, as he walked to where Keir stood over the Drow leader. "I'm pretty sure I saw every witch who came out to fight."

"You're injured!" Alyssa went to Jake's side and warmth flooded him as some of her magic started flowing into him.

The pain lessened, but the arrow was lodged deep and Jake knew it would be hell to get it out. "Worry about Hannah and Rhiannon," Jake said through gritted teeth. "I'll be fine."

"We'll check the warehouse." Silver's eyes were wide and she looked panicked. "But I don't understand why they wouldn't be here with us." Silver whirled and practically ran back toward the entrance to the warehouse, Hawk following, obviously anxious to protect his wife.

"Rhiannon and Hannah wouldn't miss a fight for anything." Copper rocked on her cast, her arms crossed over her chest, an expression of distress on her face almost identical to Silver's. "They are two of the most stubborn and toughest women we know."

"Let's get this bastard inside." Jake motioned to the Drow leader with a nod. "We'll see if he knows anything."

The Drow male growled and glared at his captors.

Keir kicked the Drow, causing the man to shout in pain. "Put him in one of the cages made to fetter magic," Keir said. "When we learn what we need to, *then* I will kill him."

The Drow leader gave a low snarl. "You will not be able to hold me."

"Uh-huh." Mackenzie wound more of her magical rope around the warrior. "Sure. So escape D'Anu magic, why don't you?"

"I will search for my mate and Hannah," Keir said before he spread his wings, lifted off, and disappeared from human sight.

Thanks to Alyssa's powers, the ache in Jake's arm numbed despite the arrowhead buried inside it. He surveyed the battle scene and the wounded being attended to by the D'Danann and his officers.

Fury made the pain in his arm lessen to where he was barely conscious of it. It looked like two of his officers hadn't made it. Most of the Drow had been killed, their bodies vanishing into sparkles, as had more than a few of the D'Danann.

"Goddamnit, we didn't need this." Jake took his bloody left hand away from his arm, gestured to his officers, and instructed them on what areas to scan for signs of Hannah and Rhiannon.

Two of the D'Danann forced the Drow leader to his feet, his arms still completely bound from his shoulders to his fingertips. They shoved him forward and guided him in the direction of the warehouse entrance. He limped due to the bullet he'd taken in the thigh from Jake's gunshot.

Five other Drow had survived and were being taken to be caged, as well. Once they were in the containment cells, the D'Anu would be able to drop their magic ropes.

As he again held his palm to his bleeding arm, Jake scanned the darkness for Hannah and Rhiannon. Where the hell were they?

"I have found them." Keir's shout came from behind Jake.

He stopped and turned as did several others and relief flooded him when he saw Hannah and Rhiannon rushing forward with Keir. The warrior had a furious expression, his harsh features even harder as he had his arm around his wife's shoulders. Rhiannon was trying to push him off, but he was obviously not letting go.

Hannah hurried ahead of them and from her heavy breathing it sounded like she'd been running. When she reached Jake she didn't look like the same unflappable woman that he'd come to know over the course of the battles they'd been in together.

"Is everyone okay?" She scanned those who remained outside. "Where's Garran? Is he still out cold?"

"Not for long." Keir scowled as he held Rhiannon tight to him. "I will kill him in his sleep for this."

"No you won't." Hannah parked herself in front of Keir and Rhiannon, bringing them to a full stop. Her eyes were hard, her mouth set in a determined line.

"Do you not see what he has done?" Keir nearly shouted.

Rhiannon finally managed to jerk herself away from Keir and stood a few feet from him and braced her hands on her hips. Jake could see the Fomorii scars on her cheek whiten in the low glow of the outside lights.

"The guy who led this whole thing did it on his own," Rhiannon said. "He's a traitor to his own people. He's pissed at Garran or something."

"Even the leaders, the Directorate, didn't know anything about it," Hannah said.

Keir narrowed his eyes. "We will discuss this further. Inside."

"You bet we will." Rhiannon marched ahead of him to the entrance of the warehouse.

Loss of blood was beginning to make Jake lightheaded.

"We've got to take care of that," the ever intuitive Alyssa said.

Jake just nodded. His adrenaline rush was fading, taking some of his strength with it. Not to mention how tired his muscles were from his workout. D'Anu magic could only do so much for bad wounds, and this was a doozy. Damn near took that arrow right in the heart, so he wasn't about to complain.

The sky was graying, a sign that dawn wasn't far behind, and these Dark Elves would be toast if they weren't taken inside and put in cells where they could be kept from the daylight. Light was also a good sign that no other Drow would be attacking.

Although Garran was able to tolerate light—he'd said the Great Guardian had given him that temporary gift. He and he alone. What if that was bullshit, and other Drow could handle sunlight?

Wouldn't that be fucking great.

Several of the D'Danann took the prisoners to the cages while his officers helped carry in the wounded and dead. Jake stumbled a bit as he watched them and his vision blurred before clearing.

Alyssa and the other witches rushed him into the kitchen and he let out a sigh of relief as he dropped into a chair by the table.

The women exclaimed over Hannah and Rhiannon, wanting to know where the two of them had been, and Keir growled his anger.

Both Hannah and Rhiannon seated themselves at the table and looked at each other before Hannah turned to Jake and said, "Take care of Jake first."

"Already on it." Alyssa was digging through the cabinets, pulling out bottles and jars for whatever magical potions and herbs the witches used.

Cassia reached Jake's side almost as soon as he sat down. He wasn't around the half-Elvin witch often, but when he was, he always got a strange sensation that sent vibrations to his gut.

She looked at him with her turquoise eyes and through his blurring vision her features seemed more Elvish than before. At least what he imagined Elvin features would be like.

Cassia's hair looked like gentle gold waves and her skin was so smooth, perfect.

Perfect . . .

While she helped him out of his Kevlar vest, he was certain he was hallucinating as he imagined himself holding her, kissing her . . .

His mind spun and he knew he was definitely losing it.

Images of Kat drifted through his mind and he found himself comparing her to Cassia. Kat was all hard edges, direct, and as black and white as you could get.

Cassia was soft, like blurred lines instead of rough corners. She was intuitive, mysterious. If he tried, what kind of mysteries would he uncover when it came to the half-Elvin witch?

As the rambling questions traveled through his mind, his head felt as if it were floating from his body.

He blinked at his strange thoughts and concentrated on not passing out as Cassia examined the wound. Her touch sent odd electrical feelings through his arm. He wondered if anyone else had felt the same thing when she touched them.

"Hold this lodestone," Cassia said as she pressed a bumpy odd-shaped stone into his hand. It gave him a little instant relief. Not a second later, rays of electricity traveled through his arm again when Cassia touched him, this time even more powerful.

When he met her eyes, her expression seemed to reflect something like wonder, maybe even fear, before changing back to neutral. "I think you're going to want to be asleep for this," she said. This time her voice had a husky quality to it that he'd never noticed before.

Jake nodded. He wasn't an idiot. That arrowhead was buried so deep in muscle it was going to be a bitch to get out.

"Hit me with your best shot," he said, sounding and feeling almost drunk from pain and loss of blood.

Alyssa arrived at his other side. The strong scents of herbs swept over him as she held up a small dark vial. "Open your mouth."

He obeyed and she tipped the bottle and put a couple of drops on his tongue. He grimaced when he closed his mouth. Nasty crap.

His whole body instantly relaxed, every muscle going limp. Voices in the room faded and his arm went numb. The spinning in his head slowed until he slipped into darkness.

CHAPTER TWENTY-NINE

DARKWOLF HAD TO GIVE Elizabeth-Junga one thing. Despite the power he now commanded, she didn't cower before him. She maintained her proud, former Queen of the Fomorii demeanor, even in the face of possible death at his hands.

The urge to kill was nearly overwhelming. He imagined wrapping his hands around her throat, snapping it with one quick twist.

Once again Elizabeth's gaze traveled over his now seven-foot height and she pursed her lips as she studied his muscles that had bulged so tightly his old shirt and jeans had shredded. Like the fucking Incredible Hulk, without the green skin. And he still looked damned good.

After having taken advantage of his new power to travel to a big and tall men's clothing store, they had used transference again to take them to an empty President's suite at the Hilton. Screw Balor finding him now. Darkwolf would use the power of the former eye anytime he wanted to.

Elizabeth tilted her head at a regal angle as she studied his chest—as if she could see the eye's power now encompassing his heart. "What do you plan to do now?"

"Find Ceithlenn." His voice had developed into a low, coarse growl. "After I fuck you."

Her eyes widened and her pupils dilated as her gaze dropped to the massive erection outlined by his jeans. His cock had grown as big around as his fist and double the length. Not to mention he was so horny he could take on a roomful of women.

Maybe he would.

Darkwolf reached up and grasped the collar of her T-shirt with his large hands and shredded it with one small movement. It took little strength for something so small as this. Elizabeth gasped as he forced her down on the floor. Her jeans went next, the thick material tearing like silk.

His thoughts twisted and churned, his vision going from gray to red to Technicolor, but the pain in his head was gone. For the first time in longer than he could remember, he felt no pain. Just power. Pure power.

Right now all he cared about was rutting inside a woman, any woman, and this one would do. For as long as he let her live.

Taking care not to ruin his own clothing, Darkwolf unbuttoned and unzipped his pants. Elizabeth's eyes grew wider when she saw the size of his erect cock up close and personal. Without giving her time to speak, he gripped her throat at the same time he forced his broad hips between her thighs and drove his cock inside her pussy.

She tried to cry out from the pain of his penetration, but his hand on her throat kept her from making a sound. Despite the blind power ripping through him so hard he felt like his skin would split, he didn't truly want to kill her.

Just hurt her.

As Darkwolf drove in and out of Elizabeth, he imagined taking Ceithlenn down the same way and repaying her for what she'd done to him. Only he'd kill *her*.

The mere thought of taking his revenge on Ceithlenn almost made him tighten his grip around Elizabeth's throat.

Shit, it felt incredible fucking her so hard and fast, her pussy tight around his cock. She whimpered, but it only drove him on until his vision began to redden, almost as red as the eye had been when it swung from the chain at his throat.

But he was free of that now and the power was his.

Despite his hold on her throat, Elizabeth climaxed first,

her body convulsing, the contractions in her core clamping down on him harder than they ever had before.

The intensity he felt in his groin and from his oncoming orgasm made stars flash before his eyes. He thrust several times more before he climaxed.

When he came he shouted, his baritone reverberating off the walls. He released Elizabeth's neck and braced his hands to either side of her tiny waist as he pressed his groin against hers. Pulse after pulse of his cock and the doubled, tripled, quadrupled pleasure he felt made him almost blind.

He felt something over his heart, digging into his flesh, and Elizabeth came into view, her arm outstretched and her hand transformed into her Fomorii claws.

The shock of feeling her jagged nails in his flesh made his vision clear.

"I could have killed you." No fear was in her eyes as she slid her claws from his flesh. "Your heart would have been in my palm and I could have eaten it before you realized what had happened. Then the power would have been mine."

His mind still spun and he glanced down to see tears in his bloody flesh healing through the rips in the T-shirt.

When his stunned gaze met hers she smiled. "Don't think for a moment that Ceithlenn won't find a weakness in you, too."

The fact that Elizabeth could have killed him so easily was like ice in his veins.

Better now, though, to find out he had weaknesses, that he wasn't as entirely invincible as he'd felt. It also told him that the god and goddess surely had weaknesses that would make them easy kills. Once he knew what those weaknesses were.

The feel of Elizabeth's nails scraping down his chest through his T-shirt brought his attention back to her. Why hadn't she killed him? What made her allow him to live?

She met his gaze, her eyes dark with desire. "Now fuck me again."

CHAPTER THIRTY

"WE WILL CHOOSE A date." Ceithlenn brushed back the short, punk-red hair she wore in her human form—that of the warlock Sara, whom Ceithlenn had shoved to the very back of her consciousness. "Every Fomorii will meet at the piers where the human tourists gather in large numbers."

Since she'd had martial law lifted by the demons she had placed in the government and military, the city would again pick up its pace, giving her and her demons greater numbers of humans to slaughter.

Tryok, the demon who served as the leader over all her legions, prostrated himself on the floor of the apartment, bowing to her greatness. "As you will it, my goddess." The demon's voice sounded odd coming from the body of the great general he currently inhabited. She almost laughed at the balding, well-fed, highly decorated general practically lying on his belly.

Ceithlenn picked up a figurine of what her human host called a Swarovski ballerina. A stupid statue, really. A statue of a weak, insipid creature—as all humans were.

Ceithlenn clenched her fist around the crystal and it shattered in her powerful grip, pieces flying and tinkling as they scattered across the burgundy carpeting. Broken crystal sliced her human palm. She held back a wince and a growl from the burning pain and opened her hand. It healed at once, small shards of crystal purging from her flesh and onto her palm where only traces of blood remained.

She brushed the crystal and blood from her hand onto the thigh of her leather catsuit, her mind turning to important matters.

Her gaze scraped the demon-man still on the floor. "Rise, Tryok."

"Yes, my goddess." The demon obeyed at once, scooping up his general's cap as he rose. He positioned the hat on his head, his jowls wobbling like gelatin with his motions.

Too bad she had chosen the body of such a fat, ugly human for Tryok. Right now she could use a good fuck. With Balor missing and Darkwolf gone, she hadn't had sex in far too long. She would have to take two or three of the better-looking men inhabited by demons and screw them all, one after another.

At least until she was reunited with Balor.

A scowl twisted her features as her thoughts turned to Darkwolf. Where was the bastard?

She needed to attempt scrying again, a skill of the warlock, Sara.

"Inform all of our legion members that we will attack two nights from now." Crystal crunched under her boots as she walked up to Tryok, who trembled in her presence. "Arrange for the demons to hide in the waters off the shore until my arrival and my signal."

The smell of human fear and sweat met her as Tryok bowed. His general's cap slipped off but he caught it before the cap landed on the floor. "Yes, my goddess."

"Leave." She watched as he backed up, turned and strode toward the apartment door, his polished shoes making soft sounds on the carpeting as he followed her instructions.

When he had closed the door behind him, she headed toward the kitchen. No more sickening odors of human cooking hung on the air. She'd had her demons clean out every piece of human food and dispose of it.

Her stomach grumbled at the thought of food. The demon-men and -women she had stationed in various parts of the apartment would need to bring more humans to dine on, giving her additional souls to absorb.

Ignoring the rumbling in her belly, she searched the cabinets in the kitchen until she came across a large metal bowl. It wasn't a cauldron or other bewitched container, but with her powers it would do.

After filling it with tap water, she set the bowl on the glass-topped table in the kitchen nook. Sunlight filtered through the flimsy sheer curtains, muted light gleaming on the table's surface.

Ceithlenn braced her hands on the glass to either side of the bowl and looked into the bowl's depths. The warlock's, Sara's, reflection stared back, her human eyes ever shifting from blue to green to brown to gray. Her short punk-red hair fell across her cheeks, and Ceithlenn pushed it behind both ears.

Gradually she slipped into a state of neither-here-nor-there and she felt as if she barely held on to the human body by a thread. Her eyes were unfocused. Images began to play out on the surface of the water and her human heart thumped against her breastbone. She dug her long fingernails into the glass to either side of the bowl. Sharp cracking sounds met her ears as her nails penetrated the glass tabletop.

Darkwolf. Balor's eye infusing him with such great power that his body glowed with it. The eye had apparently buried itself in his skin, becoming part of his heart. The muscles of his already fit body bulged with strength and his mind expanded with mastery over the weak, human part of himself. He now nearly had the strength of a god. The strength of Balor.

"No!" Ceithlenn screamed and slapped the side of the bowl with such vicious intensity that it flew across the room and shattered a window. The bowl continued through the break and sailed outside.

Water had splattered over the table's surface and on her face. "No!" she screamed again.

She lifted the glass table and slammed it against the wall, causing shards to explode across the kitchen and slice into her cheeks and the bared parts of her breasts.

This time when she shrieked she erupted into her goddess form, her fangs dropping, her hands lengthening into claws, her hair aflame and her wings spreading wide. She slammed her fist into what was left of the window, obliterating it before she pushed her way out and took to the skies.

Ceithlenn didn't give a fuck if humans saw her in the daylight. Darkwolf had taken the power of the eye for himself. She would find the bastard and rip his heart from his chest.

CHAPTER THIRTY-ONE

AFTER THE ARROWHEAD HAD been removed from Jake's arm, Hannah and the other witches used magical herbs and potions to treat the wound. The Drow diamond arrowhead glittered on the tabletop in the sunlight. Hannah shook her head. The damned thing that could have killed Jake was worth a small fortune.

Hannah breathed out a sigh of relief that he was okay as she brought her hand to her moon and crescent armband and stroked it with her fingers. Jake was one of the best men she knew and the thought of him coming close to getting killed created another knot in her belly. Banshee rested on her shoulder and tugged at strands of her hair as if agreeing with her.

The kitchen smelled of the tea tree oil used as an antiseptic, herb Robert to stop the bleeding, and comfrey ointment to speed the healing of the wound. All of these had been infused with magic to speed the healing and to take away as much pain as possible.

By the time Cassia finished binding Jake's arm with spelled cloth, he started coming around. He blinked, his sleepy blue eyes slowly becoming more alert. The man was built like a football player and dwarfed the kitchen chair.

Hannah sat in a chair next to him and put her hand on his knee. She used her magic to draw him further into the present and to help eliminate the fog in his mind. Banshee gave a soft cry as he lent her some of his own magic.

Jake shook his head twice, like he was trying to shake off the remnants of the potion. Then he looked up and his eyes appeared clear of any pain, cloudiness, or confusion.

Hannah drew her hand away, releasing the magical bond she'd used on him.

"We've got to talk." Jake's gaze moved from Hannah's to Rhiannon's. "If anything's been said while I've been out, fill me in."

"Nothing." Rhiannon pushed her hand through her hair and ignored Keir's protective stance and thunderous expression as he glowered over her. "We've been waiting for you."

"Good." Jake glanced at his bandaged arm then to Cassia and his features seemed unusually wary. "Thanks for patching me up."

Cassia just smiled her mysterious smile and turned to start throwing ingredients into a bowl. She was always cooking something, even though the D'Danann had found the legendary Cauldron of Dagda.

Unlike the kitchen at their now closed shop, Enchantments, this kitchen was large and roomy, and could accommodate five of the D'Danann, all eight D'Anu, Jake, and one of his officers.

Hannah's thoughts rested on Garran for a moment. He should be here.

"Shoot." Jake directed his command to speak at Hannah, and she sat straighter in her chair and met his stare head-on.

Automatically she wanted to close up because she never let anyone tell her what to do. Instead, she started telling everyone present about her and Rhiannon's journey to the Drow realm.

Just about every man had his arms folded across his chest, a fierce expression on his face. Hannah's body heated. Who were they to judge her choices? The witches' expressions varied from concerned to unhappy to angry.

Well, she knew just where they could put their thoughts. She wasn't an idiot. She did and she would continue to do whatever she had to in order to fight this war against Ceithlenn and keep everyone safe.

Including that bastard Garran, who had virtually traded his life for his people and hers.

When Hannah finished telling everyone in the kitchen about the visions, Keir clenched the hilt of his sword. "Drow lies. They tricked you with their dark magic."

Rhiannon got in her husband's face. "You listen, and you listen good. When I have one, my visions don't fail me and that was as clear a vision as I've ever had."

She turned and swept her gaze from one person to the next. Her anger was apparent from the stiffness of her body, and the redness of her face that caused her Fomorii scars to stand out. "The Great Guardian is responsible for Garran's power, and he has used it to help us with this war."

Hannah tried to speak without lashing out at the prejudiced people in the room. "He has endangered his life." Her next words were harder to say, as if a great weight pressed on her chest. "If he uses that power one more time, he'll probably die. We can't let him do that."

"What about the Drow who attacked and killed so many of our people last night?" Hawk asked, his arms still crossed over his chest.

"Hannah already told you." Rhiannon's scars seemed even whiter and her eyes flashed a deeper emerald color. "They acted on their own. Their leader is some guy named Vidar and he went against Garran's decision and his promise to us. Their other leaders didn't even know anything about what Vidar had done."

"Then where are the leaders, this Directorate?" Hawk braced one arm on the refrigerator. "Why have they not come?"

Rhiannon rolled her eyes and pointed to the windows where light streamed in through the fog. "Duh? The sunlight? They don't have a special gift from the Great Guardian to let them walk in daytime."

The room was silent for a moment before Silver rubbed the small pooch of her pregnant belly and said, "We have to give him the benefit of the doubt. He's been out cold, so there's no way he could have ordered that attack."

"Unless he did it ahead of time." Jake grimaced as he moved his arm and shifted in his chair, probably from the pain that magic couldn't completely take away. "He might have given his men a date and time and didn't know he'd be flat on his back." Jake brought his hand up to his bandaged arm. "He probably didn't know ahead of time about the attack on Hannah at Coit Tower, I'll give him that." With a frown, Jake added, "But he could have worked out this Drow attack with Darkwolf. After all, the Dark Elves did help Darkwolf open the door to Underworld."

Hannah's composure hung by a thread. She wanted to scream, to yell, to stomp her foot and tell the group they were a bunch of idiots not to trust Garran after he'd risked his life for all of them.

Banshee gripped her shoulder a little tighter.

She raised her chin and said, "Under no circumstances will Garran be harmed. Rhiannon and I will question him and we can go from there." She hadn't realized she was clenching her fists until she felt the ache in her knuckles. She forced herself to relax them. "I'm going to check on Garran and all of you can wait until I'm finished talking with him. Once he's awake."

With her chin raised and her back straight, she pushed the kitchen door open, walked out. She held out her arm and Banshee eased down on it before flapping his wings and taking flight.

With grim resolve, Hannah headed to the room she and Garran had been sharing.

She couldn't believe he would break his word. He wouldn't. No matter what anyone thought, Garran wasn't responsible for that attack.

GARRAN WOKE WITH THE mother goddess of all headaches. He opened his eyes and shut them again as late afternoon sunlight attacked them. It took him a few moments of blinking, but he finally accustomed himself to the light.

He frowned, trying to remember what had happened and why he was flat on his back. Smells of cedar and safflower met wood and sawdust as he took a deep breath. He flexed his hands and shifted even though every muscle in his body ached.

A light blanket covered him. He realized he was naked beneath it and he frowned again.

Memories slowly came back to him. Being in his realm and realizing in his gut that Hannah needed him. Finding her being tortured in a fiery sphere. Joining her and protecting them both from the heat before he used the power the Great Guardian had given him.

He had sent the few Fomorii back to Underworld.

But Ceithlenn had vanished.

Garran's entire being shook with his fury. The bitch had escaped.

The magnitude of what he'd done slammed into his chest as if the stone door to his realm had fallen upon him. He had used the power from the Great Guardian a second time, eliminating few of the Fomorii and not the goddess.

His people. By the gods, he had already failed them by using the power in a way that did not directly benefit them.

Yet, could even a king be expected to put his people before his family and those he loved . . . Rhiannon . . .

And Hannah?

His heart squeezed. Did he love her? Was that what the feeling was that wrapped itself around his heart so tightly he could barely take a breath without his chest hurting?

Saving Hannah had been more important to him than anything at that moment when he had used his powers.

Was it possible that he could have battled Ceithlenn in a different way? Have saved Hannah using his sword and his dark powers? He did not believe he was protected against Ceithlenn's abilities to draw the soul from a body. She could have had the opportunity to kill him.

But now . . .

He would need to use the power a third and final time. He

would have to make sure he sent the rest of the Fomorii to Underworld. And Ceithlenn with them.

Then he would likely die.

Garran brought his hand to his forehead and rubbed his eyes. His hand felt heavy as he moved it and he ground his teeth in frustration at the weakness pinning his body to the sleeping bags on the floor of the room he and Hannah had shared.

Was Hannah well? He'd assumed she was, but what if Ceithlenn had come back?

Ice coated his soul.

The click of the door had him turning his head in that direction. Relief flooded through him and a smile curved the corner of his mouth as Hannah slipped in and shut the door behind her.

Thank the gods she was all right. With the connection they had he believed he would have known if anything had happened to her—but *seeing* her well and alive made his heart soar.

A troubled expression was on her beautiful features, but she composed herself and walked toward him, where he lay naked beneath the blanket.

"About time you woke up, Sleeping Beauty." With grace she eased down and sat next to him, her legs curled to the side of her. "You've been out so long I was beginning to wonder if you were going to make it back." She gave him a look that said she hadn't been concerned, but he saw beneath that façade.

She wore a shirt and jeans and looked beautiful despite the dark smudges under her eyes. He wanted to know what had put them there. Her dark hair fell in glossy waves around her face and the one lock of blond hair was tucked behind her ear.

The heaviness in his body began to ease away and he turned on his side so that he faced her. He settled one elbow on the sleeping bag and rested his head on his palm. The blanket slid down to his hips, barely covering his cock, and his lips quirked when her gaze followed the glide of the blanket and her eyes rested on his growing erection now tenting the blanket.

"I see that at least one part of you has recovered." Her gaze met his again.

"Kiss me," he said.

Hannah blinked and just looked at him, but her nipples pushed against her T-shirt, telling him more than she wanted him to know.

He gave her a lazy smile. "Kiss me."

"Just one." Hannah lowered her eyelids and brought her face to his at the same time she braced her hand on his biceps. Her breath was warm against his lips as she brushed her mouth over his.

Garran caught her lower lip between his teeth, holding her to him, and she gave a soft sound of surprise. As she opened her mouth, he thrust his tongue inside, tasting her sweet flavor and wanting more than a kiss.

And he would have what he wanted.

In a fast movement, he turned onto his back, grasping her around the waist, lifting her, and setting her down so that she was straddling his waist.

"Garran!" Something between a laugh and concern was in her voice. "You've been ill. What in the world are you doing?"

He took one of her hands and placed it on his erection. "Does this feel like the cock of a man who is ill?"

With her eyelids lowered, she rubbed the length of it, from his balls to the head of his erection through the light fabric of the blanket. "No." She squeezed him. "It sure doesn't." Her dark gaze met his. "But you likely need more time to heal."

Garran reached up and palmed her breasts before squeezing her nipples. "I cannot think of a better way to heal than to make love to you, Hannah."

She groaned as he pinched and pulled her nipples through her T-shirt, and she rubbed his cock harder.

Garran sucked in his breath as she brought her mouth to his again and their kiss was slow and leisurely. Right now he didn't want slow. He wanted hard and fast.

He grasped Hannah's T-shirt and pulled it out of her jeans and she rose and helped him to remove it. He loved the satiny material of what she called a bra, and he ran his rough hands over both breasts, squeezing and fondling them through the soft fabric.

Hannah reached behind her and unfastened the bra, slid it off and tossed it aside. At the sight of her beautiful breasts and her rosy nipples, his erection throbbed beneath the blanket separating them. He pulled her down, latching on to one of her nipples with his mouth, sucking and licking the taut nub as Hannah gave soft little moans. He moved his mouth to her other nipple, paying the same close attention to it and making her writhe on top of him.

He didn't like the fact that she had jeans on. He wanted their naked bodies intertwined and he wanted to be pounding in and out of her as hard as he possibly could. The urge was almost overwhelming.

Before he could flip her on her back, she scooted down his body, easing the blanket away from his erection at the same time. He hissed as she looked up at him and ran her tongue along the length of his cock and fondled his balls. A deep groan rose from his throat as he watched her slip his erection into her mouth and felt her wet heat surround him.

Her tongue swirled around the head of his shaft and he almost couldn't think clearly with all the sensation concentrating in his groin. She was so good at sucking his cock that the only thing that could possibly feel better was being inside her.

As her head bobbed up and down as much as she could take of his length, she used one hand to work his cock while her other stroked, fondled, and squeezed his balls. She was so damn good he could already feel the power of his oncoming climax. It roared through his head like thunder and through his groin like a storm. She made soft purring sounds that nearly sent him over the edge as he watched his cock going in and out of her mouth while she kept her gaze focused on him at the same time.

She purred again and black spots danced before his eyes and the thunderstorm roared through him. His hips bucked against her face and his come filled her mouth. She swallowed, using deep suction, drawing everything out until he could no longer take it and reached down to grasp her by her shoulders and draw her up his body.

Her jeans scraped his belly and her self-satisfied grin made him hard all over again.

She laughed when he flipped her onto her back and straddled her. He stared into her brown eyes and she surprised him by taking his cock in her hand again and stroking it alive and harder than ever.

"I'd say you're better." She gave him a teasing smile. "But let's see just how well you really are."

"You will find this king is more than hale and hearty." Garran bent one of her knees and pushed her leg up high enough that he could reach her shoe. He flipped it to the side then peeled off her sock before releasing her leg and grasping her other foot and ridding her of her shoe and sock.

She watched him with the hint of a smile, as if amused by his aggression and how badly he wanted her naked. He quickly unbuttoned her jeans and yanked them down with her underwear, stripping her naked within moments.

"Come on, you big, sexy king." She reached for him as he knelt between her thighs. "Fuck me."

By the gods, Garran wanted to drive his cock into her slick core, but first he wanted to taste her. A sound of surprise came from her as he hooked her legs over his shoulders, slid his hands beneath her ass, and brought her folds closer to his face.

Hannah gasped as he buried his mouth against her mound, licking her folds and sucking her clit with such intensity he could feel her orgasm close to the edge already.

No, he wanted to draw out her pleasure, fill her with even

more lust and desire to have his cock inside her. He raised his head from her folds and his gaze met hers as he plunged three fingers into her core.

With a cry she bucked her hips, straining to feel him deeper inside her and also bringing her mound closer to his mouth. "Make me come, Garran." She groaned as he pounded his fingers in and out of her. "Lick my clit. Suck it."

He flashed an amused grin, loving teasing her and making her desire him even more.

Hannah moved her thighs on his shoulders as she squirmed. "King or not, I'm going to kill you if you don't finish the job."

With another grin he licked her folds, tasting her juices, smelling her feminine musk. She thrashed as he brought his mouth closer to her clit. He watched her as he ran his tongue along her folds, enjoying the flush in her cheeks as she gripped the sleeping bag in both of her fists.

When he could tell she was so close to the edge she was about to fall over, he sucked her clit.

Hannah cried out, her body trembling and shaking in his hands, her legs and thighs tightening around his shoulders. He watched her, felt her as her core spasmed around his fingers and she twisted as if seeking a reprieve, or more from him.

He could give her more.

Garran rose and moved his hands from her ass to grasp her behind her knees. He pushed her legs up so that her thighs touched her chest, her legs still over his shoulders.

Without waiting for her to catch her breath, he drove his erection inside her core and took her hard and fast. Gods, he could reach so deep inside her that he felt his cock touch her womb. She was so tight and slick and her core continued to spasm as if her first orgasm had never ended.

"Garran." She grasped his thighs as he pounded in and out of her. "Oh, goddess." Her voice was hoarse and tight. "What are you doing to me?"

"Fucking you." He reached down and pinched her nipples,

causing her to cry out and tip her head back. "One of many times, many ways I will take you."

She didn't argue as her breathing came in harsh pants. Sweat coated them both, their skin slick with it.

Her whole body started to shake, her eyes wide, and her lips parted as if facing an oncoming storm. He thrust harder, pinched her nipples tighter and she screamed. Loud enough that she could probably be heard through the entire warehouse. It pleased him to know that others would hear her and realize that he was staking his claim on her, making her his.

Her core clamped down on his cock and he could barely hold back his own orgasm. He wanted to draw hers out, make her pleasure so intense that it would border on pain.

"I can't—I can't—" Hannah said as she twisted and writhed in his arms. "Take much more. It's too much."

"You *will* take more." He would give her more than she thought she could handle and she would enjoy it. As his queen she would take everything he gave to her.

My queen?

He almost stopped his powerful strokes.

"Garran." Hannah's face flushed even rosier, sweat dripping down the side of her face. "I—oh, goddess."

He felt another orgasm building up in her with more intensity, more speed than the last. She brought her hands up and clenched his biceps, digging her nails into his flesh. She turned her head from side to side and her body shook in his arms. He thrust harder, pounded in and out of her deeper and faster.

Hannah seemed to fall apart. She cried out again, this time struggling against his hold as he took her. Her body jerked and thrashed beneath his and she made loud crying sounds that were pleasurable to his ears.

His restraint began to falter as her core clamped down on his cock, pulsing around him and pulling him closer toward his own climax.

For the first time while having sex with a woman, he grew lightheaded. The scents of sex, sweat, perfume, the feel of his flesh slapping against her, their sweaty skin rubbing together, her nails digging into his arms—it was too much for him to take any longer.

Garran gave a shout of intense pleasure and ownership of this woman. All pleasure that had been centered in his groin burst out of him and spilled into Hannah. His cock pulsed, his come filling her with every stroke he made.

When it was more than even he could take, he released her legs and pulled his cock out of her core. He drew her into his arms as he lay down beside her and intertwined her legs with his.

Her breath came in harsh pants and she looked dizzy and exhausted. "You're definitely not ill anymore," she said as she snuggled closer. "Considering you've been out for two days, I figured you'd be too weak to do much of anything."

He braced himself on one elbow, shock coursing him, sending prickles under his skin. "Two days? I have lost two days?"

Hannah nodded as she met his gaze, her expression sobering. "You didn't move. Didn't twitch. I was worried about you."

Garran pushed himself up to a sitting position and Hannah rose at the same time. *Two days?* What had he missed? How were his people doing without him? He had much to do with Carden's training before—before he used the power a third time.

And died.

CHAPTER THIRTY-TWO

HANNAH STARED AT GARRAN, so many emotions causing her chest to tighten. After the talk with everyone last night, she'd come back to the room and had slept next to his still form again.

It had irritated her that the D'Danann insisted on posting Fae outside the door. A pair of warriors stood guard now and Hannah didn't care that they had no doubt heard her and Garran having sex.

Garran shook his head as he pushed his hand through his now white-blond hair. "My people—the battle—Ceithlenn . . . What has happened during my . . . absence?"

"A lot." Her stomach clenched and she shifted on the sleeping bags as she looked away from him. "We have so much to talk about."

Garran caught her face in his hands and forced her to look at him. He looked grim. "From the beginning."

Beginning? Goddess, it already seemed so long ago. "It started with all of the other witches scrying." She brought her hands up to his wrists and pulled his palms from her face.

"You will scry again." He clasped her hands in his. "Perhaps another mirror or some other divination tool. You are a D'Anu witch and you will continue to do as you always have done."

The knots in her belly returned and she drew away from him and held one hand to her abdomen. "I've lost the only

divination tools I've ever used. And at least two of the Dragons have abandoned me."

He frowned. "What do you mean?"

"When Ceithlenn captured me, I had just finished summoning the Dragons, my spirits, my totems." Pain slammed
into her so hard her head ached with it. "The Fire and Water
Dragons made it clear they'd gone over to Ceithlenn's side."
She tore her other hand from his and clenched both of her
fists against her temples and her voice caught. "The Air
Dragon wouldn't help me. Only the Earth Dragon gave me
some of its power."

Hannah dropped her hands to her lap, her voice hoarse. "I
don't know what I'm going to do, Garran. Goddess help me,
I don't know what I'm going to do."

Garran took her into his arms and she let him, let him fill
her with the strength of his presence, like chardonnay flowing through her veins, relaxing her a little.

"We will win this war together, you and I." Garran's
words were spoken in a firm, resolute tone. "Together we are
stronger and we will not let Ceithlenn destroy this city."

Seeing Garran awake and well had pushed aside almost
every other thought from Hannah's mind. Every question,
every concern . . . everything she'd learned . . . everything
that had happened.

Hannah pushed away from Garran's embrace, rolled over
and got to her feet. His expression was puzzled as she stepped
into her panties, pulled them up then grabbed her bra.

"How could you, Garran?" She kept her gaze focused on
him as she reached around and fumbled with her bra hook.
Bless it. Her hands were shaking. "How could you let that—
that Guardian being give you the power to *kill* yourself?"
She snatched up her T-shirt and held it in front of her, her
hands still shaking. "And how could you not tell me?"

Garran's jaw dropped and he just looked at her. Hannah
jerked on her T-shirt as she waited for his answer.

He slowly got to his feet, shock evident on his features.
"You cannot possibly know this."

Heat burned Hannah's cheeks as she yanked on her jeans one leg at a time. "Rhiannon and I went to see the Drow."

Garran's muscles bunched as his body tensed. "You went alone to my realm?"

Hannah had scooped up her socks and she paused and narrowed her eyes. "The other witches scried about the Drow attacking us and believed you had used a dark power to transport the Fomorii someplace where they'll be able to attack us."

She started to tug on her socks but went completely still as she studied Garran. His jaw was set, his eyes more a shade of steel than liquid silver. Anger rolled off him in tangible waves that made her shiver. "Is that what you think of me? That I would betray you?" he asked in a deadly quiet voice.

"In my heart . . . I—I trust you." She fiddled with the socks and met his gaze. "I don't think you would do anything to hurt us. I believed that once you made your decision to help in this war against the Fomorii and Ceithlenn you would keep to your word. I still believe that."

His expression softened and he walked toward her. She backed up and he looked confused.

"Even though I feel that way, I'm angry at what you've done." She raised her voice and heard the tremors in it. "How could you do something that might kill you?"

He pushed his hand through his hair again and his eyes looked tired. In that moment she could see centuries of life in his gaze, proof that he truly was an ancient being, no matter how young he appeared to be on the outside.

The memory of the nightmare came back to her—of Garran lying sightless on the ground as rain pounded his body. She swallowed. The nightmare had been so clear and she remembered it as if she had been right there—feeling the rain on her skin, watching the carnage as the demons ripped apart humans and Ceithlenn absorbed the peoples' souls.

She blinked and found herself feeling an odd ache behind her eyes. "You can't use that power again. You *can't*."

This time when Garran walked toward her, she didn't

back up. "Hannah," he murmured. "What I will do . . . it will be the right thing." He cupped her face in his hands and studied her as if trying to imprint her on his memory. The fact that he could die was like a punch to her gut.

She dropped the socks and pushed his hands away. "Don't you start giving me some kind of self-sacrificing crap." She clenched her hands at her sides. The vision, her nightmare, and the feeling deep inside her belly told her more than his words.

Garran turned away, went to the pile of clothing and began climbing into a pair of jeans. "It is not for you to concern yourself with."

"Like hell!" Hannah's whole body was on fire as she finished putting on her socks, unable to look at him. "You'll leave the people you care about, who care about you, and the people who need you as your leader." She shoved her feet into her shoes. "Already your being out of it has screwed things up royally."

"What do you mean?" He walked back to her, grabbed her by her upper arms, and forced her to look at him. "What has happened?"

"Some of your people attacked last night, that's what." She placed her palms on his bare chest and pushed him away. "A lot of our own died—PSF officers and D'Danann—because of the Drow."

Shock followed by outrage made his fair skin flush. "This is not possible."

"A few of the Drow weren't killed and are locked up." She jerked her thumb in the general direction of the cells. The heat in her body made her words sound harsh. "According to them, they were following Vidar's orders."

Garran stilled. "Vidar?" The name was uttered like a curse. He fisted his hands. "Does he live?"

Hannah crossed her arms over her chest. "He's in one of the cells, too."

"I will kill him." Still clad only in jeans, Garran strode to his gear, grabbed his sword by the hilt, and drew it from its leather sheath. The metal gleamed in the sunlight and the jewels on the hilt glittered.

"Stop." Hannah blocked his way. "Two D'Danann warriors are guarding this door. Because of the Drow attack, they won't let you out of here until you've been summoned for questioning. And then they have to decide if they believe you."

The fury in Garran's face was so great she took a step backward and bumped into the door.

"*You* fear me now?" Garran's knuckles whitened as he grasped his sword. "*You* do not believe me?"

Hannah moved away from the door and went to him. She wrapped her arms around his neck and pressed her cheek against his chest. "I'm not afraid of you. And I believe in you."

His body was so taut, so rigid. She held on to him even though she could feel the tremors his anger caused. She expected him to relax, to return her embrace, but instead he took her arms from around his neck and stepped back.

The loss of his touch made the knots in her belly tighter. Hannah's palms itched with the desire to spell him for pushing her away. Maybe she'd even make it so he couldn't move. That would serve him right.

She rubbed her forehead, trying to collect herself. These irrational thoughts were driving her crazy.

"I will not be held prisoner." Garran brushed past Hannah and she could feel his cold, hard anger like ice against her skin.

"Wait." She grabbed his sword arm as he jerked the door open with his free hand.

Garran shrugged her off as he looked from one D'Danann guard to the other. Each man had drawn his sword.

At that moment Garran looked more like a king than ever. His presence was arrogant, powerful, purposeful, with no fear in his eyes. Only anger and an expression that demanded respect.

"Escort me to Hawk." A command.

"You must relinquish your weapon," one of the D'Danann said without flinching.

Garran narrowed his gaze but handed the warrior his sword, hilt first. The men walked to either side of Garran and Hannah. The three men strode with the masculine grace of the Fae and Elves, but it was Garran who kept her attention. His long blond hair falling past his shoulders, the muscles in his back and biceps flexed as they walked toward the main part of the warehouse. The tight jeans molded his body, his bare feet silent on the concrete floor.

D'Danann and PSF officers watched him as he passed by with his escort.

When Garran, Hannah, and the D'Danann guards reached the strategy area of the warehouse, they came to a stop in front of Tiernan, Hawk, and Keir.

Hannah stepped to the side, prepared to defend Garran if she needed to.

Keir's expression was openly hostile, one hand gripping his sword hilt. Tiernan folded his arms across his chest. Only Hawk appeared casual as he leaned one hip against the map table and met Garran's gaze head-on.

"Explain why your people attacked ours." Hawk's voice was even, but an underlying tone of anger tinged his Irish brogue.

"I cannot." Garran looked to each man as if assessing them one by one. "If what Hannah said is true, and Vidar led this attack, he acted on his own." Garran's jaw clenched. "I shall kill him myself."

"How do we know you are telling the truth?" As a former Lord of the D'Danann High Court, Tiernan's voice was more cultured, refined, his expression more unreadable than Hawk's or Keir's.

"Did I not save the life of your mate, Copper?" Garran asked Tiernan. "Did we not fight side by side against the giant of Underworld and against the beasts fleeing the door to that foul place?"

"It was you and your warriors who helped let the gods-damn demons out," Keir growled. "You allowed Ceithlenn to escape."

"This is true." Garran's expression didn't change and his powerful, kingly presence didn't diminish. "You also know that I realized I had made the wrong decision and turned the tide of battle against the beasts."

"How many times are we going to go over that? It's history." Hannah pushed her way forward so that she stood in the middle of the formidable men. "What is important is the here and now. I was in the Drow realm when we discovered what Vidar had done. His people had nothing to do with the attack." She glared at each man and almost shouted, "So let's move on."

She sucked in her breath. So much for keeping her cool.

All four men studied her. Tiernan finally nodded before speaking to Garran. "From the beginning, because of what you did for my mate, I have trusted your word. I trust it now, as well."

"Then you are a fool." Keir moved closer to Garran, crowding out Hannah. "Drow are naught but selfish, betraying bastards."

"You're talking about my father."

Hannah turned to see Rhiannon glaring at her husband, Keir. Her cheeks were red and her Fomorii scars white against her cheek.

His features and his voice softened, as they only did with Rhiannon. "But can the Drow truly be trusted?"

She moved closer to him and tilted her chin up so that her eyes met his. "Do you trust me?"

He turned from Garran and reached up to run his knuckles over Rhiannon's scars. "You know the answer." She backed away from his touch and he frowned.

"Then listen to me." Red still flushed Rhiannon's cheeks. "You're all wasting time posturing and acting like idiots when you should be taking care of the real offenders and planning together how to beat Ceithlenn."

Keir only hesitated a moment before he released his grip

on his sword. He turned back to Garran. "For my mate I agree to allow you to continue working with us and for the Drow to fight by our sides."

Tiernan unfolded his arms. "I agree to this, as well."

"As do I," Hawk said.

The tension within Hannah relaxed and she let out her breath.

Garran's expression was still proud, imperious even, as he took back his sword from one of the guards. "Show me where Vidar is."

AS HE STRODE TO the cells, Garran's grip on his sword hilt tightened as did the fury in his chest.

With Hawk, Tiernan, and Keir following him, Garran entered the darkened room where all light had been diminished due to the Drow inability to tolerate sunlight. With his keen vision he saw easily in the dark, his gaze traveling the cells where a few of his warriors remained. He knew these men, as he knew every one of the Dark Elves, including any child born into the realm.

Each man bowed from their shoulders in deference to their king. These were good men—why had they fought those working to eliminate Ceithlenn, against his orders?

Garran turned away from the men and met Vidar's dark eyes, eyes that held no remorse, only anger. For a moment Garran simply stared at the man.

Garran had no one to blame but himself, and his muscles tensed further at the realization. At one time he had trusted Vidar, had thought to place the future of his people in Vidar's hands should Garran die.

Truly Garran's failure was in his arrogance—he had never thought he would pass from this world or his own to travel to Summerland and leave his people without a strong and just leader.

The fact, too, that he had erred in judgment with Vidar was a boulder of tremendous weight in his gut.

With his teeth clenched, he bypassed his other men and strode to Vidar's cell.

The man had one shoulder hitched against one bar of the cell, his arms crossing his chest. His gaze slowly traveled from Garran's white-blond hair, down Garran's naked torso that exposed his daylight-fair skin. "So, you have taken the gift for yourself, I see." Vidar smirked. "You claim to desire the light for all Dark Elves, but you have cheated all your people."

"Under whose orders did you attack?" Garran demanded, his eyes narrowed.

Vidar shrugged. "I did what was necessary when you let down our people as king." He pushed himself away from the bar of the cell and approached Garran. "You stole from me what was rightfully mine."

"The blame lies with me—for not seeing you as you truly are, Vidar, until it was almost too late for our people." The urge to reach through the bars and throttle the man with his bare hands was so great that Garran shook with the desire. "And still it was too late for what you have done."

Vidar's eyes were dark as obsidian against his blue skin and blatant hatred twisted his expression. "We killed many, but not enough. As a failed king, you should have died, as well."

Garran's arms trembled with fury as he thought of how satisfying it would be to behead Vidar. Garran forced himself to think as a king and not as a man filled with such rage he would strike down an unarmed prisoner.

Garran loosened his hold on his sword hilt. "I would choose your life as forfeit for being a traitor to the Drow. But I will allow those most affected by your treachery to select your fate."

Vidar scowled and wrapped his hands around the bars. "The Directorate will agree that I acted for our people as you have not."

Garran gave Vidar one more hard look, then turned and walked past the D'Danann and out of the room.

When he left the room and entered the main portion of the warehouse, he saw the sunlight had faded and looked down at his arms and chest. Even as he watched, his skin turned from fair to bluish-gray, and his long hair that had fallen over his shoulders shifted from white-blond to silvery-blue.

At one time Garran had thought that to walk in the daylight was the most valued thing any Drow would wish for. But now . . . they had made a world for themselves belowground and it was a good world. Perhaps he had been too consumed with the past to live for the present. His people, as well.

Once again he had to ask himself if he had made the right decision. He straightened and looked up at the dark windows. For his daughter, for Hannah, and for their people, yes. As a father and a lover, he could not be expected to ignore their needs for his own. Carden would make a good leader—and Garran hoped to have the opportunity to see to Carden's further training before . . . before the final battle.

Angry voices came from the door to the warehouse as it was opened.

Carden and Hark.

Garran strode toward the Drow men flanked by D'Danann warriors. Two more Fae had their swords unsheathed and stood behind Garran's men as they walked into the warehouse, fog swirling in the background.

"We will see the king and the traitor, Vidar," Carden said in a voice befitting a Steward. A king even. Powerful, forceful, with justified anger behind it.

"You shall be taken to our leaders," one of the D'Danann said. "At once."

Garran had approached close enough that he could see Carden. The Steward had a proud lift to his head, his features no longer youthful but commanding. Hark stood at his side, looking just as much the warrior, but with his usual calm.

"You will also see to it that our king is present," Carden said as he and Hark relinquished their weapons to the D'Danann.

Carden turned his head just as Garran approached and a measure of relief stole over his features. He bowed from his shoulders. "My king."

Hark also bowed. "Your Highness."

"Did you order this attack?" Garran kept his voice low and hard as he looked from his Steward to the member of his Directorate. "I will have you answer me now."

"No, we did not," Carden said in a firm tone. "Vidar acted on his own."

"It is so," Hark said.

For a moment Garran studied them then he nodded to each man. Garran looked to one of the D'Danann. "Take us to Hawk."

The Fae warriors kept their features blank. "We have already summoned him and the others through mind-speak," one of the men said.

"More traitors?" came Keir's voice from behind them.

When he cut his gaze to the warrior, Garran narrowed his brows. Jake, Tiernan, and Hawk strode up behind Keir. Each man wore a hard expression. Regaining the D'Danann and humans' trust would be no easy task, no matter the innocence of his people.

One of the D'Danann guarding Carden and Hark said, "Ten additional Drow warriors are being held outside."

Tiernan gave a sharp nod, acknowledging the information.

As he addressed his two men, Garran gestured toward the Fae. "Hawk, Tiernan, and Keir, leaders of the D'Danann." He introduced the human. "Jake Macgregor, captain of the human forces."

Garran in turn introduced his own men. "My Steward, Carden, and Head of the Order of the Directorate, Hark."

Carden and Hark each gave a slight bow. "If the decision of the Directorate is so, we will see the traitor, Vidar, executed once he is questioned," Carden said, then glanced at Garran. "With our king's permission."

"It is my belief that it should be so as well," Garran said, "but I will leave the final determination to the Alliance as it is they who have suffered great casualties."

Garran could almost hear the mind-speak between the three D'Danann warriors before Tiernan addressed Garran. "We will allow you to question the prisoner, but we must assess the innocence of the Drow before we allow any decisions to be made."

The men strode toward the room with the cells where the Drow traitors were being held. Hannah and Rhiannon walked up behind the men as they reached the room.

"Carden, Hark." Rhiannon reached the two men first. "What are you doing here?"

"Princess," Carden said as he and Hark bowed to Rhiannon. "We are here to carry out Vidar's sentence."

Warmth flowed through Garran's chest on hearing his men refer to his daughter as "princess."

"And what is the sentence?" Hannah asked.

"The D'Danann and PSF must make that determination." Carden straightened. "If it is left to the will of the Drow, Vidar shall be executed, as will the remaining Drow who fought with him."

Rhiannon cocked her head. "Provided they're not innocent and were only following orders, orders they were told came from you."

Carden bowed again. "Of course, Princess."

"We'll bring them out one at a time using our magic ropes." Hannah's gaze met Garran's. "We have the right to be involved, too."

Garran's chest had tightened the moment Hannah spoke but he forced himself to relax. The D'Anu were accomplished warriors in their own right.

Each of the five Drow warriors were questioned by Hark with Garran's permission, and each man said they had followed Vidar's orders. Vidar had said the king himself had given the command to attack.

As each of the five men recounted their stories, Garran's muscles grew more and more tense. He did not like the way Jake and the D'Danann looked at him, as if they believed he *had* given that order.

When Vidar was finally brought out, both Rhiannon and Hannah had their ropes binding the fierce warrior from his shoulders to the tips of his fingers. Two D'Danann followed, prodding Vidar with the tips of their swords. Vidar limped only slightly. His leg had been bandaged, but obviously his thigh was healing with the usual speed of the Dark Elves.

"Explain your actions," Hark said, his normally calm voice holding darkness that caused Garran to lift his brows.

"The king is a fool to help these Fae and humans." Vidar raked his gaze over Garran. "So, they know not your secret?"

Carden and Hark glanced at Garran, but he ignored Vidar's question. "My decision would be in agreement with the Directorate. To execute you for your crimes against the Fae and humans, therefore against our people."

Vidar struggled in his bonds and bared his teeth.

"However." Garran's gaze met those of the D'Danann leaders and Jake. "I leave the final decision to the human and D'Danann leaders—those beings whom you have harmed."

Jake crossed his arms over his chest, not even wincing from what appeared to be a large wound beneath bandages heavily wrapping his biceps. Hawk, Tiernan, and Keir again appeared to be communicating via mind-speak.

"We will discuss this with Jake Macgregor," Tiernan said, and all four men walked away.

Hannah and Rhiannon both glared at Vidar and the warrior grimaced as if they had tightened their glittering magical bonds around him.

Little time had passed before Jake and the D'Danann leaders returned.

"We have decided to turn over the prisoners and their fate to the Dark Elves," Hawk said. "You may take them and return to the Drow realm."

"However," Tiernan added, "should our own be attacked again by the Drow, we shall take no prisoners."

CHAPTER THIRTY-THREE

DARKWOLF INHALED THE SAN Francisco air, smelling brine and fish, but not the rotten-fish stench of the Fomorii.

It was early evening and he stood beside Elizabeth overlooking K-Dock and the California sea lions that had taken up residence there. An occasional bark bit the evening air to join the noises of tourists, buses, cars, vendors, and everything else one could imagine.

K-Dock was beside Pier 39, the busiest pier and one of the largest tourist traps in the city.

A trap. That's exactly what it would be if Ceithlenn's attack was successful. The busy piers were perfect feeding grounds for the dark goddess and the Fomorii. In one of Darkwolf's visions he had seen what she had planned and it was nasty.

He glanced around him at all the people out in the evening who would be nothing but human snacks to the Fomorii. Yeah, the slaughter wouldn't be pretty.

With martial law lifted the city was almost as busy as normal. This after assurances by government officials that citizens and tourists were safe from further terrorist attacks. Of course those assurances were given by officials whose bodies had been taken over by Fomorii demons.

Another tidbit he'd learned from the eye. Or should he call it the heart? The eye no longer existed. The only way for anyone to obtain his power would be to rip his heart from his chest and swallow it whole.

The thought sobered him for a moment when he remembered Elizabeth could have done just that. Since then he'd figured out how to protect himself by pinning her hands over her head when he fucked her, or took her from behind when she was on her hands and knees. And he'd taught himself not to lose any control when climaxing.

"Right now you see Ceithlenn with your power to vision?" Elizabeth asked as she looked out toward the lights of Alcatraz. Was she missing her life as the demon queen?

The power of his senses told him Elizabeth was conflicted. Confused even. Emotions she had never felt before had left her bewildered.

"Yes, I can see her." Darkwolf glanced at the sky before looking back at Elizabeth. "She's close." With the power he commanded he'd seen Ceithlenn begin her hunt for him after she visioned that he'd taken the power of the eye for himself. It was somewhat amusing how the goddess thought she could destroy him so easily.

"What are you waiting for?" Elizabeth tilted her head and looked up at him. Considering how tall he was now, she had to crane her neck. "Why don't you just find the bitch and get rid of her?"

"I need more power." His coarse growl filtered through the loud chatter and music on the pier. "First I'll call out Balor, get rid of him, and take the rest of the god's power for my own."

She twisted her lips and frowned. "How are you so sure you can do either—kill Balor or Ceithlenn or both?"

It still surprised him how regal and queenly Elizabeth continued to appear, and how she was unwilling to back down from him despite the fact that he could almost kill her with a thought.

He narrowed his gaze at her. "I have the power of a god—I can take him on."

"*Most* of the power of one of the *old* gods." Elizabeth waved her hand like shooing a fly. "And not a great one at that." Anger at her words and dismissive gesture caused heat to flush over his body. She looked away from him, her expression not changing as she rested her forearms on a railing overlooking the bay and barking sea lions. "I was there in the days the gods ruled this Otherworld. As Fomorii, I was a sea god before we were banished. Balor's true power was in the devastation the eye caused, and now that's gone." She looked back at him. "What can *you* do?"

He dug his fingers into the wooden railing. "I have other magic the eye gave me. Don't underestimate how powerful I am now."

Elizabeth shrugged and again he marveled at her failure to recognize how dangerous he was to her. Maybe she did realize that fact and she didn't give a damn. Or maybe she trusted him enough to believe he wouldn't hurt her.

He took a deep breath and relaxed his grip then rested his forearms on the railing beside Elizabeth.

What she'd said—and what she didn't say out loud—meant nothing. She didn't have a clue.

Darkwolf had spent the past day training himself to use his powers most effectively to be prepared for his oncoming battle with Balor. Now he was ready.

A thought niggled at his brain that he'd kept pushing back. When he had his revenge on both Balor and Ceithlenn for what they had done to him, he knew his power would allow him to take theirs.

What then? What did one do with the powers of a god?

At the time he'd obtained the eye, his goals had been magical powers and aiding Balor in returning to the land where he once ruled as a god.

Now Darkwolf could have more power than Balor and Ceithlenn combined, if he was successful.

Then what? He shook his head. No freaking idea.

He closed his eyes and let his mind slide into another vision to locate Ceithlenn.

Shock traveled through him in a cold wave. He jerked his eyelids open the moment he located the goddess bitch.

She had found Balor.

CHAPTER THIRTY-FOUR

CEITHLENN DID NOT LET thoughts of her revenge on Darkwolf or her anger distract her. Instead she focused on her last scrying vision. She knew where Balor was.

Finally she would be with her love, her husband. Together they would track down Darkwolf and rip out his heart to give Balor back his powers.

Would the heart return to an eye so that her beloved could see again and lay waste to thousands at a time?

Night wind and fog slid over her wings and moistened her face as she flew to the part of the city where she knew Balor would be. The thumping in her chest grew as pleasure spread through her.

The closer to him she got, the more intensely she felt his presence. Since bringing Balor to this world, she had not been able to absorb enough human souls to find him—until now.

Countless souls released by the Fomorii filled her, strengthening her, giving her what she needed. She had fed with the demons and her might was finally great enough to find Balor.

Exhilaration prickled her skin and a thrill rose up within her the moment she saw her love. He stood on a cracked sidewalk on a nondescript but steep street, beside an open manhole to the sewers. He tilted his head as if he could see her even in his blindness.

A smile curved the corners of his mouth as he raised his

arms. Despite the empty eye socket in the middle of his fore-head, he was the most handsome being she had ever known. His body was fit and muscled, and his cock long and always hard beneath his loincloth.

"Balor!" She let the fire vanish from her hair and drew in her fangs and claws. She folded her wings away as she swooped into his embrace, wrapped her arms around his neck and pressed her body to his. She didn't care that he stank of the sewers, that his skin was coated with slime. "By all that preys upon the night, you are here," she said, her cheek against his smooth chest.

"My dreams have been filled with naught but you." Balor squeezed her tighter. "You, Ceith. My love." He grasped her face in his filth-coated hands, tilted her head up and brought his mouth to hers. A fierce kiss that she opened to and she reveled in being in her husband's arms again.

Now they were both freed from Underworld. Now they were together. No other gods survived in this Otherworld any longer. She and Balor would be unhindered in their quest to rule the Old World.

Their kiss grew hungrier. It was filled with longing and the force and joy of their reunion. His cock pressed hard against her belly and she wanted him to take her right there in the middle of this quiet neighborhood.

He raised his head and brushed his hand over her hair, which was now the soft brown it had been in the Old World, when she was a prophetess. Before Balor was cast into Underworld after the battle with the Tuatha D'Danann—when the sun god Lugh shot out his eye. The power behind the god's shot had knocked out the eye and flung it into the sea. There it remained lost for century after century, until it finally washed ashore.

Ceithlenn had been sent away with Balor and they had survived in the darkest depths of Underworld.

At this precious moment she was not going to think of the horrors they had been through over the past two millennia. Now all that mattered was that she was in Balor's arms. She would bring him to the apartment she and the Fomorii had taken over.

Together they would prepare to wrest Balor's power from Darkwolf and attack the city so that she could take more souls. Then her magic would be strong enough to help her husband on their journey to the Old World.

A blast of purple fire slammed into Balor.

The blast drove him to the ground and Ceithlenn with him.

She cried out in surprise and whipped her head up to see the now over seven-foot-tall Darkwolf standing just yards from them.

Before she or Balor could react, Darkwolf released another burst of purple fire at Balor. The intensity of the magic tore Balor away from her and threw him against a lightpost. He gave a grunt of pain as the force snapped the pole in half. While Balor rolled away, the top of the lightpole crashed to the asphalt, glass shattering and metal crunching.

"For all that you've done and all that you've forced me to do," Darkwolf growled. He focused blast after blast at Balor, who continued to attempt to get up only to be knocked down again. "Your power is mine."

"No!" Ceithlenn stumbled to her feet, transforming into her goddess form at the same time.

Fucking bastard.

She drew on her power to take souls. She would take Darkwolf's, *now*.

The moment she attempted to take Darkwolf's soul, pain shot through her chest as if she'd been pierced with a dozen arrows. She nearly doubled over from the force of it and she staggered back.

By all that survived in Underworld, Darkwolf nearly had the power of a god.

She couldn't take his soul.

While keeping an eye on Ceithlenn, Darkwolf never let up on his barrage against Balor.

Her husband cried out his agony. He was weak. Growing

weaker. With Darkwolf having taken the power of the eye, Balor lacked the strength to defend himself against the continued torrent of magic.

She would kill Darkwolf before she saw Balor die.

With a shriek, she slung a bolt of fire at Darkwolf. He held up his free hand to ward it off but missed and her magic caught him in the side, burning cloth and flesh.

Darkwolf grunted and dropped to one knee. His aim faltered, and he struck a tree instead of Balor. The tree went up in a blaze of purple flame, crackling and hissing. The sulfuric smell of their magic and the burning wood twisted in the fog.

The lapse of magic slamming into him allowed Balor to stumble to his feet. Despite his blindness, he held out his hand and flung a ball of magical fire at Darkwolf.

It buried itself in Darkwolf's belly. The warlock cried out as the magic slung him into a hedge. Loud snapping sounds of branches breaking followed his shout of pain.

Both Ceithlenn and Balor attacked Darkwolf with their magic at the same time, but Darkwolf threw up a shield of protection and their power exploded around him. The shield glittered as Darkwolf slowly pushed himself to his feet, and he snarled at Ceithlenn and Balor.

She prepared to rain her magic on Darkwolf's shield. Together she and Balor could beat it down and destroy the warlock.

Ceithlenn aimed a bolt of magic at Darkwolf's shield. But to her shock, the red of her magic was absorbed by his power. He smiled.

"Come on, baby." Darkwolf gave her a mocking grin. "Give me all you have."

Another shriek tore from her throat. She glanced up at Balor as he grabbed her upper arm, wrapping his large hand around it.

"If we fight Darkwolf together, we can destroy him," she said as she looked at her husband.

"Give me your power." Balor's words were a low, threatening growl as he gripped her arm tighter, digging his fingers into her flesh. "You need naught of it now."

The pain of his grasp on her arm was nothing compared to the pain in her heart when he gave the command. Stunned, she tried to draw away, but his grip was too strong.

It happened in a matter of seconds.

Balor started to drain her powers. Her mind spun as he began bleeding her of her magic.

Her husband, her love, was stealing from her, making her weak and vulnerable.

Anger exploded inside her like a volcano spewing lava. Now that he was without his eye, her magic was greater than his. She grabbed his wrist in her hand and mentally reversed the drain.

"What?" His cry echoed in the night as she stole his power faster than he had been taking hers.

"You bastard." Her hair flamed higher and the blaze of anger intensified inside her. "I loved you!"

Balor backhanded her so hard with his free hand that she screamed and almost lost her hold on his other wrist.

With everything she had, Ceithlenn drew Balor's magic into her.

Purple fire exploded around Balor.

Darkwolf's magic.

Flames whooshed over his body like the tree that had caught fire and still burned behind them.

At the same time, she sucked the last of Balor's power from him.

Balor screamed as he began to burn.

She released his wrist and cut her gaze from her husband to Darkwolf, who had dropped his shield.

A blast of his magic shot toward her. She formed her own shield before his power slammed into it. Already off balance, she stumbled back, barely keeping on her feet.

Balor rolled on the sidewalk, screaming, burning alive. She had taken what had been left of his power and he was now only flesh and blood.

Behind her protection she let her goddess form fall away but kept her shield around herself. She dropped to her knees and watched in horror as her husband's charred body writhed in purple flames.

The stink of burning flesh and the sight of her lifetime love dying caused her belly to heave. She puked on the sidewalk, keeping her gaze away from Balor. The smell of vomit joined the stench.

When she looked up she wiped the back of her hand over her mouth and watched as his body sizzled, burned, and finally fell to ashes. Drained of his magic, he would not move on to another world.

She had made him human.

Just as he had tried to do to her.

Despite her fury, her hurt, her pain from Balor's betrayal, tears rolled down her cheeks while she watched a strong wind brush away Balor's ashes. They swirled, scattering and vanishing into the darkened sky. Only a charred outline remained on the concrete.

She turned her gaze on Darkwolf, who had his arms crossed over his chest and a deadly smile on his face. He extended one of his arms and flicked his fingers in a bring-it-on movement.

"Come and get me, baby," he said as he made the motion.

The heat in Ceithlenn when she looked at him was so great that she could barely see. She thought about letting her shield down and fighting him now.

Even though she now had what power had remained in Balor while he was without the eye, weakness kept her pinned on her knees.

She could use the combined magic to fight Darkwolf, but it might not be enough. Especially with pain and loss filling her after the death of her husband.

Ceithlenn clenched her eyes shut, blocking out Darkwolf's arrogant, wicked smile. She fisted her hands and used the transference to take her away.

CHAPTER THIRTY-FIVE

"BALOR'S GONE?"

Alyssa's words rippled through the almost dead silence of the kitchen. The night following the visit by Garran's men, the witches stood around the table and stared at the lingering wisps of fog over Silver's pewter cauldron. Each and every one of their familiars had joined them for the scrying.

Hannah's mind buzzed as the odors of burnt sugar and wolfsbane faded, smells that had accompanied the vision. Silver had just used her cauldron to learn what was happening with Ceithlenn and Balor. As they sometimes did when Silver scried, images had risen from the mist, playing out different scenes that this time had left them virtually speechless.

Banshee lightly gripped Hannan's shoulder with his talons, his presence somehow making the vision even more real.

Darkwolf taking the eye for his own.

Ceithlenn's and Balor's reunion.

Darkwolf's attack.

A battle between Darkwolf, Ceithlenn, and Balor.

Balor's death. *Balor's death.*

Can Balor really be gone?

Silver appeared dazed as she stroked the side of her cauldron with her fingertips as the last of the fog vanished. Her python familiar, Polaris, was curled around the cauldron. "I—I. Wow."

"I can't believe it." Mackenzie stared at the cauldron from where she was standing, her ferret, Merlin, in her arms. "That just can't have been real."

Rhiannon rocked back on her heels and scowled. "No way. It can't have been that easy."

"It happened last night, while Garran's men were here." Cassia's voice held conviction and relief as she spoke, her beautiful features looking absolutely certain. "This isn't something that's going to happen in the future. It's done. Balor is gone."

"How do you know?" Hannah couldn't help the note of skepticism in her voice despite the rising hope that it was true. She felt as though the floor were tilting beneath her feet, as if she might slide across the bare concrete. "Silver often scries things that haven't happened yet. Even some things that can be changed with intervention."

"Cassia's right." Silver looked at the half-Elvin witch before meeting Hannah's eyes. "My magic tells me that Ceithlenn took what power Balor had left and Darkwolf killed him the moment he was unprotected."

"So now Ceithlenn has not only her power, but some of Balor's." Sydney removed her glasses and pinched the bridge of her nose as her Doberman, Chaos, nuzzled her arm. "She could be even harder to beat now."

"What about Darkwolf?" Mackenzie clasped the back of the chair in front of her as Merlin scrambled up to her shoulder. "Jeez, can you believe he took the power of the eye for himself?"

"And the eye is now *inside* of him?" Sydney's look of both amazement and disbelief echoed Hannah's own feelings. "I can't quite get that thought to gel."

"What does he intend to do with that power?" Copper tugged at her braid and frowned while her honeybee familiar buzzed by her ear. "Will we have to fight this new supergod Darkwolf along with Ceithlenn?"

"Since he betrayed her and Balor to begin with, I don't think he's going to join forces with her, at least." Silver let her fingers slip away from the side of the cauldron down to stroke Polaris. "And what he did—kill Balor—that's pretty much a dead giveaway."

Sydney slid her glasses back on. "What Darkwolf plans to do with his new powers, though, that's a mystery."

"Knowing him the way we do"—Copper sighed and released her braid—"he's not going to just kick back and retire, especially now."

"Dear Anu." Hannah looked to the ceiling before returning her gaze to her sister witches. "Unbelievable. That bastard now has a *god's* power."

"Obviously we need to be on guard for both Ceithlenn and Darkwolf now," Cassia said, and all of the witches turned their attention to her. The fiery look on the normally calm witch's expression made Hannah blink in surprise. "Whatever his intentions are," Cassia continued, "we need to be prepared."

Alyssa's owl, Echo, took to the rafters and gave a haunting hoot.

Kael, Cassia's wolf, howled, and a shiver trailed Hannah's spine.

TWO DAYS LATER, SANDWICHED between two Drow Guards, Hannah wandered through the underground village of the Dark Elves. It was nearly impossible to get used to the bluish-gray-skinned women with collars around their necks.

Hannah sucked in a deep breath and blew it out slowly. It wasn't right. Yet bondage was a big thing in some circles back in her own world.

To each his own.

But she was *so* never going there. Not that she'd ever personally have to worry about it.

Sounds of loud voices, a child's wailing, and an anvil striking metal rang in Hannah's ears. Garran was meeting with his Directorate and his Steward. It had irritated her when he'd dismissed her and handed her over to a couple of his guards to escort her through the city. Although she had also had the option of being taken to his room.

The image of him joining her there sent warmth straight to that place between her thighs.

She shook her head. Sex with Garran was frying her brain. But the thought of a good nap was tempting.

Smells of roast chicken, fresh baked bread, and mead made her stomach growl as she passed a tavern. She glanced down at the pendant Garran had pinned to her T-shirt before he'd sent her on her way. Intricately fashioned white gold embraced one of the largest, finest diamonds she'd ever seen. The diamond had to be worth at least half a million. He'd told her as long as she wore the pendant she could go anywhere and wouldn't have to pay for anything she wanted.

Around her upper arm, as always, was her moon and crescent armband, and she brought her fingers to it and touched the warm gold.

She paused in front of the tavern and watched both male and female Dark Elves leave and go into the establishment. Every time one of the Drow noticed her they bowed with what seemed like reverence before continuing on their way. It didn't take her long to realize it was because of the pendant Garran had given her. Must have identified her as a guest.

Hunger won out over the desire to take a nap and she headed toward the tavern doors. Before she had a chance to push them open, her guards moved in front of her and held them so that she could walk through. Both men were overly respectful as far as she was concerned. They wouldn't even talk with her.

Near darkness caused her to blink until her eyes adjusted to the dimness. Conversation quieted as she entered the room and she felt the stares of everyone in the tavern.

With her chin high, she went to an empty table. Benches lined each side of the tables, which looked a lot like the ones in the D'Danann village taverns, only these were made of granite. She slid onto one of the benches, the polished stone feeling smooth and cool through her snug jeans.

Conversations around her slowly resumed with whispers before they rolled back into a low rumble. The bits and pieces of the whispers were what had her straightening her back and making her spine tingle.

"Who is . . . ?"

". . . to a human?"

". . . here before."

"The king's consort . . ."

The last one made her ears burn. She brought her hand to the pendant, grasped it, and almost tore the diamond off her T-shirt. Instead she took another deep breath and let her hand drop away.

King's consort, my ass.

Hannah glanced over her shoulder at one guard and then over her other shoulder at the next. "Sit," she demanded.

Surprise flashed in both men's eyes, but they did an admirable job of holding it back.

She hardened her voice into a tone that had gotten her just about everywhere in the corporate world. She pointed to the bench on the opposite side of the table and commanded, "Now."

The men looked at each other and then both said, "Yes, my lady," as they obeyed.

My lady?

When they were seated, she studied first one Drow then the other, almost smiling at the obvious discomfort of the two huge men. Like most Drow warriors, they wore leather straps crisscrossing their broad chests that anchored metal breastplates. With their identical builds, matching silver hair, blue-diamond eyes, and light blue skin, it didn't take a wizard to guess the men had to be twins.

"Let's eat." She looked from one man to the other. "What do you recommend?"

One of the men cleared his throat. "My lady, we are to guard you only."

"I say you're to eat with me." She glanced at the table as if a menu might appear then returned her gaze to theirs. "So, what's good here?"

"The pork is exceptional, my lady," said Twin Number One.

"Great." She folded her hands on the tabletop. "That's what I'll have, along with some bread and that soft white cheese they served at dinner last time I was here, and a mug of mead. Also grapes. Those were the best I've ever had."

"Yes, my lady." Twin Number Two signaled to a beautiful woman carrying a tray loaded with trenchers of food. She'd just appeared from a door in the back.

The woman gave the man a nod of acknowledgment, but when she caught sight of Hannah and the diamond pendant, her cheeks turned a deeper shade of blue and she fumbled a bit with the tray.

Hannah tried to keep her face expressionless although she really wanted to shout, "What the hell is going on around here?" She studied the woman as she hurried to unload her tray, placing the trenchers in front of a group of warriors so quickly that some of the juices from the curved plates splashed onto the table.

The Drow woman must have broken a record for fastest meal served before she rushed to the table where Hannah and her guards sat. The woman was one of the few females Hannah had seen in the Drow realm who was not dressed in something extremely skimpy. She wore a simple but almost see-through sheath-style dress and, to Hannah's surprise, no collar.

"Irka," Twin Number One addressed the woman when she reached them, then told her Hannah's order.

"I said you're both to eat, too," Hannah told her guards before Irka could leave.

Both men shifted in their seats but caved when she gave them her best "Don't screw with me" stare. They ordered the same thing Hannah had.

Irka bowed. "Right away, my lady."

Hannah looked at the twins. "What are your names?"

"I am Anant. My brother is Richtor," the twin on the left said.

"Okay, Anant and Richtor." She met their gazes head-on. "What's with the 'my lady' business and how everyone acts around me?"

This time both men did show their surprise. "You are the king's consort. His mate," Anant said. "Of course our people would treat you with reverence and respect."

His mate? Hannah put her hands in her lap and clenched them into fists before forcing herself to release them. *Ten. Count to ten. Cool. Calm. Collected.*

Ten . . . nine . . . eight . . .

She was fairly certain she was managing to keep her expression neutral. "And you came to this conclusion how?"

"You wear the Brooch of Aithne." Richtor glanced at his brother before meeting Hannah's gaze. "It signifies you will soon be our queen."

Hannah barely kept her jaw from dropping.

She bit her tongue, trying her best not to correct them. Denying it here, in front of his guards and all of these people, would be an insult to Garran, and no matter how much she wanted to scream at him right now, she wouldn't make him look bad in front of his subjects.

No doubt he'd given her the pendant to wear while she was here as a way of protecting her and saying she was off-limits. Not to signify anything so arrogant and conceited and presumptuous as her being his mate.

The coppery taste of blood made her realize she'd been biting her tongue too hard. She forced herself to count backward from ten again and to take another deep breath.

Before she had to give any kind of response, Irka arrived with their meal. The woman's hands shook as she placed a beautiful silver plate and a matching mug containing mead in front of Hannah before she set wooden trenchers and metal tankards in front of the men. At the center of the table Irka carefully arranged a large silver tray filled with delicacies like those that had been at the banquet Hannah had attended the first time she came to the Drow realm.

"I hope this pleases you, my lady." Irka's voice had the slightest tremor to it.

Hannah cleared her throat. "Thank you, Irka."

The woman's eyes widened as if surprised that Hannah knew her name. She lowered her gaze and gave a deep bow. "It is my pleasure, my lady."

Irka hurried from the table as Hannah watched.

She was *so* going to kill Garran.

Then it was as if an ice-cold wave slammed into her.

He was going to kill himself.

AFTER THE SENTENCING OF Vidar with the Directorate, Garran sat in his throne, more than likely for a final time. The last thing he had expected to feel was guilt and regret when he died. Not that he had given death much thought.

Yet anger seared his skull like a hot brand, too. Anger that he must leave this world in order to do his duty as king, when as a man, he was finally again fulfilled—by having his daughter in his life.

And Hannah. Gods above, but he could not name this need to be with her always.

Love?

Garran rubbed the bridge of his nose with his thumb and forefinger.

He had been in love only once before, with Rhiannon's mother. A gentle, special love that he would always treasure.

With Hannah this feeling was intense, fiery, filling him with strength by simply being with her. All along he had felt as if they had a soul connection, and now he knew it to be true, with everything he had.

All that he had come to know of her only solidified what he felt. What they had shared with each other about their prior lives. What he had witnessed of her spirit—her desire to fight for her people and her world, and the sacrifices she was willing to make. The depths of her soul and the young girl inside her, still hurting and needing to be loved. Everything about her drew him, attracted him, made him want . . .

And love her.

Garran wiped his hand down his face and shifted on the throne.

By the gods.

"You summoned us, my king?" Carden's voice interrupted his thoughts and Garran looked at his First and at Hark who had entered with Carden.

Carden's hands were behind his back, his stance wide, and his chin raised as he met Garran's gaze. Hark stood to the side with clear disapproval in his eyes.

Garran studied Carden. "I have much to teach you and little time."

"This is unacceptable, Your Highness." Hark moved closer, no longer serene but keeping his voice calm. "You cannot risk your life. You cannot leave your people with no king."

It was more than a risk, it was a near certainty that he would die. Garran leaned forward in his chair. "Carden will be king when I pass on to Summerland. You will guide him and support him as your leader."

"If I may, Your Highness." Carden's jaw tightened. "As your First, and with great respect, I insist you stay and let your warriors battle for you."

Garran gripped the armrests of his chair and nearly growled at his two highest leaders. "Must I constantly repeat myself? My word is law."

Carden and Hark both appeared tense and angry, but said nothing.

"Your training, Carden." Garran shifted and pressed a hidden catch on the thick armrest of his chair. The padded granite top of the armrest rose as silently as a Drow slipping beneath the night sky. Both Carden and Hark looked on with surprise on their features.

From inside the hidden compartment, Garran drew out a

small diamond orb. More regret tugged at his heart as he wrapped his hand around the warm, faceted diamond. He raised his arm and uncurled his fingers. The orb immediately rose an inch above his palm and slowly rotated. Emerald, ruby, and amethyst shades glittered within the diamond.

"What is it, my king?" Carden asked in a hoarse voice.

"This was given to me by my father before he passed on to Summerland." Three millennia ago. "Other than myself, only my brother, Naal, knew of its existence." The familiar pain of his brother's recent death sliced through Garran's belly like a dagger. In his arrogance, Garran had thought only Naal needed to know of the orb.

"The Orb of Aithne is cut from the same diamond as the brooch," Garran continued, "but the orb is imbued with Drow powers that will answer many of your questions when asked of it." A sense of loss made his stomach roil as he extended his hand to Carden. "Take it."

After hesitating a moment, Carden took the orb. Fascination sparked in his gaze as he opened his hand and the orb rose to turn slowly above his palm.

Garran gave an inward sigh of relief. "My father was clear in that the orb would only serve a suitable replacement for the king. I had yet to test Vidar." Perhaps because something had held him back. A subconscious feeling that he had not acknowledged.

"I have not needed its knowledge for centuries," Garran said. "It is time for it to go to its new master. Keep it with you always and it will slowly impart its wisdom upon you until you have absorbed all that it has to share."

Carden looked from the orb to Garran. "I—I cannot—"

"You will." Garran pushed himself out of his chair so that he was standing eye to eye with Carden. "No further conversation about the subject of my leaving is to be raised, with the exception of your training."

Garran had the sudden desire to lash out at someone, to smash his fist into something. Godsdamn but he had been a fool. He had barely had time to mourn Naal's death, but for the gods' sakes, it had been his responsibility to see to this.

"Sit." He gestured to the strategy table, and after only a moment's pause, Hark and Carden obeyed, each seating themselves to either side of the chair at the head of the table. Carden slipped the orb into a pouch on his weapons belt.

Garran settled into his chair. He folded his arms on the table and began instructing Carden on what he must do if he should step up as King of the Dark Elves.

Seemingly accepting Garran's decision, finally, Hark interjected his wisdom at times and Garran was thankful as he wished to miss nothing. The orb would only do so much for Carden.

When Garran thought his head would burst from all that he had discussed with his two leaders, he pushed his chair away from the table and got to his feet. "We shall go to the troops now and speak with each commander."

He faced Carden, who had also risen along with Hark. "I will be clear that you are my Steward while I am gone, and King should I pass on to Summerland."

"Yes, Your Highness," Carden said, and Hark gave a deep nod.

"We will be going to war soon." Garran's gut churned as he thought of Ceithlenn and the Fomorii. "I will take one of the younger warriors with me to give notice when it is time to go aboveground to fight."

"So long as it is dark in that Otherworld," Hark said.

Garran nodded in agreement. "The humans, D'Danann, and I have discussed drawing the goddess and the demons out at night. We will come up with a plan and be prepared.

"The Orb of Aithne will impart the following on you as well, Carden," Garran continued. "The combined powers of all of our warriors will allow you to make the transference as one, without the use of the transference stone."

Carden and Hark looked at him in surprise. "That has never been done," Hark said.

Garran shrugged. "Such a great transference has never been needed before."

A commotion could be heard outside the throne room—Hannah's voice, loud, anger in her tone. "Let me see him *now*," she said in an authoritative manner as he cut his gaze to the doorway.

"The King's orders, my lady," one of the guards said. They had blocked the entrance. "He is not to be disturbed."

Garran couldn't see Hannah, but he could picture the imperious expression on her face. His heart twinged and regret flooded him again. She would have made a fine queen.

"I don't care what orders he gave you, I want to see Garran right this minute."

"Allow Hannah to enter the room," Garran called out to the guards before he nodded to Carden then Hark. "I will call for you when I am ready to visit the troops."

Again surprised expressions. Obviously they had not expected him to change his plans at the demands of a female. In their world it was not done.

As the guards let Hannah pass, he faced her and almost smiled. Fire lit her eyes even though she kept her expression controlled. The Brooch of Aithne sparkled where he had pinned it to her shirt.

Had he made her his queen, she would no doubt have fought for changes in their world. The thought sent another twinge through his heart. Gods, how he would miss her when he passed on to Summerland.

When she reached him her lips were pressed in a thin line. She glanced at Carden and Hark and waited until they were out of sight, and the guards outside the door, before she spoke. She set the brooch on the armrest of his throne.

"You're not going to do this, Garran." She poked one of her fingers at his chest, pressing into his skin. "No way are you going to throw your life away."

He caught her hand in his and brought her close, catching her by surprise so that she stumbled into him. Her lips parted as he brought her into his embrace and he kissed her before she had a chance to utter another word.

Instead of fighting him, she kissed him back with equal passion. Their kiss was deep, filled with desperation. Hannah took her hands from his and wrapped her arms around his neck, stretching her body up against him. His cock ached as she moved against him and she gripped his hair in her fists. The brooch on her shirt scraped his skin and added more magical warmth to their kiss.

Gods, she tasted of sweet, sweet woman and her scent was like the hint of wildflowers and spring rain. She made a needy whimpering sound that he had never heard from her before. He grasped her ass and pressed her tighter to him and he groaned.

Guards outside the entrance be damned—he had to have her here and now. He moved his hands between them and she gave a soft sound of surprise against his lips as he unfastened her jeans. But she didn't stop the magic of their kiss, it only intensified as he pushed down her jeans and undergarment. The soft thuds of her shoes met his ears as she kicked them off.

Her jeans and undergarment dropped to her feet and she stepped out of them. He broke their kiss so that he could pull her T-shirt over her head and, he set it carefully aside with the brooch. She unfastened the lace binding her breasts and let it fall to the floor, leaving her naked save for her socks.

"You are so beautiful," he said as his gaze took in her naked body. His eyes met her dark ones and he pushed the blond lock from her face so that it joined her dark hair.

"Damn you, Garran," she said before she kissed him.

He grasped her by her ass again and carried her up the dais and set her on her feet only long enough to unfasten his breeches and release his cock. He sat hard on his throne and brought her with him so that she straddled his lap.

Hannah raised herself on her knees, grasped his cock in her hand, and slammed herself down on him. She tore her mouth from his and gave a hoarse cry as she began riding him, taking him deep.

Another groan rose up in his throat at the feel of her slick, heated core grasping his cock. He thrust his hips up every time she came down on him. She tipped her head back and he grasped her breasts in his hands. He began suckling first one nipple then the other and her moans grew loader and louder.

A powerful tightening sensation expanded in his groin, an oncoming storm of a climax approaching. He tilted his head up and she met his gaze and brought her mouth to his in another demanding kiss.

He took her by her waist and moved in and out faster as he thrust up harder. Her body began trembling in his hands and he knew she was close to orgasm.

Hannah broke their kiss again, a wild light in her eyes. She clung to his shoulders, digging her nails in his skin.

When she climaxed she gave a loud cry and shuddered against him. He pumped his cock inside her, feeling every spasm of her core.

She cried out again with another orgasm. With a few more powerful thrusts he made her whimper and moan before he allowed himself to climax.

The power of his orgasm had him rocking against her, pressing his hips tight in between her thighs. His mind whirled and he felt as if he was on the transference stone and entering another Otherworld as his cock throbbed inside her.

Hannah collapsed into his embrace, her face resting at the curve of his neck. Smells of sex, sweat, and woman flowed through his senses as he held her tight.

"Don't do it, Garran," she whispered. "Don't do it."

CHAPTER THIRTY-SIX

COUNTLESS MUFFLED SCREAMS CAUSED Jake to raise his head up from studying the weapons schematics on his laptop.

His heart immediately started thundering at the strength and number of the cries.

"Ceithlenn and the Fomorii," Hawk shouted from the middle of the warehouse. He projected his voice and it echoed against the metal walls. "Through mind-speak the guards stated they see the goddess and the demons attacking the tourist piers."

Jake snapped the laptop's lid shut and bolted from his room.

"Now, now, now!" Jake shouted to his officers as his body tensed, going into battle-mode. His wounded arm had been aching, and he'd been tired, but now he was wide awake.

His officers strapped on their armor and other battle gear, grabbed their rifles and handguns, along with shields and demo tasers. With expressions of grim determination they dashed out of the warehouse.

As if the heavens above were just as furious as Jake, freezing rain and wind whipped up and assaulted them. They rushed into several SWAT vehicles and the armored Humvee tanklike transports.

The witches joined them, climbing into one of the vehicles, each with expressions ranging from fury to determination. Rhiannon and Copper already sparked with magic.

Screams grew louder as the trucks roared the short distance from the warehouse to the piers under attack.

Jake figured the D'Danann had already arrived when he saw demon heads flying through the air. No doubt the warriors were flapping their great wings as they flew above the Fomorii and swooped down to behead one demon after another.

But there were too many Fomorii. Too goddamn many.

As more demons rose from the bay onto the piers, the Fomorii attacked humans, killing them then discarding the bodies. The demon stench of rotten fish, along with smells of blood and magic, slammed into him, the rain doing nothing to lessen the smells.

Jake and his officers bolted out of their vehicles, the witches rushing out with them into the rain. The wind blew so hard the rain slashed sideways and stung his face.

"Positions!" Jake ordered.

Immediately his men and women lined up and began moving forward with riot shields in front of them, working to get close enough to their targets to use the heart-seeking bullets.

"Fire the moment you have a clear shot," Jake called out to his officers as blood pounded in his veins. "Take these bastards down."

The witches started using spellfire and magic ropes to bind or incapacitate some of the demons long enough for the D'Danann to behead them or PSF officers to use their bullets and destroy the beasts.

Sounds of guns firing, people's screams, the sizzle of magic, pounding rain, and the roars and growls of the Fomorii erupted in the night.

If only it had started to rain earlier, not as many people would be out.

An explosion of red fire came from above, snapping Jake's attention to the sky. Ceithlenn. Hair flaming, eyes glowing red, gliding as she circled the carnage.

The goddess struck. A D'Danann reappeared as he

dropped from the air and the warrior shouted before falling into the middle of the swarming Fomorii. Iridescent sparkles rose above the demons—the beasts had killed the warrior.

Ceithlenn fired her magic in the air, probably going for the invisible D'Danann. From the way her fireballs shimmered and deflected, Jake was certain the invisible warriors were blocking the magic with their swords. Soon Ceithlenn encased herself in a shield that shimmered in the artificial light and her own fire.

White and gray puffs, like streams of fog, rose from the battlefield toward Ceithlenn and she sucked them through the shield and into her body.

Souls. Jake recognized exactly what she was doing. He'd seen her do it before. The bitch was taking the murdered people's souls and making herself more powerful.

Jake raised his Glock and started to fire on the goddess but knew he'd only be wasting bullets. They'd just bounce off her magical shield. He'd have to let the D'Danann do their thing and he'd do his.

He jogged up a few steps and onto a stretch of wooden decking so that he was a little higher than the fighting. He ground his teeth and took a battle stance while holding his Glock steady with both hands.

Adrenaline kept his body so electrified that his wounded arm didn't affect his aim. He systematically began shooting demons on the outside fringes of the battle. In most cases his shot was dead-on, exploding the hearts of several demons. Their bodies collapsed into silt.

One Fomorii barreled toward Jake and he barely avoided the demon's claws by burying a bullet in the creature's heart and turning the demon into silt. More demons charged Jake's officers, who remained steadfast and fired AK-47 rifles or used handguns, depending on their positions. A few of Jake's officers were taken down by the demons.

Fury made his aim even truer. Heat swept his rain-soaked skin and a pounding knocked at the inside of his head.

Sirens screeched through the night, red and blue lights

flashing as emergency and law enforcement vehicles drew closer.

Not now. Fuck. The emergency personnel and officers would only serve as more food for the demons and provide more souls for Ceithlenn.

Where were the Dark Elves? Jake glanced around. Where was Garran? Hadn't anyone notified the Drow?

It was dark—the bastards should be here. Were they traitors after all? Were they going back on their word to help in the battle against the goddess and the Fomorii?

Sonsofbitches. They'd better arrive real quick or this battle wasn't going to last long. And it looked like it wasn't the Fomorii or Ceithlenn who were going to be on the losing end—the Alliance were way outnumbered.

Jake moved his attention to a television news station van as it pulled up to a stop at the fringes.

Kat DeLuca climbed out of the van.

Oh, fuck.

CHAPTER THIRTY-SEVEN

"YOUR MAJESTY!"

At the sound of the urgent male voice, Hannah jerked her head up from where she'd had her face pressed to Garran's warm chest. Heat flushed over her in a rush. She still straddled his lap, with only her socks on and his cock inside her.

Garran snarled as he held her in a tight embrace. "Did the guards not inform you that I do not wish to be disturbed, Carden?"

Heat still filling her body, Hannah refused to look at the other warrior as he spoke. "My apologies, Your Majesty. But the Fomorii and Ceithlenn are attacking the San Francisco Otherworld."

Both Hannah and Garran went rigid. "Take the men and transport immediately to the battle," he ordered. "I will use the transference stone."

"I must beg you one last time—"

"Go!" Garran's expression grew fiercer. "Now."

Carden's tone was anything but agreeable, but still he said, "Yes, my king."

Hannah eased down Garran's body, his cock slipping from her core as he stood. Her heart pounded so hard her chest ached. What in Anu's name was she going to do? She had to help her Coven sisters do battle, but she also needed to keep Garran from using the power the Great Guardian had given him.

Hannah scrambled to gather her jeans and T-shirt and tugged them on without worrying about her panties and bra. Garran fastened his leather pants and strode toward the black door while she finished buttoning her jeans.

"Wait here," he commanded as he made the door open, "where you will remain safe."

"Oh, no you don't." Hannah bolted after him, not taking the time to grab her shoes. "You're not leaving me!"

Before the door closed behind him, she slid across the granite floor on her sock-covered feet, lunged inside the small room, and flung her arms around his waist just as he started the transference.

The suffocating blackness overcame her and she felt as if she had her arms around nothing. As if Garran were no longer there.

In the next moment ice-cold rain drenched her, while powerful winds whipped her wet hair across her cheeks. Screams and roars shrieked through her head as Garran steadied her and set her away from him.

"Fool witch," he growled.

Hannah jerked her attention from Garran. It took her only a fraction of a second to see they'd arrived on the fringes of the battle, near Aquarium of the Bay.

And only a moment to recognize that the D'Danann, witches, and PSF were horribly outnumbered.

She held back a cry and looked back to Garran—

He was gone.

He's left to kill himself!

She started to push herself through the screaming crowd, looking everywhere for Garran. It was impossible to see through the people shoving by her and almost knocking her down.

Red and blue strobes flashed and reflected over the scene. Fire trucks. Ambulances. Police cars.

When she burst out onto the street, she widened her eyes. *Dear Anu!* High Priestess Janis Arrowsmith and the rest of her white magic D'Anu Coven were there, too! They didn't use gray magic and were virtually defenseless. They had spellshields and could perform a few charms that were not gray magic, but nothing that could help them here.

The high priestess was able to use her magical seeds that she tossed onto the ground. Immediately vines sprouted and bound some of the demons. But it wasn't nearly enough.

It looked like the rest of the white witches were doing their best to use white magic to heal, but they were open to attack and vulnerable.

Fear and anger made Hannah's whole body hurt like she'd been ripped apart. Fear and anger for all of her friends, the other people who fought the Fomorii, and the countless people being ripped to shreds by the Fomorii.

And for Garran.

Where is he?

She caught sight of some of her sister witches. Sparks flew from their magic as gunshots rang through the rainy night. Swords clanged against the demons' iron-coated claws. Cries of people being murdered and growls of Fomorii melded with the other sounds into one huge roar.

The *whump-whump-whump* sound of helicopter blades added to the noise as a police copter flew over the mayhem. It streamed its high-powered light over the massive scene and a man using a loudspeaker continually said, "This is the police. Drop your weapons." The order was nearly lost in the crazed mayhem on the piers.

Shouts of a different kind—like warrior battle cries— came from her right and Hannah snapped her attention toward it. *The Drow.* A legion of them had arrived!

But where is Garran? She shoved her way through the crowd, searching for him. She had to get to him before he killed himself!

Arrow after arrow silently whisked through the rain, piercing many of the demons' thick hides. Like Garran had told her, if the arrow struck one of the Fomorii in the chest, exactly where its heart was, the head of the arrow exploded and the demon crumbled to silt.

Still more demons climbed out of the bay and joined the battle. Some attacked the Drow from behind, slashing the warriors with their iron-coated claws, which were deadly to Fae and Elves.

As Hannah dodged Fomorii and used her spell five, she glanced up.

Ceithlenn. Dear Anu, the evil goddess hovered above the fray, shielded by her magic as she drew in human souls. White and gray forms slipped through the rain straight to her chest.

Three D'Danann surrounded her in the air, but they couldn't pierce her shield with their swords.

Rhiannon stood below Ceithlenn, her Shadows rushing from her body—but this time they couldn't penetrate the goddess's shield as they had before. Instead the Shadows crawled over the bubble of Ceithlenn's protection, shadowy man-shapes trying to get past the shield.

Adrenaline pumped through Hannah and magic crackled at her fingertips.

Ceithlenn gave a wicked smile and her mouth moved, and in her gut, Hannah knew the goddess was chanting a powerful spell.

Air sizzled and snapped near the Drow warriors, and her attention was diverted toward the sight and sounds as something wavered in the rain.

The great red Fire Dragon Elemental appeared. Solid. Real. Not the size it had been at the top of Coit Tower or on the beach. No, this time it was massive. It grew until it towered above everyone on the battlefield. The Dragon reared back, roared, and blasted a stream of iridescent magic fire at the Dark Elves.

No, no, no!

Even though she knew the Fire Dragon had gone to Ceithlenn's side, Hannah couldn't accept that one of her Dragons, her totems, could destroy these people or beings.

Many of the Drow managed to save themselves by wrapping their bodies in swirling cloaks of dark magic. For others it was too late and they gave their final death cries before their bodies faded into obsidian sparkles.

Ceithlenn laughed behind her shield, the sound traveling through the night, above the wail of sirens and the roar of the battle.

Hannah's entire body felt stretched, her skin tight. She couldn't find Garran and she had to do something against the Dragon!

The answer came to her and all she could do was pray to the Ancestors and the goddess Anu that it would work.

Frantically, she looked around for something to stand on. One of the pier's thick, wide sliced wooden pilings stood close to a sidewalk. Rocks pierced her socks and dug into her wet feet as she ran the short distance and climbed onto it to get a better view of the melee and the Fire Dragon.

Her heart pounded as she focused on drawing the other three great Dragon Elementals to the battle. She closed her eyes for a moment and pictured the Dragons she was calling while she said a chant over and over and over in her mind. With the same mental chant she called to the Ancestors and Anu, asking with urgency for their assistance.

Her eyelids jerked open.

Power rushed through her veins and tremendous magic burst within her like an explosion of fireworks. Her moon and crescent band burned her arm.

The magic was stronger than she'd ever felt before. The Ancestors and Anu were answering her plea!

She held out her arms to embrace those she prayed would respond to her call. Whether or not the Water Dragon would switch to her side, or the Air Dragon would help her, she wasn't certain. But with the aid of the Ancestors and Anu, a confidence rolled through her beyond what she'd ever felt.

Hannah tipped her face up to the rain and chanted a plea to the Dragon Elementals as she gathered strength.

When she finished the chant, Hannah held her breath, terrified that all three Dragons might not side against Ceithlenn. Yet she knew they would answer her call. Scrying mirror or no scrying mirror, the dragons were *hers*.

Wind and rain and time seemed to slow. Even the Fire Dragon's next burst of flames hung on the wind.

Shimmers like morning light refracting from a diamond appeared to the north of the Fire Dragon, a great shape coming forth. A second gigantic glimmering form rose from the bay. And a third shimmered above the battle. Enormous shapes that glistened as they appeared more clearly.

The Fire Dragon was still caught in the slow-motion spell, its fiery breath hanging in the air.

Hannah swallowed as the yellow Air Dragon flapped its expansive wings, causing great gusts of wind to join the strength of the storm. The gigantic green Earth Dragon materialized near the Fire Dragon and roared so loudly the ground trembled like a small earthquake and Hannah almost fell off her perch.

The blue Water Dragon rose from the bay. Fear yet confidence built within her as she watched it. That Elemental was the other Dragon that had stated it would join the Fire Dragon to fight on Ceithlenn's side.

Let the Ancestors and Anu sway its decision!

So much fear pumped through Hannah's body that she trembled with it. Would the Water Dragon now fight for Ceithlenn or against her? Would it see what was the right thing to do?

While everyone on the battlefield, including the Fire Dragon, continued to move in slow motion, the Air Dragon screeched. It flapped its wings so that tremendous gusts of air pushed the Fire Dragon's flames away from the Drow.

The Air Dragon was helping her!

Blue scales glittering, the Water Dragon rose from the bay and Hannah held her breath.

The Elemental paused and swept its gaze over the scene. It turned its head and spewed a torrent of water from its great mouth at the barely moving Fire Dragon, dousing the flames.

Relief weakened Hannah's knees, but she stood straighter. The Water Dragon had switched its allegiance!

The green Earth Dragon slammed its massive body into the Fire Dragon, knocking the Elemental backward and into a tall building on the other side of the battle.

Bricks, wood, glass, and metal exploded with the strength of the Dragons plowing into the building. The Fire Dragon roared as it snapped out of the spell, no longer held in slow motion, unlike those on the battlefield. The Fire Dragon tried to push itself up and out of the rubble, but the other three Dragon Elementals converged on it at once. Their great bodies shielded the Fire Dragon from Hannah's eyes.

Three of the Dragons vanished.

Only the Earth Dragon remained. It spread its expansive wings, its huge green eyes met Hannah's, and she knew it was waiting for her command.

Her body sagged in relief, but only for a moment.

Ceithlenn still hovered above the battle, growing more and more powerful.

In a snap, the battle no longer moved in slow motion. Everything continued as before. Blood splattered and bricks from the smashed building crumbled onto the crowd. Screams and sirens. The rotten-fish stench of the Fomorii.

Hannah looked up at Ceithlenn, who flapped her wings and screeched in fury as she looked to where the Fire Dragon had been attacking the Drow.

Take that, bitch!

Hannah didn't have a second to feel any satisfaction.

Ceithlenn turned her hateful gaze on Hannah. The goddess wrapped her wings around her body, spun like a top, and dropped her glittering red shield.

The force of her spin combined with the magic shooting from her body slammed into the three flying D'Danann guarding her.

Hannah's heart climbed into her throat as the warriors were blasted away from Ceithlenn. The force threw the D'Danann so far back, the goddess was free from immediate assault.

One of the warriors had been hit so badly by her magic that he dropped into the middle of the battle.

Eavan. Dear Anu, it was Eavan!

The iridescent sparkles that rose from where he'd fallen signified his death.

Rage and pain from Eavan's murder strengthened Hannah's magic.

She barely had a moment to register the warrior's death as she glanced up at Ceithlenn—

The goddess shot a fireball straight at Hannah.

Hannah threw up a shield, instinctively combining her magic with the dark power Garran had given her. The strength of the goddess's fireball was so great when it slammed into the shield that it threw Hannah backward. She fell off her perch and landed on the concrete. Pain shot up her tailbone.

She scrambled to her feet as another fireball hit the shield and sizzled over its surface.

"Help me, O Ancient One," Hannah called to the Earth Dragon.

It lumbered through the battle so that it stood behind Ceithlenn, tall enough that its head was level with the goddess's back. She didn't seem to notice the Dragon as she released her next fireball.

Grinding her teeth, Hannah gathered her own spellfire, again blending Garran's magic with her own. After a third hit to her shield, Hannah dropped the protection and released her ball of spellfire, the greatest magic she had ever used.

The spellfire shot through the air. Ceithlenn moved to dodge the ball of magic, but backed into the Earth Dragon and she couldn't avoid it. The spellfire slammed into her midsection and she shrieked.

A hole burned into the goddess's belly. Before she had the chance to regenerate or throw up a shield, Hannah shot two of her magic ropes into the air and wrapped them around the goddess's legs.

Rhiannon set her Shadows on Ceithlenn, causing her to scream and writhe against their hold.

Janis Arrowsmith's magically enhanced voice cut over the power of the noise. "No! You cannot kill Sara."

Hannah's gaze landed on Janis and her heart lunged into her throat. Holding her arms wide, her face tilted up, Janis stood directly beneath Ceithlenn. From her hands, Janis shot her magical vines of the earth around Hannah's ropes and pulled at them, trying to free Ceithlenn. "You cannot murder my apprentice, Sara," Janis repeated, her features twisted in horror and anger.

A sick weight bottomed out Hannah's belly as she struggled against Janis's powerful magic. *Not again. No, not again.* "Sara doesn't exist anymore," Hannah screamed, amplifying her own voice with magic. "Ceithlenn killed Sara and just uses her body. Don't you understand?"

Ceithlenn screeched and started to free herself from Hannah's magic ropes.

Janis attempted to throw up a magical shield to encompass Ceithlenn and herself. "I will not allow—"

Drow arrows sailed into the sky and began piercing Ceithlenn's wings, arms, legs.

Through icy wind and rain, D'Danann flew, charging the goddess with their swords.

The Earth Dragon roared as it clasped Ceithlenn in its enormous claws.

Janis screamed and dropped to her knees.

Terror cut through the wind and rain in Ceithlenn's next shriek. It was in her eyes and on her face as Hannah's powerful ropes, Rhiannon's Shadows, and the Earth Dragon's hold kept her completely immobile.

Janis's magical vines fell away as she shouted again, a moan and a cry all in one. "Noooo. Not Sara."

A D'Danann—Keir—reached Ceithlenn. With his jaw set and his sword firm in his grip, his blade arced through the air.

And severed Ceithlenn's head from her neck.

Blood splattered across the battlefield and rained down on Janis, who screamed.

A steel gray-cloud exploded and mushroomed where the goddess had been.

The cloud slammed into everyone surrounding it, flinging each being aside. The blackness rose and slipped through the Earth Dragon's claws.

"Aren't paybacks a bitch?" Hannah said, relief flooding her veins like spellfire as she smelled the burnt sugar stench of the goddess fading.

The cloud, though . . . Did Ceithlenn's magic survive in that mass that seemed to solidify as it drifted over the head of the Earth Dragon?

With its great claws, the Elemental tried again to snatch it, but its claws swept through the mass as if it were mere fog.

But Hannah knew it wasn't and a new burst of fear nearly choked her.

The Earth Dragon met her gaze, and from the look in its great eyes, she knew it was leaving. "Thank you!" Hannah cried.

After an acknowledgment with a slight nod of its great head, the Elemental vanished. It had accomplished what she had wanted of it.

Ceithlenn was gone, and the Elemental had returned to its own realm—until Hannah's need ever rose to such a level again.

But the battle raged on.

And where is Garran? The Fomorii are still here. He must still be alive!

More and more Fomorii poured from the bay, as if driven by the goddess even after her death.

Fear for Janis caused Hannah to look back to where the High Priestess had been standing. Ironically, Silver Ashcroft had herself and Janis encased in a bubble of magic, protecting them both in the middle of the battle. Ironic because Janis had been the one to banish Silver from the white magic D'Anu Coven.

Covered in Ceithlenn's blood, Janis was on her knees, her face buried in her hands.

No regrets. If Ceithlenn hadn't been killed, thousands more lives would have been lost. The Sara that Janis had known was long gone.

Quickly, as she also searched for Garran with her gaze, Hannah counted her sister witches to make sure they all were alive.

Rhiannon was drawing her Shadows back inside her as she stood below the place Ceithlenn had been; Silver still crouched in the bubble beside Janis; Alyssa and Mackenzie fought on the far side from where Hannah stood; Copper and Sydney battled side by side with the D'Danann warriors Tiernan and Conlan.

And Cassia—the intensity with which she fought the Fomorii sent a strange tickling feeling through Hannah's belly. She paused only a moment more to study the fierce expression Cassia wore as she battled, and the strength of her spellfire.

Hannah forced her attention away.

Now to find Garran.

Ceithlenn had been killed. He didn't have to sacrifice himself.

Yet with all the Fomorii still fighting, overpowering the Alliance and other human law enforcement, she had no doubt he planned to carry through with his third attempt to rid this world of the demons.

Prickles of cold raised hair on her arms and at the nape of her neck as she searched the rainy night for Garran with her gaze. She tried to blink water from her eyes and see through the red and blue flashing lights. The rain was so fierce now it was harder to see and there were so many creatures, magical beings, and humans that it was difficult to make out one individual.

While she searched for him, she noticed the huge black cloud slowly drifting northwest of the battle. Could the power in the cloud, the remnant essence of Ceithlenn, be what still drove the Fomorii to battle?

Was that a huge man standing where the cloud appeared to be heading?

Not Balor, no. Balor is dead. We know that for certain from Silver's scrying. My mind has to be playing tricks.

Right now she couldn't think about it. Her frantic heart beat faster and faster when she didn't find Garran, and knots twisted her belly.

The knots doubled and tripled when she finally spotted him.

He stood on the highest point of the rooftop of the tourist shops at Pier 39, one hand gripping a flagpole. The American flag flapped over his head in the wind and rain as he turned his head, surveying the battlefield. Red and blue emergency lights flashed over his skin.

Ice-cold terror washed over Hannah along with the downpour.

Garran was going to do it. Use the power a third time to send the demons to Underworld.

And die.

"No!" Rocks and small pieces of broken glass bit into Hannah's sock-covered feet, but she barely noticed it as she bolted toward him.

She screamed as she ran, "Garran, *no!*"

WIND AND RAIN SHOVED at Garran, but he maintained his stance on the peak of a building with the light-footed ease of the Elves. The location allowed him to see almost everything happening on what had become a bloody battlefield.

Rage tightened his muscles as he viewed the carnage below. The throb in his chest expanded until he felt it through his entire body.

A part of him had rejoiced that Hannah had brought about the demise of Ceithlenn. The bitch was gone, only a cloud of her essence remaining.

Yet the battle continued.

If he did not stop it now, too many of his people, as well as the rest of the Alliance would die, along with more humans in this world. Only he could save them and stop the massacre.

Part of what the Great Guardian had made clear knocked at the back of his mind, too.

"The humans are not to kill too many of the Fomorii. It is another act that would upset the balance in Otherworld and Underworld."

Without another moment's hesitation, Garran closed his eyes and reached out with his mind using the power the Great Guardian had bestowed upon him. Rain and wind continued to buffet his body, but it did not interfere with his mental search.

In a flash, images appeared behind his eyelids, red forms that indicated every Fomorii on the battlefield and those still rising from the sea.

Garran's eyelids snapped open as he did his best to force away thoughts of the impact of his decision.

He was leaving behind his people.

He was leaving behind his daughter.

He was leaving behind Hannah. His love.

But the sacrifice would save countless lives and end the war in this San Francisco Otherworld.

Ignoring the pain and heaviness in his chest, Garran concentrated on all of the beings he needed to vanquish. Thanks to the Guardian's gift, he had isolated the Fomorii from those they battled and the demon's forms had been branded into his mind.

He gathered his strength, the power building within him like a tremendous storm, greater than the one that raged outside.

Silver magic encased his body until he glowed and he mixed the power with his own dark magic. The power thrummed through him until he felt as if he had grown as tall as the Fire Dragon had been.

With one final, determined mental command, the magic burst from him and through the night in a rush of silver.

Triumph surged through him as the silver magic wrapped itself around every Fomorii on the battlefield.

It took only a thought, just a thought.

The demons vanished.

Returned to Underworld.

The battlefield went almost completely silent. The only sounds to be heard were the constant scream of sirens, the pounding rain, and one old witch's wailings.

Garran had no more time for thoughts or regrets. Pain from the use of the Guardian's magic lanced through him like a thousand spears. Every muscle in his body failed him. As he dropped to his knees he knew death came for him, to sweep him away and on to Summerland.

The only peace in Garran's heart came from the knowledge that the Fomorii were in this world no more and that Ceithlenn had been destroyed.

My daughter is safe. My people, and Hannah—all safe. They can make their own way from this point. Surely they can, and they will.

Darkness swirled in his mind as he fell onto his side, his head slamming against the rooftop.

He no longer felt wind or rain as his body numbed. Sounds faded.

The last thing he heard as he slid down the slanted roof was Hannah screaming his name.

"GARRAN!" FEAR RODE HANNAH in cold waves and her heart nearly stopped beating as his limp body started to move down the sloping rooftop.

Without a second's thought, she threw out a magic rope, the green glittering as it wrapped around one of his booted ankles. Blood thundered in her ears as his greater weight pulled her up while his body dropped to the next level of the rooftop. He continued to slide down the opposite side.

Gritting her teeth, she gripped the rope with one hand and

used her other hand to cast a rope that she wrapped around the base of the flagpole before she slung the end around Garran's free ankle. The rope caught him just before he would have tumbled off.

Hannah scrabbled for purchase. She managed to fling the first magic rope around the flagpole as her body slipped and she hung over the side of the top tier of the roof. The edge of the roof dug into her belly but she ignored the pain and the thundering in her heart.

Dear Ancestors. Don't let Garran be dead. Don't let him be dead!

Right now all that mattered was Garran. Everything else faded away. Sights, sounds, smells, the rain—nothing existed but him.

The next moments passed in a blur as her muscles burned and strained while she pulled herself back onto the roof.

When she was on her knees, she wrapped the rope around her waist so that it held her securely to the flagpole. Rain made the rooftop's surface even slicker, and the distance between her and Garran seemed greater.

With her sock-clad feet flat on the rooftop she jumped from the building's top tier to the level below. She slid in an arc toward Garran, the rope holding her steady until she reached him. Now that she was relatively safe from falling, she threw out another magic rope and fastened it around Garran's other ankle and tied it to the flagpole.

When Garran and Hannah were both secure she drew him back onto the roof. She used her rope and the flagpole like a pulley to get him far enough onto the surface so he couldn't fall.

Heart pounding and head swimming with fear, she knelt beside Garran. She placed her palms over his chest and searched for his lifeforce.

Only a thread of it remained. Dizziness and pain almost claimed her. He was nearly gone.

"You can't leave me, you bastard!" For the first time since

she was a child, tears poured down her cheeks. The rain washed them away, but the heat of the tears burned her eyes. "I won't let you die, Garran. I won't let you."

One of the D'Danann warriors landed on the rooftop with a thump before he raised Garran's upper body. Hawk. It was Hawk. He had come to take Garran. She sensed it, almost as if she could hear his thoughts.

She sensed Hawk believed Garran should die below-ground, in the home of his people. His body could be properly displayed, then entombed like a true king.

"No," she said, barely able to see anything through her blur of tears. "Don't you dare take him yet. I've got to heal him."

Vaguely she heard someone land on the rooftop behind her but she didn't let her focus waver. Two hands gripped her waist but Hawk said, "Wait."

As Hannah cried, her heart breaking, she poured into Garran every bit of healing magic mixed with what dark powers he had given her. The green of her magic glittered between them, mingling with the fog of his dark magic he'd given her.

Life stirred inside him and hope welled within her. Something fierce and passionate developed inside Hannah. His thread of life was growing into a rope. But a thin rope. A fragile rope.

He's coming back . . . but he needs more.

"I love you, Garran," she said as she cried and poured every last bit of her own essence into him.

She felt life fill him at the same time it slipped away from her. The pounding in her chest slowed to nothing and she slumped as she gave up the last of herself.

CHAPTER THIRTY-EIGHT

RAIN IMMEDIATELY DRENCHED DARKWOLF and Elizabeth as soon as the transference brought them to the tourist piers.

The battle he had visioned with his god's power no longer raged.

It was over. His heightened senses absorbed the remnants of Fomorii rotten-fish stench along with the coppery scent of blood, human sweat, and something different.

Magic. He smelled dark, dark magic. Voices, the screeching of sirens, and the *whump* of helicopter blades overhead were louder than normal to his more sensitive ears. In the distance additional helicopters approached.

Elizabeth caught her breath and Darkwolf released his hold on her arm. Only the witches, Drow warriors, D'Danann, law enforcement, and human innocents remained.

Some of the human survivors fought to save others. White witches worked their magic as best they could.

All except for Janis, who remained in the midst of the battlefield, shrieking and crying.

The magical beings attended to their injured before disappearing with them. Any dead D'Danann and Drow warriors would have vanished the moment they were killed.

Where the hell was that bitch, Ceithlenn?

Dead, his powers told him, but he fought the information

niggling at his mind. He still *felt* her. Smelled her burnt sugar odor.

With a sweep of his gaze, he assessed the situation. Dead human bodies littered the sidewalks and stretches of concrete, as well as the asphalt street. Rain was quickly washing away piles of Fomorii silt scattered in every direction. Blue and red lights of emergency vehicles reflected on wet surfaces and the windows of the pier's businesses.

But there was no longer a battle. No demons to be seen.

"A great many Fomorii have been killed but most were sent back to Underworld," Darkwolf said as his power fed him the information. "The demons are gone."

"What?" Elizabeth's voice choked on the word. "All of my kind are—are—"

"Gone." He glanced down at her, the former Fomorii queen once named Junga who now inhabited a woman's body.

Despite the fact she'd been stripped of her title and she had abandoned the other demons to live as a human, it was obvious she felt something for others of her species.

Her expression grew fierce. "How did it happen?"

"The king of the Drow used a power gifted to him." More information bombarded Darkwolf as he looked up at the building where the Drow warrior king was being tended to by a witch and two D'Danann. "But it may have cost him his life."

"Good." Elizabeth let out an inhuman, low rumbling growl. "He should die for sending the Fomorii back to the stinking depths of Underworld. No being deserves such a fate."

Darkwolf drew his attention back to the scene then tilted his face to the sky.

"We need to avenge them," Elizabeth said, but he ignored her.

An enormous black cloud, like thick smoke roiling from a tremendous fire, floated overhead, nearing him. It carried with it Ceithlenn's burnt sugar smell.

Darkwolf smiled.

The goddess *had* been killed. Only her power and what she had stolen from Balor remained behind.

He glanced at the former Fomorii queen. Elizabeth's voice was hoarse as she rubbed both of her wet arms with her hands. "That cloud. It feels as if it could eat us whole."

Darkwolf laughed as he looked back to the sky, pleasure warming his skin in the ice-cold rain. Thanks to Balor's power within him, he had the strength to take Ceithlenn's magic for his own.

Purple fire snapped and crackled at his fingertips as he raised his hands, palms facing the cloud. He focused on his energy, his hatred, his fury at the goddess for what she'd done to him in the past, and his desire for her magic.

Balor's black magic now encasing his heart and Darkwolf's own purple magic twisted as one. It formed a powerful stream that shot from his palm and pierced the cloud.

The black fog swirled and swirled. Using all the magic he had, he drew the blackness toward him until it spiraled down like a funnel cloud.

"What are you doing?" Elizabeth sounded frantic and concerned.

"Mine." He laughed again. "It's all mine."

His entire body vibrated and rippled from his scalp to his toes as he soaked in Ceithlenn's power. The more he seized, the more strength he had.

Even the souls she had stolen filled him. Shock stunned him for a moment and he faltered as he felt the same satisfaction Ceithlenn had in stealing human souls.

But only for a moment.

"Darkwolf." Elizabeth's urgent voice pierced his concentration. "The Drow and D'Danann—they're looking this way."

Despite Elizabeth's warning, he claimed the last of Ceithlenn's power with pleasure. The cloud no longer hovered above him but filled his entire essence. His blood vessels even glowed purple through his light skin as power raged through him.

Yet exhaustion soaked him to his bones. The force it had taken to draw such great magic left him weak. The weakness would not last, but for now it made him tired and in need of rest.

"Darkwolf!" Elizabeth shouted before she screamed, a sound of agony.

Something pierced his arm and pain seared him as the force of whatever had hit him caused him to stumble back.

He cut his gaze to his arm and then to Elizabeth, who had fallen on her back, a bullet hole in her chest and an arrow in her belly.

His gut immediately clenched at the sight. They'd been struck by Drow arrows and she'd been shot.

More pain exploded in his shoulder as another arrow buried itself in his flesh and bone. Darkwolf glanced up to see his old enemies charging toward him, along with the PSF cop, Macgregor.

Darkwolf was far too exhausted, even with Ceithlenn's and Balor's powers combined with his own, to deal with this shit. He needed rest before he had the strength he needed to take them all on.

And he needed to save and protect Elizabeth.

A volley of Drow arrows and bullets sailed toward Darkwolf and Elizabeth, but he deflected them with a magic shield. It wasn't made of the purple that had always come from his magic. It was a black, black shimmer.

He looked down at Elizabeth to see her lying slack, on the ground, another bullet in her throat.

A cry of rage rose up within him as he knelt at her side and grasped her hand. He let out a howl before he turned his furious gaze at the oncoming rush of D'Danann and Dark Elves and the fucking PSF cop.

The desire to kill them, kill them all, made his whole body burn so hot that the rain on his skin sizzled and rose up in wafts of steam.

No, now was not the time to fight.

He ground his teeth, fear for Elizabeth and fury at those who had hurt her making him shake.

Darkwolf scooped Elizabeth into his arms before he used the transference to take them both away.

CHAPTER THIRTY-NINE

TRYING FOR ANOTHER CLEAR shot, Jake kept his gun raised and aimed at the injured Darkwolf. Before Jake had the chance to fire, the warlock crouched, grabbed the wounded or dead demon-woman's hand, and they both vanished.

"Shit." Rain rolled down Jake's face as he lowered his gun, his eyes still focused on the place Darkwolf had been standing.

At least Jake had buried two bullets in the demon-woman.

Drow and D'Danann had been running toward Darkwolf but came up short when he and Junga disappeared.

What the hell, anyway? The sonofabitch had grown to stand at least seven feet tall and was built like a Mack truck.

Jake hadn't recognized Darkwolf at first due to the fog rising from the asphalt, the pouring rain, and the dark cloud that had surrounded the warlock.

It wasn't until the black cloud started to clear that Jake got a good look at him. Darkwolf was a lot bigger, but his features were unmistakable. Jake never forgot a face.

He lowered his head and looked over the slaughter and devastation and ground his teeth. So many dead.

But the Fomorii were gone. They were finally gone.

Garran had done it.

Had the Drow king died like everyone thought he would? Jake's heart rate didn't slow as his gaze swept the massacre. Where was Kat? He'd lost sight of her almost as soon as she'd arrived on the scene.

Damn it. Where is she?

What if one of the Fomorii got to her? Jake forced away the thought of Kat being murdered. *She has to be here somewhere.* He wasn't about to let himself believe she was dead.

The Drow had vanished, the D'Danann were invisible from human eyes while their wings were out, and the gray witches were nowhere to be seen. They'd probably done their glamour-thing and slipped away.

It had been almost impossible to keep track of anyone during the confusion of the battle.

Cassia, though— he'd been aware of her, catching sight of her frequently as if he sought her out while he picked off Fomorii with his Glock. He'd never seen Cassia fight with such intensity on her features and such power in her magic. To his relief she'd made it through the battle—yet she somehow looked as calm and self-assured as usual.

He hoped to God none of the other witches had been harmed. He'd seen several D'Danann and Drow taken down, and his own people, too.

At that thought he fisted his hands, his body tensed, and he wanted even more to take his rage out on *something*. He felt as if he could fight a Fomorii or two with his bare hands.

Jake shook off the tension and tried to slow his pounding heart as he forced himself to think like a cop, a professional. Not as a friend to so many of his officers and magical beings who'd been slaughtered.

I've got to find Kat.

His arm started to throb as he came down some from the intensity of the battle. He sucked in his breath and started toward the emergency vehicles and news vans. Police officers, SWAT teams, and military units had shown up and were crawling all over the place.

Jake holstered his Glock and ran in the rain toward the news van Kat had arrived in. The pounding of his heart grew harder as he dodged law enforcement and emergency personnel.

He came to an abrupt stop. Mutilated bodies slumped on the asphalt surrounding the van.

Jake broke into a run as he spotted a woman with short, dark hair lying on her side. His throat tightened and a sickening sensation settled in his gut as he reached the woman—
Kat.

He dropped to his knees beside her still body and he saw her shredded blouse soaked in blood.

An ache grew behind his eyes as he drew her into his arms. Her body was still warm, her familiar exotic scent mixing with the strong smell of blood.

Her eyelids fluttered and she looked up at him. "So," she said in a scratchy voice, "this is what you've been off doing all this time. The feed from the baseball game was real."

"Quiet, baby." A surge of hope that she'd live speared his chest. He lifted her as he rose, cradling her, and he started toward the paramedics. Red and blue lights flashed around them. "The last thing you need right now is to be grilling me."

Kat winced as he shifted her in his arms. "One of those—those beasts just slashed my side. I don't think it's serious."

"You're not taking any chances." Jake reached the paramedics and came to a stop. "You know you should have listened to me."

She coughed and winced again before giving him a half smile. "When hell freezes over."

Jake took his gaze from hers and looked at the slaughter around them. "I think it just did."

CHAPTER FORTY

DARKWOLF'S STONE-ENCASED HEART THROBBED and ached. His throat grew dry as he laid Elizabeth on the hotel bed. Blood seeped from around the bullet hole in her throat, the blood dripping down her neck to be absorbed by the green and gold bedspread. The blood surrounding the arrow in her belly and the other bullet hole soaked her dark blue T-shirt.

His own wounds had healed, the arrows falling out and onto the floor as he'd walked across the carpet, carrying Elizabeth.

The powers of two gods filled him now, and he knew she was still alive even before he pressed his fingertips to the faint pulse in her throat. Yes, she was alive, but not by much.

If she hadn't passed out, all she'd have to do was shift into a demon and she would heal. She was just as vulnerable as a human when in human form.

His mind spun as he brought his shaking hands to the bloody skin around the hole in her throat. He was a god, twice as powerful as Ceithlenn or Balor, and he could do this. He could heal Elizabeth.

Darkwolf ground his teeth. He *had* to. He wasn't ready to admit exactly why it was so important to him, but it was on the edge of his subconscious.

Anger and thoughts of revenge for what the Drow and the PSF cop had done to Elizabeth filled him and he had to force them back to concentrate on her.

She gave a shuddering breath and gurgled before blood dribbled from the corner of her mouth.

"*No.*" He shook his head. "I won't let you die, Elizabeth."

Tears bit at the backs of his eyes as he focused on healing her. He drew on his warlock healing powers and poured his god's magic into the act. His muscles tensed, his blood vessels glowed a brighter purple, and black fog rolled from him into the wound, into Elizabeth.

In healing her, he was giving her some of his magic. He knew that. He thought about stopping, but he couldn't. Wouldn't.

Tears threatened to start when nothing happened, but then the bullet purged itself, like something forced it out.

Elizabeth gasped and arched her back, more blood spilling out of her mouth, before her body slumped on the bed again.

He concentrated harder healing her. The hole started to close as the bullet tumbled onto the bedspread.

Blood still flowed out of the wound, but as his fog of black magic moved between them, it lessened to a trickle. The skin over the hole in her throat finished knitting itself together.

Darkwolf let out a deep breath, but she didn't waken. He held his fingers to her neck, searching for her pulse. He found it, but the beat of her heart was too slow.

He brought his hands and his magic to her belly and concentrated on forcing the arrow and bullet out and healing her. She coughed and the arrow moved with her body. He glanced at her face. Still out cold.

Gritting his teeth with determination, he thrust more magic into her. The arrow all but flew out of her belly and landed on the carpet followed by the slug. Blood rushed forth with them, but like her throat, the blood slowed then stopped until her internal organs began to heal and her skin formed over the wound, unblemished.

He scooted up the bed and brushed Elizabeth's black hair from her pale face. Her breathing was ragged but growing stronger.

"Wake up," he said, almost choking on the words. Even though he was almost positive she was going to live, he didn't want to take any chances. *"Wake up."*

Elizabeth's eyelids jerked open and her blue, blue eyes met his. Her skin was still so pale it was nearly colorless. What if she wasn't healing inside like she had on the outside? Was he powerful enough to save a life as far gone as hers had been?

"You need to shift." He slipped his arm under her shoulders and she gasped, pain on her face as he lifted her to a sitting position. "You'll definitely be all right if you change into your demon form then back."

She looked dizzy and as if she could barely sit up as he steadied her. With a soft moan she wrapped her arms across her belly and doubled over.

"I'll go in the next room, and you transform." He got up from the bed and walked toward the sitting area of the suite, but looked over his shoulder. "I'll give you a few minutes, okay?"

She nodded, the movement slow and jerky.

A couple of minutes. That was all he'd give her. He left her alone only because he didn't want to see her as a Fomorii, didn't want to think of her as a demon. Only as the woman named Elizabeth.

He stared sightlessly across the sitting room, his back to the door. Nothing registered in his mind but her as he waited.

One minute. Two.

Just as he started to go back to her, she spoke softly behind him. "Darkwolf."

He whirled. Relief flooded him and all the tension and pain of his concern vanished. She stood whole and perfect in the doorway. No wounds, not a trace of blood on her or tears in her T-shirt. She looked as if nothing had happened. Her skin was filled with color, her eyes sharp and bright, her stance as regal as ever.

The knot in his throat returned as he strode toward her and brought her into his embrace the moment he reached her. She wrapped her arms around his waist and he pressed her smaller form to his, her cheek resting on his chest.

When the lump in his throat lessened, he cupped her face in his hands and tilted her head so that he could look into her eyes.

She smiled, looking so much like a soft, welcoming woman. He brought his mouth to hers in a gentle kiss at first, then harder and fiercer. He needed the contact. Needed to know she was safe and alive.

When he convinced himself she was okay, he raised his head and looked down at her.

She licked her lips. "What now?"

"I have decisions to make," he said in the deep, rumbling voice he still wasn't used to.

A great sigh shook him as he released her and stepped away. He raked his hand through his hair as power rolled through him like a roller coaster.

Such great power that it caused him to shake and clench his fists.

When this hell began, after he'd picked up Balor's eye on the shores of Ireland, he would never have believed he would become a god himself. That he would have the power of not one god, but two.

Thoughts of what he could do made him heady. Cravings to dominate, to rule, grew within him.

Why not finish what Ceithlenn and Balor had started? Why not rule a place of his own? Make every person do whatever he wanted them to? Like a king of a foreign country, only with far more power.

Darkwolf turned his gaze on Elizabeth. "How would you like to be the queen of San Francisco?"

CHAPTER FORTY-ONE

LIGHT FLOODED GARRAN'S EYES so brightly he could not see and he clenched his eyes shut again. It wasn't sunlight but something that glowed and still managed to hurt his eyes.

Smells and sounds he had all but forgotten flooded his senses. Sun-warmed grass, honey from a hive buzzing with bees, the morning chatter of birds, the lilting laughter of Elvin children as they performed their daily chores—the musical Elvin voices, so different from the Drow as they had evolved into Dark Elves.

Summerland.

He had traveled to Summerland after his death.

Garran's heart expanded then ached. He had always thought one would have no regrets when passing from Otherworld to Summerland, but regret was exactly what churned in his belly.

"Wake, Garran, king of the Drow," a soft voice said.

Former king of the Drow, he thought and gave a mental sigh.

Garran blinked and squinted in the intense light, but finally his eyes adjusted enough that he was able to focus on the ethreal face above him.

He blinked again, not sure if he was seeing correctly yet certain it was her. His eyes became accustomed to her glow and then he was certain.

The Great Guardian.

With effort he pushed himself to a sitting position in the soft bed he had been lying in. Every muscle in his body ached and his head hurt as if he had bashed it into a wall.

One felt pain in Summerland?

The room he was in—he had not known what to expect when one made the journey. Ivy crept through windows and along the polished wooden walls, and the air was still and sweet. Sunlight spilled into the room and outside the windows he could see trees, rare blue-tipped orchids, and other growing things.

The room and simple furnishings reminded him of the homes of the Light Elves. Where he and his kind had lived before being cast out and into the Drow realm.

He glanced down and saw that his skin was fair, his white-blond hair over his shoulders. He was naked save for the soft embroidered white blanket over his lap and legs.

"You travel between Otherworld and Summerland?" he managed to say to her even though his throat hurt as if unused.

The Guardian smiled. "You are not in Summerland, King Garran. Because of your sacrifice, then the great sacrifice made by someone who gifted you with unconditional love, you still live."

Immediately the slight confusion cleared from his mind and his entire body tensed. What sacrifice? Who?

In his fists he clenched the soft cloth that covered him. "Explain," he said through gritted teeth.

The Guardian met his gaze. "Hannah gave you her life-force so that you would live."

"No." The word was an anguished cry and he buried his face in his hands, not wanting to believe the Guardian. For only the second time in his several millennia of existence, tears rolled down his cheeks. The only other time he had cried was when Rhiannon's mother died.

Pain was quickly replaced by rage as his gaze shot up to meet the Guardian's. "Was this your doing?" he said in a fierce growl. "Was that the condition you made when you said there was only one way I might survive?"

Because if it was, he was going to kill her, Guardian or no.

"The gift did come with that condition, yes," she said, and immediately his fury cut into his body like a sword slicing him through. The Guardian continued before he had the opportunity to react. "However, Hannah's sacrifice meant life for both of you."

Garran barely contained his anger as he narrowed his eyes and tried to decipher her words. "Cease speaking in riddles."

The Great Guardian gazed over his shoulder and made a gesture to indicate he should look behind him.

His heart thumped harder as he slowly turned his head.

Hannah.

She lay on the bed beside him under the blanket, her eyes closed, her features at peace, and her chest rising and falling with every breath she took.

Love and incredulity rose within him with fierce intensity and he tore his gaze from Hannah back to the Guardian.

"She is well, her lifeforce returned to her." The Guardian smiled again. "When she has fully healed, she will wake."

"By the gods, we are alive?" Garran could not quite grasp the reality. "My people . . . my daughter . . ."

"Waiting for your return." Her smile faded. "Rhiannon is well and anxious to see you. Your people—lives were lost in the battle, but few."

Garran released a harsh breath. "Every life has value."

"Including your own." The Guardian folded her hands together as she studied him.

Garran glanced over his shoulder before meeting the Guardian's gaze again. "When will Hannah recover?"

"It will not be long," she said.

He looked around him. "Where are we?"

"In the realm of the Light Elves." Her steady gaze met his. "Only long enough for you to heal. Then you may return to your people."

"What of the gift you promised?" The tension in his body did not easily fade with all the questions circling in his mind. "Have you bestowed it upon my people?"

"Yes." The Guardian gave a slight incline of her head. "Already they enjoy the sunrises and sunsets as they await your return. They are grateful you live and are pleased with the gift, but many are still unhappy with your sacrifice and nearly passing to Summerland."

"I expect as much." Garran nodded as he thought of the Directorate and Carden. "My Steward is well?"

"Holding the throne until your return."

He reached up and grasped a lock of his hair. "Will I experience the same condition as my people?"

"During the day while you are in the realm of the Light Elves, it will be so. At night, even while here, your skin and hair will change to that of the Drow. When you leave this realm, you, too, will no longer have daylight, only sunrises and sunsets."

Garran let out a rush of breath. "Thank you for the gift."

"It came from your sacrifice, King Garran." Something flickered in her blue eyes as she glanced over his shoulder and back to him. "You and Hannah face great choices once she wakes. I will leave that for you to discuss with her when she is well."

Garran opened his mouth to ask the Guardian what she meant, but she turned and walked through a doorway—and faded into nothingness.

He cared not about the Guardian anymore. He shifted on the bed so that he was lying next to Hannah, facing her. She looked so at peace in her sleep, all of her hard shell fallen away. He reached out and stroked her cheek with his knuckles, up to her hair where he brushed the shock of blond from her face. So soft, so real.

So alive.

Hannah gave a light murmur and rolled onto her side, responding to his touch. Still she slept, but a smile curved her lips.

Great joy filled his heart, so much so that breathing did not come easy.

Whatever choices they had ahead of them mattered not. Hannah was alive.

HANNAH SIGHED AND SNUGGLED deeper into a soft cloud. She felt so good she didn't want to wake up. Weightless, as if a huge burden had been lifted from her chest.

Yet something called for her to wake and she sighed with reluctance. So soft, so comfortable . . .

She forced her eyes open and saw Garran watching her. It was fairly dark, the only light was scattered around the room like softly glowing fireflies.

He sat at the edge of the bed she was lying in. His white shirt and pants contrasted with his silvery-blue hair and bluish-gray skin. She didn't think she'd ever seen a more beautiful sight than Garran at that moment.

At first she couldn't remember why he shouldn't be here—wherever here was.

He smiled, reached out, and brushed his knuckles over her cheek and down the hollow of her throat. "Finally, you wake," he said in that incredibly sexy Elvin accent of his.

Warmth filled her. Not from his touch, but from something deeper, stronger.

Love.

She hadn't recognized it until he lay dying on that rooftop, but when she thought she'd lost him, it had hit her hard enough to make her chest seize.

But hadn't she given him her essence? Everything she had?

"You're alive," she said softly as she remained lying down and looked up at his strong, kingly features.

He brushed her cheek with his knuckles again. "Because of you, my beautiful Hannah."

Everything seemed a little blurry on the edges. She remembered that night, yet not. "How?"

"Because you sacrificed yourself for me." His voice grew husky. "You gave me your love."

"I did tell you I love you." Hannah stared into his liquid silver eyes. "I meant it."

"I know." He leaned down and brushed his lips over hers, then said against her lips, "As I love you."

Hannah tangled her fingers in his silky hair. "What are we going to do about it?"

He nuzzled her ear, his breath warm against her neck. "I will make you my queen."

"Queen . . ." Why did she feel both pleasure and hesitancy. "Wait." Reality slowly eased into her mind. "I can't be your queen."

Garran raised his head and her fingers slipped from his hair. He frowned. "What are you saying?"

She shifted and pushed herself to a sitting position. The blanket fell to her waist and she discovered she had nothing on except for her moon and crescent armband. Naked was not the way to have this conversation—especially the way his hungry gaze dropped to her breasts and her nipples hardened.

Hannah raised the blanket and arranged it so that it covered her up to her armpits, over her breasts. "I'm saying that I'm not going to live underground."

He tilted his face to the ceiling of the darkened room they were in. The fireflylike lights played on his strong features. "It is as it was before," he said in a hoarse voice.

"Garran." She placed her hand over one of his. "Tell me what you're talking about."

Slowly he lowered his head and his eyes met hers. "I have only loved one other in my lifetime."

"Rhiannon's mother, Anna," she said, starting to understand the pain on his face at the same time she wanted to comfort him.

"She, too, would not live in my world." Garran sighed and looked away.

Hannah squeezed his hand. "You loved her a lot."

"Much." Garran faced her. "My love for you is just as great. Yet one cannot compare the two."

"I understand." Hannah raised her hand and traced the

lines on his forehead with her fingertips. "What are we going to do about us?"

"The choice is yours." He caught her hand in both of his and held it to his heart. "I cannot leave my people as much as I would give to be with you always."

Hannah closed her eyes and counted the beats of his heart beneath her palm. She'd never felt such love, such completeness as she did with Garran. How would she live without him?

There was only one answer.

She opened her eyes to meet his again. "We compromise."

He looked hopeful yet uncertain. "Compromise?"

"You trust Carden to serve as your Steward when you're not in your realm, right?"

"Yes." He held her hand impossibly tighter to him. "But I cannot and will not leave my throne to him while I am alive."

"I realize that." She smiled and gripped his shirt in her hand. "I'm suggesting that part of the time we live in my world and part of the time in yours. You can be 'on call' anytime you're needed by your people. Is that fair?"

Garran released her hand and moved closer at the same time he brought her into his embrace. "Most fair."

"Of course it is." She looked into his beautiful eyes. "After all, I didn't make my software company a force to be reckoned with without great negotiating skills."

"*You* are a force to be reckoned with," he said with a laugh as he rolled them onto the bed so that they were lying snugly against each other.

She gave him a teasing grin. "I know."

Garran brought his mouth close and brushed his lips over her. "You will make a great queen."

"Speaking of that . . ." She moaned as he rained soft kisses on her face, the curve of her neck, working his way toward the blanket still snugly crossing her breasts. "Stop that. I can't concentrate."

"Mmmm . . ." The sound came out in a low rumble as he pressed his lips to her collarbone.

Hannah sucked in her breath as a glittery sensation radiated throughout her body all the way to the place between her thighs. "If I'm going to be queen . . ."—she let out another moan—"there are a few changes I'm going to make."

"I thought so," he murmured as he tugged at the blanket hiding her breasts.

"Starting with that squeaky door."

"Done." Garran laughed as he pulled the blanket down to her waist, exposing her breasts. He flicked her nipples, making them harder and harder and had a teasing glint in his gaze. "Anything you wish to add at this moment?"

Hannah squirmed, wanting more than his touch on her nipples. "N-not right now." She cupped the back of his head to draw his mouth closer to her breasts.

He obliged, suckling one nipple then traveling with his tongue between the valley of her breasts before capturing her other warm nipple in his mouth.

"Don't wait," she said, and he tilted his head up, his liquid silver gaze meeting hers. No matter what the color of his skin or hair, he was so beautiful to her. "Make love to me. Come inside me, now."

He rolled her onto her back and slid his hips between her thighs, spreading her wide. She grasped his biceps as he braced his arms to either side of her breasts. He teased her by not entering her. Instead he pumped his hips, sliding his thick erection through her wet folds and rubbing her clit at the same time.

"Don't tease me." She slid her fingers into his hair and clamped his hips between her thighs. "I just *need* you, please."

Garran reached down and arranged his cock so that its head rested at the entrance to her core, slightly in, but not nearly enough. She wriggled in anticipation, thrills zinging from her belly to between her thighs.

With his eyes holding hers, he drove his erection deep inside her.

Hannah gasped as he stretched and filled her, reaching so deep he felt as if he were a part of her. He slowly began to thrust in and out of her slick core.

"If this is what it's always like to make love to a king," Hannah said in a hoarse voice, "no wonder I'm addicted to you."

His expression was intense as he pumped his hips harder. "For you, only this king." He brought his mouth down against hers as he drove his cock in faster and faster.

He was claiming her, taking her for his own, and she loved it. For him she would give up control. Everything she had was his to take. Just as she intended to claim him and take everything he had to give her.

Hannah gripped his hair tighter in both fists to anchor herself as her mind spun from his kiss and the feel of him moving in and out. Driving her crazy, reaching every sweet spot she had.

Their kiss grew hungrier, more frantic as she moved her hips up to meet his. Her orgasm built and built until she felt as if she were in another world altogether.

Garran raised his head and her gaze met his just before her climax hit her so hard she cried out from the strength of it. The firefly lights seemed to spin around them and her own green magic glittered and sparkled above.

The orgasm took hold of her like magic sliding through her veins. It sizzled and crackled in her blood, traveling to every part of her body. She wanted more and he gave her more until she couldn't take any more. "Come, Garran, please come!"

A growl rumbled up from him and his eyes darkened from liquid silver to steel gray as he thrust several more times. He ground his hips against hers as he shouted his release in his language, a cry she didn't understand but recognized for what it was by the look in his eyes. Words that told her he loved her.

His cock throbbed inside her and her core clamped down on him, drawing out his release the way he was driving her climax on and on until she felt as if she were nothing but a mass of sparkles and light.

With a final groan, Garran buried his face in the curve of her neck and repeated the words she was certain he had shouted before changing to her language. "I love you, my sweet one. I love you."

CHAPTER FORTY-TWO

THE WAREHOUSE'S KITCHEN WAS empty save for Jake, who tipped back his chair and took another swig of beer. The cool liquid flowed over his tongue and down his throat before he lowered the bottle from his lips.

What a goddamned mess.

Martial law was back in full force, new leaders rising up in the government, law enforcement, and military to replace those who had "vanished."

The Fomorii had taken over the bodies of so many men and women who had been in power.

But Garran had sent the Fomorii demon bastards back to Underworld.

"The sonofabitch really did it," Jake said aloud feeling amazed, yet . . . not as surprised as he should have been.

Cassia had left San Francisco for Otherworld, suddenly, for God knew what reason. He couldn't help wondering about her, thinking about her. And damned if he didn't miss her. Why? He had no friggin' idea.

According to news Cassia had sent via an Elvin messenger, Garran and Hannah had both survived.

Thank God.

And Kat. Jake blew out a harsh breath. She'd already been released from the hospital, the deep furrows in her side from Fomorii claws stitched and bandaged. She'd been so damn lucky that was all she'd suffered—as well as an egg on her head from striking the asphalt so hard when the demon flung her to the ground.

Jake set his beer bottle on the table with a loud thunk and wiped his mouth with the back of his hand. Right about now a good drunk sounded better and better, but he needed to keep his mind sharp. He needed to work harder than ever on those schematics for god-killing weapons.

An unknown remained in San Francisco.

Darkwolf with the power of two gods.

And the Fomorii queen at his side. As far as the Alliance knew, from the witches' scrying, Junga was the only demon left in the city.

What did that mean, and why did Darkwolf always keep her with him, and in human form? Was she his servant now? Or had he somehow become attached to her?

The thought was so idiotic that Jake thrust it out of his mind.

He narrowed his eyes as he scraped the beer bottle's label with his thumbnail and felt the cold glass against his palm. His muscles tightened causing the wound in his arm to ache.

A mess. A fucking mess.

Jake took another swig of beer and this time slammed the bottle harder onto the tabletop.

The Alliance had lost so many men and women to the battle that the thought of it still made Jake's gut churn. Their numbers had thinned considerably, especially the PSF and the D'Danann. The Drow—they wouldn't be much good in a daytime fight, but they'd come in handy again if it was dark. If another battle blew their way.

And that's exactly what he was afraid of.

Darkwolf was out there.

They hadn't seen the end yet.

CHAPTER FORTY-THREE

EXCITEMENT, HAPPINESS, AND LOVE filled Hannah with warmth as she and Garran arrived in San Francisco. They had waited to leave the realm of the Light Elves until darkness settled so that Garran didn't have to worry about the sun.

Hannah squeezed his hand and smiled up at him as they walked past the D'Danann guards and into the warehouse.

"You're back!" Silver ran up to Hannah and threw her arms around Hannah's neck the moment she and Garran entered the warehouse. "Thank Anu, you are safe and well."

At first Hannah stiffened, old habits kicking in of keeping herself detached. But almost immediately she relaxed and released Garran's hand to return Silver's hug.

"I'm happy to be here with all of you," Hannah said with a smile, and meant it.

"Come on." Silver took Hannah by her hand and led her to the kitchen.

Hawk had been standing by Silver, and he and Garran followed Silver and Hannah. When they entered the kitchen, all of the other witches were there, along with several of the D'Danann and Jake.

They all stopped talking, and the witches immediately converged on Hannah, hugging her and telling her how happy they were that she and Garran had returned safe and well.

For the first time, Hannah didn't freeze up when her friends hugged her. She felt their love, and squeezed each one as tightly.

The old feelings left over from her childhood would never entirely go away, but Hannah felt a renewal in her heart. An abundance of joy and love and belonging warmed her entire body and a knot formed in her throat at the power of her feelings.

Not surprisingly, Rhiannon was the last to approach, and she and Hannah paused and looked at each other. "Thanks for saving my father," Rhiannon said, then looked up at Garran before returning her gaze to Hannah's. "I'm glad you're both okay."

Rhiannon hesitated and then they both reached out at the same time and gave each other a stiff hug before quickly parting. Rhiannon turned to Garran and hugged him. She was just as rigid at first with him, but when Garran enveloped her in a tight embrace she relaxed against him before they released each other.

Hannah found herself swept up with the witches and she was seated at the large kitchen table with Garran standing behind her.

To Hannah's pleasure, Banshee swooped down and landed on her shoulder. Hannah wore one of the Light Elves' white tunics and pants and her familiar gripped the soft cloth in his talons. The falcon made a few low sounds before taking off to circle overhead and giving a loud shriek before he flew into the rafters.

"So, what's next now that Ceithlenn's gone?" Hannah asked as she looked at her Coven sisters. They glanced at each other, and Hannah's heart thumped a little harder. "Don't tell me somehow she's still alive."

"She's dead, all right." Copper frowned as she shifted her broken ankle secured in the cast she had resting on a chair. "But after she died, the goddess's power was released."

Hannah's skin itched, knowing some kind of bomb was going to be dropped.

Silver rested her hand on her slightly rounded belly. "While you were helping Garran, Darkwolf showed up." She shook her head. "Somehow he absorbed all of Ceithlenn's power."

Hannah widened her eyes. "Are you sure?"

"While you were gone, we scried," Copper said.

"And Darkwolf is pretty damn powerful now." Rhiannon scowled as she pushed her chin-length hair behind her ear. "Not only does he have Ceithlenn's power, but Balor's as well."

Hannah shook her head, her skin feeling suddenly tight over her body. "You can't be serious."

"Very serious," Alyssa said in her gentle voice, an odd look in her eyes.

"The jerk is a freaking god now." Mackenzie's cheeks flamed as anger sparked in her eyes. "And I don't think he intends to play nice."

"Not at all." Sydney pushed her chic glasses up the bridge of her nose, her lavender eyes intent, serious. "We're not sure *what* he plans, though."

"But he's a god now!" Rhiannon clenched her hands on the tabletop. "Twice as powerful as Ceithlenn was."

"Whoa." Hannah tried to absorb the news, but was having a hard time computing it. Garran's tension radiated from behind her as he gripped her chair, his knuckles against her back. "What does this mean?"

Jake hitched his shoulder against one of the refrigerators. "It means that we've got to be prepared for whatever the hell he comes up with."

"I thought it was all over." Hannah took a deep breath, feeling suffocated by the new threat. Actually an old threat, considering what Darkwolf had done as a warlock in the past.

Silver, who had been affected by Darkwolf more than anyone, looked beyond frustrated. "I wish."

"We all do," Rhiannon grumbled.

Hannah frowned as memories of the battle churned in her

mind. A vivid image of Janis Arrowsmith attempting to save Ceithlenn burned in her thoughts. "What about Janis?"

"She disappeared." Alyssa's quiet voice came from the corner. "After the battle Janis's entire Coven searched for her, but no one could find her."

"Jake wanted to arrest her for interfering," Mackenzie said with a half smirk.

"Was she eaten by one of the Fomorii?" Hannah asked, her chest hurting at the thought.

"I was with her when every last demon vanished." Silver shook her head. "After I dropped my shield, I turned away from her. When I looked back she was gone."

"I hope she's someplace safe," Sydney said, and everyone was quiet for a moment.

Copper broke the silence with a grin. "A little birdie told me Garran and Hannah have news of their own."

"Hannah and I will be joined," Garran said from behind Hannah in his sexy Elvin accent, sending tingles down her neck. He gripped her shoulders in his warm hands. "She has agreed to be my queen."

Heat flooded Hannah's cheeks as everyone looked at her and Garran with stunned expressions. Everyone but Copper, who continued to grin.

"Wow." Silver glanced from Garran to Hannah. "I had no idea . . ."

Hannah brought her hand up to clasp one of Garran's that still rested on her shoulder. "I love Garran." The words came easier than she expected.

"As I love Hannah." Garran leaned down and pressed his lips to her hair and she shivered as he rose back up.

The joy flooding her because of her feelings for Garran made her smile and she was almost giddy with happiness. She'd never thought she'd ever be giddy about anything.

"We're going to live part of the time in the Drow realm." Hannah glanced up at Garran and met his gaze before turning back to look at everyone else. "We'll spend the other half of our time here."

"Congratulations," Alyssa said, and that seemed to break everyone out of surprise mode.

"Yeah, definitely," Copper said, and everyone else chimed in with lots of grins and chatter, telling Hannah and Garran how happy they were for the two of them.

Only one person in the room hadn't said a word—Rhiannon. She sat back in her chair, her expression unreadable, and her arms folded across her chest. Everyone stopped speaking as they looked at her.

Rhiannon twisted her lips and the corner of her mouth quirked before she said, "Welcome to the family. Mom."

Mackenzie snorted and Hannah's other friends laughed and giggled.

Rhiannon met Hannah's eyes and smiled.

HANNAH MANAGED TO SLIP away from everything that was going on in the warehouse and headed to the room she and Garran had shared. So much planning and strategy were needed to be ready to fight Darkwolf and beat him at whatever game he had in mind.

They had taken out Ceithlenn. Surely they could handle Darkwolf and make San Francisco safe again.

Right now she needed a few minutes alone. When she walked into the bedroom she leaned back against the door after she shut it and closed her eyes.

It felt as though a great weight pressed against her chest because the Fire Dragon had joined sides with Ceithlenn. Still, the other three Dragon Elementals had answered Hannah's call and helped in the battle against the dark goddess.

So that was more than something, right?

Some of the tension eased from her shoulders. She opened her eyes, pushed away from the door, and went to the pack where she'd left it. The pack had remained undisturbed after Cassia had brought it back from the sacred beach.

For a moment she paused, wondering what had happened

to Cassia. Why had she returned to Otherworld? She'd only left a cryptic message with one of the D'Danann, nothing more.

Hannah knelt on the concrete floor in front of her pack and held her breath for no reason at all. She slowly forced air from her lungs as she reached the pack.

When she raised it, no glass tinkled as it shifted. Had someone removed the pieces of the mirror?

Her heart beat a little faster as she opened the pack. Scents of freshly turned earth, clean air, and rain flowed out of the pack. A knot formed in her throat and she slipped her hand inside.

Immediately, she felt something cool and smooth, and wrapped her fingers around what felt like a metal handle.

Her arm shook as she gripped the handle and drew out a large pewter-framed black mirror. It trembled in her hand as she gripped it tighter as if it might fly away.

On her mirror that had broken, only two Dragons had circled it, biting the tails of each other. This mirror had three two-dimensional Dragons that arced around the sides and the top of the frame.

Her eyes wide, she lightly ran her fingers over the one on the left, west—the Water Dragon. It bit the tail of the top Dragon, north—the Earth Dragon. She trailed her fingers along it and to the place where the Earth Dragon bit the tail of the one on the east—the Air Dragon.

Hannah's heart fell a little when her fingers reached the empty place at the bottom of the frame where the Fire Dragon should have been to make the circle complete.

The backs of her eyes stung as she touched the spot, which was surprisingly warm under her fingertips. The fact that the other Dragons were with her made the pain of losing the Fire Dragon only a little lighter.

Hannah bit the inside of her lower lip. She didn't fight the lone tear from escaping one of her eyes and it rolled down her cheek.

The tear plopped onto the empty space on the mirror's

frame. Steam rose up from the moisture and it sizzled, causing Hannah to draw her hand away. The mirror trembled in her hand as if she were shaking, but she wasn't. It was.

She gripped the handle tighter as the moisture from her tear vanished in the puff of steam. Unable to shift her gaze, she watched as the empty spot wavered, as if something were trying to get through.

In the next moment the molded form of a Dragon appeared on what had been an empty spot on the frame.

The Fire Dragon.

Hannah's heart pounded so hard now that she could hear it in her ears. The Fire Dragon opened its molded mouth and clamped its jaws over the tail of the Water Dragon. A movement to her left and the Air Dragon bit the Fire Dragon's tail.

The Dragons all went still.

So did Hannah's heart and her breathing.

She clasped the mirror and pressed it to her breasts as several more tears rolled down her cheeks. Now, not only did she catch the scents of freshly turned earth, clean air, and rain, but a touch of sulfur, too. All four Dragon Elementals.

A surge of warmth filled her along with all of her senses telling her what she already knew. She could scry again.

As Hannah clutched the mirror to her, she bent her head and said a silent prayer of thanks to the Ancestors, Anu, and the Dragon Elementals.

CHAPTER FORTY-FOUR

PLEASANT LAUGHTER AND CHATTER echoed in the great hall as Hannah and Garran were surrounded by Drow, D'Danann, the human cop Jake Macgregor, and almost all of the witches. Only Cassia was missing.

Garran looked down at his beautiful Hannah and smiled.

The Dark Elves had not taken the news of Garran's and Hannah's impending joining as well as the witches had, which was not a surprise to Garran.

Of course, the Directorate had argued against her, for being a human and a witch no less. And a woman who obviously did not fit the mold of a submissive Drow female.

Garran had been firm, leaving the Directorate no room to argue. As king the choice was his and Hannah was to be his queen.

Now it was their day. They stood upon a circular raised dais in the very center of the rounded great hall so that they might easily be seen by all those who had gathered to witness and celebrate their joining.

Hannah tilted her face to look up at him and returned his smile. In moments they would be mates forever. He saw only confidence and love in her eyes and on her expression, and his heart thumped against his breastbone.

"I love you," he murmured close to her ear, and felt her slight shiver and caught her sweet womanly scent. "When we are finished with this nonsense, I will steal you away."

"Behave." She elbowed him and he chuckled.

He straightened, but continued to look at her, even as he was supposed to be paying attention to Hark, who was about to lead the small formal ceremony.

Hannah wore the Brooch of Aithne, the large diamond glittering against one shoulder strap of her black clothing. She called the revealing creation an evening dress. It was cut low in the front, ending just above the swells of her breasts. The dress bared her back from her shoulders to the base of her spine and the hem barely reached her mid-thigh and a short slit revealed part of one thigh. Thin straps held her shoes to her feet, and the heels, adorned with diamonds, were so high he did not know how she could stand, much less walk in them.

Garran was not so certain he wanted any male to see as much of her soft skin as the dress exposed. No matter that most Drow women wore very little. Somehow Hannah was more enticing in this piece of clothing than a naked woman was. As if hiding just enough of her to make a man crazy to strip it off.

Hannah's dark brown hair fell straight to her shoulders, the shock of blond hair defining her elegant features. On her upper arm, as always, she wore her moon and crescent armband. She gave the only sign of nervousness thus far when she brought her fingers to the band and stroked it.

His cock ached at the thought of those small fingers stroking *him* and he gritted his teeth and forced his thoughts away from making love to Hannah.

When preparing for the ceremony, Garran had settled his crown upon his head. Several millennia ago his ancestors forged the crown from yellow and white gold, the strands interwoven and forming an unbroken circle.

Garran had donned his finest leather breeches and boots, and his leather and gem-encrusted straps crisscrossed his chest.

He turned his attention to Hark, who wore the black tunic and breeches of the Directorate. The only difference from what he wore daily was a large gold medallion that hung from his throat, indicating his station in the ceremony.

The room quieted as Hark ascended the dais until he stood in front of Hannah and Garran.

"On this most auspicious day, we welcome into our realm Hannah Wentworth, D'Anu witch." Hark's voice echoed in the great hall. "She who willingly gave her life essence and her love to our king so that he might live."

Mild surprise filtered through Garran at Hark's words as he acknowledged what Hannah had done for him and his people. A soft murmur rolled through the room as no doubt his revelation had astonished many of the Dark Elves.

Hark's smile appeared genuine as he looked upon Garran's mate. "Hannah of the D'Anu," the leader of the Directorate continued, "has proven to be most worthy of being queen of the Drow."

Garran felt Hannah's slight trembling as her arm was firmly against his. He took her hand and squeezed it and she squeezed his in return.

Hark turned, his back to Hannah and Garran, as he reached down to take what was handed to him from a woman at the foot of the dais.

When he faced Garran and Hannah again, Hark held a smaller circlet that matched Garran's.

Hark settled the crown on Hannah's dark hair. "Today Hannah is made our new queen, and we pay homage to her."

Pride swelled within Garran's chest and he gripped her hand tighter as he felt her shaking increase. Hark stepped back and knelt, his head bowed in respect.

Garran glanced at Hannah as everyone in the hall knelt and lowered their heads, as well.

Hannah's lips trembled. "I don't know what to do, Garran," she whispered.

"Smile," Garran murmured, "and give a slight nod of acknowledgment."

She did as he instructed her to, her lips still trembling as she smiled.

Hark rose to his feet again. "We welcome you, Queen Hannah."

Applause and cheering broke out in the hall, loud enough to make his ears ring. Garran took Hannah and wrapped her in his embrace before kissing her long and hard. The applause and cheering grew louder.

When Garran raised his head and looked down at Hannah, he saw that a blush had stained her cheeks red.

She parted her moist lips and her eyes were bright. "I love you, Garran." He smiled, and she added, "Now get me off this thing."

CHAPTER FORTY-FIVE

CHEERS CONTINUED AND HANNAH'S knees did that blessed trembling thing as she held Garran's hand. *Cool, collected, calm . . .*

To hell with that.

Sights and sounds blurred and her mind spun with the magnitude of what she'd just done. She'd married a king! The Drow king.

And by the Ancestors, she was now a queen.

She was wondering how she was going to manage the stairs in three-inch heels with her legs shaking when Garran swooped her up in his arms.

Another cheer rose and Hannah gave a cry of surprise as his powerful arms embraced her and she wrapped her arms around his neck. He looked at her and gave her his sexy, cocky grin and she smiled back. He held her tight as he carried her into the crowd that surged toward the entrance to the underground city.

Countless people congratulated them as they moved through the crowd, including her sister witches, the D'Danann, and Jake. All of the voices and faces shifted into a complete blur.

"Our people will celebrate our joining in the city," Garran said.

"Our people." She shook her head. "I don't know if I can get used to that."

"They will love you as their queen." He began to navigate in a different direction from the crowd—toward the hallway that led to his bedroom. "I can think of a better way to celebrate."

She couldn't have been happier than to slip away with him, away from the craziness of the event.

When they reached his room, Garran used one hand to slam the door before he carried her across the chamber. He set her on her unsteady Jimmy Choo heels and grasped her face in his hands before kissing her long and hard.

Hannah moaned and sank against him, bracing her palms on his bare flesh between the leather straps crisscrossing his chest. His skin was warm and tingles radiated through her fingertips to the needy place between her thighs.

Garran raised his head and she found she could barely breathe as she looked into his liquid silver eyes. His earthy male scent intoxicated her to the point she felt almost dizzy with it. She reveled in the feel of his arms wrapped around her and how his embrace made her feel secure and loved.

He glanced down at her Dior evening dress and traced one of his fingers down her soft flesh to where the fabric barely covered her breasts.

His jaw tensed. "How does one take this material off?"

"Very carefully," Hannah said with light smile, but she really couldn't care if he ripped the blessed thing off her.

She reached behind and managed to keep from trembling long enough to unfasten the dress and let it slip down her body in a silken glide to her feet.

Garran gave a loud groan as his gaze took in her naked body. She'd been entirely bare beneath that sexy little dress, and all she was wearing were her black heels, crown, and moon and crescent armband.

He brought her roughly against him, pressing her breasts against the gems and leather of his chest straps as he took her mouth in another fierce kiss. His lips moved over hers and he bit her lower lip, causing her to groan. Whenever he did that it made her wetter between her thighs and even hotter for him.

Their tongues met and they tasted each other, kissing until Hannah's mind spun and she lost all sense of anything but being in Garran's arms.

He released her long enough to step back and remove his chest straps, his sword, his black leather boots and pants. The entire time her heart beat fast and furious, as she waited in anticipation of feeling his naked body against hers.

"Goddess, you're beautiful." She drank in the sight of his large, powerful body, his sculpted muscles and that cock . . . She licked her lips and his erection seemed to grow bigger in response.

Garran moved toward her and she sank down, her knees on her dress, not caring what happened to the expensive fabric. Her gaze met his as she wrapped her hand around his erection, and he sucked in his breath when she slipped her mouth over his cock. The drop of semen at the tip tasted salty and good, and she wanted more.

"Hannah . . ." he whispered as he slipped his hands into her hair. "My sweet one, my queen."

A soft moan escaped her as he spoke and she moved her mouth up and down his length, taking him as deep as she could. She used one hand to work his shaft while bringing her other hand to her breasts, pinching one nipple then the next.

When she sucked harder, she heard his soft intake of breath. His body slightly trembled and she knew he was close to climaxing.

He clenched his hands tighter in her hair and she moved him in and out of her mouth faster. She met his gaze and his expression was pained, his jaw tense, and every muscle looked strained, as if he were holding himself back.

She'd fix that. She brought her hand from her nipples to his balls and fondled them before giving a firm squeeze.

Garran's eyes unfocused and he gave a shout before his cock pumped semen into her mouth. She hummed with pleasure as she drank from him, swallowing at the same time his unique taste rolled over her tongue.

With a groan he moved his hands from her hair to her shoulders. He gripped her upper arms and his moist cock slipped from her mouth before she rose and he kissed her firmly on her lips.

He trailed kisses down her jaw to the erogenous zone behind her ear and she shivered while her folds became wetter. "I will taste every inch of my queen."

"Don't take too long." She moaned and tilted her head back when his warm mouth latched onto one of her nipples. So hot and wet, his tongue so masterful. "I want you inside me."

He made a sound of pleasure as he moved his mouth to her other breast and began flicking his tongue over her nipple in the same way he had with the first one. She slipped her hands into his beautiful silvery-blue hair and traced the curves of his pointed ears as he clasped his hands around her waist.

When he raised her up, she wrapped her thighs around his hips and felt his cock press against her folds. Goddess, she couldn't wait.

They neared the bed and her eyes widened in surprise. The bed was covered with the rare blue-tipped orchids she had learned were only to be found in the realm of the Light Elves.

"A gift from the Guardian." He settled Hannah down in the middle of the soft petals that welcomed her in a gentle caress. "To lie in a bed of orchids on your joining night is considered good luck."

She held her arms up to him. "I have all the luck I need."

With a smile he lowered himself so that he rested between her thighs, his body so snug and warm and comforting against hers. She reached for his cock that was deliciously erect again and his smile turned teasing as he began moving down her body, his tongue and lips tasting and taunting her.

"Do *not* make me wait," she said in her most imperious tone, and he chuckled. Well, she might as well start acting queenly now. Not that he was listening.

Garran slowly glided down her body, making her writhe and groan with every touch, every caress. The unusual, sweet scent of the orchids combined with what he was doing to her was making her light-headed.

When his mouth reached the dark curls of her mound he nuzzled her and she heard him drawing in her scent in a deep breath. He placed his palms on the insides of her thighs and spread her wide as he focused on her with single-minded intent on his features.

She held her breath as she waited for his mouth to come down on her. He flicked out his tongue, tasting her only lightly. She released her breath as she groaned for more.

An orgasm started to roll toward her the moment he pressed his mouth to her folds. Her belly clenched and she brought her hands to her breasts and started squeezing her nipples, adding to the delicious shivers racing through her body.

Garran nipped her clit and she almost lost it. She barely held on to the thinnest thread of control as his tongue laved and sucked her folds and her clit. The orchids acted like an aphrodisiac to her senses—not that she needed anything with Garran.

He inserted three fingers into her core and she gasped just before he lightly bit her clit.

Hannah cried out as her entire body shuddered and green sparkles glittered behind her eyes before she realized they were coating her skin, too.

Dizziness from the orgasm made it hard to come back down from the high of her release. Her core contracted around his fingers and he gave her folds and clit final, loving strokes of his tongue.

She was still shuddering when Garran eased up her body and wedged his hips firmly between her thighs. As he brought his mouth down on hers, she wrapped her arms around his neck. She moaned as she tasted herself along with his masculine flavor that made her want more and more and more of him.

"Now, Garran," she murmured against his lips. "Enough is enough. Make love to your queen."

A smile of satisfaction curved the corners of his mouth as he rose up and brought his hand between them to place his cock at the entrance to her core.

"Yes," he said with a hard thrust that felt as if it reached her belly button and caused her to cry out. "I will make love to my queen. This day and every day."

If she could have laughed she would have. Instead she gasped and said, "I don't know if I could handle this *every* day."

"You will." A wicked look lit his eyes and she knew he meant it.

And she looked forward to every night they had together.

With hard, firm strokes he thrust in and out of her core, driving her on and on toward another climax. She looked up into his eyes and the expression on his face—the love, the caring—made her want to cry from the joy she felt.

Her orgasm started with light contractions that she knew were only a taste of something much bigger coming toward her like a storm of spellfire. Everything glittered inside and outside of her, tingles of heat and light and love.

Even though she knew it was coming, her climax still took her by surprise with its force and intensity. She gasped then cried out as her whole body shook with her orgasm's power.

Garran drove in and out of her so hard that he made her core spasm with every thrust. She held on to his broad shoulders, trying to anchor herself as if her whole body would take flight.

He pressed his hips tight to her mound and sweat glistened on his skin as he came with a shuddering groan. His cock pumped his semen inside her and she held him close as she felt every throb of his release.

Garran kissed Hannah hard before drawing her on her side and bringing her into the curve of his arm. Scents of orchids and sex and sweat and male filled her.

"You have my love always, my queen," Garran said as he brushed his lips over hers.

Hannah smiled, her heart aching with more happiness than she'd ever felt in her life. "I've found my home with you. And you'll always have my love."

For Cheyenne's Readers

Turn the page for a sneak peek at the explosive final
book in Cheyenne McCray's Magic series!

DARK MAGIC

Coming November 2008 from
St. Martin's Paperbacks

HE HAD THE MOTHER of all headaches. Something pulled at the back of his mind, faint images and sounds, but he couldn't focus on it long enough to grasp whatever it was.

Jake brought his fingertips to his forehead and rubbed his temples before dropping his hand to his side and opening his eyes.

His gaze wavered in and out as he tried to focus.

A blond woman. A smile. Fingers lightly brushing hair from his forehead.

"You're finally awake." Cassia's voice, soft, lilting. "I was beginning to wonder if you would sleep the week through."

Jake squinted and Cassia's face came more clearly into focus. She looked like an angel, sunlight shining through the strands of her golden hair so that she almost seemed to glow. Her turquoise-colored eyes studied him intently.

He glanced from her to see that he was in some kind of room with ivy crawling on the walls and through arches. The walls were a shade that wasn't white. Wasn't blue, wasn't green. Something different. Simple wooden furniture was tucked against walls and in corners. The bed had such a soft mattress he could happily close his eyes and go back to sleep.

The scent of magic surrounded him.

Jake mentally shook his head. *What the hell?*

"Where am I?" His voice came out even, his tone controlled. "What's going on?"

Cassia continued to look at him in that same calm, mysterious way that had always driven him crazy with the desire to shake her. Or kiss her.

She gestured toward the windows where he could see tree leaves glittering in the sunlight. "You are in the city of the Light Elves, in Otherworld."

He blinked. No way had he heard that. "I'm *where?*"

"Otherworld." She rested her hands in her lap. "You don't remember anything?"

Jake squinted and didn't have to reach far for memories of the attack in the park. He winced at the images and flinched as he remembered sensations of daggers stabbing him in his gut and chest. Another man had been driving a dagger toward his heart—

A female voice cut through the mayhem. Fire. Fire surrounding them. Crackling. Smells of burnt hair and flesh, and that horrible musty, sour smell.

He brought his hand to his chest to find he was naked beneath the covers. He felt rough skin, like scars. Scars where the wounds would have been. "I should be dead."

"You weren't meant to die." For the first time Cassia looked a little rattled. "I couldn't let you."

Jake scooted up in bed, the sheet falling to his lap and baring his chest. He looked down at the thick pink scars and brought his hand up to touch them. He felt no pain except for the memory of the agony of the daggers driving into his flesh, piercing deep inside his body.

An odd sensation stirred in his gut as he returned his gaze to hers. "You saved me?"

"The Great Guardian and I, yes." Cassia maintained that calm expression that still made him want to grab her and rattle her. Maybe kissing her would do just that.

Instead, he squeezed his eyes shut and pinched the bridge of his nose before looking at her again. More memories, these more vague, came to him—rain, thunder, pain, and Cassia cradling him in her lap before he was thrown into a spiraling sensation followed by complete blackness.

"But you came for me," he said with no doubt in his mind. "Not the Great Guardian."

Cassia didn't say anything.

Why did she come for him?

"What happened to the rest of those Stormcutters?" Jake asked as he thought about the fire circling them and the smells.

"Those funnel-beings?" She cleared her throat. "I eliminated them."

"You killed the bastards?" Jake stared at her. "Gray witches *never* kill."

"I am not a gray witch," she said, her voice quieting.

"What—" Jake began, but she cut him off by holding up one graceful, long-fingered hand.

"You need to sleep now, Jake."

She started to stand but he stopped her when he reached for one of her hands and squeezed. Currents of electricity shot through him. The same currents he'd felt every time Cassia had touched him in the past.

" 'Thank you' doesn't seem like enough," he said as she squeezed his hand back.

"I'm just happy you're going to be okay." She smiled such a radiant smile that his heart beat faster.

Shit. Why did he want to draw her onto his lap and hold her? Hell, he didn't even trust her. She'd deceived the D'Anu witches in the past—she could still be deceiving them with everything she did or said. She'd just admitted to not being a gray witch.

So what *was* she?

There'd be time to sort all of that out later. Right now other questions had to be asked and answered.

Jake cleared his throat and released her hand. "How long have I been out?"

"Three days."

"No fu—friggin' way." Jake started to climb out of bed, but Cassia put her palm against his chest and frowned.

Tingles radiated from her hand, straight to his cock,

which decided to harden so much his balls ached. Jake gave another mental curse. He glanced down to make sure the blankets hid that little fact.

Cassia was surprisingly strong as she braced her palm on his skin and kept him from getting up. "We repaired your internal organs, but they have needed the time to heal completely. Nothing can do that but rest."

His whole body jumped like a live wire, and not just from her touch, but from the need to get back to work. He had a lot to do to make his city safe again. Too much to do. He couldn't stay in bed. God only knew what was going on back in San Francisco.

As Cassia removed her hand from his chest, Jake clenched his fists. "How is the man who was with me at the park? How is everyone else in the Alliance? Have there been any more battles with Darkwolf and those Stormcutters?"

"Rhiannon sent word that David Bourne is fine. His wounds were nothing the D'Anu couldn't heal." She leaned away from Jake and straightened in her chair. "I've let them know you are all right, too."

For the first time he got a good look at her when she eased back in her chair. White robes parted at the slender column of her throat, separating far enough down that her cleavage was exposed, showing the gentle curves of her breasts. His mouth watered, his cock ached. He adjusted the covers to better hide his erection and mentally willed it down.

A stab of guilt hit him in the chest, the same place as one of his new scars. *Christ.* Cassia turned him on big time, but he had no business having thoughts of taking her down to the mattress, sliding between her thighs, and being inside of her.

He should be thinking about Kat. He should be thinking about getting back to San Francisco and making sure she was okay—and that she wasn't getting herself killed by trying to cover news stories involving the insanity in the city.

Jake looked over Cassia's left shoulder to avoid her eyes and sucked in a deep breath. The fact that she wasn't even *human* should be enough to squelch any other erotic thoughts about him and this beautiful half-Elvin woman.

Or was she half-Elvin? She wasn't a gray witch—so was she even a witch at all? She could be half-dragon, or a friggin' shapeshifting eggplant. What did he really know about Cassia?

Nothing but the facts that he'd seen her in battle with the D'Anu witches and watched her become the person all of the witches turned to for help and guidance. She had gone from pretending to be an inept apprentice witch to their leader.

That, and she baked one hell of a mean cinnamon roll.

"Another battle was fought." Cassia's voice jerked his attention back to her. She held her hands in her lap, her expression calm. "Casualties on both sides."

The word *casualties* hit home, and any lustful thoughts and odd feelings he'd had vanished in a snap.

Fury rode him at the news of members of the Alliance dying. This time he did manage to sit up in bed and swung his legs over the side, but kept the blanket over his lap. Her calm expression made him grit his teeth. "Who?"

"I don't know." Cassia sighed. "But the leaders of the Alliance are certain there's a leak. A traitor." She shook her head, her long, blond gentle curls swaying with the movement. "Every time the Alliance goes on a mission, Darkwolf knows and attacks."

Jake let out a string of curse words and slammed his fists against the mattress to either side of him. "I've got to get back."

"One more day." She held up her hand again, her palm facing him. "You need one more day to heal enough to be safe outside the protections and energies of the Light Elves."

"Bullshit," he growled.

Cassia stood and looked so calm that this time Jake did get up. He grabbed her by her shoulders. He didn't care that the blankets that had been covering him fell away, leaving him naked.

He knocked that calm expression right off her face as she glanced down at his body before looking up at him when he shook her. He stared directly into her eyes. "You will take me home, *now*.

She jerked out of his grip, her cheeks flushed pink. An angry glint lit her eyes that he'd never seen before. Good. Her shell needed to be cracked.

As a matter of fact, that shell needed to be cracked a lot more.

Jake caught her delicate face in his palms, spearing her silken hair with his fingers at the same time. Without pausing to think about it, he brought his mouth to hers and kissed her so hard and fierce she gasped. He took advantage of her parted lips and forced his tongue into her mouth, exploring her, letting her know he was in control of this moment.

It felt as if sparks were igniting in his belly.

Cassia grasped him by his upper arms and clung to him, her fingers digging into his bare biceps. She remained stiff and unmoving. But he didn't stop his exploration of her mouth, tasting her, teasing her, taunting her to return his kiss.

And then she finally fell into the moment, taking everything he gave. She made soft little moans that sent zinging sensations straight to his cock as she kissed him back. Her kisses were tentative, almost like she didn't know what she was doing. Innocent, pure. As if she had never been kissed before.

God, she was sweet.

She moaned louder and leaned into him. Her hands moved from his biceps, over his shoulders, until she linked her fingers behind his neck.

As he slid his hands to her waist, he brought her tight against his naked body and his huge erection, and she gasped again.

He resisted the urge to part her robe and see exactly what she was wearing beneath it—if anything.

He kissed her hard and fierce, letting all the frustration and anger turn into passion and desire.

God, he'd wanted Cassia for so long. He didn't need his cop instincts to tell him she wasn't exactly what she'd made herself out to be. But then, who was?

Everyone had secrets. Even he did.